SLATE WIZARDS
THE WHISPER PRINCE BOOK 3

THE SLATE WIZARDS
THE WHISPER PRINCE BOOK 3

TODD FAHNESTOCK

F4 PUBLISHING

Copyright © 2022 Todd Fahnestock

All rights reserved.

The characters and events portrayed in this book are fictitious. Any similarity to real persons, living or dead, is coincidental and not intended by the author.

No part of this book may be reproduced, or stored in a retrieval system, or transmitted in any form or by any means, electronic, mechanical, photocopying, recording, or otherwise, without express written permission of the publisher.

ISBN 13: 978-1-952699-37-5

Cover design: Rashed AlAkroka

Dedication

For Lara,

*Who drove the car
while I charted the stars for these characters,
way back in the beginning.*

Acknowledgements

As with the first book, it took a village to raise this series, and there are so many who made contributions. Thank you to all of my advance readers! Thank you to the fans of this story, who have followed it even though it has taken so long to reach the end. I would especially like to thank:

Rashed AlAkroka: Dude, you bring my written words to life. I literally based the descriptions of Venisha off what you created for this amazing cover. Now *that's* what a dragon god of slate and magic looks like!

Quincy Allen: You're a prince, my friend! Thank you for all of the interior design guidance and the hours you put in. You always come through. Always.

Lara Fahnestock: My love. Thank you for the support of this story, from that first brainstorming in the car to everything after. SEVENTEEN years after. ☺

Andy Grover: Thanks for continuing to remind me that I needed to finish this series. You're one of the true fans.

Mandy Houk: Thank you for making sure that my scrawlings are organized and not embarrassingly riddled with typos. You're the best!

Tami Miller: *Fairmist*'s #1 fan! I'm sorry you had to wait so long. Thank you so much for hanging in there, and for driving me to get back to it. Every time I wrote on *The Whisper Prince*, I thought of you.

Steve Patterson: I haven't forgotten about your dedication to this series, my friend. Nor have I forgotten about that six-pack of Corona that you left on my doorstep to incentivize me to finish *The Undying Man*. That's a dedicated fan.

THE SLATE WIZARDS

THE WHISPER PRINCE BOOK 3

Prologue

Adora woke for the last time.

She sat up, the blankets slipping from her naked body, but she didn't shiver. It was warm in the ice hut. It was freezing outside, the most inhospitable place on the entire continent of Devorra, but because Grei wanted it to be warm inside this dome of ice, it was.

The bed had blankets, too, because he had wanted blankets. That was what he did. He could take what hadn't existed and make it exist. He could change the nature of ice and make it warm.

He could take someone who was dead and force her to be alive again.

Adora had died. Lyndion had raked her open with a knife and pulled her guts out. She'd been "saved" by Velak, the murderous Faia banished from Devorra hundreds of years ago. He had bound her body together with fire. But when he'd withdrawn his magic, Adora's body had returned to the ruin it had been after Lyndion's knife.

After the intense pain and her sudden death, she had found herself surrounded by a green light. It had been gentle and lovely. It had whispered all the assurances she had longed to hear: *You will never again be betrayed.... You will never again be manipulated for another's purposes....*

You will never again burn people alive, watching as their bodies blacken and curl into themselves—

She closed her eyes, pressed the heels of her hands to her head and wished the image away. She'd almost escaped the horrors that Velak had forced her to commit. She had floated away from the wreck of her body, into the green light. But Grei had snatched her from that place and shoved her back into her body.

Now he slept next to her on their bed made of ice which was, because he had willed it, as soft and warm as a goose down pillow.

He was a good man. Fallible, impetuous, oblivious, but a good man. She was sure he didn't know what he'd done to her, the gorgeous peace he'd ripped her away from, the burden he'd forced her to pick up again. If he'd known, he would surely have let her die.

So she had made love to him last night. She had given him what he wanted. She had taken up the mantle of Adora. She'd allowed herself to live the lie one more time.

She stood, moved toward the snowy door of the hut. Beams of ice crossed overhead. Walls of ice somehow held in the unnatural heat.

She slid her fingers through her black and gold hair, restored to its luxuriant length because he'd wanted it that way. When he had called her back to life, he hadn't brought back the shaved-headed, scarred Adora. No, he had returned her to the way she had been before Velak, before Lyndion. The vixen who slung drinks and flirtations across a foot of polished mahogany. The woman he saw as the "real" Adora.

Except there was no real Adora. Even the name was fake. She had lived three lives and worn three different names, each with its own birth and a death, and each more painful than the last.

Her first had been Mialene, the princess of Thiara. A scared girl with a heart full of trust, she had ridden to her death on a betrayer's horse.

Her second had been Adora. A determined girl with a heart full of hope, she had marched to her death on a path of lies.

Her third had been Velak's avatar. A furious girl with a heart full of hate, she had charged to her death down a road of bloody slaughter.

She'd been all of those people, and she'd hated each in turn, transformed into a marionette for others to tug this way and that. Her father had used her as a sacrifice. Lyndion, to increase his power. Velak, as his fiery sword of vengeance.

Now Grei used her too. He'd given her the gift of life, and all she had to do was be his fantasy girl.

But she understood the truth now. Her father had been flawed, yes. Lyndion had been a villain. Velak had been a literal monster. But they were not the culprits. Not really. Life itself was the horror. It was a crop that harvested only pain, no matter how many times she started anew. Everything only became…worse.

There were so many moments that seemed like promises of happiness but were only carrots dangled in front of her to lead her off a cliff.

If Jorun Magnus had defended her on the slope of the Slinks that fateful day, had fought for her innocence, then perhaps…

Or if Grei had saved her from Baezin's Order in the South Woods on that fateful day, had built her young life around his love instead of the Order's deceptions, then perhaps…

Or if he had just stayed with her that night in the Thiaran palace after they'd made love, had fought Lyndion off and opened up a future for them to be together, then perhaps…

But no. These were only the hopes of moments gone past. Those happy futures didn't exist any more than Grei's fantasy girl did. Life didn't lead to happiness. It led to pain, the only destination at the end of any road.

She drew a deep breath and glanced down at the slumbering Grei, then at the foot of the bed. He had created clothes for her, but she didn't want them. She didn't want anything.

"Goodbye," she whispered.

She opened the door, stepped out into the snow, and closed it behind herself. Once shut, the aura of Grei's magic vanished. The icy chill stabbed her like knives.

She grit her teeth, lowered her head, and trudged through the snow, sharp ice cutting into her feet, deadly air piercing her skin like needles.

All she could see was her blackened, curling victims in her mind's eye: the sad resignation of the Green Faia, the terror of the Orange Faia, the surprise of the Blue Faia. She recalled the desperate effort each had mustered in their last moments, trying to turn the tide as Velak raged through her and burned them to ash.

Her legs went numb. She staggered and leaned over, shoving her arm up to the shoulder in deep snow to regain her balance. She shivered uncontrollably, but she staggered ever forward, forcing her body to work just a little longer.

She stumbled on a rock, went down beneath a three-foot snowdrift, and viciously scraped her shins on a hidden rock. Bright red blood dotted the snow when she stood.

She kept going.

Her eyelashes froze. She couldn't feel her cheeks anymore, and her vision blurred. She peered blearily back at the hut, but it was no more than a dot of irregularity in the never-ending ripples of white.

Breathing became painful, her lungs trying to suck in this air that wasn't fit for people. The killing wind was a skeletal hand scraping along her cheeks, sucking the warmth from her chest.

But she forced her stiff legs forward and reached her destination at last. The snow rose a little at the edge of the cliff before rounding off and falling away.

She didn't know where in Devorra this was. She doubted Grei did either. She doubted this frozen wasteland even had a name.

A nameless chasm for a nameless girl.

The drifts rose thigh-high as she pushed forward, then waist-high. Her left foot slipped, and a cascade of snow fell away to reveal the hard edge of the cliff. She windmilled her sluggish arms and regained her balance.

Wind swirled, tossing snow about, and she thought she heard whispers beckoning her. She gazed straight down at the sharp rocks poking up from the white far below.

And she jumped.

Part 1

The Return
of the
Whisper Prince

Chapter One

GREI

"*Picture it inside.*" The Slate Spirit's voice, always accompanied by a soft hiss in the background, spoke inside Grei's mind. "*Speak to the earth, pull it through. It will come.*"

Grei stood before Fairmist Falls, and he envisioned it as it had once been: a supernatural spout of water shooting over the Highward to plunge a hundred feet into the pool, hitting like a fist, throwing water into the air.

Because of the Blue Faia's magic, that water had once stayed aloft, wobbling and becoming huge droplets, then drifting down the slope toward the town.

But Velak had run the Blue Faia off or killed her. In her absence, the floating droplets had ceased, leaving the city of Fairmist bright and bare and dry under the hot sun. The falls had been reduced to a thin sheet of water trickling from the Highward. Diminished. Unremarkable.

Grei clutched The Root, the artifact which had saved his magic and to which his magic was now bound.

He tried to concentrate, but his thoughts strayed. He kept wanting to look down the hill, to look for Adora. Ever since she had thrown herself off the cliff in Benasca, he couldn't escape the thought that he had failed her.

Grei had stopped Kuruk, destroyed Lyndion, and killed Velak. He had taken control of the most powerful magic on the continent of Devorra: the field of blue roses. He'd pushed his way through death and pain and enemies so powerful they had broken the lands.

But he'd failed Adora, and by everything holy, he wasn't going to fail again. He was going to take a hand in human affairs.

He was going to mend the broken things.

Fairmist wasn't supposed to be a city of sun and heat. It was supposed to be cool and wet and dark, a place with hidden nooks and secret coves, with mysteries behind every corner and adventure flitting between the trees.

He whispered and thrust his fist into the solid rock, making it as malleable as soft clay.

"Feel it," the Slate Spirit said. *"Call upon the blue roses. Master them. Make them obey your call."*

Grei pictured the vast frozen field of blue roses and narrowed his focus to a single bloom. He imagined an invisible hand slowly closing around the delicate petals, reaching beneath the snow to the roots.

"Come to me," he whispered to the rock encasing his fist, envisioning the message going into the earth and racing all the way to that rose far in the north. He told the magic of the rose to come to this place.

He released the final whispers from his mouth, pulled his hand from the rock, coaxing the liquid stone upward. The pillar of rock rose, the width and height of a finger, then shimmered and became a green stalk. The stalk twisted, throwing out one, two, three leaves that widened and opened to the sun. At the top of the stalk, a green bulb appeared, swelling then unfurling, spreading the petals of a blue rose.

"Well done," the Slate Spirit murmured in Grei's mind. *"Gods of old, Grei, well done."*

Elation swept through him. But then it abruptly faded, like the joy had attached to his bones, his organs, his vitals, and then been yanked out with a string, leaving his body a hollow shell. He swayed on his feet and almost fell. He looked down at the rose.

Its power thrummed through him, a heart pumping life and vitality into the lands. It caused the world to shimmer like ripples on water, moving outward. Slowly, the hollow sensation inside Grei faded as the magic of the rose filled him and everything around him.

"The rest, you know," the Slate Spirit said. *"Do it."*

Grei raised his hands, faced the ordinary falls, and bid them to become as they once were. He asked the water to charge over the Highward, smash into the pool, and fling droplets into the air.

The river surged, suddenly ten times its previous size, as if a lake had been dumped at the top of the cliff. It hit the pool with thunderous force. Huge droplets flew into the air, and Grei whispered to them, telling them to float like dandelion fluff. He coaxed them to remember what the Blue Faia had asked of them, to do exactly as they had before.

They did.

The water rose, joining and forming large droplets. Some of those split and formed smaller droplets. They slowly filled the cove with sparkling abundance, then began to drift downstream one at a time.

The falls looked and acted the way they should. He glanced downhill at the dry city of Fairmist as the army of raindrops slowly marched toward it.

"Yes," he said.

"As it should be," the Slate Spirit echoed.

His thoughts, as always, flicked to Adora, and his triumph died. One success. One failure.

"Let's get about it," he murmured, his elation gone.

"The statues in The Garden." The Slate Spirit echoed Grei's thoughts.

It bothered Grei, the voice having the ability to enter his mind any time he touched The Root. He wondered if the

Spirit could be reading his mind. The Spirit certainly seemed to know Grei's intentions. But he had been nothing but benevolent so far. Every single suggestion he had offered had been helpful.

Grei flicked open a hatch on The Root, dropped into the hole that opened in the earth beneath him, and bid the air to slow his descent. He landed softly in the middle of a rock-walled corridor. He flicked the hatch shut. The hole overhead closed, plunging him into darkness.

Grei whispered to the air, asking it to mimic sunlight, and a soft glow lit the tunnel. He jogged toward his next destination, to the next atrocity he was going to undo, to the next broken thing that he would mend.

Chapter Two

GREI

Grei alighted on the ground before the tortured statues in The Garden. Some crouched, some reached forward, trying to grasp their long-absent tormentors. He shut the hatch on The Root, and the hole in the ground behind him rumbled and became normal dirt and grass again.

"Yes," the Slate Spirit said. "You are the master of the blue roses. Use them."

So far, the Slate Spirit was everything he'd promised to be: helpful, a source of unending information.

But Grei never forgot that he was beholden to this magical spirit, and the demigods of Devorra had a history of hurting mortals. The Faia had stood by as the Slinks devoured one innocent after another. Velak had waged a murderous war against his family without thought to the cost in human lives. Cavyn's ruthless obsessions had burned down the city of Thiara and tortured Blevins to the verge of insanity.

So Grei held back any affection for the Slate Spirit, and the moment he didn't need the Spirit's advice, he preferred to break his connection to The Root.

He started to do so now, slipping the artifact back into its pouch—

"Wait," the Slate Spirit urged him. "If you would."

Grei hesitated. "What?"

"I call in my first favor," the Slate Spirit said. "The first of the three you owe me."

And here it is…. Grei's stomach twisted. "What do you want?"

"I wish you to free the people of this horrible place, this…garden. Make them alive again. Turn stone to flesh."

"I was already going to do that."

"I know you were."

"Then why make that one of your favors? Why waste it?"

"Grei…you're bringing Devorra back into balance. Every time you correct one of these twisted aberrations—at the falls, here at The Garden—it tips the lands back toward balance. Waste it? No. I have no greater purpose than to help you if this is your crusade."

"I just don't…you could get something that would…" He trailed off.

"Is it so hard to conceive that you and I are aligned in purpose?"

Grei hesitated. "Very well. As my first favor to you, I'll set these people free."

"Good."

Grei dropped The Root into the pouch and cinched it shut. The voice in his mind went quiet, and the persistent hiss also vanished.

He turned his attention to The Garden, encircled by the broken wrought-iron fence. Once, this had been a forbidding place, shadowed figures frozen in a dark haze of floating droplets, repelling anyone who dared come near.

Now, bathed in sunlight, The Garden smelled of heated pine sap instead of the once ever-present scent of water. It had dried out for the first time in centuries and the sun revealed in sharp clarity that the haphazard statues, leaning this way and that, weren't terrifying monsters of rage. They were desperate men and women who had failed to protect their loved ones, a testament to what happened when those without magic tried to fight those who had it.

He felt a sudden urgency to go to The Floating Stone, to return to Adora's room, that little apartment up the rickety wooden stairs.

He tamped the desire down. He would mend what was broken. This must come first.

Opening the wrought-iron gate, he entered The Garden and stopped before the woman who had haunted his dreams as a child. Her furious face remained unchanged. She still reached for the Highwand who had transformed her, a foe long gone.

He closed his eyes and listened to the whispers. He could feel more than he'd felt before he'd bonded with the blue roses. Beneath the strong whispers of "stone...stone...stone...stone..." he now heard something else, the unique personality deep within each statue, the whispers of the people inside.

He could still hear the souls of those within, most of them. Just like when he'd been turned to stone, they were still in there, trapped, trying to find a way out.

He drew a deep breath and closed his eyes.

This would require more power than he had at his command.

He knelt, put his fist into the cracked and dried-out earth, and again saw the field of blue roses in his mind. Like he had done at Fairmist Falls, he beseeched the nearest blue rose to come forth. He drew his hand upward and, as with Fairmist Falls, the rose sprouted at the feet of the woman who had once haunted his dreams.

The power of the rose filled him, surged into him, ready for his spell, and he talked to each of the statues—all of them at once.

And he changed them back.

Chapter Three

GREI

An hour after the spell's mighty transformation, Grei trudged away from The Garden and the lingering sounds of sobbing. It had taken him time to work his way through all the survivors, calming them, piecing together their shattered souls. Someone must have seen him or heard the wails of the newly living statues, because the people of Fairmist began to converge on The Garden. As Grei comforted each of those who had been transformed, more and more people arrived until it seemed all of Fairmist had come to The Garden. Even Grei's father was there, tearfully reunited with his stepmother Fern.

As Grei left, sobbing filled The Garden, yes, but there were also soft cries of joy. Unconsciously, Grei slipped his hand into his pouch and closed his fingers around The Root. His anchor, his "haven," immediately rejuvenated him, replenished him.

"You have fulfilled your first promise to me," the Slate Spirit said. *"Thank you. You have honored your debt, and part of it is now cleared."*

Euphoria washed through Grei. A weight lifted from his shoulders, and he gasped.

"What is that?" he said.

"When you bound yourself to The Root, you bound yourself to your promises. They are connected to the very soul of you, as I told you, and that was one of them releasing. Those who keep their promises are always rewarded by the world. This is just more...direct."

Grei stopped in the middle of the street. Floating droplets touched his cloak and became water, sliding in rivulets down the oil-treated surface. The hazy glow of the sun filtered through, mostly obscured now. The city was almost back to normal.

"Why are you helping me?" Grei demanded.

"We are helping each other," the Slate Spirit said.

"How?"

"Why do you ask?"

"Because I think you want more than you're letting on."

The Slate Spirit went quiet.

"I needed your help to get my magic back. And you delivered. And it helped destroy Velak. You helped me save the lands, and I will honor my promises to you, but..." Grei paused. "Your request doesn't make sense to me."

"I can't want to help the people of your hometown?" the Slate Spirit asked.

"You can. But why would you?"

"Because it is the right thing to do."

"I don't buy that." Maybe Grei was simply too untrusting, but he'd never encountered pure philanthropy. "I've never met a magical being that wanted to do the right thing. Tell me what you actually want."

The Spirit went silent.

"What are you?" Grei felt an insidiousness creeping over him, like an ocean rising to cover his head.

"Very well," the Slate Spirit admitted. *"I have not been completely honest with you."*

"Then start."

"You once asked me if I wanted the god Venisha to invade these shores. I didn't answer. I do not, but you were right to fear such a thing. Three immortals called the Slate Wizards are coming."

"I thought Slate Wizards were…*priests of the god Venisha.*"

"*No. Priests are priests. The Slate Wizards are Venisha's chosen. Made immortal by His hand.*"

"Immortal?"

"*For at least three hundred years.*"

Interesting. That was about how long the Thiaran Empire had existed.

"And the Slate Wizards are Venishan users of magic. They make artifacts like The Root."

"*And more dangerous.*"

"Why invade now after all this time?"

"*Before, the Faia always stopped them.*"

"And now the Faia are gone." Grei's heart went cold. "Very well. Once the Slate Wizards are here…then what?"

"*They do what they have longed to do all this time, make Devorra part of the Venishan kingdom. They will enslave this land and do what they did to their homeland.*"

"What did they do to their homeland?"

"*The country of Venisha is not green like it is here, Grei. It is a land of metal and oil. A land of magical artifacts, but not of life. The Slate Wizards crave what you take for granted.*"

Grei clenched a fist. He didn't want another war. He wanted to be done.

"And your pact with me. What do you want?"

After a long pause, the Slate Spirit said, "*Freedom. I want you to free me.*"

Grei glanced at The Root. "You're a prisoner?"

"*Did you think I was always just a voice, a whisper inside your head? I was once flesh and blood. I was once one of them.*"

"A Slate Wizard?"

"*We were created in the bowels of the Slate Mines by the god Venisha himself. But when Vaeron started down a dark path, I objected, and Vaeron brooks no opposition. He imprisoned my soul in this artifact, and my body remains trapped in a magical stasis in the Slate Mines of Venisha.*"

"Wait. Vaeron? *The* Vaeron? The king of Venisha?"

"*Yes.*"

"The king of Venisha is one of the Slate Wizards? How is that even possible? The king of Venisha is a descendant of the original Vaeron, named for him. They had a coronation for the new king only five years ago. He's not immortal."

"*It is the same man. Vaeron was an original Slate Wizard. Yes, the kings of Venisha are all called Vaeron, but that they are different men renamed is a lie. It is the story fed to the peasants. There has only ever been one King Vaeron. He fakes his death every fifty years, changes his appearance, and has his 'successor' take the throne.*"

Grei reeled. An undying man, like Blevins.

"*Vaeron became immortal three hundred years ago, as did all the Slate Wizards, transformed by a powerful magic. Him, his sister, his beloved, and me. When I opposed them, they took steps and imprisoned me. After more time than I would like to count, I was able to effect an escape…of sorts. I imbued part of my soul into this artifact, The Root. It took centuries as I was passed hand to hand, but finally The Root made its way over the Sunset Sea to you—one of the few people who might be able to free me.*"

"Your actual body is in Venisha."

"*You must go there, for both our sakes, to brace the Slate Wizards in their homeland and to free me.*"

Grei shook his head. "No."

"*Grei—*"

"I am not abandoning the people of Thiara to run off to Venisha."

"*If you do not, they will bring the fight to you—*"

"If they come, I will make them wish they hadn't. But I'm not going somewhere to start a fight. I'm going to mend what was broken. And that's all."

The Slate Spirit went silent.

Grei was about to say more, but he took his hand off The Root, pulled the pouch's drawstrings tight, and began walking again. The sun slowly vanished into the thickening haze of water droplets. The normal light of Fairmist returned: a mystical golden glow as the floating droplets refracted the sunlight.

He stopped at the mouth of the alley to the south of The Floating Stone. Adora's Alley. He stood there, the droplets drifting into him, turning into light splashes on his cloak. This was where he'd first asked her to show him her heel. She'd distracted him with her bedroom eyes and the swing of her hips. She'd delayed the answers he had craved to pull him into the Order's prophecy.

No, he couldn't go to the kingdom of Venisha. He hadn't yet mended the most important thing. He hadn't, and he didn't know how. He climbed the creaky steps one at a time and opened the door.

Adora turned to face him, the amber glow from the window lighting her beautiful profile.

Chapter Four

GREI

Adora stared at Grei with the dead gaze that made his heart hurt before she turned to look out the window once more.

She wore the clothes he had made for her, a brown skirt and dun-colored tunic.

He paused, caught by her beauty. She looked vital and desirable, just like she'd looked before they'd both been battered and twisted by forces beyond their control. Now Grei *was* one of those greater forces, and he was never going to let anything hurt her.

"Is it everything you wanted?" she asked softly. Still facing away, she took a long lock of her hair and slid it through her fingers. "Adora the vixen?"

Grei swallowed, feeling like he was walking into a room filled with traps. He had been awake for days, beseeching the very air to keep him alert. If ever his eyes drooped, a gust rushed into his face, forcing its way into his mouth, nose, and eyes.

Being away at Fairmist Falls and The Garden had been a kind of torture for Grei. Using his *dasha*, he could keep track of Adora from a distance, but that meant constantly looking over his shoulder, waiting for the moment he'd have to rush to her side and stop her from hurting herself.

Yesterday had been the fifth time she'd forced him to resurrect her, and he didn't want to have to do it again.

He wanted Adora to come back to herself. He wanted her to remember the simple life she'd imagined back in Thiara. She had talked of a small house with a chicken-scratched yard. She'd told him she'd imagined a little girl with wavy brown hair and blue eyes perched on Grei's shoulders. That's what she'd said she wanted.

And Grei was going to give it to her if it was the last thing he did. He was going to mend what had been broken.

He was the only one who could. Once he did—once he restored the lands to what they had been before—he would cast off the mantle of the Whisper Prince and take up Adora's simple life. He would take her somewhere away from all the emperors and empresses, all the Ringblades and Highblades, all the demigods of Devorra. He would take them somewhere they'd never be found.

"I want you to be happy," he said softly.

"So you've said." The edges of her mouth curled in a flat smile.

"Adora, you just need time to heal."

"You dress me in these clothes." She gestured at her body. "To make *me* happy."

"You can wear whatever you like. Just tell me what you want."

"I've told you what I want. I want—"

"No," he cut her off. "No."

"—to die," she finished. "Let me die."

"Please..." he said hoarsely. "You don't want that. You know you don't."

"And yet here I am, telling you otherwise."

"What about the chickens? Or-or pigs, in the yard. I'm a farmer and we have...a little girl with brown hair and blue eyes."

She turned away and looked out the window again. "One of the women I once was said that. I'm not that woman anymore. Nor the woman before her or the girl before that. I'm not anyone, Grei. I am…a cup passed from hand to hand, filled with the desires of men."

He approached her like he would a skittish deer. "Please, Adora. You once said you trusted me. Trust me now. Trust that you'll feel better in time. Would you try? Would you just try?"

"Do I have a choice?"

"Adora—"

"How much time?"

"What?"

"How much time do you need before you let me die?"

Silence hung in the room. He wanted the perfect words to mend her, but he didn't know what they were.

He cleared his throat, changed the subject. "I returned the statues in The Garden to normal."

"To normal," she echoed.

"Yes. To…I brought them back to life."

"Did they want to be returned to 'normal?'"

Frustration rose inside him. "They were trapped. I brought them back to life."

"Did you ask them?"

"They were stone, Adora. How should I have asked them?"

"Isn't talking to stone pretty much what you do?"

"I was a victim of that spell once, Adora. It is *brutal*. They were trapped in a shell where no one could hear them or see them. They didn't want to stay there. Believe me."

"Trust you believe you trust you believe you…." She murmured, still staring out the window.

"They couldn't move, couldn't breathe. They were suffocating, held in place by forces they couldn't hope to overcome," he said.

"That must feel horrible," she said flatly.

Her verbal lash stung, and his frustration flared. He fought to calm himself.

"Maybe the lands don't need you," she intoned. "Did you ever think of that? Maybe everything is proceeding exactly as it should."

"I *shouldn't* have saved them?" he asked incredulously.

"You think this newfound power gives you the right to decide what's normal and what's not. You can't wipe away the scars of the world, Grei. That's why they're scars."

"You don't really believe all of those people deserved to be statues, trapped in that...that horror. You can't believe that," he said.

She crossed her arms beneath her breasts. A muscle in her jaw twitched. "It appears I don't get to believe anything."

"I know you're hurting," he said soothingly. "You have so many reasons to be angry. But please Adora. Trust me—"

"And yet you don't trust me," she said.

"I love you!"

"Then let me die."

"That's not...trust.... You're just...how you're feeling now is going to change. It's going to get better."

She didn't reply.

It felt like hope was draining out of his body, down through his legs, out his boots and onto the floor. His fatigue pulled at him. His muscles felt like lead and his eyes burned. He looked longingly at the little bed against the wall.

"I...I have to sleep now, Adora," he said. "I've got to sleep—"

"I'm not stopping you," she said.

"But I need you to...to just stay here. To not—"

"Kill myself?"

"Don't make me bring you back again. Please."

"You're the only one making people do things here," she said.

Grei wanted to pull his hair out. "Will you just...stay here with me?"

"Would it make a difference if I leapt off Fairmist Falls the moment you closed your eyes?"

He hung his head.

"Then why even ask?"

"Adora—"

"Sleep, Grei," she said.

"It's going to be better soon. You'll see."

She didn't respond.

Whispering to the air not to wake him, he staggered to the bed and fell onto it. "Don't..." he mumbled. "Please just don't...." His eyes slid shut. The fatigue of the day's events swept over him like a wave, and he finally slept.

Chapter Five

VAERON

"The Faia have fallen. It is time."

The sudden voice in Vaeron's mind surprised him, and he almost died for it. The automaton that Pliothe had built nearly skewered him through the heart. Its sword was a blur, slipping past Vaeron's block, and if it weren't for Vaeron's supernatural reflexes, it would have found its mark.

He twisted. The blade punched through his chainmail, slicing across his ribs.

Vaeron hissed, anger flaring, but the automaton didn't care about his rage, didn't care that he was the king of Venisha. It had been designed—at Vaeron's behest—to care only about testing Vaeron's swordsmanship. Its sole purpose was to give Vaeron a foe that might challenge him. It would continue until commanded to stop with the correct—and only the correct—command.

But Vaeron didn't have time to take a breath, let alone say a word. The automaton pressed the attack so viciously that if he took his attention from his defense for even an instant, its next strike would kill him. Vaeron backed up, trying to give himself time, but the automaton had already anticipated that. It thrust. Vaeron blocked, barely deflecting the attack.

"You will travel to Devorra, my wizard," Vaeron's master commanded, voice loud in his mind as though Vaeron was not fighting for his life.

Vaeron's heel hit the wall. The automaton sensed the weakness and thrust. Vaeron spun, just avoiding the blade and pivoting to flank the magically animated armor.

It gained him half a second.

"Inert!" he gasped. The automaton froze, already pivoting to kill Vaeron. It had raised its arms and had almost brought the sword down in a counter to Vaeron's sidestep. The overhand blow—meant to cleave Vaeron's skull in two—hovered a foot above his face.

Sweat dribbled down Vaeron's face, and he gripped his sword in fear for the first time in a long time. To have such a near scrape hadn't happened to him in centuries. If his opponent had been flesh and blood, Vaeron would have surely killed him for his insolence. He was tempted to melt this automaton out of sheer rage.

Or if a servant had called out to him, causing this kind of hesitation, he'd have slain the servant on the spot. But the voice in his head—the voice of his master who had given him his powers—was the only person in the world Vaeron could not rail against. The god Venisha had not spoken to Vaeron for decades. Whenever and wherever He chose to speak, Vaeron would listen, no matter the cost.

Vaeron walked away from the inert automaton, away from the center of the audience chamber, past the two dozen thick, triangular pillars that thrust up to hold the slanted ceiling of the room. The pillars created an approach the width of a road from the double doors on the far side to the dais of his throne.

Steep angles climbed from the seven-foot-tall walls lining the triangular room all the way to the peak of the pyramid. Eight-foot-tall banners hung on each side of every pillar, depicting the Slate Wizards. There was Vaeron with his two-handed sword on a field of red, Fylomene on a field of blue looking predictably elegant and radiant, and Pliothe on a field of brownish yellow, a wide-eyed girl that chilled you to look upon her. Beside each facet rose a tall, wrought-iron candle holder and a trio of burning candles.

This room had once been used to hear petitions from citizens of Venisha back when Vaeron had bothered himself with such foolishness. Now, though he still held his important meetings in this place, he mostly practiced his swordplay.

He moved into the shadows, paying no mind to the religiously silent Slate Priests, who would only say or do something if he ordered them, and knelt in the corner.

"Master," he murmured. "It has been so very long."

"Call your wizards together," Venisha said. *"We have an opportunity, but we must move quickly. Devorra's lands are wounded, and we must not give them a chance to heal."*

"Our invasion is finally at hand?" Vaeron asked in disbelief. The Faia had kept the Slate Wizards out of Devorra for three centuries. The Slate Wizards had tried everything within their power to pierce their barrier. They had attacked the Faia in every way possible from this distant shore. They had even tried to infiltrate Thiaran culture with Venishan religion to gain a stronghold in that land.

All attempts had met with failure.

"Only one Faia remains," Vaeron's master said. *"Uriozi. The Black Faia. But she cannot maintain the barrier alone."*

"How did they die?" Vaeron asked.

"Cavyn's constant meddling proved to be her undoing. Her banished son returned in fire and vengeance, and he destroyed her and her daughters. We are not the only ones who hate Cavyn and her little aberrations."

"So it is time…." Vaeron said.

"Call your wizards. To Thiara you go."

"I will muster the army immediately."

"No. Thiara is in disarray. Their leaders are dead or at each others' throats. You will use the chaos to destroy any hope that the empire will re-organize. But first, you will kill the last Faia and this mortal upstart who wishes to become a Faia."

"A mortal?"

"He has stolen the field of blue roses," Venisha said.

"How?" Vaeron asked incredulously.

"Uriozi gave it over to him."

The blue roses. Those little fountains of magic were the source of Devorra's considerable power, and the key to Venisha's resurrection.

"The barrier has fallen?" Vaeron asked.

"It is gone."

This was what Venisha had wanted since he'd created the Slate Wizards. The so-called Thiaran Empire was ripe for the plundering. The blue roses ripe for the plucking.

"Pliothe will bring Uriozi into the fold. And the roses."

"And my brother?" Vaeron asked.

"He is still there."

Elation spread through Vaeron like warm water poured over ice. "At long last, my traitorous brother will pay for his betrayal."

"Keep your eyes on the true victory, Vaeron. Do not disappoint me."

"Of course, Master," Vaeron said. "We take the Faia. We kill the boy. I understand."

"After, you may do whatever you wish with Baezin. The roses first."

"Yes, Master. Uriozi and...what is the boy's name?"

"Grei Forander."

"Grei?" The name struck a chord. "I know this name."

Venisha had spies in Thiaran society. There had been a report of a boy who had turned stone into water in the town of Fairmist. That boy's name had been Grei Forander.

"The Whisper Prince," Vaeron murmured. "They call this boy the Whisper Prince."

"That is correct."
"I thought he was a rumor. Peasant gossip."
"Now you know otherwise."
"Yes, Master."
"Call your wizards."
"Yes, Master.

Chapter Six

FYLOMENE

Fylomene was seductively unbuttoning her dress in the cramped little stateroom of the dashing captain's ship, holding his eager-eyed gaze, when her earring whispered to her.

"The time has come. Return immediately."

She stopped unbuttoning the side of her dress as if she'd been paralyzed. Vaeron hadn't spoken to her in years. His voice—even the whispered version that filtered through Pliothe's little device, made her shiver in pleasure.

The dashing Captain Kor hadn't heard the voice, of course. He continued kissing her neck and slid his hands up her sides. He undid one more button, then another, exposing the length of her leg all the way to the top of her hip.

She concentrated on Vaeron's whisper, waiting, eager. She hated him, of course. She had hated Vaeron for centuries, but that was love, wasn't it? When he called, her body stiffened like a lightning rod in a storm. Even after all this time—after all his neglect—his voice still coursed through her like pure joy.

"The barrier is down. The Faia all but gone."

Captain Kor reached the end of the buttons along her ribs. He slid the dress over her head and tossed it on his small bed. She strained to hear the rest of the message.

"I need you, Fylomene. Come to me..."

Vaeron's dark voice stopped speaking. She waited for a long moment like a thirsty woman lengthening her tongue to catch another drop of water. But that was all.

The pleasure of his voice left her, and she awoke to Kor's increasingly frantic movements. He peppered her with kisses as his hands roved down her back to her buttocks.

"Oh, my love," Fylomene purred, drawing away. "I'm afraid I must go."

Kor chuckled, like it was a joke, and he moved forward again, continued caressing her.

She pushed at his chest, her arms straining, but she was barely able to get his lips off her collarbone. His hand clutched her breast.

"Enough, my dashing captain," she said.

"Gods, you're divine. You know exactly how to enflame a man," he responded, as though her resistance was part of the flirtation. He crushed her to him, and she thumped into him, lacking the strength to stop him.

A hot sliver of annoyance jammed into her heart. Physical weakness. This was the bane of her life.

Centuries ago, when the all-powerful Venisha had asked her, "You may have one wish, Fylomene. Above all things, what would you have?" she had answered with the vanity of an empty-headed girl.

"Make me irresistible to all men," she had said. "Make me young and beautiful forever."

Make me young and beautiful forever....

She could have chosen anything, but she'd chosen that. If she'd asked for physical power—as Vaeron had—she could have forced this insistent captain away.

If she had chosen to be a master artificer—like little Pliothe—she could have turned him into a mechanical slave.

But no. Youth. Beauty. Irresistible allure. These she had chosen, for all time. And in this moment, her power only strengthened the bonds she now wished to cut. It was maddening.

At the tender age of nineteen, she had convinced herself her sexual allure was the only power she had. She'd thought controlling the minds of men would give her everything. She'd thought it would give her Vaeron.

With a sigh, she ceased her useless push and wrapped her arms around Kor, laced her fingers into his hair.

"Captain Kor," she said. "I really do apologize, but I must go."

He leaned away, the love-drunk haze over his eyes finally clearing. He hesitated, as though it was the first time he'd actually heard her. His hands slid from her breasts to her arms and he gripped her there, gently but firmly, as though he was reluctant to give her up, as though she belonged to him.

"You're joking," he said.

"Alas," she said. "I'm not. I've been summoned."

He glanced at the little door to his cabin, quiet and closed. "What summons?"

"It was for my ears alone." She gave a sensuous shrug to her shoulders, indicating he should let her go now. He didn't.

"I'll be quick." He winked with that charm that had made her choose him in the first place.

It was romantic, and he was so delicious.

"A tempting offer," she said. "Perhaps another time?"

His face darkened. "Another.... You're joking."

"I am not."

"Oh, I think you are. Do you imagine that you can simply come here, tease me like this...." He glanced down at her naked body. "Then walk out?"

"I do apologize, but I suddenly have more pressing matters—"

"No you don't." He shook her a little. It hurt.

"Oh...I see how it is," she purred.

Once, she would have tried to talk to him. She would have encouraged him to show a bit of gallantry, to forego the driving need to carve another notch on his headboard. She would have reminded him that there would be other nights for the two of them. Why not give those nights a chance rather than taking something not freely given?

Long ago, she would have. But it was pointless to stand between fools and their mistakes. There was no saving them.

"You're a strong man," she continued. "A man who takes what he wants and damn the cost. You wish to…" She raised a seductive eyebrow.

He smiled, lifted her up and threw her onto the little bed.

She bounced on the surprisingly soft mattress, then rose on her elbows, languidly working her way backward one hip at a time, and brought her knees up in invitation. He slid between them, pressing down upon her. She rolled him over, and his eyes lit with desire as he crudely knocked against the bulkhead and shuffled to get underneath her.

She straddled him and sensuously shook out her arms. Pliothe's steel bracelet slipped down her forearm to her wrist, then squeezed like a snake, ready. She leaned down to put her lips against Kor's ear.

"You wish to sheathe your dagger, milord?" she asked breathily.

"Oh yes," he whispered.

She put both fists against his chest, just under his ribcage and activated Pliothe's bracelet. A thin shaft of steel shot up and into Captain Kor's heart. His back arched like he'd been struck by lightning, lifting Fylomene into the air. Eyes wide, he sucked in half a gasp, hand extended toward her—in supplication or violence, she didn't know—and then he fell back, dead.

"Me first," she murmured.

The thin dagger pulled back, dragging a line of red across her wrist before it reassembled into Pliothe's bracelet. It fragmented into smaller slivers that stacked one across the other in a pretty pattern around her wrist. There was barely any blood on Kor's tunic, only a pin prick on the front of the smart, half-unbuttoned uniform.

His glassy eyes gazed at nothing, and the intense "O" that had been his mouth at the moment of death softened into the slack-jawed expression of a village idiot.

She leaned over him and kissed his pale forehead, gingerly lifted her leg up and over him, and stood. He lay on her dress, so she painstakingly rolled him over and tugged it out from underneath him. The silken, sand-colored dress was intricately sewn with taupe embroidery, and was one of her favorites. She paused at the coin-sized dot of blood just to the right of the plunging neckline. Right where Fylomene's own heart would be.

She wondered if that was a nod from Venisha somehow. She put the dress back on, sliding it into place with that little cold, wet spot against her breast.

She slipped her shoes on, went to the cabin door and turned to look at the stiff, pale captain.

"We all make choices, my love," she said. "And then we live with them."

She turned and left the ship.

Chapter Seven

PLIOTHE

"*Pliothe...*" Vaeron shocked her, speaking through the earring he'd forced her to make, jammed through the lobe of her ear, and warned her to never remove. "*Venisha has spoken. Return at once. We have work.*"

Vaeron's voice struck like a whip, and she flinched, clenching her fists, waiting for more.

"*Pliothe...*" Vaeron's impatient voice returned. "*Don't make me wait.*"

She winced.

Vaeron was upset with her. He was always upset with her. Once, that hadn't mattered. She was his sister, and brothers were supposed to love their sisters, so she'd followed him around, convinced that soon he would become a real brother.

Now she just wanted to hide so he wouldn't see her—or worse, ask her to make something. She didn't like him seeing her. She didn't like anyone seeing her. She didn't even like to look into a mirror.

But Vaeron and Fylomene were Pliothe's family. And you couldn't escape your family. Well, maybe if you had good friends, the kind of friends that could take you away and protect you. She had tried to make such friends—she tried all the time—but Pliothe made people nervous. A person couldn't really be friends with someone who made them nervous. Not really.

The smell of the sea wafted up to her, strong beneath the pier where she sat, but despite Vaeron's warning, she remained where she was. Many places in Venisha had sand, but this spot had smooth, round stones the size of Pliothe's fists. The stones were hard and damp beneath her, but not wholly uncomfortable.

She liked dark corners where people couldn't see, alleyways where people didn't go, old rooms within the temple that no one had visited in years. This space beneath the pier was like that. No one spent time here because sea serpents crept out of the sea, looking for food. Every now and then, when the citizens of Venisha weren't careful, the monsters would feast on some drunken sailor who'd passed out or some child who'd come adventuring too far.

She squinched her eyes shut, then opened them. She tried to rub away the lashing pain of Vaeron's whip. This was a good place for that. Away from people. Only her and the sea and the pebbles.

And her friends, of course.

A sudden pain stabbed her heart like a quick needle, in and out. At first she thought it was Vaeron exercising some new magical power, but then she realized it was one of her artifacts. The pointy bracelet. Fylomene had used it.

With narrowed eyes, she clenched her knees to her chest until the captain's death faded, the needle pulled slowly from her heart.

Long ago, she had asked Vaeron and Fylomene not to do that, not to use her artifacts to hurt people, but they didn't listen. They never listened.

It will get worse if you don't go, she told herself. *Vaeron will be so angry.*

She almost stood up, resigned to her fate, when one of the softly rolling waves beneath the pier rolled differently, splashed oddly. She focused on that particular wave, and as it smoothed out, she saw the head surface.

A sea serpent. Her pulse quickened.

The sea serpent wanted to see Pliothe as well, it seemed. Its dull red eyes fixed on her, and it slithered forward. Water splashed beneath it as it created its own little wave, jets of water shooting from its body, holding it aloft as it left the sea.

"Hello," Pliothe said as the sea serpent reared up before her, two long fangs unfurling from a mouth full of teeth. "Will you be my friend?"

The serpent hissed, poised to strike, but it hesitated. Its head jerked as its gaze went beyond Pliothe to the shadowy depths of the pier. Pliothe's friends clicked on the rocks as they clustered around her.

Dozens of rats scampered into the scant light, their bodies gleaming, interwoven with strips and shards of steel, copper, and iron. Assorted bugs scuttled forward as well, made from metal shavings or snips of wire. There were also two snakes, a half-dozen ravens, and a skinny dog. They encircled her and continued forward toward the sea serpent.

The serpent hissed in alarm and drew back. Most living creatures became alarmed at Pliothe's friends, which made it hard to make more friends. At least, the kinds of friends that Pliothe didn't have to create.

The sea serpent, suddenly seeming to realize it had become the prey here, turned and jetted back toward the sea.

Pliothe frowned.

Her little creatures squeaked in their mechanical voices and leapt after the sea serpent.

All she wanted was another friend. Was that so much to ask?

Her little horde clicked on the stones as they pursued. The sea serpent hissed when the ravens dove down from the underside of the pier, plunged their gleaming metal claws—

as sharp as the tines of the pitchfork Pliothe had used to make them—into the serpent's neck. It whipped around, trying to bite the ravens, and the dog caught up, jumping on the sea serpent's back and tearing with teeth that Pliothe had snapped from the ends of kitchen knives.

The sea serpent screamed, thrashing in the now-bloody surf. The rats caught up then, and the snakes. Her creatures didn't eat the serpent, but they liked to bite and tear. This helped with the transformation.

"I just wanted to be your friend," Pliothe whispered to the dying serpent. "Would that have been so hard? To listen to me? To be nice to me?"

By the time the host of tiny metal roaches, beetles, and centipedes reached the sea serpent, it had gone still. Pliothe stood up and approached it. Her little boots touched the edge of its teeth, toeing the two long fangs. She memorized the shape of its head, the sinuous length of its destroyed body, and she thought of what materials she would need. Scallops of metal—so many of them—for the scales. She would need two daggers for the fangs, thin ones. Vaeron had those. He had so many weapons.

A sea serpent would be a fine addition—

"Pliothe!" Vaeron's voice whipped her. *"Need I send someone to collect you?"*

She cringed.

Perhaps she wouldn't be adding a sea serpent to her collection today. Perhaps not....

She left the underside of the pier, climbing up the slope of smooth stones. Her host of friends, claws and teeth and beaks dripping blood, followed.

Chapter Eight

GREI

Grei jolted awake to an empty room. Adora was gone.

Panic blossomed in his chest. It was just the same as the five other times: Grei slept, and Adora sneaked away and put an end to herself.

He didn't even know how long he'd been asleep. One hour? Ten?

He pushed himself up. He hadn't undressed when he'd fallen onto the bed—hadn't even taken his boots off—so he simply ran to the door and pushed it open.

He burst onto the tiny landing and almost tripped down the steps. He barely managed to catch the rickety handrail to keep himself from pitching headlong onto the cobblestones. He gathered his wits, closed his eyes, and reached out with his *dasha*.

He expected to find her body face-down in one of the tributaries that flowed through the city or dashed apart on the rocks at the base of Fairmist Falls. He expected it to take him some time to locate her—

It didn't.

Instead, he found her nearby and alive. She was just inside The Floating Stone, barely a hundred feet past the wall to his right.

His heart thundering in his chest, Grei cautiously approached the side door of the Stone and opened it. Pipe smoke and the strong scent of ale wafted out, as did the raucous noise of dozens of patrons talking and clinking glasses.

Seydir, filling a flagon behind the bar, spotted Grei instantly. The owner of the Stone topped off the flagon and pushed it expertly down the bar. The ale slid to a stop softly enough to touch Grei's hand.

"To the wizard of Fairmist!" Seydir said proudly, lifting another mug. "To the man who gave our city back to us!" The closest patrons of the bar turned to see who had entered, but instead of cheering, they went quiet.

When Grei had first tasted his powers as the Whisper Prince, back when only that nursery rhyme repeated over and over in his head, he had seen into Adora, seen confused ribbons of colors and felt her emotions. He hadn't been able to sort it out then, but it all came to him in an instant now.

He saw the ribbons of sallow yellow and frosty blue wafting up from the hunched patrons of the bar like they were all smoldering, like they were lit from the inside by colored coals. It was fear, different colors of fear. The lot of them, afraid of him. He had healed the wounds Velak and the emperor had inflicted upon his home town. He'd mended the broken things. Why were they scared?

He tried to push down his frustration.

"You blighters," Seydir boomed angrily, echoing that frustration. The barkeep's face went red. "Raise your mugs. To the wizard of Fairmist!"

A few mugs reluctantly went up, and a tepid cheer rippled through the room. Then everyone turned their attention away, suddenly fascinated by the rims of their tankards. Grei gave a wan smile, picked up the mug and raised it in return, but he didn't drink.

"It's a Thiaran Dark." Seydir worked his way out from behind the bar.

"I'm fine." Grei set it back down.

"If that's not to your liking, my boy, I'll get you something else."

He saw the red ribbons of anger rising from Seydir, but they were interwoven with ribbons of fear as well. For all his bluster, Seydir was also afraid of Grei.

He held the barkeep's gaze. "You've known me since I was a child, Seydir. Do you really think I'd hurt you? Or anyone in Fairmist? You don't need to be afraid of me. *They* don't need to be afraid of me." He jerked a finger at the subdued room. "I only came here to make things right."

Seydir's eyes turned sad. "I know that, lad. I know. That's not it. I...." He sighed, and Grei suddenly realized he'd read the man wrong. He wasn't afraid of Grei. He was afraid for a different reason. Something having to do with Grei was making him nervous, but not Grei himself.

"Where's Adora?" Grei asked, even though his *dasha* told him she was in the darkened corner of the bar, just beyond the crackling fireplace in the shadows.

Grei started in that direction, and Seydir caught his arm. "Lad..." he began, but he didn't seem to know what else to say.

Grei gently disengaged Seydir's hand, walked around the bar and into the shadows. At the first table sat a big man, a lowlander by the look of him, with long hair and a three-day growth of beard. He had powerful shoulders and muscled arms beneath his leather tunic.

Adora straddled his lap, kissing him passionately, her fingers in his hair. His big arms wrapped around her, and one hand cupped her behind.

Grei stumbled to a stop. For a moment, he couldn't feel anything. It was as if his heart had stopped beating. His hands and chest suddenly felt cold. A roaring filled his ears. He opened his mouth, like his body knew he had to say something, but his throat constricted.

They continued to grope at each other right in front of him, and Adora seemed to be initiating the embrace. She caressed the lowlander's face, kissed his lips with abandon.

"Son," Seydir said from behind, and Grei suddenly realized the barkeep had followed him. He tried to draw Grei away. "Come on."

Suddenly, Grei's heart pounded madly. He clenched his fists. The power of his magic hovered near, close at hand. He could hear the whispers of everything around him. The wood in the floor. The smokiness of the air. The damned excitement in the damned lowlander in front of him.

The whispers filled him and seemed to make the room lighter. He could command the air to lift the lowlander up, slam him against the wooden wall. He could command the wall to swallow the man, shackle him in a human-shaped prison...

And what? Have it cut him in half like a guillotine? Kill him?

Grei swallowed, fists quivering at his sides.

Adora drew a breath and took her face away from the lowlander. She twisted on his lap and glanced over her shoulder as though she'd known Grei was there the whole time, as though she'd been waiting for him.

It was like a slap.

She had been waiting for him. To show him this. To show him that she could hurt him for denying her suicide.

Or was this a way to get *him* to hurt *her*?

What did she think he would do? Kill her for kissing another man?

Grei cleared his throat and said, "Adora..."

"Yes?" Her hand was still tangled in the lowlander's long hair, caressing his scalp. The man belatedly realized she'd stopped kissing him, and his glazed eyes focused past her on Grei.

"Ay," he said. "Piss off. I'm workin' something here."

The lowlander's words were the tines of a fork pushing into Grei's cheeks. His fists clenched so tightly his nails bit into his palms, and he suddenly realized he *could* kill this man. Grei bared his teeth, ready to do something horrible…

He glanced at Adora's eyes again and saw the challenge there. She *wanted* him to do something horrible. She wanted him to come apart, to lose the high ground.

At least I don't go around killing people, Grei. I just want to die.

He forced his fists to unclench, and he swallowed hard. "My apologies," he said hoarsely. He looked directly at Adora. "Please, don't let me interrupt."

"By the twisty beard o' the emperor, I won't," the lowlander slid his hands along Adora's back and pushed her head back to his. She vigorously joined the kiss.

Grei tasted bile, turned stiffly and walked to the other end of the bar where Seydir had slid the Thiaran Dark. Seydir followed nervously.

Grei still didn't know what to do, only that he couldn't just kill someone because they were kissing Adora. He picked up the Thiaran Dark and drained the entire flagon without taking a breath.

"Give me another," he rasped. Seydir hesitated, then scuttled back behind the bar. He took the flagon and refilled it, slid it back to Grei.

He thought of the first time he'd met Blevins in this bar, of how much the fat man could drink. Ox Beer after Ox Beer, one after another until it seemed like even such a large body couldn't possibly contain that much liquid.

Grei drained his second ale and then a third. When he lifted the fourth to his lips, the lowlander stood, threw a couple of coins on the table, and lifted Adora in his arms. He carried her to the back of the bar toward the rooms Seydir provided for travelers.

Adora looked over the big man's shoulder, her dead eyes boring straight into Grei's soul.

Chapter Nine

GREI

Grei awoke in Adora's room without her. The glow of Fairmist's daylight slanted in through her single window, pressing at his eyes. His head pounded like someone was striking it with a tiny mallet. The room smelled like ale, and the vile aroma made Grei want to vomit. He didn't remember coming here, only remembered drinking ale after ale after ale.

He tried to hold very still. It seemed less painful if he didn't move, but by the Faia he needed air. He had to get out of this stifling, stale-beer room.

Clenching his teeth against the horrible, watering taste in his mouth, he staggered to the door and threw it open. He leaned over the rail and threw up onto the cobblestones far below.

Last night, he could barely understand what was happening, let alone what to do about it. All he'd known was that he had to stop himself from using his magic in rage. So he'd forced himself to keep drinking.

Adora was trying to make him hate her. Maybe she felt if she could achieve that, he wouldn't care about her anymore. He'd just let her...

He breathed hard, head hanging over the rail, lips dripping bile.

It isn't going to work, he thought. *I swore to protect you, and I will. No matter what. You want to drag me into an abyss? I will go. And we will come out the other side together. I will mend this just as I mended Fairmist Falls. I swear.*

It was only a new challenge, Grei tried to tell himself. He'd survived the tortures of the Delegate's men. He'd survived Selicia's betrayal. He'd survived the onslaught of Lyndion and Kuruk and Velak. He would survive this.

He wanted to lie down again, but the idea of going back to that sickening, stifling room was almost more than he could bear.

Instead, he staggered down the steps and into the city. He hiked uphill, following the fresh air and letting the floating droplets drench him. He hiked all the way to Fairmist Falls where he stripped down and leapt into the pool.

He tried to forget everything as the falls pounded into him, washing away the filth, washing away the entire night. He stayed under the falls until he was numb, and then he climbed to the shore and lay naked on the bank, staring up at the floating droplets.

This changes nothing, he thought. *Adora's actions. My drunken night. I move forward. I fix what I came to fix. And if, at the end of that journey, Adora still wants to kill herself...*

He stopped the thought before it came to completion. No. He wasn't going to think that. He wasn't ever going to think that.

He put on his clothes, feeling somewhat better, and walked slowly back to town. His stomach roiled, but at least he didn't feel like vomiting at every moment.

Using his *dasha*, he searched the city below him and found Adora. She was still at the Stone, so that's where he went. They were done in Fairmist. It was time to move on.

Opening the door, he expected to find her in the arms of her lowlander, but she sat alone at the bar with a tankard and some kind of metal flask lying next to it. The Stone was nearly empty—only a couple of people at tables against the wall. Grei didn't know what time it was, but based on the Stone's occupancy, it had to be morning, sometime before Highsun.

Adora swiveled as though she'd been waiting for him. She lifted the tankard, sipped it, and smiled.

He sat at the stool next to her as though they were two normal people. He wanted to say half a dozen things to lash her, like, "Did you sleep well?" or "Where is your friend?" or "Shall I run you a bath?"

But he didn't say any of those things. That's what she wanted. She wanted him to rage.

"We're leaving today," he said.

"You know, I used to hate Blevins," she slurred. She grinned and drank again. "Thought he was a no-good wastrel, drinking and concocting stupid dares to get you into trouble. I couldn't understand why a man with such an obviously keen mind would choose to drink instead of doing something useful with his life. Such a waste, I thought."

She upended the tankard and slammed it down on the bar. She stared at it for a moment, as though letting the notion sink in that it was empty, then she pushed up and leaned over the bar, her bare feet straining against the support struts of the stool. She tucked the empty flagon underneath a spout and expertly twisted it with one hand. Once it was full, she settled back and carefully centered the flagon in front of herself.

"But you know what I've learned?" She took a long drink. "Blevins was a Faia-be-damned genius."

He didn't say anything.

"And this..." She picked up the metal flask. It was small, the size of a hand. "This is my new best friend. Have you ever heard of Serpent's Tears?"

"No."

"S'new. Seydir just got it in before…everything. Before the whole thing. It's s'posed to be twice as potent as Dead Woods liquor. I never cared 'bout that before. Seems more important now." She unscrewed the cap on the flask and lifted the tiny spout to her lips. She barely tipped it up before bringing it back down and wheezed. "Just a drop'll do for you."

"Is there anything you would like to take with you?" he asked.

"Just my lovers." She gathered the flask and the flagon to her bosom.

He swallowed. "We'll get you riding pants."

"Ooo, good idea. You know, I once rode halfway across the Felesh Plantations in a shift. Me and Galius. Galius…. I killed him, too, you know. Killed him. Set him up for my father to stab him through the heart." Her brow clouded for a moment, then it eased with an expansive smile. "Just like everybody else. I killed a lot of people, Grei. Did you know? But I'm sure it's going to be alright, because I'll feel better in time. Right?"

"We're riding out today. I'll get horses."

"Won't that be fun," she murmured.

"Will you be here when I get back?" he asked.

She grinned and put her arms up in the air as she twisted slowly on the stool. "Where else in the world would I want to be?"

Grei sighed. He turned and left *The Floating Stone*.

Chapter Ten

GREI

Thirteen flying hares soared overhead as Grei and Adora rode south toward the Badlands. The sun beat down as they wound their way through the dry, blackened trunks. Sweat trickled down the back of Grei's neck as he watched the hares—who were obviously keeping pace with them on purpose. Grei had heard about flying hares his whole life. A drove of the giant-eared creatures would snuggle a child, tickling him with their soft coat and delighting him with their clicking purr.

But a single flying hare was crazy enough to attack an army.

Most animals became bold in groups. Wolves hunted in packs. The wild Twisthorns of Trimbledown protected their young by forming a circle and facing outward, the sharp horns of their namesake pointed toward any who might dare hurt them. People, of course, were the most aggressive in groups. Mobs. Conquerers. Wars.

But flying hares were the opposite. "Mad as a hare" as the saying went, because their strange behavior went against all logic. For the first time in his life, Grei felt he understood the hares.

He felt he didn't have a family anymore, but the loneliness didn't make him want to crawl in a hole, to distance himself as people sometimes did. No. He felt like he wanted to rage against the unfairness of it.

But he tempered the feeling and focused on his purpose.

When Emperor Qweryn had come for the Faia of the Vheysin Forest, when he had ripped the magic away from her and her domain, the other Faia had done nothing.

When Grei had fled to Fairmist Falls, evading Highblades and a murderous Slink, the Faia had turned away.

Now Grei would be damned if he was going to sit around and do nothing like the Faia. He had thought Adora, above all other people, would understand this, and it was all he could do to tamp down the glowing anger burning deep within him. Adora's indifferent attitude was a sliver in his mind that threatened to drive him mad. Only his iron purpose kept his rage in place. He wasn't an animal. He was the Whisper Prince, and he couldn't behave like some insane flying hare.

He shook his head and let out a snort.

Adora chuckled in response, and he looked over at her, trying not to glare. She watched him with a detached amusement, swaying gently in the saddle as she sipped from a wineskin filled with Thiaran Dark.

"Y'look like a water toad," she slurred.

Water toads were orange-skinned creatures that lived on the banks of the Fairmist River and its tributaries throughout the city. Strangely, the magical droplets did not lose their magic, becoming normal water when they touched water toads, like they did when they touched anything else. It was as though the toads were somehow compatible with the magic.

That would have been all well and good, and probably no one would ever have noticed this subtle phenomenon, except that water toads liked to swallow the droplets. They leapt about, chasing them. And if the frog actually managed to swallow a large enough droplet, it would pick the toad up and carry it a dozen feet before the brainless creature regurgitated it, dropping to the ground again. It was a popular child's game in Fairmist to chase water toads that had swallowed too many droplets, waiting for the moment they vomited and dropped back to the ground.

"A water toad?" Grei asked evenly, letting out a measured breath. He'd sworn to himself to be gentle with her, no matter what.

"Y'look like y'swallowed a huge droplet." She gestured with both her hands, stretching them as wide as possible, almost falling from her horse and spilling a swallow of Thiaran Dark onto the dry ground. "You're all stuffed up. 'Bout to pop!"

Grei turned away from her.

Getting out of Fairmist had been hard. Adora had gone along with him docilely enough, but she wasn't—she refused to be—the Adora he knew, the Adora he had loved. Instead, she'd played a twisted version of the wanton vixen she'd first portrayed to catch his attention.

On the way out of the tavern, she had made a spectacle of herself. Not only had she insisted on bringing *four* jugs of Thiaran Dark with them, but she had flirted with every man within reach, winking, giving sultry smiles, touching arms suggestively. Her fingers had lingered in the beard of a stunned—and married—Thoral Guildford, whispering enticing promises in his ear as Grei had pulled her out the door.

He supposed he should be happy that she had stopped trying to kill herself.

He had considered using The Root to travel to Thiara. It would have been faster, but like a lone flying hare, he felt a rabid resistance to doing what was easy. He didn't want to pass over even one place that Velak had ravaged. He needed to see every bit of what the demigod's attack had done to Thiara. Hundreds—perhaps even thousands—of people had been controlled by Velak's red mist. Grei had to retrace

Velak's footsteps and erase as much of the demigod's destruction as he could.

They had already found dozens of bodies alongside the road, some caught in the twig-thatched eddies of the Fairmist River. He could only imagine what had happened to those poor souls. Dead of thirst or starvation on the road, marching at Velak's command until their bodies simply collapsed? And those in the river…had they retained enough of their own minds to go mad at the horror of what was being done to them? Had they sought escape through drowning themselves?

He had buried every body they found, whispering gently to the dirt and sand to sink the bodies deep underground. He'd then created stone the color of marble, stronger than steel, and had it rise at the head of each grave.

He couldn't help thinking about those people now—so many dead—and wondering where their families were. What did they think? Would they come looking? Those poor survivors had deserved something, some monument to the passing of their loved ones. The road south of Fairmist now wound through a somber forest of blank white headstones.

"Y'know if you don't—" Adora began, but interrupted herself with a loud burp, which sent her giggling again.

They had reached the place Grei sought, and he reined in his mount amidst the burned trees. Adora continued riding as she giggled.

"If you don't, y'know…." she said, then blearily realized he wasn't riding next to her horse anymore. She craned her neck and looked back, fumbled with her reins and pulled her horse to a stop.

With surprising grace, she turned her mount and came back to join him. "You should vomit."

He sighed.

"If you don't—" She bent over and gave a mock retch, then popped back up and grinned. "Vomit, you know. If you don't vomit, y'could explode. Like a water toad. Explode like a toad. Right on the road."

"I appreciate your concern," he said, but he wasn't listening to her. He was listening to the murderous, seething whispers of the Dead Woods. The angry pines were just barely visible through the charred trunks of the Badlands.

He moved his horse off the road and between the burned trees, picking his way like he was following a dream. The marks of Selicia's wagon were long gone. The marks in the dirt where Blevins had slain Highblade after Highblade as Grei had escaped were gone. But he knew this was exactly the path he'd taken toward the Dead Woods that day he'd sprinted away from Selicia.

When he and Adora reached the desiccated remains of Grei's previous mount, he paused. Its dry hide had split, exposing the bones. His own horse bobbed his head, nostrils flaring, and he whispered to calm it.

Ahead, barely a hundred yards away, the jagged pines of the Dead Woods rose into the air, implacable like a line of spearmen awaiting a charge.

Adora clopped up alongside him and stopped. She looked down at the skeletal horse. "This looks like a good place to vomit."

He grunted, wishing she would stop talking.

For a moment she seemed like she might take her own advice, then she looked away from the carcass and spotted the trees. "This where you went into the Dead Woods."

"Mmmm." He was remembering the searing pain when the spirits came for him, ran their ethereal claws through him.

"And they didn't kill you," she said.

"They almost did."

"But you're the Whisper Prince, and nobody can kill the Whisper Prince." She grinned, her eyes half-lidded. "Everybody loves you. Don't they?"

He let out a measured breath and encouraged his horse forward, away from the carcass and toward the forbidding pines. He considered bringing Adora with him inside, but the spirits of the Dead Woods killed everyone who entered. Everyone, as Adora had pointed out, except for him. The spirits had told him not to return until he had defeated the Lord of Rifts—Velak—and he had fulfilled that promise. But they hadn't invited anyone else.

"Why're we here?" Adora asked.

"Unfinished business."

"With the Dead Woods?"

"Yes."

"This..." She drew a breath in the middle of her sentence like drunk people did, like she'd forgotten how to breathe normally and had suddenly remembered she needed air. "Looks like a really good place to die. Can I go with you?"

"You're staying here."

She chuckled, took another pull from the wineskin. "Of course, my liege."

He dismounted and tied his horse to a tree, pulled out the oat bag and affixed it to the horse's bridle. There was nothing to eat here, hadn't been anything to eat in some time.

"You should feed yours as well," he told Adora.

"Yes, my liege."

"Adora," he began, clenching a fist.

"Yes, my love?"

He sighed. "Never mind. Please just stay here."

"A please!" She feigned surprise. "Oh, he said please. I am overcome." She raised her flask. "Go, my liege. My master. My overlord. Do what you must. I shall stay, the docile and obedient little captive."

It was all he could do not to snap at her. He swallowed and turned away.

The insidious whispers filled his mind as he entered the Dead Woods, slipping between two of the tightly clustered, angry trunks.

As it had the first time, the sky went from bright sunlight to darkness, the trees leaning close to blot out the sun. His eyes adjusted quickly to the dim light and, just as before, he had gone about two dozen paces into the woods when the malevolence of the forest heightened. Its general hate coalesced into a specific fury focused on him.

The spirits came for him again, but this time they did not look like Adora. He saw them for what they truly were—swirls of yellow magic, twists of souls that suffered from a never-ending pain, from the loss of the joyous center of what they had once been. The Yellow Faia. Their anger would always be as fresh and raw as their memory of when the Yellow Faia had been ripped from them in a brutal fire of selfish magic.

The yellow spirits swirled around him like sharks for a moment, then stopped, flaring upright like giant yellow flames, each the size and height of a person.

"You have returned," one of the flickering swirls said. He didn't hear her words with his ears, not like he would hear a person talking, but instead within his mind. It was as if the words flowed on a wind that no one could perceive except The Whisper Prince.

"I kept my promise," Grei said. "The emperor and the Lord of Rifts are no more."

"We felt the passing of the Lord of Rifts," the spirit said. *"You have done a great service for your grove. And you also opened the lands to a great destruction."*

Grei nodded. "That is why I am here."

"Is it?"

"I am the new steward of Devorra. Of the blue roses." He didn't know if these spirits knew of such things, but it was possible they did. The Yellow Faia certainly had.

The spirit didn't respond.

"The Faia have passed," he continued. "Where once they took care of their domains, now there is only me, and I would do right by you. I would mend what was broken when the emperor killed the Yellow Faia."

The yellow flame-bodies flickered faster, as though caught in a breeze.

"Come with me," the spirit said. One by one, the person-sized flames flowed into the air, turning into those long, shark-like swirls of yellow, and darted deeper into the woods. Grei jogged after.

He knew where they were going. The first time he had come to this place, these spirits had wanted to kill him. They had attacked him, inflicting excruciating pain. He'd fallen unconscious and when he'd awoken, they had brought him to a great white tree in the center of the forest. Under his protest, they had somehow shoved him inside it.

In that moment, he'd thought they'd killed him, but it had been a kind of spell, an unexpected method of communication.

Now, of course, Grei understood the whispers far better. He could feel the increasing concentration of magic as the yellow flames led him into a huge clearing where the enormous white-barked tree grew upward, encircled by green pines like an emperor encircled by spearmen. Its gnarled branches twisted outward, and its great white leaves caught the sunlight, each bordered in a slim outline of green.

Grei studied that. The last time he'd been here, the leaves had been bordered in yellow. A slight change, but probably a significant one.

The yellow spirits swirled around the tree, then settled back into their person-high flames.

"You have been here before." The closest spirit spoke in Grei's mind. *"This is...."* the spirit said a word, but Grei didn't understand it. The word lingered, a nonsensical hum,

as though Grei's mind simply couldn't grasp the meaning. After a disorienting pause, the unknowable word translated to, *"...The White Tree."*

But though Grei had no word for what the spirit had tried to convey, he didn't need a word to feel the immensity of what the White Tree meant to the spirits of the trees that hovered around him. The White Tree was vast, beyond the rest of the pines in the Dead Woods as Fairmist Falls was beyond one of its floating droplets. Its whispers flowed to him so strongly it felt like they were about to carry him away like a feather on a hurricane.

Images and colors came to him. Ribbons of green and white, growing things and the power of truth. Suddenly Grei knew that the White Tree had been there for a long time. A very long time.

It was...ancient. It had been here since long before the Yellow Faia had arrived.

Last time, Grei had been so disoriented he had not understood the power of this place. Now he did. There was a kind of...similarity between this place and the field of blue roses. This was a place of great magical power.

There were places of great power in the lands, nodes of magic. Fairmist Falls. The Jhor Forest. Grei had always thought those places were powerful because of the Faia who resided there—that it was the presence of the Faia that *made* them powerful. Now he wondered if it was the other way around, if the Faia had chosen their havens because magical power was already there.

"When you were here before," the yellow spirit said, *"we forced you to speak to...."* Again, there was a pause as Grei's mind failed to understand the word. *"...The White Tree.... Do you need our assistance again?"*

"That won't be necessary." Grei walked forward. The yellow spirits flickered faster, agitated, and several moved closer. He listened to their whispers as well as the whispers of the ground beneath him, the pine trees at the border of the clearing, the very air between them, and the White Tree. Its whisper was different than the rest, a litany that wasn't so much words as a feeling of ancient calmness.

None of the spirits stopped him, and he came to stand before the White Tree. He reached out and put his palm flat against its smooth white bark. Last time, he'd fallen inside the tree, and its memories had become his memories. This time, he didn't need to see the past. He wanted to help with the future.

He let his mind drift on that powerful wind, letting its feelings come to him. He opened a bridge between his human consciousness and whatever was within the White Tree.

Those unintelligible whispers made him suddenly feel like the boy he'd been when the Delegate's men had tortured him, when he had struggled to understand what was happening to him.

But learning to translate the whispers of another creature had been his first lesson. Slowly, he began to understand.

"*You…are…The Whisper Prince…? You…are…The Whisper Prince…? You…are…The Whisper Prince…?*" The voice droned, as though it had said that same sentence over and over again for the last minute.

"Yes," he finally answered, and the repeating sentence stopped. The whispers went quiet in his mind. Then, after a delay in which Grei's mind seemed to work the translation…

"*You can hear me?*" the White Tree asked.

"I can now."

"*You have come far. Since you partook of my roots and the…*" The White Tree said a word that didn't translate. Grei's mind fumbled with it until it finally came up with "*…Times-and-Events-Within-Me.*"

"Yes," Grei acknowledged.

"*This is unexpected. Never before has a human heard my voice.*"

"I've learned a great deal, and I've come to offer a gift. A…recompense for your trials. It was humans who did this to you." He waved at the pines, at the angry yellow spirits. "The Faia who resided here, who used her power to protect you, was taken by humans. That makes it my responsibility. And while I realize that what was done can never be undone, perhaps I can help a little."

Grei took several steps away from the White Tree and knelt in the meadow. He touched the grass lightly, pushed his fingers deeper into the dirt, and called on his connection to the blue roses.

The power roared through him, and he slowly pulled his fingers out of the dirt. A blue rose sprouted, going from tiny sprout to seedling to a full, shimmering rose in seconds. Far to the north, he felt one of the roses in that far-off field shrink down and vanish.

The whispers all about Grei intensified. The White Tree shuddered, leaves shaking, and the green outline of those white leaves changed to blue.

Grei stood up, wobbling. Every time he used such powerful magic, it left him disoriented. His body brimmed with power, but his mind seemed to detach, like he was unanchored on a vast sea.

"It is…" Grei murmured, working to regain his senses. "Not the Yellow Faia, but it is something."

For a long moment, Grei heard hums and rustles in his mind from the White Tree, but apparently none of it was communication. Or if it was, none of it translated to words.

Finally, the White Tree said, *"Thank you."*

The swirling flames of the spirits flickered, and their edges also became blue, just as the White Tree's leaves had done. When he'd first come here, they had screamed at him so horribly he'd had to grab his head at the pain. But this time, they sang, and it lightened his heart: the joyous call of the wind, the playful rustling of leaves.

"I am the steward of the blue roses," Grei said. "Of the continent of Devorra."

The White Tree shuddered, and the song of the spirits heightened. Then, after a moment, the song quieted to silence.

"We thank you, Whisper Prince," the White Tree said. *"Your gift is beyond measure."*

"You are welcome. And I'm...so sorry. I will ensure humans will not act in this same manner toward your lands again. The Faia were wrong to stand aside. The mother of these lands went insane, I think. Perhaps that is why she hoarded the power of the blue roses, and why the Faia pulled back."

The White Tree shook lightly, and a single blue-bordered leaf drifted down, alighting softly on in Grei's shoulder. He reached up and took it reverently, held it cupped in both hands.

"Cavyn was troubled," the White Tree said.

"You knew her?"

"Of course. Deilli was saddened at her slow transformation."

"Deilli?"

"Deilli was the one you call the Yellow Faia."

"Ah."

"Cavyn bent the natural order, yes. And some of her creations were wondrous—like Deilli who made my grove her home. But some were catastrophic, like the Lord of Rifts. I honor her passing for the good she wrought as well as the bad. But you are mistaken. Cavyn was not the mother of these lands."

"Wait. Cavyn wasn't...she didn't create Devorra?"

"No. She was—as is everything in this land—the child of Devorra."

"Devorra...the continent."

"The continent is named for its creator. Devorra the mother. Venisha the father."

"Venisha?"

"She and Venisha created everything you know."

"The god Venisha?" The creator of the Slate Wizards. He tried to piece it together.

"Yes."

Grei fell into stunned silence.

"Humans consider the Faia to be gods," the White Tree continued, *"but Venisha and Devorra made the world. They made everything you see, long long ago. Devorra nurtured me. She was the first thing I knew as I awakened to life."*

"Where is she now? How could she allow Velak to…how could she allow all this to happen?"

"She went away some time ago. She did not return."

"Of course. That seems to be a hallmark of her entire family."

"Your ire does not become you, Whisper Prince. I do not think Devorra's intentions were to leave us forever. Venisha came for her lands. She had to fight him."

"Fight him?"

"They were lovers before the world existed. It was their lovemaking that breathed life into the lands. It began in the lands named for Venisha. They were the first birthed. The trees. The ocean. Even humans. And then Devorra came here, created this place away from Venisha."

"Away from him?"

"They fell to bickering, and she left him. Venisha took and twisted the life around him, sometimes extinguishing it and sometimes transforming it into new and abhorrent forms. Devorra opposed this, but he was too powerful for her. She could not break that bond, so she fled what you know as Venisha and birthed these new lands you have named for her. She used what she had learned with Venisha and created a bastion of life and beauty on this faraway shore."

Grei tried to absorb everything he was being told. There were beings more powerful than the Faia, more powerful than Cavyn.

"Devorra created you?"

"*I was one of the first to awaken to self-awareness, to see and understand that I was alive. Devorra was delighted by this. In those early days, she would often come to my grove, adding to it, encouraging me. This is how I learned of Venisha and how the world came to be. It was a time of sublime peace for me. I looked forward to her visits, and I thought that was how life would always be. It might have been to this day if not for Venisha.*"

"He came here. He tried to take it," Grei guessed.

"*When he saw what she had made, he wanted it. He flew across the Sunset Sea and tried to take it from her. He drove his roots deep into her lands and tried to form the same bond that he had formed in his own lands. She fought him again, but this time she won. Her creations came to her aid. She called upon me and every other creature and we gave our life force willingly. She siphoned just a little from every living creature. She created the blue roses from it, a bastion of pure life fed by every living creature she had nurtured. This fountain of power enabled her to fend off Venisha.*"

"She forced him back over the sea?"

"*Yes, but he didn't stay there. Again and again he tried, and again and again she used the blue roses to repel him. This was when I learned that the world wasn't just peaceful, that there was a threat that could destroy us all, destroy what Devorra had longed to build. Then one day, she simply vanished, and I never saw nor felt another battle in these lands she loved. Oh, when I felt her vanish from these lands, I thought for certain that Venisha would arrive the next day, that he would suck the life from us, that he would enslave us. But he never did.*"

"What happened?"

"*No one knows for sure. We all believe different things, the longest lived among us, those who remember Devorra. Some believe the lovers killed each other. Some believe they took their tempestuous love affair to some other reality we cannot perceive. But I believe he lured her away to his lands, where he was strongest. I believe he has her trapped there still.*"

"Why do you think that?"

"Because Devorra would never leave her creations, not willingly."

"But you don't think he killed her?"

The White Tree shuddered, and the sounds it made faded as though it was contemplating that terrifying fate.

"Do not say such a thing," the White Tree said. *"It is not fathomable that the mother of the world, that such a being could die."*

"I've watched such beings die," Grei said.

The White Tree shuddered again, and this time its leaves descended randomly, not with the pinpoint precision from before. *"If she were dead, I would feel it. I would know it. But all I feel is a great sadness, a…longing. She is out there, Whisper Prince. She is somewhere in the lands ruled by Venisha. And you must find her."*

That startled him.

"What? No. I'm going to mend the wounds of *this* land. Then I am done. And once I'm done, I'm going to take Adora and vanish from all of this nonsense. We are going to live a simple life. That's what she wants. That's what I want."

"You must save Devorra. If you do not, Venisha and his Slate Wizards will come, and they will do to these lands what they have done to their own—"

"Enough!" He took his hand off the white bark. "It's too much. I will mend what I can mend. I'm not a demigod and I don't want to be one."

"Grei, you must."

"No." He backed away from the White Tree. The flame-like spirits surrounded him, as though they would stop him. He let the flood of the blue roses flow through him. He didn't want to fight them, but he would.

"No," the White Tree said. *"We do not fight The Whisper Prince."*

The tree spirits stopped their advance.

"I'm sorry for your loss," Grei said. "But I'm not looking for this goddess of yours. I can't. I promised you I would mend the rifts. And that's what I'm going to do."

"The rifts will never be fully healed—this land will never be whole—until Devorra returns."

Grei shook his head, not wanting to talk about his real reasons. The truth was, the lands had moved along just fine without Devorra. In the wake of Velak's destruction, the last thing Grei wanted to do was loose another nigh-omnipotent demigod on the Thiaran Empire.

"I'm sorry," he said.

He turned away from the White Tree, began walking through the forest. When he'd first come to the Dead Woods, he'd instantly become lost in the angry trees, but now he knew the whispers of the ground, the bark, the very air. He knew exactly where the sun touched the top of the forest's canopy. He felt the pulse of the world like it was his own pulse. He headed back to Adora.

"You will save Devorra," the White Tree said softly, its voice seeming to emanate from the pines he passed.

He shook his head.

"You will," the White Tree's voice echoed. *"You will see."*

Chapter Eleven

GREI

As Grei emerged from the Dead Woods, he reached into his pouch and withdrew The Root. The Slate Spirit's creaky voice filled his mind.

"Hello Grei," the Slate Spirit said, then paused. "I sense magic all around you. Where have you gone?"

"Into the Dead Woods."

"Ah," the Spirit said. "There is a strong entity who lives there."

"I am well aware."

"She is very protective of her boundaries."

"What do you know about Venisha?"

"Everything there is to know," the Slate Spirit said. "It is where I was created, where I am imprisoned. The kingdom is ruled by—"

"Not the kingdom. The god."

The Slate Spirit went silent. "Ah."

"Is he real? Is there a god named Venisha?"

Again, a hesitation. "Very real."

"Did you know him?"

"Know him? He was a god. No one knew him."

"Was a god?"

"He has not been seen in centuries. Since before he created me and the Slate Wizards."

"He was the one who gave the Slate Wizards their power?"

"Of course."

"Why didn't you tell me this before?"

"I..." The Slate Spirit paused. "It didn't occur to me. The Slate Wizards are the danger to you. And they are my jailers."

"What about Devorra? What do you know of her?"

"The goddess, not the continent, I assume."

"So you've heard of her."

"A little. According to an ancient myth, she was Venisha's lover. His counterpart. A goddess nearly as powerful as he. This continent is named for her. Perhaps she was to Thiara what Venisha is to Vaeron's kingdom."

"What happened to her?"

"Am I to know this? I am not a god, only a spirit trapped in an artifact. There are myths, to be sure, but are they true? I don't know."

"What myths?"

"It is believed that she and the god Venisha killed each other in a great war three hundred years ago. The Slate Wizards and I were given power to fight that war, meant to come and claim this land for him. But the war was cut short when Venisha vanished. The Slate Wizards tried to continue it, but they were kept at bay by the Faia, as I have already said."

And the Faia were now gone, along with this barrier they had supposedly created to keep the Slate Wizards at bay.

"I told you. If they are not here already, they are coming, Grei."

Through the trees, he saw Adora by the tethered horses. She sat on the ground with her back against a tree, one knee cocked, and drank from her wineskin as she loudly sang a bawdy tavern song.

The Badlands had undergone a startling transformation. It was as though a waft of life and humidity had swept through the place. The ground felt moist under Grei's feet. Small patches of green grass clustered near the bases of the still-dead trees. But on a high branch above Adora's head, a single green leaf had sprouted, an emerald splash of color on the gray-brown bark. The blue rose had brought life, even out here. Soon, the Vheysin Forest would be what it had once been. The thought made Grei's heart ease.

I will mend the broken—

"I would like to make my second request of you now," the Slate Spirit said.

Grei's sense of easiness curdled, and he armored himself again.

"What do you want?"

"I would like to show you something about The Root, something you may not know."

"You want to show me something?"

"A function that you may find helpful."

When Grei had made the deal with the Slate Spirit, he'd thought he was making a Slink's bargain, that for the power he needed, he was setting himself up for disaster. But he'd taken the risk because Adora's life—the very lives of everyone on Devorra—had depended on it. Now, that price was coming due, but....

It barely seemed a price at all.

"That's all?"

"That is all."

"Very well, show me."

"You wish to go to the crown city of Thiara next, is that correct?"

"Yes."

"I would like to show you a faster way of using The Root for travel."

"Faster?"

"Collect your beloved," the Slate Spirit said.

As Grei approached, Adora was still raucously singing, and she raised her wineskin to him in salute:

The great Zed Hack, he drank deep
Danced all night without sleep
Swept the ladies off their feet
And he made do
With one or two
And left them smiling in a heap

"Open The Root," the Slate Spirit said. "We will use it to go to the crown city of Thiara today."

"Today?" It was a three-day ride from here.

"This instant," the Slate Spirit said.

Adora stopped singing as Grei spoke to, apparently, nobody. She cocked her head.

"How do we get from here to Thiara in an instant?" Grei asked.

"Collect your musical lady and enter The Root. I will show you."

"Are we going somewhere new?" Adora slurred.

"Still to Thiara," he said. "But we're using The Root."

"Back to the mud tunnels! Every girl's dream." She tried to rise, lost her balance, and fell back down. Grei took The Root from his pouch and flicked open a hatch.

He envisioned it opening beneath all four of them, and so it did. Grei, Adora, and their two horses dropped into the earth. He whispered to the air to slow their descent, and they all alighted softly.

He looked down the long tunnel—straight as an arrow—that went completely dark beyond the light from the open hatch.

Adora modified her drinking song.

Into The Root
Into The Root
I'm tumbling down a dirty chute

But I'll make do
Yes I'll make do
And offer up my best salute

She raised her wine skin to Grei, then tipped it up and drained it, shaking the last drops into her mouth.

"Focus on The Root," the Slate Spirit said.

Grei listened to the whispers of the earth around him, felt the shape of the tunnel in its strength, and its connection to the little artifact in his hand. It hummed as though it knew that he was thinking about it.

"The Root is straight," the Slate Spirit said. "It's always straight, going from point A to point B without winding around the folds of the land. This is one of its greatest advantages. But, unless you use it as I am about to instruct you, it still passes the same distance you would pass on the land above, simply without obstructions. But The Root can do more. I want you to imagine your destination."

Grei thought of the Red Wall outside of the crown city of Thiara. He thought of the mighty gates, the city beyond with its seven white towers, and the Sunset Sea behind it all. He recalled it like he'd seen it with Selicia that first time.

"Do you have it in your mind?" the Slate Spirit asked.

"Yes."

"What do you see?"

"The Red Wall. The gates of Thiara."

"Good. Now connect The Root to that place. Imagine where it will stop beneath the earth, just before the gates."

He did. "All right."

"Focus on the end of the tunnel, on that spot where you will open the hatch again. Imagine opening that hatch, looking up and seeing the sky just near the city."

He imagined it.

"Now imagine the long, straight tunnel curving just a little. Imagine it bending just a little with every foot of it, bending bending bending. Do you see it bending?"

"I...yes."

"A little bit at a time, bend it all the way, like a loop where the beginning and end are parallel to each other, touching."

Grei struggled with that. "Bend it back on itself?"

"Exactly so."

He envisioned it like he had folded a cord in his hands, with the two ends parallel and pointing the same direction.

"The ends are side by side?"

"Yes."

"Now... have them touch."

He touched them. The tunnel shook, and little bits of dust and rock showered down from the ceiling overhead.

"By the Faia!"

"Hold the image. Do not lose your concentration."

Grei redoubled his effort. He envisioned the end of the tunnel and the beginning of the tunnel next to each other, pointing the same direction, and the long middle looping around and back on itself.

"Now..." the Slate Spirit said. "Dissolve the wall between the end and the beginning of the tunnel."

Grei whispered to the tunnel wall—not the one in his imagination—and asked the rough rock and dirt to become liquid. It flowed away, revealing an exact duplicate of the tunnel on the other side.

"Walk through quickly," the Slate Spirit said.

"Adora," Grei murmured to catch her attention. He was afraid the moment he stopped picturing the curved tunnel so clearly, it would vanish. If he stopped to think about what he was doing, about the sheer madness of it, would everything collapse?

The duplicate tunnels shook, and more dirt and rock sifted down. Adora continued her song, but she swaggered through the opening, leading her horse. Grei tugged at his.

"Rebuild the wall," the Slate Spirit said.

Grei whispered to the debris of the liquid dirt, asking it to reform, to build up and close the circular portal between tunnels. It leapt to his command and soon, Grei, Adora, and the horses stood in a singular tunnel again.

"Now you may release your concentration. Imagine it going back to the way it was, long and straight, except now you are at the end, and the beginning is far away, back by the Dead Woods."

Grei nearly lost his concentration at that. He clenched his fist, fighting to keep the image. He had no idea what would happen if he lost the picture in his head. Slowly…he straightened the imaginary tunnel. The actual tunnel where he and Adora now stood stopped shaking.

"Well done," the Slate Spirit said. "Startlingly well done. You have a gift for magic that rivals anything I have ever seen. My second request has been fulfilled. Consider your second debt paid."

A sweeping euphoria rushed through Grei, and he took a swift breath. He felt like he was floating, like a hundred-pound sack of sand had been lifted from his shoulders. He felt like he could bound up and touch the stars.

Grei held up The Root and flicked open one of the hatches. The ceiling opened, and daylight flooded the tunnel. Adora squinted up and changed her song again.

The bright, the bright!
I'm soaking up the light
Just like I'm soaking up the ale
To keep me feeling right.

She saluted the daylight. The air lifted them and their horses gently out of The Root until they stood on normal ground atop The Crown—the rocky outcropping that surrounded the city of Thiara.

"That was…amazing," Grei murmured, looking behind him at the leagues and leagues they had just crossed in an instant. It made him dizzy. But they were here. They were actually here in…

His thoughts dried up as he looked down at the city of Thiara. He could feel the wrongness of the place. In the distance, Thiara's majesty looked the same: the seven white towers thrust high in the sky, the Web of Blades hung high between them, glistening like it was awaiting the return of some giant spider, and the Red Wall encircling the city shone wetly as if it were covered with fresh paint.

But its whispers were different. The entire city shivered quietly like a beaten dog. None of the cacophony of whispers rising from that place were happy. Of course, he hadn't expected rejoicing or celebrations at the death of Velak—most citizens of Thiara didn't even know of the existence of Velak—but he had expected at least a sense of hope.

It felt as if an axe were poised above the city's neck.

"What's happening here?" Grei murmured to himself.

"I think…" Adora swung up into her saddle. She leaned back like a child who wanted to see how far back she could go, arms winging out to the side. "I think that the sky is getting farther away. That's what's happening. I think it's actually getting farther away. Doesn't it seem taller to you?"

"Never mind," Grei said, but she popped upright, red-faced and blinking as she focused on the city. "Hey, it's Thiara! The beloved cradle of my upbringing. My childhood source of love and support. The place where parents would never throw a child into the burning arms of fire monsters. Are we here so soon?"

Grei tried to ignore her and concentrate on the pall of emotion he felt. He immediately thought of Kuruk and his brothers. Had they returned? Had they come back to Thiara for revenge?

But…no. If Kuruk was here for some kind of revenge, there would be screaming. There would be dying. Grei felt none of that. He just felt…apprehension.

"Something's wrong," he murmured.

Adora chuckled. "Something's wrong? In Thiara?"

"Adora—"

"That's like saying 'This bucket of water might be a bit wet.'" Her chuckle turned into laughter, then into uncontrollable laughter. She swayed sideways and fell off her horse.

With a whisper, he bid the air catch her and put her back in the saddle.

"Whoop! How about that? I fall. You put me back. I fall. You put me back. It's like a girl can't fall out of the saddle even if she wants to. Remind you of anything? Is there a subtle parallel here?"

She leaned toward him, smiling, and tried to take another drink from her wineskin. Finding it empty, she tucked it away, then fumbled to retrieve the hand-sized metal flask.

Grei didn't say anything.

"Oh, I'm sorry. I should mind my manners. Something big and horrible is happening and the Whisper Prince is worried. And if the Whisper Prince is worried, we should all be worried. Or else—"

"Adora!"

She hiccuped.

"Your sister and your mother are in there," he said.

"My mother. As if I want to see my mother."

"I can't imagine running an empire has been easy these past weeks."

"My mother gave me up to pirates!" Adora hissed dramatically, waving her arms.

"Adora—"

"Well, maybe they weren't pirates. But they were Slinks. Except they weren't that either, really. They were figments of our imagination. My mother gave me up to figments! She deserves to get slapped around a little."

"And your sister?" Grei asked.

Adora's jolly attitude faded. She took a deep breath and let it out, swaying in the saddle. "No. Vecenne didn't deserve anything that happened to her. Rape. Beatings. To be crushed under the heavy fist of Velak's mind...." She trailed off, and her arms sank down to her sides. The flask hung from the tips of her fingers. "Yes. Thank you for that. For reminding me of the ruin I've made of her life."

Grei clenched his jaw. "Adora, we're going to fix it."

She blinked, looked over at him with dead eyes, and then the sparkle returned. She grinned and sipped from the flask. "Of course we are. All we need is a hammer. And the Whisper Prince is the biggest hammer in the land. Slam slam slam."

Grei mounted and urged his horse forward, down the slope toward the Red Wall. After taking a pull from her flask, Adora dutifully followed.

No sooner had they joined the imperial road than the gates of the Red Wall opened and a cohort of seven Highblades came through at a gallop, heading toward them with obvious purpose. They wore the imperial colors: gold pantaloons and red X harnesses.

The Highblades stopped. Three stopped short, pulled bows and nocked arrows, training them on Grei and Adora. The other four sidled closer, drawing swords.

"Hospitable, aren't they?" Adora noted and hiccuped.

Grei let the whispers flow into his mind. He heard the steel in their hands, the metal helms, the reins and saddles, the X harnesses the Highblades wore, the wood of the bows and their strings of sinew, the horses and their nervous energy. He whispered and the air between them went as solid as a shield.

"Whisper Prince!" The lead Highblade pointed his sword at Grei's face, though there was still half a dozen feet—and an invisible wall—between them. "You are to come no further. The emperor has decreed you an ill omen, and you shall not set foot within Thiara."

"The emperor?" Grei asked.

"Turn around and go back," the Highblade commanded.

"Which emperor?" The more Grei looked at the man, the more he noticed certain things. His unshaven face, his unkempt hair. He wore his X harness like he wasn't quite used to it, and he had an air that seemed too brutish, even for a Highblade. Grei wondered how long this man had actually been a Highblade.

"I did not come to parlay with you. Emperor Biren has commanded you leave," the Highblade said. "I won't warn you a second time."

"Well, I'm not leaving," Grei said.

Adora giggled.

Sneering, the Highblade held up his hand and three arrows sang from ready bows.

They hit Grei's invisible wall. Two ricocheted. One snapped in half and fell.

The lead Highblade's eyes went wide, then narrowed. He let out a bellow, lifted his sword high, and kicked his heels into his mount. With a whinny, the horse leapt forward—

And smashed into the same wall, its head and neck forced down, and its back legs leaving the ground in a fierce bucking motion. The mounted Highblade crashed headfirst into the wall and dropped like a stone, unconscious.

The other six Highblades roared and charged, riding around in a circle to flank Grei and Adora.

Grei whispered, melting their helmets down over their faces, then solidified them again. Suddenly blind, the Highblades panicked. They shouted and pulled on their reins. Two horses reared. Three of the Highblades fell to the ground, wrestling with their heads.

Two others swung blindly with their swords, coming dangerously close to decapitating each other, as the last Highblade leaned into his horse's neck, grabbing tightly like a scared child grabs its mother.

"So this is how it's going to be?" Grei murmured, moving his horse between the Highblades as they struggled. He turned to Adora. "Who's Biren?"

"My intended," she replied. "My affianced. My mandated beloved. When I was ten, it was decreed we would marry. Alas, it appears he is through waiting. One can hardly blame him."

"Your intended?"

"Before I died. The first time," she said.

They approached the gates of the Red Wall, and the stunned Highblades atop it shouted to each other. The great wooden doors began to shut. Grei narrowed his eyes.

As if a gate was going to stop him.

Chapter Twelve

BIREN

Emperor Biren shoved a grape in his mouth and chomped down. A squirt of juice escaped and trickled down his chin. He wiped at it with his sleeve and, at the last second, realized the white cuff was now stained.

That annoyed him.

But then, really, what did it matter? He'd have the imperial seamstress make him a new robe. Perhaps he should have one for each day of the week. Perhaps a dozen if he wished. Why should an emperor care? After all, it was his job to do whatever he wanted, and it was the job of everyone else to serve him.

He looked over at Via. She was sitting on the stone floor in the outfit he'd commanded she wear, made of a gauzy dark material that showed off her pleasing curves. It showed off that she was the most beautiful woman in the empire.

He'd had his men remove her cushion today, though. She'd decided to talk back to him about it when she should have been grateful, so she didn't deserve a cushion. She hadn't said a thing since, still wearing that defiant look on her face.

She seemed to feel his eyes on her and turned to glare at him even as she tucked two fingers underneath the steel collar around her neck to ease its weight. The attached chain trailed away and connected to the leg of Biren's throne. That collar was heavy, he had no doubt, but if she didn't want a collar, she shouldn't have tried to escape last week.

She should be grateful. She'd realize that soon.

He looked away from her, annoyed. The day's audience was sparsely attended. Word had gotten around that Emperor Biren didn't tolerate silly requests. If he deemed a petitioner frivolous, he saw no reason to allow that petitioner to ever have the chance to bother him again. After all, an emperor was far too busy to waste his time with inconsequentials.

Biren's archon, a steward from Felesh named Tyshant, had assured him that open audience time with his subjects was an important part of being emperor, but Biren didn't see the advantage. Giving commoners the opportunity to interact with the emperor…just didn't seem natural. He was definitely going to do away with this custom. If Tyshant thought it was so important, *he* could talk to the unwashed masses.

Biren reached over for another grape from the tray and popped it into his mouth. He chewed it thoughtfully as he looked down at the miserable petitioners. There were twelve of them today. He mentally swore that if one more person brought up the Phantom War and the Red Haze, as they were calling it, he was going to execute them right here in the throne room.

At least that might be amusing.

Dozens of Biren's loyal Highblades flanked the main floor. There were probably more Highblades than petitioners, and that was the way Biren liked it. When the Red Haze had ensorcelled the minds of everyone in the palace, Biren and his small army were in the southeastern edge of the city. They'd gotten word about the red mist and had evacuated before it had reached them.

That had been the brilliant stroke of luck that had delivered the throne to him. After the Red Haze had wiped out the city, it had been simple to move in, as easy a conquest as any in history. But he hadn't gotten cocky about it. No. His father had shown him that you should always strengthen your position. Pendulums swung back and forth all the time.

So before Via, her Highblades, and her pet assassins had come to their senses, during that befuddled fog that had followed the release of the Red Haze, he had struck. He'd killed her top Highblades first, cutting down the leaders of her force, and then began hunting down the rest.

There was only one flaw in that plan, and it nattered at his mind. He'd killed a number of Highblades, ensuring his forces were the strongest in the capitol, but he hadn't been able to find any of the Ringblades. When he'd begun slaying Via's Highblades, the Ringblades just vanished. Cunning little rats.

That made him a little nervous.

He popped another grape into his mouth and chewed viciously. In retrospect, he should have gone after the Ringblades first. He'd perceived his biggest threat to be the fighting men, but now those Ringblades were out there...somewhere. And he knew Via wouldn't be half so defiant if she didn't believe her pet assassins were slinking through the shadows, preparing to rescue her. Biren wanted her without hope. He wanted Via's will battered down. The missing Ringblades made that difficult.

One of the side doors behind the throne opened forcefully, slamming against the wall with a boom that echoed throughout the chamber. Eltioch rushed through, breathing like he'd run the entire circumference of the Red Wall.

Biren clenched his teeth and threw a grape at the attendant with the tray. It bounced off her belly and fell on the floor just as Eltioch crashed to his knees by Biren's throne, causing the girl to stumble back and almost fall.

Grapes, sweetmeats, and succulent cuts of pineapple fell onto the floor as she tried to save them, overbalancing the tray and dumping even more onto herself.

"Baezin's Blood, Eltioch. A fine show you're making!" Biren snarled. "What could possibly—"

"The Whisper Prince!" Eltioch gasped. "He's here."

Biren paused for just a moment, then his anger flared. He was surrounded by incompetents. He wanted to stab Eltioch through the heart with his dagger right here and now.

"I told Sheffic to take six Highblades and kill him," Biren growled.

"They…couldn't. They tried. He just…" Eltioch fought to catch his breath as he waved his hand vaguely. Like that was supposed to mean something. "He did his whisper thing…I think."

"You think," Biren said, his hand gripping his dagger. "Your incompetence is—"

The giant double doors at the far side of the throne room opened by themselves. Usually it took one man on each door, but some powerful force had shoved them wide from without.

A ponytailed man wearing traveling leathers entered. He had dark, angry eyes and a clenched jaw, and he was followed by a woman with a large, floppy hat. She cocked her head back and forth as though she had just acquired it and was flaunting it for others to see. She appeared as frivolous as the man was serious, and she walked with the rubbery gait of someone five tankards drunk.

The man strode up the aisle toward Biren, and the petitioners who took up the center of the throne room melted away from him. His dark gaze flicked to Biren, to the attendant to Biren's left who had stopped in the midst of her frantic cleaning, then to Biren's right where Via huddled on the floor.

"You are the so-called emperor?" the man asked.

Biren sneered, stood up from his throne and pulled his dagger, even as he gave a nod to his many Highblades.

"And you're the so-called Whisper Prince?" he said as twenty Highblades stalked toward the man, swords drawn. A dozen archers in the gallery overhead rose, pointing crossbows.

"Oh Biren," the drunk woman with the floppy hat said. "You're looking good. That big jiggly belly makes a girl go weak."

Biren frowned, peering at the woman...and recognized her! By the Faia, was that Mialene? Wasn't she supposed to be dead?

The sight of her stunned him. Mialene. His betrothed. The princess he was *supposed* to have married.

He shook his head. No. That was the past. That was the prize of a duke's son, not the rightful consort to the current emperor. Mialene didn't matter. He had her mother. And after that, if Via couldn't be cowed—or if he grew bored with her—Princess Vecenne was being held in reserve.

"Kill them!" Biren growled.

A dozen crossbows twanged, but instead of feathering the stupid Whisper Prince, the arrows shot every which way, bouncing off the ceiling, floors and walls—one even thunked into Biren's throne, right beside his hand!

The archers suddenly fell through the floor of the gallery, crashing hard onto the ground-level throne room. Bones snapped as ankles and legs gave way.

The Highblades rushed the Whisper Prince, swords drawn—

And fell into the floor like it had become soupy mud, all the way up to their necks. The floor froze into stone again the moment only their heads were visible.

Biren's mouth went dry. In seconds, every single one of his Highblades was out of the fight. The scruffy-looking

Whisper Prince strode up the middle of the throne room. Biren raised the dagger, but it trembled in his clammy hand.

To his right, Via slowly stood, her chain clinking. Her eyes flashed and she smiled as she watched Biren.

"I command you to stop!" Biren said to the damned Whisper Prince. "My word is law. I am the emperor!"

The Whisper Prince shook his head. "You're cruel, is what you are. One glance at this throne room and I can see it. The whispers of this city and its beaten-down people denounce you. And I'm sick of you. I'm sick of all of you."

Biren's trembling dagger melted to silver water, dripping down his hand. He gasped and jerked his arm back like he'd been burned, droplets flying, but the liquid metal was cool.

"Stop it!" Biren piped, holding up his dripping hand.

"Sit down." The Whisper Prince gestured with his palm. The air hit Biren's chest like a fist, and he sat down hard on his throne

Moans from the broken crossbowmen beneath the gallery echoed in the otherwise silent throne room as the Whisper Prince reached the base of the dais. Behind him, Mialene crouched in front of one of the terrified Highblades buried to the neck in the marble floor.

"What does *that* feel like?" she slurred. "Is it comfortable like a glove? Or does it squeeze you?"

The Highblade whimpered, his frantic eyes showing the whites.

The Whisper Prince ascended the steps one at a time until he was level with Biren. Biren's gaze flicked about the throne room, looking for some kind of protection. To his right, Via's chain clattered to the stones as her collar melted just like his dagger had done. She rubbed her chafed neck. Then, even as Biren watched, her gauzy clothes became opaque, thicker, covering up her tantalizing nakedness.

Biren swallowed hard down a dry throat as he turned his focus forward again. He'd never felt so powerless. All his resources, all his strength, all his Highblades and weapons, all gone in an instant. How could one man *do* that?

"I can see..." Biren managed to say, "that you're a man of power. I respect that. I respect *you*. Your emperor could use a man like you."

The Whisper Prince narrowed his eyes, cocked his head ever so slightly, and Biren knew he had him.

He warmed to his narrative, talking faster, with more confidence. "I can see you want something, and your emperor is the man to give it to you. Allow me to orchestrate a royal audience. Just the two of us. Together, let us talk as men do."

"Talk all you want," the Whisper Prince murmured. "I have no time to listen to you."

Biren gasped as his entire throne plunged downward into the marble dais. He shouted—maybe he even screamed—as the marble and granite rushed in on him. It was like he'd plunged into the ocean. Gray and red and white colors flowed past him, and he desperately held his breath. The fall seemed to go on and on, multi-colored water rushing past him, and then suddenly he was falling through air, droplets of liquid stone raining all around him.

The throne slammed to a stop in utter darkness, and the impact sent Biren sprawling to the ground. The stone beneath his hands and knees was damp, and it smelled wet and earthy. As his eyes slowly adjusted, he realized he wasn't in pitch blackness. Torchlight flickered on the wet iron bars of a prison cell.

Biren lurched to his feet and grabbed the bars.

"I'm the emperor!" he roared into the darkness. "You can't lock up the emperor!"

"...emperor...emperor...emperor..." His own voice echoed down the long corridor. Slowly, he turned and faced his new throne room.

"You can't..." he whined softly, but only the echo returned to him. "I'm the emperor...."

Chapter Thirteen

REE

Ree walked the length of the royal meeting room, turned and paced to the other side. The open shutters let in a breeze, pleasant and fresh with the tang of the sea.

Emperor Baezin, who for some reason still insisted on being called Blevins, sprawled in one of the chairs, dwarfing it with his huge, muscular frame, one leg up on the table. Uriozi sat on the windowsill, legs tucked up, chin resting on her knees, arms wrapped around her shins as though she longed to be out in the breeze. She seemed almost part of the archway, like if Ree blinked, Uriozi would become a random shadow *shaped* like a Faia. Her tiny, compressed body was a diminutive counterpoint to the huge and sprawling Blevins.

Ree had traveled the length of Thiara with the Black Faia, an actual goddess from myth and legend. And Baezin the Conquerer, too. Emperor Baezin. The father and founder of the empire, three hundred years old. Sometimes, it seemed she was walking through a dream.

And that wasn't the most ridiculous part.

They had returned to find that the crown city of Thiara had undergone not one but two coups since Ree and Grei had fled the Red Haze. Biren, that greasy-mouthed son of the dead Archon, had stolen the throne from Via. Then, in a display of the uncompromising justice that followed Grei like a cloak, the Whisper Prince had returned and put Biren in his place.

Now there was no emperor or empress at all. Grei had literally removed the throne.

After Baezin and Uriozi had arrived—and secured surreptitious lodging in Lowtown—Ree had gone in search of Grei. She hadn't needed her Ringblade training in information gathering to hear about the coups. Everyone was talking about it. Their group heard a dozen comments between the gates of the Red Wall and their Lowtown lodgings.

The Whisper Prince has returned....

He lifted the throne with his mind and smashed it down on Emperor Biren!

The Whisper Prince is going to be the new emperor....

He is marrying a Faia, and they will rule Thiara together....

The rumors flew, but one thing was sure. Grei was here. The thought made Ree feel like the empire was finally turning in the right direction again.

Grei and Ree were still connected by the blood bond she'd made with him, so she had pinpointed his location easily. Apparently, Emperor Biren had killed as many of Via's Highblades as he could, and Biren's remaining Highblades had fled. So there had been no guards posted anywhere. Ree had moved quietly through the palace at will to Empress Via's apartments in the royal wing. But as she'd approached, the door had opened and Grei stood there, waiting for her like he'd seen her coming a mile away.

"Ree," he'd said. Ree had briefly glimpsed three women in the room: Princess Vecenne, Empress Via, and a third woman with a big floppy hat. "Let us talk tomorrow. I will meet you in the western meeting room on the third floor at Highsun."

Before Ree could object, Grei had shut the door, and she'd had the sudden, foreboding feeling that if she knocked on that door again, something bad would happen. She had turned and left.

Now, the following day, she and her two mythical traveling companions waited like petitioners in the western meeting room. According to the water clock against the wall, it was nearly Highsun. She'd told both Baezin and Uriozi what Grei had said and done. Uriozi hadn't responded, but Baezin's countenance was dark.

"I wonder if he'll chastise us like the previous emperor," Baezin rumbled.

"Don't be ridiculous." Ree interrupted her pacing to stop in front of Baezin. "This is Grei."

He chuckled. "If you think this is the Grei you knew, you're fooling yourself."

"What are you talking about?"

"That boy did what Uriozi refused to do, and she had good and moral reasons. He's taken control of the blue roses."

"You don't know that."

Baezin darkened. "Oh, I do know it. Better than anyone on Devorra. Better than anyone could. I know what vast power does to a person."

"He removed Emperor Biren. That makes him a hero."

"And replaced the emperor with himself."

"No."

"And he's trying to cut ties with anyone who might remind him that he's not the emperor."

"What are you talking about?"

"Us, of course."

"He's not trying to cut ties!"

"He wants us to know that he is our ruler, not our friend."

"You're being paranoid."

"Is this how you would greet your friends?" Baezin gestured at the table.

Ree glanced at it. There was no food. No ale or water. No refreshments of any kind. In the palace, food was always provided for honored guests, even if it wasn't mealtime.

"He doesn't know about social protocol."

"He has the ability to know whatever he wants to know. He doesn't want us here."

"He's our friend," Ree insisted.

"He *was* our friend. Now he's the emperor."

"He's not the emperor. He doesn't want to be the emperor!"

"He created a new throne and sat down in it, Ree. What do you think that says?"

"Baezin, he—"

"The power is taking him."

"He's one of the few people who actually knows what to do with power. He is doing what is right."

"Everyone in power thinks they're doing right."

"It *was* the right thing to unseat Biren. He had Empress Via chained up in the throne room for all to see."

Baezin shook his head. "Not the point."

"How is it *not* the point?"

"Did Grei try to reason with Biren? Did he pull together a faction of people to give alternate points of view aside from his own? No. He just made a decision and forced everyone to his will. He did exactly what Biren did."

"Grei is not Biren!"

"One human's nightmare is another's dream," Uriozi said softly, joining the conversation for the first time. She still stared out to sea. "It is always so. A savior to one is a villain to another. This is the reason my sisters and I stepped away from humanity."

"You think Biren should still be on the throne?" Ree asked, hardly able to believe what she was hearing.

"I think humans are humans," Uriozi said.

"What does that mean?" Ree asked.

The Black Faia said nothing.

"Apparently Grei just squashed Biren like a bug—"

"This is Grei!"

"We don't know what Grei did with Biren," Baezin said. "Whether he imprisoned him or cut him into quivering pieces."

"Grei wouldn't do that!"

"Wouldn't he?"

Ree felt hot in the face. "What about you, Emperor Baezin? How many people have you killed?"

"Plenty. Too many to count. It's how I know I'm right. I've seen this before. I, perhaps more than any other."

Ree shook her head. Grei would never transform into the villain. He was the opposite of that.

Silence frosted the room. After a time, Uriozi spoke again.

"For many years, my sisters and I struggled to perceive what might be best for humans. In the end, we determined that if the power to choose is taken away from them, they fight to restore it, no matter how horribly it ends. Our answer was to let humans sort out their own problems. Whenever we intervened, it always became worse."

"But Grei is fighting for *right*. He doesn't want to be emperor. He's doing it because clearly Biren was awful. He will help to install an appropriate ruler."

"And who will that be? Via? Or is she too much of a schemer for his taste? Selicia? Or is she too ruthless? And Vecenne? Too young, perhaps?" Baezin shook his head. "No. Mark my words. Grei is the new emperor. It can go no other way."

"Grei isn't you."

"All men with power are the same man. It twists—"

The door opened and Grei entered with a woman, a courtesan by the look of her.

Swaying a little, the woman stepped forward. She wore a short skirt of red silk and a brief sash across her breasts. A bright red ribbon wrapped her forehead but did little to tame her mass of black and gold hair. Her left hand pinched a silver flask and her right gripped the handle of a huge tankard, frothing over with dark ale. Her tall wooden shoes clacked on the stones as she came forward behind Grei, and a shaft of light illuminated her face. A chill ran up Ree's spine and she glanced at Baezin, whose eyes had narrowed.

That was Adora!

Grei had vanished in the middle of the night with Adora's body. They'd all thought he had wanted to bury her himself, to mourn her alone.

But he had brought her back to life....

Ree's heart hammered, and she felt cut adrift. Blevins's dire warnings suddenly seemed all too true. What kind of man brought the dead back to life?

Adora sauntered past Grei, and he shut the door. She didn't seem like the Adora Grei had described: bright-eyed, passionate, and dedicated. This woman seemed like a drunkard and a wanton.

"Thank you for waiting," Grei said.

"Got your hands full, do you?" Baezin asked. His black eyes never left Grei's face, and his tone sounded like an accusation.

Baezin was spoiling for a fight. It seemed he always was. Half a dozen times during their journey back, they had been accosted by Benascan or Thiaran troops. Baezin had always wanted to use his sword. Ree had stopped him four of those times, but two had ended in blood. Baezin seemed happiest when he was killing someone. Now he looked at Grei with that same gaze.

"Of course we don't mind waiting," Ree cut in. "You're probably the busiest person in the empire."

She snapped a glance to Uriozi to see if the Faia would help, but she still stared out the window at the sea.

"I do have my hands full, actually," Grei responded to Baezin's question. He had dark circles under his eyes, but they didn't make him look tired; they made him look dangerous.

"Busy cutting a swath through the empire, are you?" Baezin said.

Grei opened his mouth to say something, but Adora sauntered in front of him and put her the flask on the table. She spun it.

"I thought we were going somewhere interesting," she said over her shoulder to Grei. "I dressed up and everything, but there isn't an eligible man in this room."

"Adora—"

"No offense, grandfather." Adora ignored Grei completely, sat on the edge of the table and struck a pose. You look absolutely strapping, but I recently discovered that we're related and…ew. There are some things even *I* won't do."

Baezin's brow furrowed like he didn't know what to make of her. She smiled widely as if that were the point.

Grei cleared his throat. "I brought you all here because I need your help. There are questions that need answering."

Baezin smiled thinly. "We need answers from you, Stormy. Like what exactly do you think you're doing?"

Grei's eyes flashed. "What anyone with a conscience would do. What *you* should have done when you sat the throne. What *she* should have done." He tipped his chin at the silent Uriozi. "I'm making things right."

"You have the biggest sword now, is that it? And by the gods you're going to swing it."

"Right into the faces of every lying, power-hungry monster who thinks other people are disposable."

"You're in charge, and you're going to make sure everyone knows it. Right?"

"I'm going to do what I can to mend what was broken. For that, I need answers. You have them. You and Uriozi. All this time, and you never told me about so many things.

Cavyn. Velak. Devorra. The Slate Wizards. I'm beginning to wonder why."

"I see. I'm the enemy now. Going to swing your sword at me?"

Grei showed his teeth, his fist clenched.

"All right," Ree said. "That's enough."

"Ooo," Adora said, shivering. "It's so chilly in here all of a sudden."

"Grei," Ree said. "I'm just...maybe we can help with what you're doing here—"

"I know what he's doing," Baezin growled. "I've seen it all before."

"Ooo. I think you need to join me for a drink, grandfather. You sound too angry by far. I was angry, too, then I started drinking Serpent's Tears." Adora spun her flask on the tabletop, stopped it with a slap of her hand, and shoved it down the table to Baezin.

Baezin glanced at the flask but didn't touch it. He turned his full focus on Grei.

The hilt of Baezin's sword and dagger were exposed, and Ree knew it wouldn't take much to draw either one. In fact, from his position, Baezin could throw his dagger straight from the sheath with a backhanded flip. Ree had practiced that move herself. It took skill to do it right, but this was Baezin the Conqueror, after all.

The former emperor looked lazy, but Ree knew better. He was a coiled serpent. She'd seen that look before. She'd *used* that look before.

"Stop what you're doing, Grei," Baezin said softly. For the first time his words didn't sound like a challenge, like Baezin was talking to Grei friend-to-friend. "It goes to a place you don't want to go."

"And stand by and do nothing?" Grei shook his head. "I won't allow lying, power-hungry monsters to torture people who cannot defend themselves."

"What about those who can't defend themselves against you?"

"Let them run in fear. Let the word spread across the empire. Let the Birens of the land shake when they think of me."

"You took Thiara by force," Baezin said. "If you take something by force once, you'll do it twice. Once you do it twice, it's a habit. And that's the style of ruler you will be."

"I'm not a ruler," Grei said.

"You most certainly are. You just deposed the rightful emperor single-handedly. You're a ruler now whether you want it or not."

"Rightful? Biren was not the prince or princess. He had no claim to the throne."

"So you're going to re-install Via? She *is* the rightful ruler."

Grei hesitated.

Baezin gave a tight-lipped smile. "Except she's not good enough either, is she? One of those lying, power-hungry monsters. So you're going to choose someone better. Who will that be? Who knows better than you what must be done?"

"I am not taking the throne."

"Someone needs to. Is it going be Qorvin? If you think Via's power-hungry, wait until you meet that boy. You can be assured of a half-century of war with Benasca under Qorvin. Or do you plan to install Vecenne? A sixteen-year-old girl. She has the makings, but is she ready? Will you throw her to the wolves and hope they don't tear her apart?"

"I would help her."

"Ah. And when Qorvin returns and demands the throne? Will you bury him wherever you buried Biren?"

"If someone threatened the rightful emperor, they would fail," Grei said.

"So you plan to rule from *behind* the throne," Baezin said.

Grei held up a fist, closing his eyes and turning his head like he would erase Baezin's incendiary words. "Blevins. Enough. I know you like to play with words, but I don't have time for your games anymore. I'm not the boy you once knew."

"You certainly aren't," Baezin said.

"Are you going to help me or not?"

"And if we don't?" Baezin asked.

"Of course we are," Ree interrupted. Grei glanced at her, and she saw his distrust there, the same distrust she thought they'd moved past during the war with Velak. "Grei, of course."

Baezin stared daggers at Grei. "You're not asking for help. You're asking if we're going to get in your way."

"Are you?" Grei asked.

"That depends."

"On what?"

"On what you plan to do."

"The right thing."

"You can't save the empire by yourself," Baezin said.

"I'm the *only* one who can. I trusted my father to do the right thing. He refused. I trusted Emperor Qweryn. He burned down the Yellow Faia. I trusted Empress Via. She gave her daughter over to murderous old men. I trusted the Faia. But they stood aside and did nothing. I'm done trusting others to do the right thing."

Ree glanced at Uriozi, but she still hadn't moved, just kept gazing toward the horizon. Suddenly Ree felt an incendiary frustration with the Faia. She was doing exactly what Grei accused her of doing: nothing. Ree felt that if the Faia just spoke up, uttered some calming words of wisdom, it might keep this conflagration from burning out of control.

"What you're doing, Grei," Baezin said, "we call that a tyrant."

"That's so funny." Adora emptied her tankard and clacked it on the table. "That's exactly what *I* told him."

"I'm not a tyrant," Grei whispered, his voice brimming with emotion.

"That's what Velak thought," Baezin said.

"I'm not Velak."

"That's what Cavyn thought every time she brought me back from the dead." Baezin deliberately turned a glance on Adora.

"You don't know—"

"Every time I *begged* her not to," Baezin growled, trampling over Grei's sentence. His black eyes flashed.

"I'll drink to that." Adora put her tankard to her lips, upended it, then frowned. She shook it upside down over the table and a single drop darkened the wood. She sighed.

Grei's gaze hardened.

"Grei…" Ree flashed a frustrated look at Baezin. "Baezin is just—"

"I've discovered what I needed here," Grei said. "I think I know where everyone stands."

"Don't go," Ree said.

"There is nothing more to say." Grei took Adora's hand. She went with him docilely, arching her back and flinging her hair dramatically. Her high heels clacked on the stones.

"Wooo!" She grinned as she stumbled and bumped into him. She wrapped an arm around his waist to steady herself, then lifted her leg high and marched toward the door. "To the bedroom, lover?"

With a clenched fist, Grei followed. The door slammed behind them without him touching it.

Chapter Fourteen

REE

"That," Baezin said, "may be the most dangerous thing I've ever seen. And that's saying something."

Ree rounded on him. "*You're* the problem! I thought we were going to try to *talk* to him."

"I *was* talking—"

"Accusing is more like it," she snapped. Emperor or no, three hundred years old or no, Baezin thought like a damned Highblade. Direct assault was what he knew. "A bit of subtlety was needed here."

"Because lying to the Whisper Prince always works so well."

"I'm not talking about lying. I'm talking about finesse."

"He's already made up his mind. He came here to see if we would blindly follow him."

"You don't know what he wanted," Ree said. "You didn't give him a chance to tell us!"

"I was right about everything, Ringblade. He took the roses. He brought Adora back against her will. He's caught in the grips of it. You're a fool if you don't see it. If we don't fix this, he's going to become another Velak."

"Of course he's not. How can you even say that?"

"The boy I knew in Fairmist fought for those who couldn't fight for themselves. He uncovered truths and smacked down the arrogant. Now he *is* the arrogant. He's not using the roses to help others. He's using them to get what he wants for himself."

"He said he's trying to mend what's broken—"

"Cavyn didn't interfere," Uriozi interrupted.

Baezin and Ree turned to face her. The Black Faia still stared out the window. "Say whatever you want about my mother, but she left humanity alone. She let them make their own decisions, reap their own victories, and stumble over their own failures. Grei is not going to do that."

"Exactly. How is that wrong?" Ree asked.

"Grei didn't come looking for our counsel," Uriozi said softly. "He came to tell us what to do. Baezin is right."

"What if Grei knows what he's doing?" Ree said. "What if we *should* be following his lead? Have either of you considered that? Biren was a tyrant. Grei took care of it."

"And dredging Adora back to life? He took care of that, too, didn't he?" Baezin asked. "She seemed pretty happy and normal, didn't she?"

"Choosing a leader like Biren over a leader like Via is like choosing one curling wave over another," Uriozi said.

"He's fighting for right!"

"And who determines what's right?" Baezin asked.

"He's not—"

"He's destroying the blue roses," Uriozi said softly.

Ree stopped, thunderstruck. "Destroying them?"

"To resurrect Adora," Uriozi said. "I can feel it when a blue rose dies. He has destroyed five of them."

"Adora has died...five times?" Ree asked.

"I know that trapped look in her eyes," Baezin said. "There is no more helpless a feeling than knowing that your life—or death—no longer belongs to you."

"He *loves* her," Ree said. "He's crossed the continent twice to save her—"

"If he's destroyed that many roses," Uriozi murmured, "he'll destroy more. The power is seducing him."

"He's not going to stop," Baezin growled. "Cavyn brought me back to life again and again for centuries. Now Grei is doing it to Adora."

"We might be able talk to him," Uriozi said. "It...might not be too late."

"We *did* just talk to him," Baezin said. "You saw how that went."

"You put him on the defensive!" Ree said. "He thought he was walking into a room of friends and you made it clear you were his enemy. Of course he resisted."

"It wouldn't have mattered," Baezin said. "It would have ended the same. He's too far gone. There's only one thing to do—"

"Don't even say it," Ree warned.

"I stood by once before while catastrophe befell this empire," Baezin said. "I'm not going to do it twice."

"This is Grei we're talking about!"

"It's the only thing that will stop him."

"You bloody-handed butcher!" Ree spat.

"Are you going to lecture me, assassin?" he drawled.

"He's our friend." Ree turned to Uriozi. "*You* were supposed to be the steward of the blue roses. Stand up and do your job now. Take the roses. Become their steward now."

"I don't know if I can," Uriozi said.

"He'd fight for them now," Baezin said.

"Just give him a—"

"I agree with Ree," Uriozi said softly. "This is my fault. I was the logical successor to Cavyn, and I stepped away from my responsibility. I thought Grei was the one destined to take up my mother's mantle, but he is, in the end, just human. He has already exhibited a willingness to put the lands in danger for his personal desires. That willingness will only grow."

"We can't wait," Baezin said.

"Give me one day," Uriozi said. "Allow me to prepare myself, see if I can wrest control of the roses from him, quickly and completely. It will take me only a day to know if I can. And if I cannot..." She left the sentence hanging.

They were actually talking about killing Grei! She had to warn him. She couldn't just let them—

She glanced up and found Baezin's black-eyed gaze boring into her.

Ree suddenly realized her mistake. She hadn't played the politics of this situation well at all. They'd entered this room as friends, but on this subject, there were no friendships. They'd kill her if they thought she'd run off to warn Grei. Ree schooled herself, let her feelings drain away from her face.

"All right." She put on a show of reluctance. "I see what you're saying. It's just...I don't want to believe it."

Uriozi nodded.

"You're going tonight?" Baezin said to Uriozi, though he continued to stare at Ree.

"Tonight," Uriozi echoed. "Now."

She stood up on the windowsill, wings flicking. She leapt into the air and vanished into the darkness.

Ree let out a breath.

"Your loyalty is admirable," Baezin said, "but Grei's not really human anymore. He isn't trustworthy anymore."

Ree said nothing. Baezin wasn't going to be an ally, so she had to let that go. It was just her and Grei again, like it should be. And the sooner she left Baezin behind, the better.

"Well, I'm going to get some sleep." She headed for the door—

"Have a drink," Baezin said.

She turned.

He spun the flask, slapped it to a stop with his hand as Adora had. The cork pointed at Ree. She glanced at it, then back at his hard eyes. With every bit of her will and training, she forced down her fear and acted naturally. She raised an eyebrow and smiled, giving him the face he wanted to see.

"That sounds nice, actually," she lied, drawing away from the door. She tried to stay calm, tried to remind herself that she still had time. Uriozi said she had to make preparations.

"We've got all night," Baezin said, uncorking the flask and taking a sip. He expertly slid the flask to her without spilling it.

She sat down casually, as though she didn't want to bolt for the door, but she chose her chair carefully, with plenty of space on her right side where her ringblade hung on its hook.

"What is this again?" she asked conversationally, though she had heard Adora perfectly clearly when she'd identified it as Serpent's Tears. She picked up the flask, raised it to her lips, and took a sip.

"The latest liquor from Fairmist, apparently," he said.

Her throat burned and her eyes watered as she swallowed. She blinked, forced a smile, and passed it back to him.

"It's not Ox Beer." His eyes glittered as he took a swig like it was water. "But it'll do."

"For what?" she asked as he passed it back. She took another sip.

"Let's toast to our friend," Baezin said, like the Grei they knew was already gone. Like he had died.

Her smile faltered, and he saw it. She recovered, pretending she hadn't heard his ominous tone. "To our friend." She smiled, ignoring the words that Baezin wasn't saying....

May he rest in peace.

Chapter Fifteen

URIOZI

Uriozi spoke to the wind. She flicked her wings as it lifted her up. She flew for a time, high above the seven towers, circling the Web of Blades strung between them. She remembered the days when she and her sisters had built that web for their father, when he had no clue they were his daughters, when he'd thought they were simply benevolent spirits who had come to assist him.

Mother and Father had seemed happy back then, but now Uriozi wondered if that had been an illusion. It seemed their relationship was a disaster from the beginning. Mother had lied to Father about her children until she'd finally given birth to the one she thought he would accept. Father had been ignorant of his influence on the lands, bent on conquest. It was miraculous that they'd ever had any bright moments at all, really. But that was "being human," Mother would have said.

Each time Uriozi circled the Web of Blades, it deepened her sadness. Perhaps this had been her and her sisters' grand mistake all along, trying to impress Father with gifts, trying purchase his love while remaining enigmas. Perhaps, despite Mother's wishes, Uriozi and her sisters should have revealed themselves to Baezin from the start and let the cards fall where they may. They had spent so much time trying to circumvent the natural order of things that they had altered the natural order of things.

Finally, Uriozi soured on looking at the Web of Blades, and she descended to the streets. For some reason, it felt good to put her bare feet on the damp cobblestones of the city.

It was quiet now—it had been this way since she, Baezin, and Ree had arrived. The Phantom War had flowed through the city, reinvading the terror of the first Slink War. Then the Red Haze had stolen everyone's freedom to even think on their own, and ripped them from their homes, then Emperor Biren had put his stranglehold on the tattered remains of the citizenry, and now the Whisper Prince….

The beleaguered people of Thiara didn't want to leave their homes for fear of what would greet them on the other side of the door.

With her diminutive size and midnight skin, Uriozi was frightening to humans: a monster or a goddess, and nothing in between. A Faia walking the streets would normally draw a crowd, but there was no crowd to draw now. She moved through the city with ease. Still, despite the quiet, she kept to the alleyways, away from the main streets and canals.

Perhaps, though, the Faia should have walked the streets of Thiara just like this from the start. Perhaps, from the outset, she and her sisters should have tried to live among them, to let the shock of their appearance stand and slowly become a part of human society. Would that have made things better?

Had Devorra walked among her creations without feeling the need to hide? When she had created these lands, had she treated her creations as something of an equal? Uriozi suspected she had. So maybe that was the mistake.

Every time Mother had talked about Grandmother, it had been with bitterness. According to Mother, Devorra had left Cavyn to steward an entire continent with no instructions.

Mother had been so angry at Devorra, believing Grandmother had left in order to teach Cavyn a lesson, to force her to be independent. Uriozi had always taken that at face value before, but now she wondered.

Mother had been capricious, deciding one thing and then deciding the exact opposite a few years later. If Devorra had been the same, perhaps she had simply decided one day to go wherever goddesses went after creating life. Perhaps Devorra was, even now, making a new world with new people somewhere out there.

Thinking of Devorra made Uriozi think of her sisters. Dead. All dead now. And her brother, too. Only Uriozi had escaped.

She hadn't spent much time with her sisters over the last century. They'd all had such different ways of looking at the lands, at humans. There had been decades where Uriozi hadn't so much as thought of her sisters, let alone visited them, but now…to know they were gone forever…it created a vast empty space inside her that she knew would never be filled.

She was the last, the only remnant of Devorra's line, Cavyn's line. The only Faia in the lands. Should she have taken up stewardship of the roses? At this moment, she felt that maybe she should have, that she had again made the wrong decision.

At the time of that choice, she had thought the best thing to do was let the roses lie fallow and allow the lands to move forward without the meddling of the Faia or their mother.

But she should have known better. Humans never left well enough alone. It was their defining quality. And while she had felt Grei was a different kind of human, she'd been proven wrong yet again. Of course he'd been tempted by the idea of greater power. That was what humans did. And now there was a human floating about with Mother's power.

Father was right. Despite whatever good intentions Grei might have had, the power would eventually consume him. Rising so far in such a short time would surely unbalance his mortal mind. Uriozi had no desire to saddle herself with the responsibilities Mother had shouldered, but perhaps that was the lesson. Perhaps the alternative was worse, and Uriozi should have stepped in when she—

"Will you be my friend?" a soft voice came from the shadows ahead of Uriozi.

She snapped her gaze up, realizing she'd meandered down a narrow alley. There was only darkness ahead, and she wasn't sure where the voice had originated.

Uriozi listened to the whispers of the air, of the walls of the buildings and the ground beneath her feet. Her natural connection to the whispers allowed her to feel when someone was near, but instead there was only a low hissing sound. Why hadn't she heard that before?

She turned all of her attention forward, to pinpoint whomever had spoken. The hissing heightened, as though trying to cancel her magic, but Uriozi was a Faia. The whispers of the world were like the thoughts in her own mind. When she focused on them, they leapt forward and she heard past the incessant hissing.

The person ahead was a human girl, maybe twelve years old, but not an ordinary girl. *She* was the source of the hissing, and Uriozi realized she recognized it.

The artifacts of the god Venisha made that sound.

"Who are you?" she asked, and she caught the sound of another person in the alley. The whispers sketched the woman out in Uriozi's mind, though it was too dark for her eyes to see. A larger person. Taller. An adult.

"So you're the last Faia." The adult woman sauntered forward. Black hair flowed down around her face and over her shoulders like water. Her large dark eyes seemed almost hypnotic. She wore tight, revealing clothing, but not in the way a courtesan would, more like a young empress. She held a thick, fur-lined cloak draped over one arm.

A human would have found this woman irresistible. She reminded Uriozi of Mother, except Cavyn's human form had been tall and blonde with the light skin of the Benascans. This woman wasn't quite so tall, and she had the dark eyes, bronze skin, and black hair of the Venishans.

But like Mother, the woman's allure came from strong magic. She had been constructed by a powerful being, by those hissing whispers. Venisha.

Something was very wrong here, and Uriozi had the strong urge to leave. There wasn't much in the lands that could threaten a Faia, but these people possessed an old and unfamiliar magic.

She whispered to the wind. It gathered beneath her body and her wings, lifting her up. She told it to shoot her into the sky like an arrow—

"No." The young girl stepped forward and held up a hand.

Snakes of glittering metal shot out from the girl's wrists, a dozen of them. Each was made of a thousand jagged scales. They wrapped around Uriozi's ankles faster than she could react.

Instinctively, Uriozi spoke to the metal in the jagged little snakes, intending to turn them to water.

The hissing jammed into Uriozi's ears like daggers, blotting out the whispers. The wind faltered. The snakes yanked brutally.

She crashed to the damp cobblestones at the feet of the alluring woman, skinning her knees and elbows. Uriozi looked up, craning her neck, horror dawning inside her. She couldn't hear the whispers, couldn't use her magic. The hissing was like a roar.

The beautiful woman moved forward again, swinging her hips like she was trying to catch a mate, and a third figure emerged from the shadows...

"Father?" Uriozi said incredulously.

Tall, muscled, with thick black hair pulled into a tight ponytail, the man moved just like Father. He bore an enormous sword slung across his back, nearly as tall as he was.

But this wasn't Baezin. No. Baezin simmered with strength and arrogance like this man, but this man's bearing was cruel. Also, now that he was closer, Uriozi could see that his long nose had been broken at least once. His eyes were set slightly further apart, but aside from that, he might have been Baezin's twin.

He wore loose black pantaloons and a billowing black shirt with a pyramid embroidered on the breast. He crouched before Uriozi, deftly managing his enormous sword.

"So this is the mighty Faia who have thwarted us for so long." He spoke in a voice that sounded exactly like Baezin's. He cocked his head. "She's tiny."

The beautiful woman put her hands on her hips. "What did you expect? The divine intermingling with the mortal. The result was bound to be...twisted."

"You're the Slate Wizards," Uriozi said.

The man bowed his head ever so slightly.

Uriozi desperately reached out to the elements, but all she could hear was that hissing. She was as helpless as a mortal. She pulled at her bonds, but they yanked back.

"You said you could take the roses away from the Whisper Prince," Baezin's doppelganger said. "How did you plan to do that?"

"How did you know that?"

"We listened to your conversation," the man said.

"How did you...?"

"With them, of course." The man tipped his chin past her shoulder. "Pliothe is very useful."

Uriozi flicked a glance in that direction and her breath froze in her throat. The mouth of the alley was filled with dozens of rats, all of them made from metal like her bindings. They clustered together with purpose, their glistening little noses pointed at her, their red eyes focused on her.

"No!" Uriozi leapt into the air, pushing hard with her wings—

The man's huge hand clamped on her entire leg from knee to ankle and ripped her from the air. Pain knifed into her hip as something gave. The man slammed her into the ground.

"Now now," he said in a dark voice, bringing his huge face close to hers. "You've denied us for centuries. I think it's time you give a little."

The pain was excruciating. He'd pulled her leg out of joint!

These were the ones she and her sister had held the barrier against. These were the ones Mother had warned about. And they were here. The barrier was down, and the Slate Wizards had come.

Suddenly the problem of Grei seemed inconsequential. Uriozi desperately wished he were here right now. With the power of the blue roses, he could cut through that hissing. He could send these Slate Wizards fleeing.

The rats, their bodies made of mashed-up shards of metal and twists of wire, surrounded her, stopping a finger's-width from her body, noses twitching, sharp teeth gleaming. There were also tiny bugs scuttling around the feet of the rats.

"Can you really do it?" the man asked. The bugs and rats, so close now, smelled like oiled metal. "Can you take the roses from the Whisper Prince?"

"No."

The beautiful woman laughed. "She's lying."

"So she is, Fylomene. So she is. Well then. I think we have nothing more to say," the man said. "Pliothe, take her."

Nearly submerged in the darkness, the girl wrung her hands, looking at Uriozi. "Will you be my friend?" she whispered.

"Pliothe!" the man barked.

Pliothe closed her eyes, and the rats leapt upon Uriozi, digging their teeth into her.

She screamed.

The pain was beyond belief. She screamed until her lungs were empty, then she drew a ragged, shuddering breath and screamed again.

The bugs burrowed into her skin. They tore flesh, devoured muscles.

The agony took her past madness, and she fell back into herself, deep and far away from the pain like she was falling down a well. Somewhere above, her scream continued, pitiful and hoarse as she ran out of breath a second time.

The rats and bugs consumed her—skin, muscles, and bones—leaving twists and shards of metal in their wake. They replaced her flesh and blood with metal and wire.

When most of her flesh was gone, the pain slowly left with it, and Uriozi found that she was still—impossibly—alive. From that deep dark place within herself, she watched as her entire body turned into the same kind of metal construct as the rats.

Then it was over. Uriozi lay on the cobblestones looking up through shimmering metal eyes, and her half-consciousness rose back to the surface. The hissing became a clear voice in her head. The voice of the little girl.

"You are my friend now," she said.

Uriozi sat up, feeling the scraping, bending and sliding of her new metal body. She raised her hand, gazing horror-stricken at the coils and shards of her glittering arm.

"You're all right," Pliothe said, her voice loud and ringing inside Uriozi's mind. *"You aren't scared."*

And then, Uriozi wasn't scared.

"Now," the man said. His voice sounded metallic to her. "I will ask my question again. Can you take the power of the roses from the Whisper Prince?"

From that deep place inside her mind, Uriozi knew she shouldn't answer that question. She resisted and kept her new metal lips shut.

"You want to answer the question," Pliothe said into her mind.

Uriozi rasped, "Yes," before she could stop herself. Her voice no longer sounded like her own, the soft lilt made of wind and throat, flesh and life. Now it sounded like a file scraping against a spoon.

"Good," the man said. "Pliothe, to the north, if you please. To the roses. Don't waste time."

Pliothe set down a little box made of tiny, thin metal spars assembled in a square. She clicked something and stepped back.

A portal opened in the air above the box, bordered in a glowing blue light. Beyond it lay fields of cold snow and starry skies. Blue roses dotted the white in the moonlight, and a freezing wind blew into the warm Thiaran alley.

"Bother," Fylomene said, taking the thick fur cloak from her arm, shaking it out and slinging it prettily over her shoulders. "It's going to be freezing."

"Shut up," the man said.

Fylomene sighed in resignation and stepped through the portal.

"You want to go through the portal," Pliothe said in Uriozi's mind.

Uriozi's metallic wings flicked, and she bounded after Fylomene. Pliothe and the man followed. The portal closed behind them.

"Now," the man said, his eyes narrowed against the icy wind. "Take them."

"You want to take the blue roses, make them your own," Pliothe's voice filled Uriozi's mind.

Uriozi tried to resist, but she could see exactly how to do it now. It would be so easy.

"You feel at peace. You want to do this."

Uriozi's doubts and worries vanished. She reached out…

…and took the roses away from the Whisper Prince.

Chapter Sixteen

GREI

Grei and Adora returned to the room he'd slept in after the Phantom War, where she and he had first made love. It seemed a lifetime ago, before Velak's rage exploded to encompass the entire continent.

Nothing had changed. The corner of the room, where Adora's secret door had been, was melted and misshapen. Some of the floor was still liquid, and he could feel the whispers of the invisible air barriers he had so hastily constructed.

He hadn't wanted to come back here. He'd created such a disaster letting the Red Haze loose, but this was a broken thing. He had to mend it.

Grei whispered to the floor, the wall, the agitated air itself. Slowly, with great care, he returned everything to normal.

"Ah." Adora kicked off her Thiaran wooden shoes, sauntered to the bed and threw herself onto it. "I remember this place. Let's get to it, lover."

He let out a long breath and his heart ached. She gazed back at him with an inviting smile, half-lidded eyes. It was torture, because he knew she was faking it. She knew exactly what he wanted, and she was giving him a twisted parody of it. She wanted him to suffer.

"Let's repeat the magic," she said coyly. "I'm ready."

"Can't you be...just for one night, can't you just be *you* again?"

"I *am* me, lover." She rose up, standing on her knees. She held out her arms. "Come to me. I'll make all your fantasies come true."

Though she'd emptied her tankard of ale in the meeting room, she had her wineskin back in hand. She tipped it up, took a long drink, brought it down and swayed on the bed. She cocked her head and watched him.

He had little doubt that if he went to her, she would lay with him. She wanted to trample over their previous lovemaking, to replace the beauty of what had happened here with something tawdry and meaningless.

He walked to the balcony instead.

"Will you leave me so unsatisfied?" she asked.

He pressed his hands onto the rail, still warm from the heat of the day, and let his head sag between his shoulders. Maybe she was right. Maybe he should just let her die. Maybe Blevins was right. Maybe Grei didn't have any right to depose a feckless thug like Biren. Maybe he should just throw the cards to the wind and see which way they came down. Maybe Grei should hide in the cracks of history and do nothing with his power, just let evil men and women decide the fates of the innocent, now and to the end of time. Maybe he should be like Cavyn and the Faia had been.

"Lover," Adora said in a pouty voice. "You seem upset."

He half-expected her to saunter across the distance and wrap her arms around him, try to seduce him that way, but the truth was she hadn't touched him. Not once, not since he'd first brought her back to life. She never recoiled when he touched her, took her wrist to lead her one place or another, but she had never instigated contact with him. Her invitations were all words. He was sure that wasn't an accident.

Sure enough, she stayed where she was, standing on her knees on the bed, watching him with her seemingly-seductive gaze.

He couldn't go on like this. Every night he didn't sleep he became increasingly angry, increasingly frustrated. His head ached constantly, a dull throbbing that wouldn't go away. He was going to break at some point, and he'd do exactly what Adora wanted him to do. Snap at her. Shove her. Spit some unforgivable vituperation. She would prove he wasn't altruistic at all, that he didn't care about her, only what he wanted.

He pressed his eyelids shut.

No. He wouldn't. He would never give up on her—

Below, a single thin scream pierced the air. It stretched horribly—a hopeless, agonized sound—and then it died. A cold sweat broke out on Grei's scalp.

The night went silent, and then a second scream split the night, desperate...and then it died.

He threw his *dasha* toward the noise and immediately felt something. Four streets down in an alley.

"I have to go," Grei said.

Adora chuckled. "That sounds familiar. Are we doing this again?"

"Adora—"

"No no, I like it. I'll play along." She drew herself up. "No, Grei," she mimicked her own voice. "Don't go. Please stay. For me. For our love. If you leave me here, something bad may happen to me. Like I'll get ripped apart with a knife and thrown to a god of fire."

"Did you hear—?"

"Or is that too ridiculous?" She interrupted him. "Who would ever believe that?"

"I'll be right back." He leapt over the railing and beseeched the air to catch him. He heard Adora's laughter follow him, and he glanced back in time to see her jump off the balcony as well.

Panic lanced through him, and he quickly asked the air to catch her before she hit the stones.

"Wheee!" Adora said as he lifted her up next to him. "Oh, that's refreshing."

"Adora, you should stay in the room—"

"Where it's safe? No, I don't think so. I did that once and it wasn't safe at all." She paused, pensive. "Oh wait. No. I *should* stay. It's the surest way to die. Just like before. Just like the script says—"

"I'm not repeating some script!" he snapped.

"Oh, but you are. Over and over again. It's funny that you don't see it."

Grei clamped his lips shut, then asked the wind to bring them to the ground safely. They alighted and he ran toward the place he'd heard the scream.

"Who do you think is screaming?" Adora asked.

"Quiet. They could hear us coming."

"Who do you think is screaming?" Adora yelled.

He glared at her and she winked.

"I don't know," he said. "If I knew I'd—"

"Rescue her from death?"

Grei turned his head away. He had to ignore her. Just ignore her. Nothing good would come of this unwinnable banter. Adora would make sure of it. She only spoke to trip him up, and if he engaged, she'd just twist the words around and around.

He threw himself into sprinting and listening for the hiss. It was louder this time; he pinpointed its location. Two streets more and into an alley.

"This is invigorating," Adora said, her bare feet slapping the cobblestones as she sprinted, breathing hard and pushing herself to keep up.

The hissing grew ferocious in Grei's mind, and a blue light lit the alley just ahead. Just as he and Adora drew near, the blue light vanished.

He skidded to a stop at the mouth of the alley. A few rats skittered away into the darkness, but aside from that, there was nothing.

His neck prickled as he felt the residue of magic in this place, like the air just before a storm. He started into the alley, and Adora moved to follow him.

"No. You stay here."

She chuckled and ignored him, stayed right behind him. He sighed.

He scanned left and right, seeing nothing out of the ordinary on the walls, but then he looked at the ground.

"Wait," he said, stopping and crouching.

The was a stain on the cobblestones, small and almost invisible in the darkness. He reached down and touched it. Sticky. Blood.

But it was only a little, and it looked like it had been smeared...or cleaned...

Or licked away.

He yanked his hand back in revulsion. His heart beat fast. Something horrible had happened here.

"What is it?" Adora asked, and this time it seemed a genuine question, free of her usual sarcasm.

"I think someone just died here."

"It doesn't seem like a lot of blood," she said.

"It's been...licked away."

Adora made a face as Grei stood up. "All right. That's vile."

Who had magic except for Uriozi and Grei? He thought about Ree and Selicia, the limited magics they had implemented. Little artifacts with limited powers. Could this be their handiwork?

Grei searched the alley, but all he found was grit, grime, and that smear of blood. Adora grew bored and leaned against the wall, cocked one foot up behind her while she sipped from the wineskin.

"You brought that with you?" he said.

"My other lover." She winked. "I didn't want him to feel jilted."

"Tell me you and I are going to have a real conversation soon."

"Whatever you want, lover," she said.

"I think if you—"

An invisible sledgehammer hit Grei in the chest. It hit so hard, so swift, that he didn't even have time to gasp. It knocked him backwards into the wall, and he fell to his knees.

Adora's eyes narrowed, and she stopped drinking, but she didn't rush to him.

"Adora!" he gasped, falling onto all fours. It felt like the invisible sledgehammer was now pushing into his chest, pushing a blunt, painful hole all the way through him, pushing his organs out the back of him. He gasped again and fell face forward.

He tried to summon the magic of the blue roses—

But they weren't there.

That was what was leaving him. That was the huge hole he felt through the center of him. Something—or someone—was ripping away his hold on the magic of the blue roses, ousting him from his haven and taking his place.

But there was only one creature who could possibly do that: Uriozi.

"She's...taking the roses," Grei said. "I have to...get to the field. I have to fight her."

Adora raised an eyebrow, then took another drink. "Do you?"

"Adora...help me!"

She hesitated, and for a moment it seemed she would come down on his side, but then she slowly shook her head.

Growling, he fought the pain and grappled with his pouches, finally finding the one with The Root. He fumbled with the laces, and finally got it open—

A shimmering portal grew before Grei's eyes, a circle of blue light that opened onto the wintry snow of Benasca and the field of blue roses. For a moment, Grei thought it was the roses calling out to him, helping him get to them....

Then three figures emerged. A beautiful woman in a fur cloak, a child wearing worn, stained leathers, and...

"Blevins?" Grei exclaimed.

Chapter Seventeen

GREI

As soon as Grei said it, he knew he was wrong. The man's eyes were wider apart than Blevins's. The cruel set to his mouth was different. This was...what? His twin?

Grei's connection to the blue roses was gone. That never-ending well of power drained away, but Grei could still hear the whispers. He still had his connection to them and, unlike the Faia, Grei had created two havens to anchor his magic: one to the blue roses and one to The Root.

He reached out, listening to the whispers of this imposter's body. Once upon a time, Blevins's body had no whispers. Grei could always identify him instantly simply because there was a quiet space where he stood. But since Cavyn had died, Blevins's body whispered just the same as anyone else's.

The moment Grei heard this man's whispers, he knew for certain it wasn't Blevins, only someone who looked like Blevins. The man sounded—all three of the newcomers sounded—like the hissing Grei had experienced in the Slate Temple after he'd been stabbed with the emperor's twisted dagger.

"You're..." Grei murmured. "You're the Slate Wizards."

The Blevins doppelganger reached over his shoulder and dramatically drew his enormous sword. The thing was six feet long and the blade itself had to be a handspan wide. Its two-handed hilt was encrusted with jewels and topped with a wide, ornate cross guard.

"I'm so pleased to meet you, Whisper Prince," the man said. "I am King Vaeron. This is Fylomene and Pliothe."

A tiny fourth figure emerged from the portal—smaller even than the little girl. It was some form of metallic creature with wings. It landed next to the girl, not quite as tall as her. Its little wings folded against its back, and the figure hung its head.

At first, Grei thought this was some elaborate artifact, some construct of the kingdom of Venisha. Everyone knew that magical artifacts came from across the Sunset Sea, but as he looked closer, he realized that, despite the shards and spars of metal that comprised the creature's body, there was something familiar about her.

"Uriozi!" Grei blurted, suddenly seeing the Faia in the metal construct before him. "What did you do to her?" he snarled at King Vaeron.

"A gift from Pliothe. It means the last Faia now belongs to Venisha. So do you, in case you were wondering."

The man brought his blade around in a blur, but Grei was getting efficient at fighting swordsmen. He whispered the air solid, and—

The blade hit the hardened air, crackled like it was sheathed in lightning, and Grei exploded backward. He landed on the cobblestones and slid almost to the mouth of the alley. Stunned, he looked up.

"Oh," Vaeron said, striding forward. "Try that again. I like that."

Grei's ears rang, and he tried to shake away the numb feeling. Adora stood against the alley wall, watching like this was a play. She had that sardonic smile on her face, and she sipped from her wineskin.

Fylomene glanced at Adora. They exchanged a single look, whereupon Adora raised an eyebrow.

"We know what you are, Whisper Prince," Vaeron said. "And we know how to deal with you. We've been preparing for the Faia for three hundred years. And you...you're barely a Faia at all."

Grei scrambled backward, awkwardly staggering to his feet. Instinctively, he reached out to the bottomless well of the blue roses—

But it was gone.

Damn it! He cursed and spoke to the air, bringing another invisible wall between himself and the charging swordsman.

Again, the man's blade struck, again lightning leapt across his blade, and again the wall collapsed, blasting Grei backward into the street. Ready for it this time, he rolled with the force and managed to pop upright again.

Vaeron chuckled. "Well, this is going to be easier than I thought."

A host of rats poured out of the alley, flooding around Vaeron's legs like a river. All of them looked like Uriozi, transformed from flesh and blood into steel and wire. They scurried toward Grei, red eyes glowing in the dark.

"Slate Spirit!" Grei called, clasping The Root. He felt its steadiness, and his focus returned. He had to protect Adora. She was behind them now, back in the alley. They hadn't seemed to care about her, but that couldn't last long.

Vaeron stalked Grei, swinging his giant sword back and forth as though it were a stick.

Grei peered into the alley, looking for Adora. She stood next to the striking female Slate Wizard, Fylomene. And it....it looked like they were chatting!

Adora made relaxed hand gestures as she talked, but between his ringing ears and the thirty feet of distance, he didn't know what she was saying. What could she possibly be saying? She seemed to be explaining something. Fylomene, with an amused expression on her face, listened with her arms crossed.

Grei's momentary stupefaction nearly cost him his life. He jolted out of his reverie to find Vaeron lifting his blade over his head. Grei whispered, turning the cobblestones beneath Vaeron to water and throwing himself to the side. The blade clanged on the hard stone as Vaeron dropped into the now-watery stones. But he slapped his hands on the hard stone at the edge of the spell, stopping himself from sinking below his waist.

"Hard," Grei murmured, and the street encased the man, trapping him in solid stone from the hips down.

With a roar, Vaeron twisted, breaking stone. He surged upward, ripping out one leg and then the other. Stone and dirt exploded outward. Grei shielded his eyes and backed up.

With a mighty surge, Vaeron lunged before Grei could even throw up a wall. The man's sword came straight for Grei's heart—

Steel clanged on steel. A silver, circular blur smashed into the blade, and Vaeron's perfect thrust went wide, nicking Grei's shoulder.

The ringblade ricocheted and flew back the way it had come.

Right into Ree's hand.

"Ree!"

Blevins strode out of the darkness behind her, a gleaming sword in his fist. "Vaeron?"

Vaeron straightened. "Brother..."

Grei looked back and forth between the two huge men. They looked almost identical, even down to their over-developed muscles. Same hair. Same height. Same ridiculously wide shoulders. But their faces were slightly different. Vaeron's eyes were wider set, his brow thicker. Blevins's face had a brooding cast to it that Grei always felt must be from the many horrors he'd seen. This look was missing from Vaeron. In its place was...a cruelty, a slant to his brows that made Grei feel that, like his brother, Vaeron was ready to kill, but unlike his brother, Vaeron took great pleasure in it.

Vaeron smiled wide, revealing straight white teeth. "I was looking forward to this more than anything else, I confess. I was so glad to hear that you had survived these past centuries. You always had a knack for escaping your due."

"You shouldn't have come here, Vaeron."

"You're giving me orders? Is that it? You should bow to me, brother."

"You were never my king."

Fylomene, Pliothe and Adora emerged from the alley. Fylomene purred as she looked at Blevins. "Oh, he's still as handsome as ever, isn't he?"

"Shut up, Fylomene," Vaeron growled.

She shrugged with a little *I just can't help myself* smile. Adora took a drink from the wineskin, one eyebrow raised as if she was amused by this entire confrontation.

"Take your brood and leave," Blevins said, moving to stand in front of Grei. "You don't rule here in Thiara."

Vaeron glanced at Grei, then back at Blevins. "Wait.... Do you serve this one? Are you a lackey to the Whisper Prince?"

"More or less," Blevins said.

"Blevins, is King Vaeron your brother?" Grei asked.

"Unfortunately."

"Wait," Vaeron said. "Blevins? You're Blevins? My spies reported that the Whisper Prince traveled with a giant fat man named Blevins who was amazing with a blade. That was *you*? *You're* the fat man! What happened? Did you lose your middle jogging across the continent?"

"Something like that," Blevins growled.

"Well," Vaeron said. "This is just...it just goes to show that those who serve Venisha *do* get their fondest wishes. I'm going to enjoy having you as a mechanical slave, brother. Stick you in my temple like a sculpture, watch the intelligence slowly die behind your eyes."

"Then maybe stop yapping like the dog you are. Whenever you think you're strong enough to face me, Vaeron, I'm ready. We both know how it turned out last time."

"You mean three hundred years ago?" He waved his sword before him. "Fylomene, you have the woman in hand?"

Fylomene chuckled. "She's thoroughly pleasant. More interested in drinking and watching, it seems."

"Keep an eye on them."

"Yes, my beloved."

"Pliothe, take the rest of them. Make them your new 'friends.' I have a long-overdue reckoning with my brother."

Vaeron charged Blevins.

Grei reached out, intending to drop Vaeron—and Fylomene and Pliothe—into the ground. He whispered to the stones—

The whispers of the air around him suddenly changed, and two invisible walls smashed into him. Grei dropped to the ground, dazed. His vision went black, then slowly returned.

He blinked. Through blurry vision, he saw Uriozi—or the mechanical thing that looked like Uriozi—hovering over him, wings flicking, making a noise like falling coins.

Oily tears leaked from her eyes. The sheer power in her strike had staggered him. She had the blue roses at her command now. And he didn't.

She gestured and the walls came together on Grei again. He barely had time to whisper to the air, to try to stop it. He slowed them, but they still slammed into him. His head rang, and he was sure the next time, the strike would split his skull.

He checked to see if he could count on help from any of his friends.

A cadre of metal rats swarmed over Ree. She fought and dodged, but they clung to her.

Adora stood next to Fylomene, who was doing the talking now. Adora looked entranced, nodding and smiling as though a desperate battle wasn't raging right in front of her.

Vaeron had driven Blevins back under a brutal onslaught. Blevins blocked Vaeron's strike, but it drove the big man to his knees, as though Vaeron's muscles were twice as strong as Blevins's.

We're losing, Grei thought. *They knew exactly how to hit me, to weaken me. And now we're all going to die if I don't do something.*

An hour ago, Grei would have known exactly what to do. He would have thrown them all into the sea with the power of the blue roses. But now, he could barely keep himself alive, let alone help his friends.

They had to get away from this place, to regroup, to return to the field of blue roses and take them back from this thing that was now Uriozi.

Grei looked down at The Root clenched in his fist. He could open a hatch. He could drop his friends into the ground, bend the tunnel and create the portal the Slate Spirit had shown him, transport them virtually anywhere else in an instant.

And anywhere else would be better than here. Where to go?

To the field of blue roses? No, that was exactly what they'd expect. They'd use their glowing blue portal and go there first. Grei didn't know how long it would take him to undo whatever Uriozi had done. He didn't even know if he *could*. He needed time to study the problem.

No. Not the field of blue roses. They needed a place to regroup, to plan, a place that would be hard for the Slate Wizards to find and harder to follow—

The thought hit him like a lightning bolt. The Dead Woods. The domain of the White Tree. These Slate Wizards *seemed* to know everything, but it was possible they didn't know about the Dead Woods.

That was where they had to go.

The plan flashed through his mind in an instant. Wind rushed at him as the invisible walls approached, ready to crush him again. Grei flicked open all four hatches on The Root, envisioning one opening under Adora, one under Ree, one under Blevins, and one under himself.

Grei fell through the ground. The air smashed together above him, its collision blasting such a wind at him that he slammed into the dark dirt floor of The Root's tunnel.

To his left, Blevins thudded into the earth. To his right, Adora fell and then Ree, still covered with metal rats. They clawed and bit at her, but she was using her wooden arm to scrape them off. Grei slammed the hatches shut.

They heard Vaeron bang his sword against the street overhead. It created a *thoom* in the tunnel. It came again and again, over and over, as he tried to hack his way down.

Grei heard Uriozi's whispers, beseeching the earth to turn to water, wash away and allow her access. He fought her, asking the earth to stay firm, stay solid.

Then with the rest of his attention, he told The Root to go to the Dead Woods, reversing the course he had made to come here in the first place.

The tunnel shot out in front of him, disappearing into the darkness. Sweat beading on his forehead, still holding Uriozi at bay, Grei envisioned the tunnel of The Root bending…bending…bending….

"Come…" he gasped, "with me." It was so hard to keep Uriozi from overwhelming him. She held nothing back. It would be only seconds before she'd crush his will.

He envisioned the two ends of the tunnel touching, then he whispered to the tunnel wall, asking it to fall away. It did, revealing a duplicate tunnel on the other side.

He lurched through it. Blevins followed. Ree, still battling rats that clung to her like burrs, staggered through. Adora hesitated.

"Adora!" Grei said.

She sighed, then walked through.

Gasping, Grei asked the tunnel walls to fill back in, and then he let go of the loop.

Ree was still ripping rats and bugs from herself, and Grei let his mind dive into their whispers. These were much harder to manipulate than the normal elements. They resisted him, their hissing sound rising to a crescendo like some kind of guardian, like these whispers were protected by another magical being. The elements were obliging, but the magic binding the rats was not. They wanted to stay the shape they were.

But this time, Grei was stronger. He forced their integral wires, the little bits of them that held them together, to turn to liquid.

The dozen rats on Ree fell apart. Little *spang* noises filled the tunnel, and a shower of parts fell to the floor at her feet. Ree kicked at them and backed away. She had nicks and cuts all over her hands and face. Her leather Ringblade clothing was scarred and punctured in multiple places.

Grei collapsed to his knees. No more thundering sword strikes *thoomed* overhead, and he couldn't feel Uriozi whispering her way through the dirt and stone above.

"They're gone," he gasped. "We're safe…. For now."

Adora blinked and shook her head as though coming out of a dream. "Ooo, I think Lady Fylomene put a spell on me. The more she talked, the more I wanted to look at her lips."

Ree winced, gingerly touching the places where she'd been bitten.

Sweat streamed down Blevins's face, and he looked haggard. "Where…where are we?"

"The Dead Woods," Grei said. "It was the only place I could think of that would be far enough away, and safe enough to give us a moment to regroup. Is everyone all right?"

"I may need…" Ree winced as she touched her arm. "Some bandages. And alcohol."

Grei nodded. "We will get you taken care of. There's a stream here that does wonders for wounds."

He opened a hatch on The Root, and he beseeched the air to bring them up to the surface. It barely worked. The whispers above seemed muted, barely half their normal intensity. Slowly, ponderously, the air lifted them up and set them on the ground.

The dim sky was filled with dirty clouds, layer upon layer of them. To Grei's right, an enormous pyramid rose in the distance. All around, metal cylinders as tall as the Thiaran palace belched smoke into the air. The streets were paved with flat square stones, and the lamp posts had tiny cylinders that shot lightning back and forth between them.

The air tasted like oil, and his eyes stung.

"Where are we?" Ree marveled.

"It's the Dead Woods," Adora said brightly. "Except all the trees turned to steel."

"This isn't the Dead Woods," Blevins growled. "This is Venisha."

Part II

Venisha

Chapter Eighteen

FYLOMENE

Fylomene sighed as Vaeron grabbed the lip of the cracked cobblestone and heaved it aside with one hand. He slammed Kingkiller, his two-handed broadsword, down on the earth again and again, trying to dig deep enough to follow the magical hatch that had swallowed his brother Baezin.

It was futile of course, trying to dig through stone and dirt with a sword, but with Vaeron's supernatural strength and single-minded fury, he clearly believed he could reach his foes.

Fylomene glanced at Pliothe. Vaeron's little sister made her uncomfortable. Fylomene had never liked children, really. Her parents had been poor dirt farmers who believed the more children they had, the more successful their farm would be. As a young woman, the third child of thirteen, Fylomene had been forced to care for her younger siblings, and she'd hated it.

At fifteen, she'd thought life was just like that. You grew up with barely enough to eat, helped out at the house, took care of the younger children, and when you were old enough to have babies of your own, your parents married you off to another dirt farmer to start your own brood.

But Fylomene's entire life had changed when she was fifteen. She'd already been matched with a boy two towns over, a goodly distance from home, earlier than her two older sisters. By fifteen, Fylomene's beauty was already well known. Everyone had told her she was pretty since she was old enough to know what that word meant. The early marriage was a source of great pride to her, setting her apart, making her special.

She'd met her betrothed once, and he was fine, she supposed. She'd actually looked forward to it. Certain feelings had begun to surface within her—she'd even kissed a few local boys—and she was eager to explore that feeling with abandon.

One fateful day, with thoughts of having her own house far from squalling babies and ruthless toddlers, she went into town with her oldest sister to buy milled flour. Father's harvest had been unusually good that fall, so they had a rare bit of money.

While she was waiting on the miller's stoop, a carriage pulled up to the livery across the street. She had never seen anything like it. It was painted bright red with golden borders, and it was drawn by no fewer than four horses!

A rich woman from the crown city of Venisha stepped out of the carriage, sweeping aside her fine silk skirts, and went into the livery flanked by two men who looked like guards. Fylomene waited, holding her breath, until the woman emerged again. One of her servants actually put a gilded stool beneath her feet so she could climb into the carriage more easily. The other servant closed the door behind her, climbed up, flicked the reins, and drove her away.

That quickly, Fylomene's future changed. It was like a door had opened that she'd never known existed, and beyond it she'd glimpsed a treasure more beautiful than she could have imagined. The windows of the brightly painted carriage had had *curtains*. Curtains on a wagon! And they had been made of a white frilled cloth that was finer than anything her eyes had ever seen.

That door would never close again, she realized. There was something more out there. There were people who rode in bright red carriages with frilled curtains, with servants catering to their slightest whim. There was an alternative to being a brood mare to a poor farmer.

And she had to have that life.

After that moment, nothing from her poor life could satisfy her. She began to see it for what it really was. Everything was so drab and common. Baby howls were like spikes in her ears. Mother's constant demands were the screeches of a harpy. She fought with her sisters about every little thing. She felt like she was sinking in mud a little bit more every day. She knew if she didn't do something soon, that mud would cover her head, and she would suffocate. Her parents and her siblings behaved no differently than they'd done for the last fifteen years, but Fylomene suddenly loathed them. That they behaved no differently was the *reason* she loathed them.

Her older sisters' hands already looked rough from the lye of washing dishes and clothes. She realized that her mother's wrinkles and the dumpy, sagging ruin of her body was exactly the fate in store for her.

Father often told the story of how he and Mother had met, of how beautiful she had been, the finest looking girl in the whole village. Mother's eyes always lit up when he told the tale, and she would give him her worn smile.

Fylomene had assumed Father was lying. She'd thought Mother had never been a real beauty—not like Fylomene was. How could she have been, to look like she did now?

But Fylomene suddenly realized Father wasn't lying. Mother *had* been a beauty, and this life of babies and labor had reduced her to a gray-haired hag whose only hope for beauty was to remember it, to recall that brief instant she had been pretty.

You're so pretty, Fylomene.

Such beautiful hair!
Those eyes…

She had heard the comments people made about her. She had felt the eyes of the boys follow her. At fifteen, she knew it gave her a kind of power over everyone, but how long would that power last? A year? Five years if she was lucky? How many days would she spend scrubbing clothes, changing diapers, and pushing out babies before her body was the wreck that Mother's was?

Horror-stricken, Fylomene spent the next week in a daze, staring down the hopeless, one-way path of her life. At the end of it, in the evening when the family gathered together to tell stories, Fylomene went to her room, packed her best dress—and her sister's best dress—wrapped it all up with some food she'd pilfered from the kitchen, and escaped out the window.

She left that little shack with its squirming children, dirty walls, and gray dreams. She never looked back.

The road was long, and she relied on the kindness of strangers over and over, but she made it to Venisha. Those first few years were hard. She had been forced to do things she'd never dreamed she'd have to do, things good little farm girls would never do, things Mother and her sisters would have gasped at.

But she'd made her way. Most importantly, she'd never had children. And she'd never had to take care of anyone else's children. And then she had met Vaeron, and he had fallen for her well-honed charms….

She extricated herself from her reverie. Vaeron still hacked at the ground like an animal.

No, she'd never liked children. She hadn't liked Pliothe before they'd all been made immortal by the god Venisha. The girl had been a strange little tagalong. And after their collective transformation, Pliothe had only become… stranger.

Of course, she wasn't really a child anymore, was she? She wasn't a little girl any more than Fylomene was a young woman. They were both over three hundred years old. But the girl still acted ten years old. She was grimy most of the time, played with her magical artifacts like toys. That was when she wasn't playing the murderous little henchman for Vaeron. Holding the girl's gaze was ghastly, those round eyes with their whites showing.... She always looked at Fylomene like something between a mother and a meal. It was unnerving.

Still, the girl's artifacts were a wonder.

"He's digging a hole in the ground for nothing, isn't he?" Fylomene said. "They're not down there."

Pliothe shook her head.

"My love," Fylomene said.

Vaeron ignored her. *Hack hack hack.*

"Vaeron," she said louder. "They're gone, my love. Pliothe says they're not there anymore."

He kept hacking. She wasn't even sure he'd heard her. When Vaeron flamed into a rage, it sometimes required shaking him to snap him out of it.

She could go over there and put a hand on his shoulder, she supposed, but that was a good way of getting oneself chopped in half.

"Vaeron!" she shouted. She hated raising her voice. Real ladies never raised their voices. Women sounded shrill when they shouted.

He stopped and raised his reddened face, huffing and puffing.

Fylomene cocked her head. By Venisha, he was handsome man. All bulging and sweating and breathing hard like…

Her heart fluttered, and she wanted him all over again. It always happened. Fylomene could make any man fall in love with her—and some women—but with Vaeron it was always backwards. He could yell at her, dismiss her, degrade her in front of others, but she never stopped wanting him.

"Pliothe says they're gone," Fylomene said.

Vaeron showed his teeth, then stalked toward them.

"We will find them," Fylomene said. "It's just a matter of—"

"Shut up," he growled, then to Pliothe. "Pliothe!"

Pliothe flinched like she'd been whipped. She always acted that way with Vaeron.

"That was one of your artifacts. You can control it?"

"Yes."

"And what did I tell you to do?"

She cowered.

"Pliothe!" He shouted, towering over her, gripping his sword like he was going to chop her head off. "Where did you send them?"

"Where you told me to," she said in a small voice.

"Then where are they?" Vaeron raised his hands and turned in a slow circle, an expectant look on his face. "I told you if he tried to use The Root that you were to send him back to us."

"I did send him back."

"Then where is he?"

"I sent him back home."

"Yes, back to— What?"

"I sent them home."

Vaeron clenched his sword so hard his entire arm trembled. Pliothe cringed, holding her hands close to her chest and bending over as if he might strike her. Except Vaeron had never struck Pliothe. And he never would. Even as mindless as he became in his rages, he would never hurt her. She was far too valuable to him. The power given her by Venisha was infinitely versatile, and more powerful than Vaeron's or Fylomene's abilities combined. One on one, Vaeron's strength and supernatural skill with a blade could best any man. But he couldn't spy on someone on the third floor of the Thiaran palace. He couldn't change a Faia from enemy to slave in seconds.

Pliothe could. She could do just about anything given the time to craft the appropriate artifact.

Vaeron looked apoplectic. His face had gone beet-red. "You...sent them where?"

"Venisha," she said.

Vaeron turned and slammed Kingkiller into the ground, cracking a thick flagstone with the point.

"You said to send them home." The girl began to cry.

"Now you've done it," Fylomene said.

All the artifact creatures that had rabidly attacked the Whisper Prince and his followers now skittered and scuttled across the cobblestones, gathering around Pliothe. Even the transmuted Faia fluttered down to stand beside her. The show looked like a rallying of forces to withstand an attack, but it wasn't.

Whenever Pliothe broke down and cried, her creatures gathered near as though comforting her and...Pliothe would completely lock up. She would fall down and remain inconsolable—and incommunicative—for hours.

Vaeron whirled, belatedly coming to the same realization as Fylomene. "No, wait. I apologize."

But it had already begun. Pliothe was crying. She slumped to her knees, and her creatures clustered around her. She put her face in her hands and sobbed, then fell over on her side.

"Sister, no. Please. Look, I'm putting the sword away." He sheathed Kingkiller. But Pliothe didn't see, didn't stop crying. He shot a frustrated glance at Fylomene, but all she could do was hold out her hands and shrug.

"Listen, Pliothe. Everything will be all right. I was simply angry, and not at you. Please stop crying. I need you to make a doorway. Use that portal of yours and take us back to

Venisha, to the exact spot you dropped them. Can you do that?"

Pliothe sobbed harder. The Faia put her arms around the girl. The rats and bugs made a little pile that half-covered her.

"It's no use, my love," Fylomene said. "You're just going to have to wait."

"The last thing we can do is wait!"

"You're not chasing anyone for the next hour at least."

"Fylomene—"

"Don't blame me. You shouldn't have yelled at her. You know how she is."

He glared at her like he wanted to chop her head off, and Fylomene felt herself go cold. Once again, she'd incautiously let her sharp tongue have its way.

Like Pliothe, Fylomene was useful to Vaeron, too, but unlike Pliothe, she was not indispensable. And Vaeron seemed far less interested in availing himself of Fylomene's charms than he once was.

Fylomene stopped talking, feeling like her tiptoes were at the edge of a precipice where the slightest shiver could pitch her to her death. Vaeron glowered at her, and she knew if she even breathed wrong in that moment, he would kill her.

"So we wait," he growled.

Her heart thundered in her chest, but she put on a well-practiced smile.

"Yes, my love...."

Chapter Nineteen

GREI

Grei looked around them, shocked. Everyone in Thiara knew of Venisha, of course. He had even met some Venishans back in Fairmist. He'd heard the tales of how Venisha was a city of industry and culture, that it was more advanced than the Thiaran Empire in so many ways, that the city teemed with magical artifacts created by the priests of the Slate Temples. But he could barely comprehend what he was seeing now. Never had anyone described it such that he could have pictured this.

The main roads in the Thiaran Empire were raised. If you weren't walking on the road, you were looking up at it. Here, it was the opposite. It was the walkways of stone that were raised, flanking the flagstone roads which were lower than the walkways by half a foot. It looked like a shallow trench for a canal. Practically everything in sight was made of steel and stone. Some of the houses were made of wood, but they were banded by steel, as though a frame had been constructed and wood had been used to fill in the walls.

In fact, Grei couldn't see any trees at all. Even in the heart of the crown city of Thiara, there were gardens and green spaces, not to mention canals that were fed from the Fairmist River. He spotted a few planter boxes with edible vegetation in the windows of the buildings, but there wasn't a patch of grass anywhere on the ground. Oily dirt lots between buildings were filled with twists of discarded metal and stone, as though the city's builders had no interest in anything that wasn't a construct, and no one had ever cleaned them up.

They stood alone in an alley, but a few streets down, Grei could see people walking, horses pulling carts beneath the erratic lightning-like street lamps.

He looked at the tall smoking pipes that towered over the buildings. They seemed like twisted cousins of the seven shining towers in Thiara. He tried to understand their purpose.

But all the jarring sights were nothing compared to what had happened to the whispers of the elements all around him. He couldn't hear them.

He strained and finally found them, but they were so quiet that at first it had seemed like some giant had clapped a lid over the entire world. It was though the very nature of this place had been buried under oil and metal.

How could anyone live here? How could they make their homes here?

He'd always felt the crown city of Thiara was confining, with its imposing Red Wall, close-together buildings and masses of people, but it was nothing compared to this. This city of oil and industry had no single-story houses. Every house was over three stories, as if each competed with all the others, with the towering smokestacks themselves. The tall buildings seemed to lean in on him, and he felt suffocated. They blocked out most of the night sky, and what the buildings didn't block was obliterated by dark clouds.

In Fairmist, there were a few two-story structures, like The Floating Stone or the Delegate's palace. In Thiara there were even more with the palace, the Web of Blades, and the seven towers, but this city with its tall buildings and trench-like streets felt like some ugly maze where he and his friends could only scurry about like rats.

He wanted to cover his nose and mouth against the fumes. "What...why is it like this?"

"This," Blevins rumbled, "is where I was born."

Grei suddenly remembered that Baezin the Conquerer had originally come from across the Sunset Sea. Everyone knew him as the visionary—the builder—who established the towns of Thiara, Fairmist, Trimbledown, Moondow, and Cliffgard. But he'd come from this place first.

"Why did you bring us here?" Blevins asked.

"I didn't," Grei said.

"That's not good," Blevins growled. He glanced around, as though expecting enemies to come charging out of the darkness.

The Slate Spirit had been silent since Grei had picked up The Root in Thiara, and usually when Grei picked the thing up, the spirit was quick to speak. Grei hadn't noticed it at first because he'd been busy trying to save his own life. Now, though, it concerned him.

He longed to say something, but felt self-conscious in front of Blevins. He'd read Blevins's whispers clearly when they'd had their last meeting. The man had been preparing to kill him. Grei didn't want Blevins to know that, if he still wanted to do such a thing, now would be the perfect time. Grei hadn't felt this weak since he'd been stabbed with Selicia's magic dagger and lost his powers.

"I invoked the artifact," Grei said. "I told it to go to the Dead Woods."

"The Slate Wizards created that thing you're holding," Blevins said. "They could wrench it away from you. Did you see what they did to Uriozi?"

"We'll fix it," Grei said.

"Will you?" Blevins looked around, shook his head ruefully. "I never wanted to come back here."

"Did it look like this three centuries ago?" Grei asked.

Blevins glared at the smoky, oily city, but he didn't answer the question.

"Can you take us back, Grei?" Ree asked. She had procured a cloth and was dabbing at her many wounds.

He glanced down at The Root, imagined using it, and found himself reluctant. He hadn't felt any outside influence when he'd used it for their escape, but how could he be sure? What Blevins said made a certain sense.

"I think I can," he said.

"Throw that thing away," Blevins said. "Better yet, destroy it, and then throw it away. We'll sail back to Thiara."

Grei held The Root tighter. He knew so little about it, but he and his magic were bound to it. A sick feeling filled his belly. With the field of blue roses wrenched from him, The Root was the only haven he had left, the only anchor for his magic, and in this foreign land, he needed that more than ever. Without it, would he be able to use magic at all? He didn't think so.

He simply knew too little about this thing to which he'd bound his magic and his life. The Slate Spirit had said that he and the Slate Wizards were enemies, but could he have been lying?

Of course he could.

Every way Grei turned, he was caged. He couldn't throw The Root away, but he couldn't trust it either. He couldn't see the way out, couldn't see what his next move should be.

"Grei," Ree said quietly. "Take us back."

"We'll find a ship," Blevins insisted.

"That will take weeks," Ree said. "What will become of Thiara in that time?"

"He uses that thing again, we're going to end up in a prison cell," Blevins said. "Or worse."

Grei thought of returning to that fight on the streets of Thiara. They weren't ready. They'd fled to regroup. They couldn't jump into the middle of that again. They had been completely overmatched. They'd die.

He thought of trying to flee to the Dead Woods again…but even if he could wrench The Root to his will, what would he do once they got there? The White Tree would only tell him to return here and find the goddess Devorra.

Adora began to sing another bawdy drinking song. She winged her arms out like a child and skipped along the curb, bending left and right to catch her balance.

Unreliable friends. Rabid enemies. He couldn't see a path no matter which way he turned. He wanted the lands to work like they should, to be a place where those with power were benevolent and those without were treated fairly. He wanted a world where he could love Adora and have her love him back. He just couldn't see how to get there.

"Grei," Blevins rumbled. "The docks are this way."

Once again, power-hungry demigods were trying to kill him, to remake the lands. Once again, they wanted him running scared.

"No," Grei growled.

"What?" Blevins asked.

"I said no," Grei repeated. He wasn't running. He refused to fear these new enemies. They had weaknesses like everyone else. He just had to find them. Even now, he could feel the power in this place. It wasn't like the power of Devorra: the whispers of healthy life—trees and clean water and solid earth—but there was something else. These artifacts of metal and oil hissed, that same hiss that always pushed into his mind when he used The Root, when he was close to other Venishan artifacts. If he could learn the language of the hissing, speak to them like he spoke to the elements….

Blevins darkened. His black eyes flashed. "That's a Venishan artifact, Grei. Even money says the Slate Wizards control it. Throw it away. Let's trust our wits, our strength, and the ocean."

"I'm not going anywhere," Grei said. "Maybe you're right, maybe they redirected us to keep me away from the blue roses, to make me vulnerable. Maybe they wanted to trap us close to the heart of their power. Fine. Let's show them just how dangerous it is to put us close to their heart. We are taking the fight to them."

"You're going to take the...." Blevins shook his head. "You saw what they can do. They'll be twice as powerful here. They'll destroy you."

"No," Grei said. "I'm going to destroy them."

"Going to conquer Venisha now, too?" Blevins's lip curled.

"Blevins, I wanted to mend the broken things. I wanted to complete that one task, then make a simple life without politics or power. But apparently, I have one more job to do before I can stop being the Whisper Prince."

"One more job," Adora said in singsong. "Then I'll stop. Fight the mob. One quick chop. And more and more and more.... One more job, then I'll stop...."

Grei flicked an annoyed glance at her, but she smiled and repeated her new song.

"Look at you," Blevins spat. "You talk about the power hungry, about how they want to reshape the lands, but that's exactly what *you* want to do."

Grei showed his teeth. "I don't want any of this! But I'll be damned if I'm going to walk away and let *them* have it. No more demigods."

"No more demigods indeed." Blevins put his hand on his sword.

"Don't," Grei warned.

Ree slid between Blevins and Grei, dagger in hand. Blevins showed his teeth.

"Look at him, Ree," Blevins said. "Look at what he's saying. He's making excuses to gather more power. And more. And more. *That's* how it happens. Look at him!"

"Grei has never let me down before."

"He resurrected her!" Blevins jerked a thumb at Adora, who continued to sing as though she didn't care about the entire exchange. "Again and again. I should kill him for that alone!"

"He's our only defense against the Slate Wizards," she said quietly.

"Defense? He deposed an emperor, took over Thiara. Now he wants to conquer Venisha."

"You'd rather the Slate Wizards take it all?" Grei asked.

Blevins growled. He clenched the hilt of his sword. With a shout he whirled and stalked away, disappearing around the corner of a tall brown building.

Adora stopped her song and let out a forceful sigh. "That was invigorating!" She hopped off the curb, shook her hair out and whipped it behind her head. She took a drink from her wineskin.

"We're running low on allies," Ree murmured, her hawk eyes flicking from shadow to shadow, looking for Blevins to return with a surprise attack.

Grei felt hollow. "If he can't trust me, he's not our ally." His heart twisted as he said it. Blevins had been by his side from the beginning. But dammit! The Thiaran Empire—the entire continent of Devorra—was at stake. Grei didn't need Blevins blocking him at every turn. "If he can't see what I'm trying to do, let him go."

"I'm not sure *I* see what we're trying to do, Grei," Ree admitted.

"What I do best," Grei said.

"Oh purr," Adora said in a saucy voice, giving him bedroom eyes as she bit her bottom lip. He clenched his teeth and ignored her, focusing on Ree instead.

The Ringblade looked confused. "You can do just about anything, Grei. What is it that you do best?"

"Listen," he said. "I am the Whisper Prince, and the artifacts of Venisha whisper in their own way."

"Slate Wizard magic?"
"I'm going to take it away from them."

Chapter Twenty

GREI

Grei led them up the narrow street, frantic flashes of white light splashing across the slick stones from the silently violent lightning lamps.

"Are you sure about this?" Ree murmured, looking left and right. "You're going to learn an entirely new form of magic and then use it against beings who've been using it their whole lives?"

"Several lives," Adora said. "They're centuries old."

Grei flicked a glance at her.

"Fylomene told me while we were talking. When you were playing with Vaeron."

"I wasn't playing. I was trying to stay alive while you were doing nothing to help," Grei said.

"You should stop."

"Trying to stay alive?"

"It makes everything far less complicated when you don't care about dying."

Grei turned away from her. He didn't have time to play her games. He had to concentrate. When he'd first learned magic in Fairmist, it had been purely intuitive. He'd been led forward as though the whispers themselves were dying to talk to him. He'd…listened, and then he had uncovered secrets no one else knew. Now, he just had to do the same thing.

Aside from the busier thoroughfare two streets over, Grei saw few people. He saw two drunkards sleeping in an alley to their left, but aside from that, their chosen street was relatively empty.

At first, he had worried Adora would take this moment of disorientation in a new city to attempt an escape. Or, failing that, she would just refuse to follow him, but she didn't. She simply drank from her wineskin and staggered along behind, a smile on her face like this was some kind of game.

"Are we looking for anything specific?" Ree asked.

"I'll know it when I hear it," Grei said. He had been testing the extent of his diminishment. He'd asked the stones to turn to water. They had responded, but the response was sluggish and the results less than impressive. The stone had become malleable like clay, but only the first inch or so. The center had still been hard.

He stopped in the middle of the street, and Ree stopped with him. Adora sauntered past them until she realized she was alone, then turned and ambled back. Grei stood beneath the light of a lightning lamp with a stylized dragon on top. The dragon's steel head pointed to the sky, its fanged jaws open, and the crackle of lightning shot two feet up from its throat, lighting the street. The thing was a work of art, meticulously and lovingly sculpted.

There was no wood inside the thing, no oil. Grei's powers were weak, but they were strong enough for him to sense the pole, the dragon's head, the flame, and what they were made of. There was no fuel for the fire. It came from the dragon's head, from the air within its throat, similar to how Grei could cause one element to behave like another. In Fairmist, there were many artifacts left by the Faia, spells that lingered long after their creation, like the Lateral Houses and the seven main bridges over the Fairmist River.

The hiss of the dragon artifact sounded in his mind. He tried to talk to it, but either it refused to listen to him, or it wasn't like the whispers of Devorra. Perhaps it *couldn't* listen to him.

How do they do it? he thought.

"What if Blevins is right?" Ree asked.

Adora began humming. Thankfully, she didn't sing.

"About the Slate Wizards coming after us, you mean?" he asked.

"If they orchestrated your arrival here, wouldn't it make sense they'd rush headlong after you?"

"I suppose."

"So why haven't they?"

It was an interesting question. Grei had thought they'd soon be fighting for their lives when he'd realized they were in Venisha. But there hadn't been a single sign of danger.

"Maybe The Root got affected by all the magic being thrown around in Thiara," he said. "Maybe The Root meant to go to the Dead Woods, but actually put us here by accident."

"That seems a highly unlikely coincidence," Ree said. "Why not throw us to Trimbledown? Or Fairmist? Or Benasca, even? Why all the way across the ocean?"

He didn't say anything.

"The only thing that makes sense is that the Slate Wizards somehow got a hand on your spell with The Root, and they flung you here, to their place of power, away from yours, to put you at their mercy. So why aren't they taking advantage of it?"

"I don't know."

"Me neither, but I'm wondering if we should get as far away from here as possible. What if they meant to put us in the palace but, as you say, the spell got jostled and put us only *close* to the palace."

Ree wasn't wrong. Grei didn't want to take on the Slate Wizards again with his currently meager powers.

"You're right," he said. "Let's find a hidden place. I need to study one of these artifacts without being bothered."

"Kind of what I figured. Come on," she said. "I see something promising ahead."

Chapter Twenty-One

FYLOMENE

Vaeron slammed his sword into the cobblestones again. Chips of stone erupted. Vaeron hit it again and again and again, creating a sizable crater as Pliothe continued to sob inconsolably.

Fylomene turned away. She'd seen a hundred of Vaeron's tantrums, and it was best to face away rather than risk having his wrath turn in her direction. So she studied the architecture of the palace while Vaeron bled out his anger in a futile display. The palace was quaint in its simplicity, with archways and columns and thick walls. In Venisha, they didn't rely upon stone to build tall structures. They used steel, refined and perfected in the great smelting guilds. Steel didn't rely on gravity to bear heavy weights. The potential configurations of steel were limitless. And with a little bit of Pliothe's magic, bound in artifacts attached to the structures, Venishan architecture could be wondrous, with entire arms and walkways that seemed to float while people walked on them—

"You!" Vaeron shouted, and Fylomene's heart spiked. Perhaps turning away wasn't going to be enough to stop herself from becoming the target of Vaeron's rage this time.

But Vaeron wasn't looking at Fylomene. He glared at the Faia Pliothe had transformed. The creature stood with her hands at her sides, seemingly staring at nothing. Her head perked up when Vaeron shouted, though, and she turned to face him.

"What is the point of you if you can't stop the Whisper Prince from escaping? You have the blue roses!" He lunged at her and struck the little creature with a thunderous backhand. The metallic Faia flew a dozen feet, crashed across the cobblestones and trailed sparks. Little bits of wire bounced behind her.

Pliothe whimpered as though Vaeron had struck *her*. The Faia slid to a stop face-down on the ground, metallic arms and legs limp. Vaeron leapt after her and landed with a thunderous boom beside her. He raised his sword overhead like he planned to decapitate her.

"No!" Pliothe cried. Fylomene looked sharply at the girl. That one piercing cry stopped Vaeron in his tracks.

"Stop!" Pliothe said. "Don't..."

Vaeron slowly lowered his sword, his face reddening. "What did you say to me?"

"You'll lose the blue roses," Pliothe said.

That got through to him. He sneered down at the unconscious Faia like he wanted to kick her, but he didn't.

He strode toward Pliothe, and she cringed away from him like a beaten dog. "Well, well. You're awake. Good. Take us to the Whisper Prince."

She swallowed, nodded.

"Back to Venisha we go," Vaeron said.

"We just...leave things as they are?" Fylomene glanced at the silent courtyard, the silent palace.

"Why did I come here, Fylomene?" He asked in the tone he always used when the answer was obvious.

"To conquer Devorra," she said.

"And who could possibly stand in my way?"

"The Whisper Prince."

"Who else?"

"I…" She faltered at that. "I don't know."

"Exactly. There is no one else. The Faia are dead or under our control. Cavyn is gone. Only the Whisper Prince is a threat, and now where is he? In the heart of our city, far away from his home. We return to Venisha. We slaughter him and his friends, and then we walk through this continent unimpeded." He reached down and touched Pliothe's head in a loving gesture. She actually didn't flinch away this time. Instead, she held perfectly still, like she always did when he touched her.

Vaeron grunted. "Pliothe, give the Faia the command to kill anyone who tries to take the throne or organize any kind of government here."

Pliothe hesitated, then nodded. "I did."

"Good. Take us home immediately. Before they have a chance to get away."

Chapter Twenty-Two

FYLOMENE

Light strings whipped around them, kinking and snapping as Pliothe activated her teleporting artifact. Without a stumble, they vanished from the Thiaran streets and appeared in the Slate Temple back in Venisha, flying across the entirety of the Sunset Sea to Vaeron's stronghold in an instant. What was impossible a month ago now was as easy as blinking an eye, at least for Pliothe.

Fylomene envied Pliothe's immense magic, but it was hard to envy the sad girl her lot. She stood, shoulders slumped, eyes downcast at the gray slate stones of the throne room. Fylomene had barely known Pliothe before their transformation, but in the brief interactions they'd had back when they were mortal, Fylomene didn't remember the little girl being particularly happy either. She wondered if Pliothe had ever been happy.

Fylomene had been, at least for a time. In the beginning, right after they'd all been transformed, she had reveled in her beauty and youth that she knew would never fade. She'd reveled in the things Venisha had given her that she hadn't actually asked for. Sexual attraction. A supernatural ability to turn a man's head, to make him think of her, to make his blood rush when he looked at her, to make him mad with lust. The Slate Spirit had read her innermost desire and given it to her: to capture and hold Vaeron's attention.

And it had worked. Oh, those beginning days were heady. They'd broken from the mines and Vaeron had gone on a rampage to remove his father from the throne. Systematically, he had cut his way from one bastion of strength to another, slaying the old king's captains on the outskirts of the city in a single combat, then cowing the remaining guards and soldiers. One by one they fell, as no single warrior—nor any dozen for that matter—could best Vaeron in combat. And he had done it so quickly that before the old king had even realized what was happening, Vaeron had a third of the city's military behind him, and the chant of reformation swept through the city. By the time Vaeron had charged the Slate Temple where the king resided, his father's fall had been inevitable. The old king had fulfilled the prophecy he'd so feared: that one of his spawn would dethrone him. The steps he'd taken to curtail that future—trapping his direct descendants in the Slate Mines—had sealed his fate.

During those bloody days, Vaeron had done what he did best. Conquer and subjugate. Grab and hold power.

And Fylomene had done what she did best. During the nights, she had been his queen. He would return to her, flushed and spattered in blood, and she would clean him, letting her magic build around him until he could not stand it any longer. Then he would rip the clothes from her body and have his way with her.

It had been divine. Fylomene had been truly happy perhaps for the first time in her life. She had her prize. She was no longer a hungry peasant girl doomed to a life of aging before her time, a face of weather-beaten wrinkles, and arthritic hands. She was the lover of the most powerful man in the kingdom. She loved him, and he loved her.

But in the months and years after, Fylomene come to a painful realization. Vaeron enjoyed her for temporary pleasure, but he loved only one thing: power. Just like that realization she'd had at age fifteen, she saw her future in that moment. She watched the golden moments of her life set like the sun, melt into the flat line of the sea and leave only the endless waves of one day after another.

And each of those monotonous waves whispered the same words: *You will never have him. He is married to another.*

That was the first time she had come to envy Pliothe, who had made a wiser wish than she had.

It hadn't been apparent at first, not during those passionate days of bloodshed and sex. During those days, Vaeron had ignored his sister. Vaeron and Fylomene had barely noticed that Pliothe tagged along on the battles, watching the carnage. They hadn't even known about Pliothe's power until they'd noticed the mechanical rats following her around. Fylomene remembered Vaeron had, at first, turned his nose up in disgust and told her to keep the damned things away from him.

But in time, they had recognized the nearly limitless flexibility of Pliothe's gifts. That was when Vaeron had begun to use her, to have her craft more and more artifacts and, with artifacts that could transfer a portion of her gifts, to teach the Slate Priests how to do the same, albeit making weaker facsimiles of Pliothe's originals.

Oh, Fylomene had envied Pliothe then. She'd not only made better use of the wish the Slate Spirit had granted, but she had Vaeron's attention. Fylomene had even contemplated killing the girl in those initial days.

But not now. Even though Fylomene, curse her soul, still wanted Vaeron's attention above all things, to be the center of Vaeron's attention was like holding a flame in your hands. It could warm you, but it would almost certainly burn you as well.

Vaeron looked around, eyes narrowing. Two Slate Priests flanked the throne, as they had been commanded to do. They hadn't flinched as the portal opened and their masters had emerged. They witnessed magic on a regular basis. Two Slate Priests also flanked the double doors on the far side of the huge room, undisturbed.

"What—" Vaeron snarled as the crackling whips of lightning faded away. "—is this? Where is he?"

"You said to take us…home," Pliothe said, already withdrawing into herself. Her entourage of mechanical animals skittered around her, agitated.

"Pliothe…" Vaeron turned his reddening face toward his little sister. "I told you to take us to the Whisper Prince. Where is he? Where is my brother?"

Pliothe wrung her hands and glanced around the room. Her creatures milled aimlessly, agitated, reflecting her emotions. "I sent them here. I sent them here. I sent them here," she murmured.

"You incompetent little wretch." Vaeron stalked toward her, his hand falling on his sword.

"Vaeron, don't," Fylomene said. He whirled, his sword leaping from his scabbard.

"Are you defending her?" He walked toward her, aimed the point at her throat. At first, she thought he was simply trying to scare her, but when he didn't slow, she stumbled backward, trying to stay away from that deadly sword. She smacked into the wall and thought, for a breathless instant, that he would run her through.

But the deadly tip stopped just before her flesh, steady as a rock. The snarl on his red face seemed inhuman. He raised a fist like he would strike her, and she prepared for it. It wouldn't be the first time.

The fist uncurled and he rested the sword on her shoulder. Eyes wide, she swallowed as he slowly reached for the front of her dress. He twisted his fingers into the fabric and brutally ripped the cloth away.

She gasped. Beads bounced on the floor as he exposed the entire front of her body from clavicle to waist.

Fylomene breathed hard, but she didn't dare move.

"Don't...ever...think that you control me, slut," Vaeron said. "If I choose to mete out punishment to my sister or to whomever else, don't you ever question me. If I ever sense that you are even *trying* to use your magic on me, trying to bend me to your will, it will be the last thing you ever do."

Fylomene longed to open her mouth, to say the words that would soothe him, but her throat tightened. She *had* used her magic on him. Countless times. To do exactly what he feared. To calm him. To guide him. And at that moment, she knew that he would be watching like never before. Perhaps he already suspected her. Now he was looking for proof. Now he was looking for any excuse to kill her.

"I need you for two things, bitch. To do exactly as I command you, should I need you to seduce some wayward lord or captain. And to gratefully fall to your knees when I myself require your one talent. I do not need your counsel. I do not want your opinions."

Even as he spoke, he looked down at her naked breasts. His gaze shot back to her eyes, and anger flashed again. Anger at himself. Anger that he still desired her. He searched her face to see if she held even a glimmer of triumph in her eyes.

Thankfully for her, she was so genuinely frightened that she didn't feel the least bit triumphant.

"If you cannot accomplish these two barely consequential items," he continued, "then I have no use for you at all. Do you understand me?"

She gave the barest nod.

The anger in his eyes banked, and his flush receded. Now his gaze roved freely over her naked flesh. He removed his blade from her shoulder and sheathed it. The muscles in his jaw clenched.

He seemed to want to turn back to Pliothe, to continue railing against her failure, but his nostrils flared.

"Get on your knees."

Fylomene flicked a glance at the Slate Priests across the throne room on either side of them, but they were wisely staring straight ahead as if there was nobody around.

At her hesitation, Vaeron's eyes went flat and he clenched his fist again.

Fylomene slowly descended to her knees.

"Yes, your Majesty."

Chapter Twenty-Three

FYLOMENE

When Vaeron was through with her, he walked away, lacing up his breeches. Fylomene stood slowly, pulling up the scraps of her dress to cover herself, though the Slate Priests had wisely continued to stare straight forward. If Vaeron thought for even a second they had watched, they would die. He'd done it before, killed priests right here in this very chamber.

Vaeron's great chest expanded and contracted as he breathed, then he turned his gaze back to Pliothe. He narrowed his eyes. "Where is the Whisper Prince?"

"He is in the city," she said immediately.

"Where?" Vaeron growled.

"I...maybe the docks. Or the road out of town toward the Slate Mines. Or the player district."

"He's in three places?"

"I saw three flashes when he used The Root," Pliothe said. "He could be at any one. It is...difficult. His will is strong, and I couldn't completely control him. But I know he is here somewhere."

"In three places."

"One of the three."

"Very well." The tension went out of Vaeron's shoulders. He slammed his blade home with a clang, and

Fylomene knew the danger was past. "I will take the docks. Pliothe, the player district. There are a lot of alleys for your creatures to search. Fylomene, you take the road out to the Slate Mines. And for Venisha's sake, take someone competent with you. If you get into a fight, you'll need more than your long lashes."

"Yes, Your Majesty." Fylomene gave a wooden smile. She had loved this dress, and now it was ruined. She could never repair the intricate beadwork. She'd have to throw it away.

Vaeron started toward the double doors.

Pliothe set her little artifact on the floor and, before Fylomene could ask for transport to her rooms so she could change her clothes, the artifact flashed and Pliothe—and all her little creatures—vanished.

Fylomene turned to one of the Slate Priests.

"Get me a carriage," she said, moving toward the door that led to her apartments in the Slate Temple, holding her tattered dress to her chest. "Make it ready for me in fifteen minutes."

Chapter Twenty-Four

GREI

Grei let out a frustrated breath and sat back. It wasn't working.

They had stopped behind an abandoned building—there were more than a few of them—and Grei had practiced on the stuttering lightning lamp behind the building. He saw no reason for a lamp behind an abandoned building. He could only guess that at one point this had been a place where people had gathered. Apparently, the lamps continued unabated no matter what. In the hour or so that he'd been working, he hadn't seen a single light—lightning lamp or normal flame—in the windows of the three-story building.

In this strange land, this abandoned space seemed as safe as anywhere. But Ree stayed alert, and thankfully Adora had stopped singing and humming. She lay on the dirty ground, staring at the cloud-choked sky overhead. Her short red skirt and brief Thiaran wrap—already soiled by this greasy city—weren't ideal for lying on the ground, but she didn't seem to care.

Ree heard his sigh and emerged from the darkness. "Not working?"

"I was hoping to find some kind of reception from the hissing, but it doesn't seem interested in being understood.

It's very different than the whispers of the elements. I've learned so much, but apparently I don't know it all."

"I don't either," Adora said. "A moment ago, I really tried, but I just couldn't know it all."

Grei closed his eyes. Every time Adora spoke, it hurt. They were stranded in Venisha. The Slate Wizards might conquer Thiara, might find them and kill them all. But she didn't care. She acted like she didn't care about anything.

At first, he had felt sorry for her. He'd seen it as his duty to humor her until she recovered her senses. But with every hour that passed, she sank deeper into this new persona, and he began to wonder if she had actually transformed into this drunken, singing wanton. He wanted to shout at her to shut up.

And he hated himself for it.

Ree stopped, crouched before him and studied his face. He saw the concern in her eyes.

"I'm not surprised you can't learn an entirely new type of magic," she said softly. "You probably couldn't learn how to bail water from a leaky boat in this condition. You need sleep."

"You know what I need? More ale." Adora raised her wineskin, then let her arm fall back to the dirty paving stones, the wineskin limp in her hand.

"Sleep, Grei. While you were working, I took a moment to explore." She tipped her chin at the darkened windows of the three-story building. "No one lives there. I found a bed that is in good condition. Rest for now."

"I can't." He nodded significantly at Adora.

"He's afraid I'll kill myself if he falls asleep, but I'm past that." Adora waved a hand. "I have moved on to a better plan. I am going to sail across the night sky on a river of ale, manning a ghost ship of failed dreams and abandoned hopes. But I'm going to need more ale if I'm going to make a river of it. So I might go searching for some, unless you want to make some for me, beloved? Can you turn these bricks beneath my feet into ale? How about the air? I bet you could."

"I'll watch her," Ree said. "You sleep."

Grei looked at the building. A bit of rest sounded divine. To lay his head down, just for a second.

"All right," he said.

"Come on." She helped him to his feet and, after waiting for Adora to rise and follow, they went into the building. There were many rooms. Most had broken furniture and straw mattresses infested with mice. Their droppings were scattered across the floor, and he saw two of them scurry into holes as they passed.

True to her word, Ree led him into a spacious room that looked like it had been lived in recently. A layer of dust covered the floor, but everything was organized, as though someone had cared for it. A wood-framed bed stood in the corner with a mattress atop it. It seemed safe enough, downright cozy compared to the other rooms.

And that bed looked heavenly.

"I'll walk the perimeter," she said, leading him to the bed.

"I'll go with you," Adora offered.

Grei lay back against the mattress, wondering if he could fall asleep with so many things on his mind....

He drifted into sleep immediately, like he was falling into thick, dark oil.

Chapter Twenty-Five

GREI

Grei awoke with a start. Something had moved in the room, but neither Adora nor Ree had returned. He had visions of the mice scurrying under the closed door to investigate this new interloper.

The closed door...

He hadn't closed that door. He tried to remember if Ree or Adora had closed it on their way out, but though he'd been halfway to sleep already, he was pretty sure they'd left it open.

A cold prickle walked its way up Grei's neck and across his scalp. He sat up. It was still dark outside. Of course, for all he knew, the entire country of Venisha spent its days beneath a haze of smoke and clouds. Perhaps, like Fairmist, Venisha never saw the sun, except instead of a cool blue or soft orange glow lighting everything, this city simply crouched in darkness all the time.

Grei reached into the muted whispers all around him. Trying to listen for the whispers of nature in Venisha was like being half-blind after a lifetime of sight. He sought out any living intruder, listening for whispers that weren't the floor, the air, the walls.

That Venishan hissing sound grew suddenly louder and a little girl stepped from the shadows in the corner of the room.

It was the same little girl who had been in the courtyard back in Thiara. The one with the pack of mechanical rats and bugs following her around. A Slate Wizard.

"Will you be my friend?" she asked in a hopeful voice.

Grei squinted, tense. "What?"

Her expression soured, like that was the wrong answer. Her brow furrowed, and she shuffled forward a few jerky paces. He backed up on the bed, his back hitting the wall.

"I brought you here to be my friend." She looked annoyed, like she'd just explained everything and that he should understand.

"*You* brought me here—"

A loud hiss sounded in his mind. A half-dozen rats crept onto the bed. They glittered dully, made of wire and bent bits of steel, just like Uriozi had been.

They leapt on him.

Grei called on the whispers in desperation. He tried to turn the air hard all around him, make it solid as steel, but the whispers were so weak that he didn't get the full effect. Three of the rats bounced off. Two slowed, like they were wriggling through invisible mud. But the last got through. Its spiky metal teeth sank into Grei's thigh.

He screamed, and the hissing filled his entire mind just like it had the night he'd been stabbed by Selicia. The scant whispers vanished, and he yanked the thing away, threw it across the room.

He staggered to his feet, but the rat wound burned. A piece of metal remained—its tooth or part of its wire jaw... and it began spreading across his own flesh. The hissing now completely obliterated his connection to the whispers. It was inside him now, coming from the site of the wound.

To his horror, he watched as his flesh around the wound became metal, wires sprouting like weeds.

"No!" Grei shouted.

When Julin had shot him with a Highwand's weapon and turned him to stone, it had felt like this. This time, instead of stone, it was bits and parts of metal.

"I wanted to be your friend," Pliothe said. "All of you. If you would just let me. But you won't."

Grei reached out to her with one hand as the gleaming transformation continued, spreading up his leg to his belly, his chest, his neck.

Her magic ate into his mind.

The hissing drove Grei deeper into himself. That relentless noise! All of his senses vanished like they had when he'd been turned to stone, leaving him floating in a darkness so deep that it seemed he was no more.

Distantly, he realized he was dying.

The hissing droned on for what seemed like a lifetime. In every moment, he felt as if he must cease to exist, yet he endured.

His whole body was turning into twisted wires and shards of steel....

Except for the arm the Faia had created. Grei's mind had hidden in his Faia-created arm the last time his body had been transformed by magic. Now, again, it became a refuge for the small part of Grei who remained free from the girl's powerful spell.

With the Highwand, the magic had been fueled by a dead Faia's will, a repetitive droning of "*stone stone stone stone.*" This spell was held together by the girl. Instead of a repetitive singular word, he heard that relentless hiss and then, overlaid so subtly that he'd missed it until now, the girl's own voice. A litany. As though she were reading aloud from a book.

Grei listened to the ramblings, emotional and volatile, like an angry child berating its doll, but none of her words were actually words. They sounded like words, but they were indecipherable. Her babbling seemed closer and then far away, louder and then softer, like the girl was a curious yet skittish dog trying to get closer to inspect him.

And then her indecipherable words became clear. As the whispers of the elements had transformed for Grei so long ago, the girl's words suddenly made sense to him. It *was* like reading from a book. She was telling a story about a little girl named Pliothe…

Chapter Twenty-Six

PLIOTHE

Pliothe was sleeping when they came for her. She wore her sand-colored nightdress, the one with the flowers on the hem, the one her brother Baezin had given her.

Her governess had been after her for two days to wash the thing—she'd worn it every day since he'd left—but it was one of her few presents from Baezin, and she just couldn't fall asleep without it. It quieted her nightmares, pushed away the fear that came for her in the dark.

But tonight, her nighttime fears became chillingly real. The door burst open, the latch shattering and wood flying even though it hadn't been locked. Her father strode in, eyes blazing, with six guards behind him.

Father had become steadily meaner since the beginning of the year, but nothing like the last few days. Three days ago, her brother Baezin had taken over a hundred ablebodied men and half as many women from the court, the city, and the countryside. He'd stolen three ships from Father and sailed away across the Kingsea. Father had been in a rage ever since.

Now he towered over her, spittle at the corner of his mouth, eyes wild. She whimpered and cowered against the headboard.

"I suppose you think you're clever," Father snarled. "So clever. Just like your brother."

She didn't know what he meant. Was he mad because she was wearing the nightgown Baezin had given her?

The king gestured, and two guards hauled Pliothe out of her bed and threw her at the door. She sailed over the footboard and crashed into the floor. Pain lanced through her elbows and her hips as they struck, and she cried out. She tumbled to a stop, battered and dazed, and looked up at Father.

His lip curled in a sneer. "I should have them tear you apart. Limb from limb. That's what you deserve. That's what you all deserve."

"Daddy!"

The guards yanked her up and shoved her out the door. Their mailed fists hurt like dull scissors, and she sobbed. Her feet didn't even touch the ground. They carried her down the hallway and out of the palace. She cried the whole way, from the pain of her fall, from the look in Father's eyes, from her own confusion. Father thought she had done something horrible, but she didn't know what it was!

The guards threw her into a small steel carriage. This time, she tried to roll, she tried to stop the hard floor of the carriage from hurting, but it didn't really work. She winced, lying on the cold steel, feeling the pain throughout her whole body as they slammed the door behind her. The bolt slid home.

Shivering, she raised her head and realized there were four other people in the carriage. One was her eldest brother, Vaeron. He lay unconscious on the floor. Blood leaked from a cut above his brow. Next to him, her eyes wide and scared, sat the pretty woman Pliothe had seen a few times with Vaeron. The woman had a very long name that was hard to remember. She acted like Vaeron's betrothed, but when Pliothe had asked Father if they would marry, he'd spat and muttered a word Pliothe didn't understand: whore.

Pliothe had tried to find out what a whore was, but no one in the palace seemed to want to tell her.

Behind the pretty woman with the long name, on a steel bench built into the side of the carriage, sat Pliothe's two cousins: Loradile and Mezzryn. They were both much older than Pliothe. On many occasions, Pliothe had tried to tag along with them, but Loradile always rolled her eyes and told her to leave. And Mezzryn was downright mean. Once, he'd thrown a rock at her like she was a mongrel dog. It had hit her in the shoulder and ripped her dress. She'd had a bruise for a week.

Mezzryn wasn't sneering now. He looked scared. Loradile was crying, her cheeks wet with tears. She looked just as confused as Pliothe.

The steel carriage jerked and started forward.

"L-Loradile," Pliothe stuttered. "What's happening?"

"Shut up, you little rat!" Mezzryn stood and raised his fist. "We have to think of what to do and we can't do that with you jabbering. Make so much as a peep and I'll shut you up for good."

"Sit down, Mezzryn," the pretty woman said. "Can't you see she's scared?"

"Shut your mouth, whore," he said, turning to face her. "You don't matter."

The woman's pretty eyes, so wide and beautiful a moment ago, narrowed to slits. "What a crude thing to say."

"You're not one of us. You don't even belong in the palace," Mezzryn said. "So shut your mouth. I don't want to hear another sound out of you."

"And if I don't, you're going to make me, is that it?" Her voice dripped with contempt.

"Bitch." Mezzryn lunged at her, bringing down his fist like a hammer—

He screamed.

Pliothe didn't even know what had happened, but Mezzryn staggered back. His sudden retreat seemed to jerk the pretty woman to her feet by her arm, as though her hand was attached to him. Mezzryn slammed into the side of the carriage, clutching his forearm. Blood blossomed on his white shirt. He sucked in a breath and screamed again.

The pretty woman clutched a thin dagger, dripping red. She'd stabbed him! When his fist had come down, she'd stabbed him.

"I am not your 'bitch.' Nor am I your 'whore.' My name," the pretty woman said softly, "is Fylomene."

"Look what you've done!" Mezzryn clutched his bleeding arm. It looked like she had stabbed a hole clean through it. "I am the king's nephew! He'll kill you for this, whore!"

Fylomene slipped up next to him, graceful as a dancer. It was such a soft and beautiful movement, Pliothe thought she was going to hug him. Maybe kiss him. He tried to turn away, but Fylomene's bloody dagger flashed in the scant light.

Mezzryn jerked and screamed again, then crashed to his knees, clutching his belly. Blood leaked between his fingers. So much blood.

His wide, disbelieving eyes rolled up into his head, and he fell face first onto the floor with a thud. And now Loradile was sobbing.

"My name," the woman said to the unmoving Mezzryn, "is Fylomene."

Pliothe felt she had tumbled into some strange world where fathers kidnap daughters and pretty women stab princes. It made no sense. Screaming. Blood. Killing. Pliothe's mind felt like a thin board that was bending... bending more than a board could bear.

Fylomene swiveled, skirts swirling, and looked at Loradile. Her sobbing turned into little bursts of screams as she babbled. "Mezzryn! Ahhh! What have you done? Ahhh! Where is the king?! Ahhh!"

"The king *put* us here," Fylomene said. "He's not going to protect you. He's going to kill you. He's going to kill all of us."

"Ahhh!" Loradile screamed again, like she couldn't think of anything else to do. "We've done nothing wrong!"

"Clearly the king is insane," Fylomene said.

They all sat in silence as the carriage drove through the night. Only Loradile's whimpers broke the silence. Pliothe stared at the pool of blood around Mezzryn's body. It had mostly collected around her cousin's middle, and his head bounced whenever the carriage went over a bump.

After a long time, the carriage's slight rumbling turned into a pronounced bouncing. They had gone off one of Venisha's many paved roads onto a dirt road. Or perhaps no road at all.

Just then, Pliothe's brother Vaeron stirred. He came to life like someone had jabbed him with a spear, jerking and sitting up in one movement, his fists ready. Blood from the cut on his forehead ran down into one eye, but his other eye blazed. He got to his feet and glared at everyone.

"He's imprisoned us," Vaeron growled.

Fylomene leapt to Vaeron, holding her bloody hand behind her back like she didn't want him to see. She pressed her body against his and kissed him on the neck. "Oh my love, you're all right. Thank the gods you're all right."

Vaeron tolerated her first kiss, then shrugged his wide shoulders and dislodged her. She stumbled, gracefully recovered, and still touched his arm with her un-bloodied hand. She didn't seem upset, just gazed up at him with love.

"Ahhh!" Loradile screamed. "Why? Why did he do this?"

"Shut up," Vaeron growled. He went to the door, took the bars in his big fists, and shook. The door didn't move at all.

"Ahhh!" Loradile screamed. "Why? We didn't do anything!"

"We're going to have to wait for them to open it," Vaeron calculated.

"Ahhh!" Loradile continued, as though she couldn't stop.

Vaeron glanced at Fylomene's bloody hand, which she had neglected to hide, then at Mezzryn's body. He gave Fylomene a grim smile. "You have a weapon?"

She produced the dagger, red with blood. One minute her hands had been empty, and the next minute she was holding it. Pliothe couldn't tell where she'd been hiding it.

"Ahhh!" Loradile screamed.

"How did you get it past them, my love?" Vaeron ignored the hysterical girl. "They didn't search you?"

"They searched me." She gave him a winsome smile and passed the dagger over. "Quite thoroughly in some ways. Not so much in others. Men get absentminded when you give them something interesting to touch."

Vaeron grinned. "You are a demon in a silk skirt."

"I'm *your* demon," she murmured.

"Ahhh!" Loradile continued.

With a snarl, Vaeron spun and stabbed Loradile through the throat. Her shrieks stopped, and her eyes flew open wide. Blood spurted from her neck and she grappled with it, as though her fingers might stop the flow.

She let out a little sigh and toppled over, slumping into the steel wall as her blood drained onto the steel floor. She gave a gurgling little hiccup, and then the light in her eyes went out.

"Vapid banshee," Vaeron growled.

Pliothe pressed her lips tightly together. She didn't scream, didn't cry, didn't even whimper.

Vaeron's baleful gaze moved to regard Pliothe.

"What will we do?" Fylomene put a hand on his arm. She winked at Pliothe, as though she knew she was taking Vaeron's rage and directing it elsewhere. Pliothe loved her a little bit just then. "When they open the door?"

"We fight," he said. "We surprise them, then we fight our way free. I need a sword. If I can get a sword in my hand, it won't matter if they brought half a dozen men."

"How do we surprise them, love?"

He cast his eyes about the carriage as though looking for the answer. His glare fell on Pliothe.

"We throw my sister at them," he said. "They won't expect it. By the time they recover, I'll kill one of them, maybe two. Then I'll have a sword."

Pliothe swallowed. The board in her mind began to crack, close to its breaking point.

She thought of a story that her governess once read to her, about a fox that traveled the woods looking for friends. With each new animal the fox encountered, he would ask, "Will you be my friend?" Some of the animals said "no" and attacked the fox, but the fox was fast, and he would run away. Some of the animals said "yes," but each that did required the fox to perform some task or test.

Pliothe looked up at her brother Vaeron. He was family. He was blood, but he wasn't Baezin. Baezin had been kind to her sometimes, like giving her this nightgown. But Vaeron acted like he had never wanted a little sister, that he'd be just as happy if she had never existed.

She had always feared Vaeron and never tried to get his attention like she did with Baezin. She had known that if Vaeron ever turned his angry gaze upon her, nothing good would come of it.

But now that gaze had found her and, more than that, he'd found an important use for her. She knew he would not hesitate to kill her if it gave him even a slightly better chance at survival.

The board of her mind cracked a little more, and Pliothe spoke. She didn't even tell herself to speak; the words just came out.

"Will you be my friend?" she asked timidly, like the fox in the story.

"What?" Vaeron frowned.

"Will you be my friend?" Pliothe repeated softly.

She saw Fylomene's face soften, concern in her eyes, but Vaeron's lip curled like one of the animals that would try to kill the fox. And Pliothe was not so very fast. Not fast at all trapped in a steel box.

The scant moonlight, which had illuminated the carriage in tones of gray and black, suddenly vanished. They had entered a place of pitch blackness. Pliothe blinked and her slowly adjusting eyes detected an orange light at the barred window, coming from the lantern on the front of the carriage.

The ground slanted suddenly, as though they were going down a steep slope, and Vaeron and Fylomene fought to keep their footing, sliding toward Pliothe. The angle pressed Pliothe into the steel seat behind her, and Vaeron's boot heel landed on her hand, crushing down. It stayed there for what seemed a lifetime as the carriage went down and down. Pliothe bit her lip to keep from crying. She yanked at her hand, but Vaeron's entire weight pinned it to the steel floor.

The carriage jolted to a stop. Fylomene and Vaeron stumbled forward. With a gasp, Pliothe yanked her hand free, cradling it to her chest.

The horses outside whinnied. Vaeron went to the window and grasped the bars.

A man outside said, "Cut it, just cut it!"

The horses whinnied again, and there were sounds of retreating hoofbeats and footfalls.

"They're running." Vaeron pressed his face between the bars.

"Where are we?" Fylomene asked.

"Underground. A cave of some sort."

Pliothe barely heard them as she held her hurt fingers. Her ring finger was twisted and bent at an odd angle. Vaeron had broken her finger.

Vaeron turned away from the window. His gaze swept over Pliothe, but his eyes were unfocused, like he was thinking.

"The Slate Mines," he said.

"The what?" Fylomene asked.

"That's where we are. He's taken us to the Slate Mines."

She glanced at the door. "Why here? If he wanted to lock us up and starve us to death, he could have done that in the prison cells. Or just outright kill us. Why not just kill us?"

"We're a sacrifice," Vaeron said, pensive.

"A sacrifice? To what?"

"My vicious father has been an impious man his entire life. The Slate Priests have petitioned him over and over to let the church have a greater influence in the rule of the city. He has ignored them. He has kept an iron fist around everything. During his reign, the church has waned in power." Vaeron glanced at the tiny window. "But as Father's health has failed, his grip has weakened. His brains have addled. So too has his rule begun to fail. He knows this is happening, and I think he has been grasping at how he can maintain control. The last two short conversations I've had with him he rattled on about Venisha and the Slate Priests. He thought the priests were actively conspiring against him. That he needed to maneuver them to his side once and for all."

"Venisha the god?" Fylomene asked.

"Yes. Father rambled on about serving him, after so long refusing the priests, like Venisha was standing right in the room, judging him."

"Then why are we here instead of at the temple?"

"Supposedly, this is where Venisha first appeared to the faithful."

"In a mine?" Fylomene wrinkled her nose. "What becomes of us, then? The priests will come? Try to kill us?"

"Unlikely," Vaeron said, going back to the door and shaking it ineffectively again. "The old man probably didn't think past just leaving us down here. Let us starve in a cage." He glanced back at the corpses of Loradile and Mezzryn. "Or let us kill each other."

"Is that what the priests demanded? That he throw us down here to die?" Fylomene asked.

"Who knows? Ever since my damned brother left, the old man's mind has unhinged. Baezin's betrayal set him to looking for betrayal around every corner."

"We have to get out of here, my love," Fylomene said.

"Tell me something I do not know, *my love*." He glanced down at the small, slender dagger in his hand and then at the door, as though he was thinking he might stab it. "This works wonders on vainglorious fops, but I daresay it will make a lousy pry bar." He gave a grim look at the corpses. "Though it may serve as a fine carving knife for cannibalism, if it comes to it."

"Don't say that."

He grunted, and a distant rumble shook the carriage like some horrible reply. It sounded like heavy stones striking the ground far away. Then all was still.

"What was that?" Fylomene asked.

"They've not only shut us in here, now they've shut us in the cave."

Fylomene's eyes grew wide. She swallowed. "They collapsed the cave."

"That would be my guess."

For the first time, Fylomene lost her composure, and Pliothe felt the pretty woman's terror mirror her own. Trying to beat a steel door down was daunting, but still possible. But being trapped beneath tons of rock in a place with no doors? A pry bar or a clever bit of locksmithing could not move a boulder.

Pliothe could barely breathe at the thought of dying in a hole in the ground. She understood Loradile's panic. She felt like she'd been put in a coffin and buried, except she was still alive. She wanted to scream and scream and keep on screaming.

She didn't.

She had to keep silent, or what had happened to Loradile would happen to her.

Vaeron paced back and forth. He didn't look afraid. Just angry. Fylomene looked at him with adoration, like she knew he would figure out this problem and, when he did, she would be ready to help him implement it.

Suddenly, Pliothe felt something. A...presence. Something the others seemed not to notice.

At first, she thought it was just a growing foreboding that they were trapped, the sudden realization that the lantern would eventually run out of oil, and then they would not only be buried, but they would be buried in the dark. This terrifying thought grew and grew, like she was being filled up with icy water.

But as the terror grew, it became a palpable presence that wasn't inside her anymore. It wasn't just her fear. It was coming from somewhere. She felt it behind her, toward the front of the carriage, the direction that went deeper into the mine.

Before she knew what she was doing, she had stood up, climbed onto the steel bench and touched the front wall of the carriage. Terror overwhelmed her, but like when she became a fox in her mind, like when she spoke words she hadn't intended to speak, her body rose and climbed onto the bench. She put both hands, even her broken one, onto the flat steel.

"What are you doing?" Vaeron demanded.

"It's...coming," she murmured.

"Venisha's hollow eyes," Vaeron cursed. "You're as crazy as father."

He grabbed her arm like the handle of a shovel. It felt like he was going to rip her away from her perch and throw her across the carriage at the corpses on the other side, at the deadly metal bench. That would crush her body, smash her head. She had made the mistake of drawing his attention to herself.

But he stopped, his powerful hand clenching. He froze as though the moment he came in contact with her, he sensed the same thing she was feeling.

"What is that?" Fylomene whispered. Clearly she felt it now too. "Gods, Vaeron, what is that?"

Vaeron had no answer this time. He let go of Pliothe and went to the steel door, pressed his face between the bars again. He peered as though he might be able to see forward, around the carriage.

With a gasp, Vaeron pushed away from the door and slammed into the other side of the carriage. For the first time, she saw fear on his face as he stared at the door.

"Vaeron—"

"Shut up," he whispered. Every muscle in his forearms and upper arms tensed as he gripped the dagger tightly.

Pliothe turned toward the door. The presence had shifted. It was right outside now.

Steel shrieked as the door twisted, folding in half and flying away. It clanged against rock somewhere out in the darkness. But nothing stood on the other side.

Vaeron didn't move. Fylomene and Pliothe froze as well. Only moments ago, all they had wanted to do was get out of this carriage, and now the door was open, but not even Vaeron seemed eager to leave anymore.

Pliothe giggled. It was funny, after all.

Vaeron glared at her as though he understood exactly what she was laughing at, and he seemed ready to kill her right then and there. Maybe he would have even done it, but that's when the voice spoke.

"Step forward, my children. Step out of the cage that I may see you."

The voice spoke from everywhere, as though the very air suddenly had a mouth.

Fylomene and Vaeron looked at each other, stunned. Their eyes were wide, but neither of them moved.

Pliothe had the crazy idea to run to the door, jump out, and talk to the thing.

So she did.

She didn't even choose to do it. She didn't think she even meant to do it, but her body didn't wait.

Vaeron snarled and grabbed at her, but like the fox she was too quick. She ducked deftly under his hand and hurtled through the doorway.

She landed on the rocky, uneven cave floor, then looked up. The cavern was immense. The huge lantern the driver had left barely lit a third of the great space. High above and back the way the carriage had come, she could see only darkness, so she turned…turned…looking for the source of the voice. All was still, quiet.

"You are brave, little one," the deep, sovereign voice said.

Pliothe could hear it better now that she was out of the carriage. It wasn't coming from everywhere, but from high above.

A terrible bulk moved in the darkness. Something immense. Something unfathomable.

She looked up, up, up, and the leviathan lowered its head into the ring of light.

Pliothe's breath caught in her chest.

It was a dragon!

The thing's muzzle emerged first, a flat nose of stone with two vertical slits for nostrils. The box-like snout sloped backward into human-like cheekbones. Its thick lower jaw was divided down the center, as though it didn't open like a human jaw, but instead would split sideways to reveal a horror of teeth that could barely be conceived.

The frightening head lowered further. Glowing turquoise eyes moved from the darkness into the sphere of light. Black smoke curled up from the edges of its eyelids like the eyes were burning a foul sludge. Horns of jagged slate rose up just above and behind its eyes. Each of the horns was longer and thicker than the tallest trees she'd ever seen.

She had never been more terrified in her life, but a rogue thought scampered across her mind.

An hour ago, she had been sleeping in her bed at the palace. She'd been tucked into her warm covers, her bare feet making a twist of them at the foot of the bed. She had been doing all the normal things a normal girl should do, drifting into dreamland, thinking about what she would do on the morrow, all the adventures she might have in the morning.

And now she stood in her nightgown facing a dragon.

She giggled.

The dragon cocked its great head and the jaw worked in what she decided was a smile.

"I," the dragon said, "am Venisha."

"Will you be my friend?" Pliothe asked.

The vertical split in the thick jaws opened, and she saw a flash of those dark, pointed teeth. Each was taller than she was, jagged like shards of broken rock. For an instant, she thought she'd killed herself with her impertinent request. Everyone knew the name Venisha. Venisha was a god. The Slate Priests worshipped him. Her father's country was named for him.

But those odd jaws didn't envelop her, the god didn't chomp her in half. Instead, a thumping, grinding sound emerged from somewhere deep in the dragon's chest, a rhythmic chuffing.

The god was laughing.

The sound shook the cavern, and little bits of dust fell into the ring of lamplight.

"Yes, little one," the god said in its dark voice. "I will. A friend like no other. Would you like that?"

"I would like it very much." Pliothe clasped her hands.

"As would I. As would I."

Most of Pliothe—the greater part of her for certain—cowered in fear, deep within the recesses of her mind. But the rogue thoughts, those errant splinters of her broken mind had control of her body, so she clasped her hands to her chest and danced as though she stood in a meadow of flowers.

"Tell me your name, little one," Venisha said.

"I am Pliothe. And you're Venisha the god."

Again, those vertical jaws shifted outward, revealing the jagged teeth. A smile. "I am indeed, and I have three wishes to give. Would you like one of them?"

"I would like that very much."

"That is well and good. Tell me what you would like, my dear, and you shall have it."

"I would like friends. I should like the ability to make whomever I encounter a friend." She gripped her hands together so tightly, bouncing up and down.

The grotesque grin split wider. "A worthy wish. You shall have it."

The turquoise eyes flashed as though something had exploded within the dragon, and for one instant the entire cavern lit up. The curling smoke at the edges of Venisha's eyelids thickened and roiled upward...

...then it twisted, turned and floated toward her. The black smoke hit her like a spear, stabbing into the center of her chest. She screamed, her body thrown back and landing in a heap upon the stone.

He'd killed her. The smoke flowed into her arms and legs, into her belly, her chest and her head. It filled every part of her. She gasped for air, but there was no air to breathe, nothing but the black smoke.

Finally, it filled her completely, and Pliothe's writhing body went still.

Am I dead? she thought. *Is this what it is like to be dead?*

But she could still feel her arms and legs. She could still feel the rocky ground beneath her, biting into her back.

She sat up and opened her eyes.

The whole world looked different. The walls and ceiling and metal carriage and dragon were all still there. They still had the same shapes and textures as before, but now there was...more. She could see triangles of light within each—within Venisha especially.

"You'll have more friends than you know what to do with now," Venisha said.

"How?" she whispered, marveling. She looked at her own hands and saw those same sparkling triangle lights.

"Just ask them. I don't think they'll refuse you now."

A thump sounded behind Pliothe, and she looked back. Vaeron had jumped down from the carriage. Behind him, Fylomene extended her hand, expecting Vaeron to help her down. He didn't, wasn't even looking at her. Instead, he stared upward at the enormous face of Venisha. Fylomene frowned and gripped the edge of the cart and, without a trace of the daintiness she'd pretended a second before, dropped deftly to the ground.

Vaeron stepped forward. "You're...Venisha."

The dragon's head lowered. Its body shifted behind it, and Pliothe could not only feel the shudders in the ground as its bulk moved, but she could see those glittering triangles in the darkness, showing every bit of the god's body. She wondered what the triangles meant.

Two giant claws made of jagged rock scooted into the light as Venisha settled himself down, resting his head on his claws like a dog. Vaeron barely came up to the god's nose.

"That is correct," the god said. "And I shall give you one wish, prince. What is it you long for above all else?"

Vaeron didn't hesitate. "I wish to be the most powerful man in the world, a fighter so devastating that none can beat me. No one."

Pliothe saw the glittering triangles within Vaeron, too. They clustered together in his heart, illuminating his desires, and she finally understood why Vaeron hated their brother Baezin so much.

Not because Baezin had left the crown city. Not because Baezin always seemed to get away with everything. No. It was because he was the better swordsman.

In a flash, Pliothe saw Vaeron's greatest passion. He felt he should have been the superior blade. He practiced more. He was older. But Baezin had always bested him.

Pliothe had watched them spar twice, and both times Baezin had proven not only the better fighter, but so much better that even Pliothe could tell he had held back to keep from humiliating his older brother.

In those triangle sparkles, Pliothe saw it all, the raging fire of anger within Vaeron, the source of it. All these years, that's what rankled the most.

"Ah…" Venisha said, as though he could see the same thing Pliothe could see. "And so it shall be, great prince. I think, also, it will not be long before you are a great king."

Vaeron seemed to grow taller at that statement, and he smiled so wide he showed his teeth.

Again, the smoke from the corners of Venisha's eyes curled into a column and flowed into Vaeron. He shouted, clenching his fists and throwing back his head. His great arms flexed and he howled at the cavernous ceiling.

Sweat beaded on his forehead as though he'd run a dozen miles. He fell forward onto his hands and knees, lank hair falling in his face. Only then did the smoke leave him, curling around and floating away.

"How does it feel," the god asked, "to know that you can now best any man, any two men, any dozen?"

"Yes…" Vaeron whispered. "Yes!" He raised his sweaty head, and his eyes seemed to glow. The glittering triangle lights flew around him like fireflies now, ten times as many as before. "Oh yes," he repeated, and he stood up, looking at his clenched fists as though they belonged to someone else.

Fylomene stepped forward, and Venisha turned his glowing gaze to her. "And you, beautiful daughter, I shall grant you your fondest wish as well."

She snuck a glance at the kneeling Vaeron, still engrossed with the newfound strength that flowed through his body. Pliothe read the triangle lights clustered around her chest. She loved Vaeron. She loved him beyond all sense. She wished to please him, to be first in his thoughts.

"I would be young and beautiful all of my days, lord of lords," she said. "I would be…irresistible."

Venisha nodded, and again the smoke came from his eyes and shot into her. She screamed, but whether from joy or pain, Pliothe couldn't tell. She rose up, floating above the floor. Her hands moved over her own arms, her sides, her hips. The smoke slowly left her, causing her to alight on the ground once more, and when Fylomene looked at Vaeron again, a sly and knowing smile came to her face. Vaeron climbed to his feet and looked up at Venisha once more.

"My eternal thanks, lord of lords," he said.

"Yes," Fylomene agreed, coming forward to stand next to her sweating man. She put a light hand on his forearm.

"Vaeron, you will be my fist," Venisha said. "You, beautiful Fylomene, my tongue. And you, little Pliothe, my heart."

"You have a task for us?" Vaeron asked.

"Oh, indeed."

"Then instruct us, lord of lords, giver of gifts."

"It is already done. The maps written upon your hearts will guide you. Simply follow the ambitions you have always had and you shall be my avatars more surely than if I gave you written instructions. Go, my glorious servants. Do those things you crave, and all will be well."

"I want my father's throne," Vaeron said.

Venisha laughed, and it shook the cavern. Bits of rock and dust fell from the ceiling at the booming sound. "Yes," he said. "You shall have it. Who may stop you now?"

"No one."

Fylomene raised her chin, beaming, leaning into Vaeron's arm. Neither she nor Vaeron thought to look at Pliothe, so engrossed were they in their dreams of conquest.

But Venisha looked at her, a sidelong glance that the other two didn't see. The triangle sparkles danced about his eyes, and she heard his voice in her mind.

You, little Pliothe, shall be the most important of all. You, I shall protect above all others, for you shall carry my heart.

Pliothe swallowed. She suddenly felt ill, but she wasn't sure why. She smiled and forced joy to flow over that thick pit in her stomach, forced it to fill her entire body. She imagined the triangles dancing for joy about her, and as she imagined, so they did. For she knew that Venisha would see the triangles as easily as she did, even if Vaeron and Fylomene did not. Unless she covered her foreboding, Venisha would surely know how she felt. It made her ill to be his heart, but he must never know.

Thank you, lord of lords, she thought back to him, using the title Vaeron had used.

The god nodded.

"I am going to kill my father tonight," Vaeron declared.

"Go then, and begin your good work."

Vaeron strode toward the cave's opening, the tunnel that would lead back to the surface, back to the city, back to the palace. Fylomene followed, head high, striding as though each step made her feel glorious.

Pliothe hesitated. She didn't want to kill her father. She didn't want to kill anyone.

"Go with them, little Pliothe," Venisha said. "They will need you."

Suddenly, Pliothe felt like she was falling down a well, the steep curved walls flashing by her, and her without the ability to grab hold. She knew she would hit that water. It waited with absolute certainty. She knew she would sink beneath it and she would never come to the surface again.

And there was nothing she could do about it.

Part III

The Rise of the Slate Wizards

Chapter Twenty-Seven

BLEVINS

Blevins stalked toward the docks, furious. He wanted to kill someone. He hated this place. He'd always hated this place. He had left this life behind long ago, and he'd never missed it. Not once. It represented everything he'd never wanted to be.

And it highlighted every mistake he'd made in his life. He thought he'd escaped the legacy of his father and his brother, but in the end, it had followed him, hadn't it?

He'd escaped with such hope, like he'd been wearing a cloak of rotting flesh his whole life and he'd finally been able to shrug it off. With the sun rising ahead of him, he had glanced back only briefly at this gray, grease-choked city with a contemptuous salute. He had known for certain that he was sailing to something better across the Kingsea.

By the Faia, the Kingsea…

The name bobbed to the top of his mind like it had been waiting for centuries. On this side of the water, this was the Kingsea because everything was about the king or the Slate Priests.

But on the other side of the water, it was the Sunset Sea because Blevins himself had changed it. That had been his first command. He had crossed that sea and it had become the dividing line between him and his origins. He had never wanted to look back, and continuing to call it the Kingsea would forever remind him of his place of birth. He had refused let the sea link him to Venisha because of something as small as a name. So the Sunset Sea was born and with that simple act, his past was erased.

That moment had represented everything to him: a new land with the sun setting over the old. It had changed him. He had planned to be a new kind of ruler, to do everything his father had not. He would rule his people like a leader should....

Blevins's boot thumped on the wooden planks of the pier. It was a dilapidated construct, clearly out of use, and he hesitated there. His intention had been to go to the center of the wharf, find a boat that could be manned by one person, and steal it. But he stopped there, then headed down the weather-beaten pier to the end and looked out over the dark waters. He ran a hand over his forehead, his nose and cheeks, and let out a breath.

A ruler different from his father, indeed.

Baezin's father had sown strife amongst his sons, amongst the Slate Priests, amongst his nobles. Like the pyramids throughout Venisha, his father's kingdom had been built at angles, all its metaphorical walls leaning on each other yet somehow keeping the balance. Constant strife. Constant opposition. His father had believed that if everyone fought each other, no one would have the time to mount a united force against him. And it had worked for half a century.

Blevins had sworn he'd never do that, but as he looked out over those dark waters that had chopped off his old life and given him a new one—to do with whatever he chose— he had to face the truth that he had done no better. He'd made so many poor decisions. His love of Thiara, for whom he would have sacrificed anything except his own damned pride, had been a disaster. The loss of his children the Faia, whom he had frightened so much they'd been afraid to reveal themselves to him, had been a tragedy. His war with the Benascans, even though Thiara tried to show him the beauty of their culture, had been a legendary mistake.

He'd been so sure of himself, but what had he sown in the end? Animosity between himself and his beloved. An eternal war between the Thiarans and Benascans. A corrupt royal line that had spawned a creature like Lyndion. A hatred from his son so incendiary it had burned down his entire family.

Blevins wrestled with his culpability in these horrible events. Had it all happened because he had, in the end, been a tyrant like his father? Had he come to new shores and destroyed them as surely as his father would have?

But then, had anything that happened in his life been within his control? For centuries Blevins had been Cavyn's puppet, drifting from one life into the next, unable to die, unable to remember who he was. Was it really his fault at all?

Strangely, his father's words bubbled up in his mind: *Normal people may blame others for misfortune. A king may not.*

Baezin recalled that day, when his father had said those words. It had been a rare moment where the king actually tried to be a father to his ten-year-old son. Baezin had sat on the steps at the base of the throne. He'd been forced to sit there for eight hours straight while his father dispensed justice to his petitioners.

"All they do is complain," Baezin said.

"Yes," Father replied.

"What do they expect you to do? They act like it is *your* fault."

"It is," Father said.

Baezin had looked up and seen a rare thoughtfulness on his father's usually angry face.

"What? Why?"

"If you are not smart enough to make the right decisions—if you are not strong enough to enforce them—then you should not be king. Venisha exists because of what I do or fail to do. Normal people may blame others for misfortune. A king may not."

The memory faded. Blevins had not thought of that conversation for a long time. It had been a rare glimpse of what a good king might be, instead of what his father became.

Blevins's father had been right, in that singular moment at least. Sometimes all it took was one decision to change a life.

After all, Blevins had chosen his own fate in the one moment when it had mattered. He'd spurned his wife's entreaties about the Benascans, ignored Thiara's wisdom. He'd arrogantly assumed she was too close to Benascan culture to see how it was a hideous offense to women and their freedom. He'd told her he would bring the enlightenment of the Thiaran Empire—of his rule—to the Benascans, whether they wanted it or not.

She'd begged him. Oh, she had begged him. His glorious, radiant queen had fallen to her knees and clung to his pant legs, tears dripping down her face.

He remembered it all. Though she had wiped it from his mind a hundred times, it now came back with a startling clarity....

Chapter Twenty-Eight

BLEVINS

Thiara knelt before him, holding onto his leg, but the sobbing stopped. She went still, her hair hanging down to the floor, back sagging as though the floor itself were pulling her down.

"Obey my will, Thiara," he said. "I know what I'm doing. You're too naive to negotiate these matters of state."

He waited for her to capitulate, to support him as she had done in every other endeavor of his fledgling empire. She stayed like that for so long, head bowed, that worry flickered in his mind. But he stayed firm, brow furrowed.

She raised her head, her dark silky hair falling back from a face that had gone to stone. She stood like she had no weight, like she'd been picked up by an invisible hand and set on her feet.

"You are blind," she said, the desperate passion gone from her voice. She sounded how a corpse would sound if it spoke. Tears still marked her beautiful cheeks, but other than that, there was no evidence she had ever been crying. No flushed face. No anguish in her features. "I thought I could show you. I tried to open your eyes, but you are arrogant and intransigent."

"You are the blind one," he growled. "The Benascans essentially enslave their women. They use them as brood mares, and I'm going to end it."

Her gaze bored into him. Her eyes seemed to be changing, from dark brown to a lighter brown, lighter and lighter with each passing moment. Her hair began to shimmer with blond highlights. "I thought I could tame your intolerance, but you want to tear down this land and make it over in your image. You cannot see its beauty, and if you cannot see the beauty of the Benascan culture, how can I hope you will ever see the beauty of our children?"

Her transformation startled him, but her words hit harder. The word *children* cut through his angry haze.

"Children?" He was bewildered. "We have one child. Thiazin."

"We have ten children, beloved."

The words rocked him.

"By the Faia, woman, you're babbling," he whispered, but it felt like the wind had been knocked out of him. Against all reason, it felt like...truth.

"By the Faia, indeed," she murmured. "Those are eight of your children. What you call the Faia. They're yours. Mine. Our firstborns."

Her eyes continued to lighten, changing from light brown to blue. The highlights in her hair continued to spread. It was more blond now than black. He stepped back from her, eyes wide. A cold wind blew through him, a premonition, like he'd known this information already. Like he had known it all along.

"Thiazin is our firstborn," he murmured. "She is our only child."

"Is she?"

Suddenly, he didn't want to know what she was saying. "Shut up. Just...stop. You don't know what you're talking about."

"I'm talking about your human seed in my body, beloved," she continued relentlessly. Her hair went completely pale blond, just like the Benascans. "I'm talking about the progeny that grew inside me before I knew how to be…human. Seven daughters and a son. Jevare, Deilli, Pyll, Lankoli, Sherim, Besni, Uriozi, and Velak. And later, a second son. Saebin."

Baezin's jaw slowly dropped as a door in the back of his memory cracked open, a door that someone had shut. The memory stepped through, fragmented, an incomplete picture.

He saw Thiara in the first weeks they had known each other, in the first month after he had arrived on these shores. She had stepped through the door of the sturdy tent his followers had built while they constructed the beginnings of the capital city of his burgeoning empire. Her belly had been distended, nine months pregnant. He remembered his shock, like the bottom had dropped out of his belly.

Yesterday that belly had been as flat as a maiden's. They had made love for only the third time last night. He lurched to his feet, pointed a finger at her, called her a demon. She had looked horrified, raised a hand and…

And that was it. There was no more to the memory. There was nothing after that.

The sudden, brutal memory rocked Baezin, and he staggered back, steadying himself with a hand on the wall.

"That's not…it's not possible." He fought his disorientation. It couldn't be true!

"So many things are possible," she said. "You simply are incapable of accepting them. The third time we made love, I allowed a child to be created inside me. Except I didn't consider how you and I might mix. The children came to term within days. I thought you would be happy. I thought I would see that human excitement light you up, but when I walked into that tent, when I saw your horrified face, I instantly realized my mistake. Because of how you reacted—because of how you are acting now—I knew you would not accept them. So I took your memory and fled. I gave birth to our eight children in secret."

"Took...my memory?" Too many things flew at Baezin at once for him to fully comprehend them. Pregnancy. Eight children. "How can you...take my memory?"

"Because I am not human, beloved. Any more than our children are. I do not fit into your narrow-minded view of what is acceptable, far less so than the Benascans in fact. I also hid our second-born son."

Baezin twitched as a fragmented memory of her second pregnancy came through that door in the back of his mind. Another memory she had stolen that returned in brutal clarity.

She had swelled over the course of nine months. He had been so excited. Then, as they approached the eve of the birth, she had vanished. She'd last been seen walking through the royal gardens, and then she was gone. He remembered the frantic search for her, how he'd scoured the city and the countryside. How he hadn't slept. And then she had returned. No pregnant belly. No child in her arms. He had raged. He'd demanded to know what she'd done with their child. He'd...he'd hit her.

He had remembered none of this until now.

He grappled with his head. "Second born..."

"Sweet Saebin. I managed to get the timing correct for that one. A perfect nine months, just like a human woman, but I failed to produce...other aspects. Our second born stands eight feet tall, beloved. He has hooves, not human feet. His noble head is that of a great beast of the woods, with glistening soft brown eyes and curling horns. He is beautiful, but you would call him an abomination. From the moment he was born, he understood his circumstance. He wanted to hide from you. I think he absorbed my own fears through my body as he grew, fears that you would never accept him."

"S...Stop." Baezin held up one hand even as the other held his head. "What are you doing to me?"

"Revealing to you that which you already knew, beloved. That which I took from you."

"You...took my memories!"

"What else should I have done? When I returned after giving birth to Saebin, you struck me. Had I been a real human, I think you would have killed me."

"You...took my child away!"

"A child you would have reviled. Had you seen him born, you'd have killed him as a monster."

"No! No, I-I wouldn't have done that...."

She shook her blond head. "It is a quintessentially human foible to lie to yourself. But I know you. I know everything about you. You'd have named him a demon just as you named me that night in your tent when I came to you pregnant with your first children. Just as you wanted to name me now. I couldn't allow that. I couldn't let you harm the boy."

"You...tricked me!" he said.

"I knew you."

"You...tore memories from my head. What else have you done?"

She narrowed her eyes. "What else? I have done everything. I *am* everything."

Baezin's anger came to his rescue at last. "You deceived me. You wore the face of someone I could love. You lay with me like a human woman, but you are...what? What foul magics have you cast upon me to make me love you?"

"Here it comes at last. The judgement you feel will give you rights to do violence upon me. You cannot control me, cannot command me. So you must fear me. You must kill me, just like the Benascans," she said.

"You stole my memories and manipulated me!" he raged. "You are a demon! A foul, manipulating beast!"

Her lips peeled back from her teeth. "You're the beast, Baezin. Do you know how insignificant you are? Do you? I thought you were something special. I loved you. But that is done. Your...arrogance. Your intransigence. Let us see what kind of realm you command without me. Do you think these walls would stand? Do you think this empire would exist?"

Baezin grabbed the sword hanging on hooks over the fireplace.

"At last, we come to it. The violence." She shrieked, "I was right to keep your children from you!"

"Begone, foul spirit!" Baezin waved the sword.

"Do you think that pathetic metal stick can hurt me? You do not possess the power to harm me, *beloved*," she said venomously. "You are nothing!"

He advanced on her.

"I hate you!" She screamed.

Baezin swung, but she held out a hand. The blade exploded. Shards of metal stung Baezin's arms and face as they cut him.

"This is the last mistake you will ever make," Thiara said. She turned, glancing at the window as though expecting something.

A boy sat on the windowsill. He had not been there a second ago. No...not a boy. He was...smaller. His skin was dusky red, and as Baezin looked closer he realized the boy had horns curling up from his forehead.

"Baezin, meet your son Velak." She walked toward the window. "Velak, this is your father. He hates you."

"What is that?" Baezin pointed the shard of his broken sword at the demonic creature.

"This human no longer wants my protection. Do what you will." She leapt out the window, twirling in mid-air. Her dress became bat wings and she flapped away.

The demon boy leapt to the floor. He was like a human in miniature. Like the Faia. He grinned, showing sharp, pointed teeth.

"FFFFather," he said, like it was the first time he'd ever spoken. He bowed mockingly, then leapt out the window and flew away like his mother. Baezin ran after, slamming into the windowsill, but he could see nothing of either creature. His heart hammered. His mind raced.

Fire rained from the sky, burning into the buildings he and his people had painstakingly built over the last few years. Destroying Baezin's city. Killing his people. Obliterating the new empire—the new life—he had hoped to build.

Chapter Twenty-Nine

BLEVINS

Blevins twitched, bringing himself back from that horrible memory, back from that singular moment of his life where he had changed his trajectory forever. There had been no turning back, no amending that one mistake. He'd paid for it for three hundred years since.

He shook his head, banishing the memory, and looked out over the dark waters. Was there any way to start a new life? To use the horrible mistakes he'd made as lessons? To cross the Kingsea again and start anew once more?

The very idea exhausted him. He'd spent his ambition and, it seemed, the only thing left was bitterness and anger. He'd thought for a brief moment when he'd met Stormy that there was hope. But the mantle of power had taken Grei like it had taken Blevins's father, like it had taken Blevins himself. Grei now wore the same arrogance Blevins had worn when he'd made his horrible decision.

Blevins had left Venisha to be better than his father. To be more accepting, not less. To be more compassionate, not less. He had failed spectacularly at exactly the wrong moment because of his arrogance. And by the Faia, he and everyone he loved had paid. He had never stopped paying for that moment.

It stabbed him in the heart to see Grei following in those same footsteps—

"Hello, brother." Vaeron's voice came from behind him.

Blevins turned. Vaeron, three priests of Venisha, and a hulking man clad head-to-toe in black plate mail armor, stood on the dock behind him.

In another day, at another time, Blevins would have been frightened by this scene. Certainly before he'd left Venisha so long ago, being cornered on a dock by his brother, three priests with magic, and what was clearly a powerful fighter would have had spooked him. He'd have been thinking through the strategy. He'd have drawn his sword and surprised them, trying to make a pathway to escape.

"What do you want?" Blevins said.

"Justice," Vaeron said.

"That would be a first."

Vaeron showed his teeth, but it wasn't a smile. "Call it what you will."

"Revenge?" Blevins said. "For doing what you didn't have the courage to do. To leave our father behind."

"This kingdom doesn't belong to Father. It belongs to me."

"So I see. Father would be proud. You are his spitting image."

Vaeron's face reddened, and Blevins waited for the attack. Vaeron never could control his temper.

But surprisingly, with effort, his brother calmed himself. "Let me tell you what is going to happen, brother."

"This should be rich."

"I am going to give you one chance. Lay down your arms and put on the Night Cage." He pointed at the man in the suit of armor.

"The Night Cage..." Blevins murmured, studying the man. Except it wasn't a man in armor, was it? It was an artifact. One of Vaeron's clever artifacts. A suit of armor that was a trap. A cage. The Night Cage. Vaeron was opening the door to a cell. Blevins could only imagine what horrors befell a man who put on that armor.

"I see."

"You know I can beat you," Vaeron said. "You were a step from death in Thiara."

Blevins drew his sword slowly and deliberately. "Do you really think I'm going to lie down and submit to your will?"

"No. No, I don't."

Blevins chuckled. "Good."

"There is nothing good in this for you. Of that, you can be sure."

"I'll tell you what I'm sure of. This is the best moment I can remember. For the first time in a long time, I can't lose. I'm going to kill you. And if I don't, I get to die. Either way, you lose, brother."

"Die?" Vaeron grinned, a malicious grin that suited him perfectly. "Oh no, brother. You don't get off that easily."

For the first time, a sliver of fear pushed its way into Blevins's heart.

"You've escaped your due for far too long. It's time for you to pay up. You're going to finally get what you deserve," Vaeron said. "Forever."

He drew that monstrosity of a sword from his back and started forward.

Chapter Thirty

GREI

Grei lived Pliothe's story as though he had been her, as though Pliothe's soul had been laid over his for an instant, and he'd absorbed the heartache at her very core. He blinked and realized that almost no time had passed in the room in the abandoned building in Venisha. Pliothe had barely moved. She still pointed at him as her magic ate into him, and he knew she had no notion of what she'd just pushed into him, the visions he'd seen of her life.

The story unlocked secrets, gave Grei a brief glimpse of Venishan magic. He saw the sparkling triangles of light and knew they were the magic's essence. All this time, Grei had been trying to hear language in the hissing. What if the language wasn't auditory?

Instinctively, desperately, Grei stopped fighting the hissing. He let the girl's transformation in, let it run through him. He didn't try to understand it like he would the whispers. Instead he thought of those triangles of light, tried to shape the hissing, to make it—

The room exploded in glowing triangles. Grei squinted at their sudden brightness, and he realized they had always been there, every single tiny triangle of light. They hovered around the girl like bees. They swarmed over Grei like ants.

A single giant triangle of light hung in the air right between Grei and Pliothe.

The language was in the light. It was in the light!

With a guttural cry, Grei pushed at the triangles all over his body. He commanded them to get out, to take their magic and go back to the girl.

It felt like he was pressing his head against a boulder, but he shouted again and commanded them to undo their magic and…

Go…

Back…

To the girl!

Grei slammed his fists together in front of himself. The hissing rose to a deafening height. The triangle lights scurried all over his body, twisting, turning, frantic to undo their work. Then they leapt from him like spooked fireflies, charging back through the giant triangle of light that hung between him and Pliothe.

It was like he'd thrown a stone into the middle of a pool. Ripples radiated toward the girl, carrying the triangles of light on them like crumbs of bread. They hit her, clinging to her.

Pliothe stumbled. Her back hit the wall, and she stared at him with wide eyes. Her attack ceased.

"What…" she uttered, "did you do?"

Grei's heart beat so fast he thought it would pop out of his chest. He scrambled up from the bed, panting, looking down at his body. His tunic and breeches had holes all through them, but the flesh beneath was pink, unmarred, unbroken. The metal and wires that he'd been transformed into were…gone.

He couldn't believe it. He patted himself all over. No metal. No wires. He was himself.

"You…." Pliothe said, eyes wide. "How…?"

Grei didn't know how. The glowing triangles still lit up the room, but they were slowly fading. He thought of attacking her with the triangles, but he'd used the Venishan magic instinctively, in a panic. Would he be able to do it twice?

Could he bet on that?

He decided that intimidation was the better road. If he could just get the girl to leave him alone....

"Don't do that again," he said with all the authority he could muster.

Her eyes narrowed, belying an intelligence he hadn't seen before, as though this child were only pretending at being a child. "You stopped me. You can't do that."

"I've been told that before," he said.

"Whisper Prince...." she murmured.

He kept his hands out, ready, like this was some kind of brawl, but he honestly didn't know what he'd do if she came at him again with her magic, ordered her creatures to attack him again.

"Whisper Prince..." she murmured again, then she turned with the unpretentious efficiency of a child and walked out the door. Her mechanical rats and bugs immediately followed.

Grei stood there for a long, silent moment, keeping his authoritative air in place in case she burst back through the door with her monsters to give it another go....

She didn't.

The moment he knew that she wasn't returning, he began to shake.

He glanced down at his raked and bloody arms. That had been so close. By the Faia, that had been close.

But he had seen the light of Venishan magic; he'd seen its essence. He had manipulated it! It had been panicked and hasty, but he had *used* Venishan magic. And if he could understand it once, he could understand it again.

That would have to come at another time. He couldn't stay here. Clearly, the Slate Wizard knew where he was. Pliothe had left, but she would be back with reinforcements.

Grei had to run, but he wasn't running home. This magic was knowable. The Slate Wizards were expecting him to be afraid, to be lost, to be powerless. So he must be the opposite. He was going to take the fight to them, use their power against them as they'd used his power against him.

He was going to end this.

All he needed was time, a precious bit of time to further his education, and Pliothe had given him exactly the key he needed.

He wondered where he might hole up to continue learning....

There was no house that these Slate Wizards couldn't trace him to, not in this foreign land where he knew no one, where there was no refuge and there were no allies....

Wait.

Maybe there were. Maybe, like Venishan magic, he was simply not seeing things correctly. He might actually have allies here; he'd just shied away from using them.

The Slate Spirit needed Grei's help, had begged him to come to this place to free him. The White Tree had begged Grei to go looking for the long lost Devorra.

What if that was the missing piece in this convoluted problem? What if the very problems Grei had avoided getting involved in were actually the solution?

What if Devorra was here, trapped by these Slate Wizards and their god Venisha? What if this goddess, once freed, could tip the scales? And what if the Slate Spirit, once freed, could do the same?

What if all he needed to do was shift his perspective? To trust...instead of suspect.

The path became suddenly clear. It was risky, but Grei knew there was only one place to go. There always had been. He was going to learn Venishan magic in the place where it had, apparently, all begun.

The Slate Mines.

Chapter Thirty-One

GREI

Ree pointed up the street. Following her finger, Grei saw the pyramidal building in the distance. It looked like it was trying to copy the enormous, powerful pyramid that rose above everything in the middle of the city. This one was small, shabby, and it looked like its point had been removed.

"I don't need another place to hide," Grei said. "What I need is—"

"You need rest."

"I don't."

"You barely slept. And your minuscule nap was interrupted by an attack."

"There is one end to this."

"Uh huh." She ignored him, gave a quick look up the street. She had been indispensable in getting them across the oily, smoky city without being seen. At least it was in the right direction. Thanks to Pliothe's dream, Grei had some idea of the direction the Slate Mines lay, and he'd pointed them right toward it.

It was after dark, but in the part of the city nearest the huge pyramid, horses and horse-drawn carts filled the roads. People in grease-stained leathers and dirt-smeared faces moved about their business as though this was normal.

Grei had seen poverty in the Thiaran Empire. Nobles had their privilege, their white horses and jeweled masks. The thin middle-class, like his father, curried favor for jobs and hoarded the coins they made. And, of course, there were the Lowlanders who seemed to have nothing save the old dray horses that brought their crops in during the harvest.

But these sad and dirty people looked—every one of them—like they had left hope behind long ago. They lacked...fire. They went about their business much like the people of Fairmist, but they seemed to lack any desire for a brighter day. This was life, it was the only thing they'd ever known, and it was always going to be this way.

"Stay here," Ree said, then crept up the street.

Grei leaned up against a wall, and he hated to admit that Ree might be right. His eyes kept wanting to slide shut.

"I wonder how long it takes for feet to get tough." Adora leaned against the wall beside him, inspecting the bottom of her bare feet.

"You never got shoes," Grei realized.

"Well, that cobbler's shop we browsed for hours had some beautiful boots, but none were in my size," Adora said.

"We have to get you something."

"No, this is my new leaf."

"Leaf?"

"I'm turning over a new leaf. I think barefoot is my new leaf."

He closed his eyes.

"All right," Ree said from right beside him. Grei jumped.

"We should push through and get out of the city," he said.

"Uh huh. You're sleeping." She motioned with her hand, and the two of them followed her through the shadows.

The pyramidal structure was partly made of wood and brick, and partly made of steel that had collapsed toward the top, as though there had been the skin of something hung on the steel like bones, but it had long since been removed or torn down by the elements.

"It's abandoned. We can avoid the guards here."

The guards she referred to were the functionaries of Vaeron's kingdom. The priests. Most wore yellow robes, though Grei had seen two priests in red robes and one in blue. The robes looked exactly the same except for the color, and he had to believe the colors designated rank.

The priests seemed to be mobilizing for something, running this way and that. No doubt looking for Grei and his friends.

"I don't need sleep the same way that you—"

"Save the argument. Go." Ree led them along the alley around the dilapidated building. They crept through a broken window to find a huge empty room with a few contraptions made of rusted iron, a floor scattered with old straw, dust, and dirt, and walls smoked black by soot. It looked like a builder's guild of some kind.

Grei could hear the hiss all the time now, but it was stronger in some places than others, and there was an echo here. He thought of trying to summon the triangles of light again, but the very thought exhausted him. He also wondered what kind of magic had once been done here, what kind of Venishan artifacts this place had made.

"There is so much we don't know about Venishan magic," he murmured.

Ree went to the far side of the room, inspecting the debris, no doubt looking for a good place for him to sleep. He was about to look away from her when she swayed, almost stumbled, and put her good hand on the wall.

"This is so homey," Adora said, not really talking to either of them. She ran a finger along the soot-stained wall and held up a black finger.

"It will do for now," Ree said. "We've put a good deal of distance between us and those searching for us. They were concentrating on the western edge of the city." Ree flexed her wooden hand, and it moved stiffly.

It suddenly occurred to Grei that the magic of Ree's wooden hand, like the whispers, might be weaker here. His own Faia-bolstered hand hadn't shown any difference, so he'd never thought about it. He came closer to her. "It's troubling you."

"It's fine." She stopped flexing the hand and hid it behind her hip. Her features were shadowed by the erratic light flashing through the open windows from the lightning lamps on the street.

"It's stiff."

She hesitated, then nodded.

"I think the magic is distant. That's why. I'm...sorry. What does it feel like?"

"Like the hand of a seventy-year-old woman."

Grei came closer and Ree raised her head. He had been so preoccupied with absorbing their new surroundings, with fending off Pliothe, with trying to learn Venishan magic, that he hadn't noticed that Ree looked awful. Her face was pale. There were dark circles under her eyes, and he'd never seen her stumble like that before. She was dead on her feet and trying not to show it.

He put a gentle hand on her shoulder. "You're exhausted."

"No less than you."

"You can see the stars from here!" Adora said from the center of the room, staring up through the enormous hole in the ceiling. "Or, well, you could if not for those lightning things. And all that smoke." She squinted up at the haze that lay over the city like a blanket. "If there were stars to be seen, you could see them from here!"

Grei clenched his teeth and tried to ignore her. Every word she uttered was like another pin in his heart, and he didn't know how much longer he could take it. When they had been in Fairmist—when all Grei had to do was use his vast power to mend the land—he'd been able to tolerate it, to give Adora whatever time she needed. But here…he felt like she was a block of sandstone, rubbing…rubbing…rubbing against him, stripping away the skin. The muscle. Now she ground on bone, and he didn't know how much longer he could take it.

"When was the last time you slept?" Grei asked Ree.

Adora twirled in the open space beneath the mottled sky. "It's not—"

"Faia's blood, Ree. Answer my question."

Ree's shoulders slumped. "I honestly cannot remember."

"Sleep."

"I have to guard you."

"Rest, Ree. Adora will guard me tonight."

"Oooo. Yes. We can drink all night. These are our kind of stars, lover." She leaned her head back and drank from the wineskin, throat moving as she swallowed hard. Grei wondered why that damned wineskin never seemed to run dry.

He put his other hand on Ree's shoulders, squeezed reassuringly. "You've said Ringblades can get by on little sleep. Just half an hour, then. Will you close your eyes for that long?"

Wearily, she nodded her head. "Yes, all right."

Ree found a relatively clean corner and curled up against a wall, dagger in one hand, ringblade in the other. She was out almost immediately.

Adora continued to twirl and spin beneath the dirty sky. Grei took a deep breath, then went to a window that had a view of one of those lightning lamps.

He sat down before it and got to work.

Chapter Thirty-Two

GREI

After a full hour, Ree still slumbered like someone had felled her with a hammer, and Grei let her. She made no sound, not even the slightest whuffle or sharp indrawn breath, as though she had been trained as a Ringblade to even sleep completely silently. It surprised him a little that she hadn't woken on her own. Certainly, she was more exhausted than she'd ever been before, which was saying a lot. Grei, for his part, was beginning to think that stopping in this old workshop had been a far better idea than making straight for the Slate Mines.

He couldn't get the triangles of light to reappear.

He tried to follow the hiss. He tried to force it into showing its true language. For the entire hour, he tried, but there was nothing. His breakthrough under Pliothe's onslaught had come to him in a panicked moment, and now he couldn't seem to duplicate it. All he could hear was that monotonous hiss.

He tried until tears of frustration burned his eyes.

Adora, who had spent the time skipping around the building, exploring the second story walkway, touching all the posts, and spinning beneath the open sky, suddenly started chuckling.

Somehow Grei knew it was about him, and he whirled on her. Sure enough, she was watching him, the mirth directed right at him.

"You think this is funny?" he asked. "I know *you* want to die. What about Ree? Will you consign her to death as well? If I can't figure this out—"

That made her laugh harder.

With that, something snapped inside Grei. He stopped talking. Instead, he stood up and strode toward her.

She raised an eyebrow, watching him come. No matter what other ridiculous thing she chose to do, it seemed Adora was always half watching him, waiting for a reaction. She smiled as though she'd finally gotten what she'd wanted. A reaction.

His fatigue nettled him. His failure frustrated him. Blood pulsed in his temples like tiny hammers.

"Adora," he said huskily.

"Yes, lover?"

He closed his eyes, clenched his fists and tried to master himself.

"What if I told you I would give all this up? Spend our lives avoiding the Slate Wizards instead and let them have what they want. Would that satisfy you?"

"Oh, are we giving up now?"

"Please stop taunting me for a moment and listen to me."

"Oh, I'm all ears." She gave him a winsome smile.

"Adora…please answer me. Would it make you happy if I just left this? If instead of me trying to figure out this frustrating magic, trying to stop Thiara from being overwhelmed by villains from this Faia-forsaken land, trying to do the right thing…if I left this all behind. Do as Blevins said. Grab a boat and sail back to Devorra. Hide. Let the Slate Wizards—"

"A ship?"

"What?"

"You said boat. I think you mean a ship."

He ground his teeth. "Does that matter?"

"I just thought you'd want to use the correct terminology. I don't think a boat, such as it is, would make it over the Kingsea. Do you know they call it the Kingsea here?"

He clenched his fist in frustration. "Just answer me. Would it be enough? To get out of the way of history, vanish into the fabric of the world. Live a life. What if I gave up my quest? Would you come back to me? Would that be enough?"

"Ah, I see. You want to listen to me, to my desires. You want to know what would be enough for me?"

"Yes." Relief flowed through him. Finally, a normal response!

She moved to him, and his heart leapt. Lifting her beautiful arms, she put her hands on his shoulders and leaned close. He thought she might hug him, maybe even kiss him, but she stopped six inches from his face. Her smug smile, that glazed look, both of them vanished to reveal pain glistening in her eyes.

"Let... me... die..." she said. The desperation in her voice struck him to the heart.

"Adora—"

"I'm not yours." Tears brimmed in her eyes. "If I ever was, I'm not anymore. I'm not supposed to be here. Maybe I never was."

"Please—"

"You envisioned me the way you wanted to see me from the very beginning, from the moment you saw me in The Floating Stone. And I fed that fire, because that's what Lyndion bade me do. I did what was demanded of me. But I don't think I was really that girl. She was a creation of Baezin's Order. And even if I ever was—even if it was true at the time—she's lost."

"You are still—"

"No." She shook her head violently. "It was a fiction. Maybe one I would have been happy to indulge in once upon a time. But you know what I've done. You keep dredging up that thing I said before Lyndion ripped me apart and Velak stole my body. A little cottage. A chicken-scratched yard. A child? By the Faia, a child? How could I possibly raise a child when I've killed other people's children?"

"That wasn't you," he said hoarsely. "It was Velak."

"Velak's weapon of vengeance. Adora the bartender. Mialene the princess. It's all the same, Grei. Don't you see that? I've never made a choice on my own. My one choice, the only real choice I've ever made in my life, is to end it. And you've taken that away from me. This life, whatever it might have been, was a mistake—"

"Don't say that!" He tried to hug her, but she stiff-armed him, holding his shoulders tightly, holding him away.

"I'm not yours," she repeated. "The only thing you can do for me is let me make my last choice. Let me go."

His lip trembled, and his vision blurred. "Adora..."

She shook her head. "That girl died in the Temple of the Faia. She died again under Lyndion's knife. *She* was your lover. Not me. You can only be one of two things to me now, Grei. My jailor or my friend, and I've been begging you to be my friend. Let me go."

Tears burned his eyes.

"I don't want to."

"I know, but I'm asking you to. For the lover you once loved, if you must see it that way. For the human being I am right now, right in front of you, begging. If you can see clearly enough to feel compassion for a woman who simply wants to go her own way, who wants nothing of your plans or hopes."

Grei bowed his head, exhaustion and hopelessness crashing around him. He fell to his knees and sobbed.

He wanted her to relent, to kneel next to him and take him in her arms, to comfort him and to tell him she didn't mean any of it. He wanted her to tell him they would be together, that it wasn't too late, that he hadn't made a fatal mistake when he'd left her in that bedroom in the Thiaran Palace.

But she didn't. She stood there, looking down at him like a stern parent, waiting for him to stop throwing his tantrum.

"I'm sorry," he murmured. "About…everything."

"I know."

"And that makes no difference?"

Her expression didn't change. "*Nothing* makes a difference, Grei."

"Tell me there is no chance for us. Say it out loud. I have to hear you say it—"

"There is no us."

He bowed his head.

"I see," he breathed, staring at the cobblestones. He couldn't stand to look at her anymore, couldn't stand to see the face of the woman he had loved so passionately, who he'd assumed he would spend the rest of his life with, looking back at him with no feeling for him at all. His head swam and he placed a hand on the sooty stones, lest he fall over.

It felt like his heart was tearing slowly in two. Cruel clawed hands ripping apart muscle and hope.

"Fine," he finally murmured. It was so soft even he could barely hear it.

"Did you say fine?"

He turned his gaze up at her, and he felt sick. "Go, Adora. I will try to find a way to live without you. I hope…I hope in your final hours you'll remember I loved you. That you meant everything to me, that I never intended to be your jailor. That I wanted to be…everything to you, too."

She narrowed her eyes, looking down at him skeptically.

"Go," he said.

She took a few steps away from him, and it hurt him to see her body language, to see that she didn't expect him to let her go. But he didn't chase her. He wasn't going to chase her anymore.

"I'm sorry I hurt you," he said. "I really thought you would change your mind."

She continued backing up like a wild animal that was afraid if she moved too quickly, the hunter would notice. She reached an empty window frame. Keeping her gaze on him, she lifted one leg up and over the frame, then the other, then vanished into the night.

She was gone.

Even if he'd wanted to go back on his promise, it was too late now. He hadn't revealed to Adora or Ree just how helpless he was here in Venisha. Without the whispers, he couldn't track her here like he had in Fairmist.

But even if he could, he wouldn't. It was over. She wanted freedom.

Freedom from him.

He raised his head. Every muscle in his neck screamed for rest. With a grunt, he got to his feet and staggered to the window on the opposite side of the ruined factory. He looked out at the smoky sky, at the powerful, greasy buildings.

He knew the way to the Slate Mines. He'd seen it in Pliothe's memories, had seen the road back when Vaeron had begun his war. Instinctively, he knew how to get there. And at this point, what else was there?

Grei didn't have a future anymore. After his tasks, after his promises to mend the broken things, he had envisioned being with Adora. She had been his future, and now that future was gone.

All he had was left was this war. All he had was justice for villains.

He squeezed his eyes shut and put the palms of his hands against his eyelids.

And wasn't that what he'd wanted? Wasn't the war what he'd chosen over Adora that fateful night in the Thiaran Palace when she'd begged him to stay? That was his pivotal moment. Not now. Now was too late. He could have listened to her then.

But he hadn't.

He opened his eyes again and looked out the window. The horrible, heart-rending pain in his chest settled like it was going to be there forever. There was no happy ending here, and that was a bitter draught he would simply have to swallow.

He was the Whisper Prince. Not Adora's lover. Not a husband. Not a father. Not a man who was able to have these things. He was the last, the only dispenser of justice in this benighted place.

He'd better get about it.

He glanced over at the slumbering Ree. His first thought was to wake her, but what was the point? Grei was most likely going to his death, just as Adora was. Ree had served him faithfully throughout everything. Perhaps the last bit of compassion he could show her was not to drag her down with him.

It had occurred to Grei back at the last abandoned building that each time the Slate Wizards had found them, it was after he'd used or touched The Root. So he hadn't touched it since. Now a plan formed in his mind.

Ree would wake on her own soon, and he needed to be long gone by then. He would get as far away as he could in the next half hour, then touch The Root again. If it somehow alerted The Slate Wizards as he suspected, that would draw them away from here, give Ree time to rest, to wake, and to make her escape from this horrible kingdom.

It was the least he could do for her, and perhaps the last gift he could give.

"Goodbye, my friend," he whispered. "You deserve better than to die here in this dark and dirty kingdom. When you wake, return to Thiara. Go live the life you were meant to live before you ran afoul of The Whisper Prince."

He went to her and carefully wrote his goodbye note in the soot of the floor.

Goodbye. Go home. Thank you for everything.

He padded away as quietly as he could, climbed silently up and over the window frame, and vanished into the night.

Chapter Thirty-Three

GREI

Grei walked for two hours, avoiding Venisha's guardians. He walked along greasy packed-dirt streets lined with misshapen canvas houses propped up by spars of rusted metal. He'd thought he'd seen the poverty of Venisha near the center of the city, but it was nothing compared to this. Grimy, barely-dressed people drifted like ghosts between the walls of the "houses" that fluttered in the hazy breeze.

He had touched The Root after that first half hour, just as he'd promised himself he would. The Slate Spirit's voice had instantly spoken.

"You're closer," the Spirit said. *"You're in Venisha."*

"I'm coming to get you," Grei said. He told the Spirit what had happened since they had last talked.

"Bless you, Whisper Prince."

"You're in the Slate Mines."

"Yes."

"Then I'm coming for you...if you can answer one question."

"Of course."

"I saw the creation of the Slate Wizards in Pliothe's memories. I saw everything that happened. Vaeron, Fylomene, Pliothe, given powers by the god Venisha."

"You...saw into Pliothe's memories?"

"And you weren't there."

The Slate Spirit said nothing.

"You said you were one of the Slate Wizards, that the god Venisha created you with them, that you objected to Vaeron's methods, and that he imprisoned your spirit in The Root. Except, you weren't there."

"You saw everything Pliothe saw?"

"Which begs the question: why are you lying to me?"

"I am not lying."

"There was no fourth Slate Wizard, Spirit. There were only three people in the carriage when Venisha arrived."

"No, Grei. There were five. Vaeron, Fylomene, Pliothe, my dead sister...and me."

The name flashed into Grei's mind. "You're Mezzryn?"

"I am."

"But she stabbed you. You died."

"She stabbed me. She thought she had killed me, but I passed out from the pain. I would have died, would have bled out right there in that carriage if Venisha had not healed me...changed me."

"You weren't dead yet," Grei murmured, and the Spirit's words rang of truth. Pliothe's vision had not gone beyond the point where she, Vaeron, and Fylomene had received their blessings.

"I went with them," the Spirit said. *"I was there when they made war upon the king. I wanted to stop Vaeron, but I was too scared. I couldn't stand up to him then. Not right away. Later, after he was king, I thought I could challenge him, take the throne for myself. I built a secret cabal to overthrow him, but he sent Fylomene to me one night. She pulled the details of the plot out of me, and then Vaeron knew. He couldn't kill me, of course, but he found a way around it. Pliothe ripped my soul from my body and put it in The Root."*

"Why couldn't he kill you?"

"That was my power, Grei. With my life's blood leaking out of me, with Venisha levitating me from the carriage, I wanted only one

thing. I was terrified of dying. When he asked me my wish, I told him to make me immune to injury and death. I was Vaeron's perfect opposite."

Grei regarded The Root. "So Pliothe put you in here…"

"Yes."

"I'm sorry."

"So am I. But if you can find my body, if we can put The Root into my hands, I can live again. Live as a human." The Spirit sighed.

"Well, then that's what we're going to do."

"And once I am free, I am your ally against them, Grei. Believe me, I've waited a long time to pit my immortality against Vaeron's sword arm. And I will not go down so lightly again. I've had a long time to think about how to get around him and Fylomene. And Pliothe, of course. There are ways around Pliothe…."

"First things first."

"Yes."

"Tell me, is it possible for the Slate Wizards to find me using my connection to The Root?"

The Spirit hesitated. *"I think yes."*

"You think?"

"The Root is one of Pliothe's creations. Now that she knows you possess it…yes, I think she could find you. You must hurry."

"But only if I use its magic?"

"I think talking to me is also using its magic," he said reluctantly.

"All right then. I'm going to put it away until I reach the mine. Then I'm going to free you. Then we may have a fight with the Slate Wizards on our hands."

"I long for that fight," the Spirit said.

"Good." Grei put the artifact back in his pouch, pulled the drawstring, and continued to the edge of the city.

The poverty-stricken sheet hovels fell away behind him and he took the cobblestone road out of the city. The road lasted for almost a mile, bisecting a field. It had been built to last and well maintained, but after that, it became packed dirt and, soon after, a crossroads. Five different paths stretched out before him like a snake with five heads.

Wagon wheel grooves had sunk deep in the earth, solidified by many wagons over time. Each wound in a different direction, the rightmost path appearing to hook around, circling the edge the city. The one on the left appeared to do the same. The other three curved toward the dark horizon, one toward an ominous-looking forest off to the right, one toward the continuation of the sere plains to the left, and the widest and most well-traveled ran straight up the middle.

Because of the emotions and memories thrust upon him by Pliothe when she'd attacked him, this place was like a scratch across his soul. She had known this crossroads well.

The loudest source of hissing came from path to the left.

He started walking.

Another hour took him to a tumble of boulders, and his soul practically vibrated with the intensity of the hissing.

He had never been to a mine, but the Lowlands below Fairmist had a few mines, and he'd heard the Lowlander miners grumbling about them from time to time. Mines were in hills—an opening in the side of a mountain. This pile of stones before him barely qualified as a rise.

The smoke had partially cleared from the sky this far from the city, and a mottled moon illuminated the cluster of boulders. He walked around the little knoll, looking for an opening. He found nothing, other than a place that looked like it might have been some kind of entrance in the past. Two towering boulders—each misshapen and fifteen feet tall—flanked a pile of haphazard rocks, as if a mine shaft had collapsed. He wondered if Vaeron had done this to ensure that no one else could go into the ground and be rewarded with the gifts of the Slate Spirit. It sounded exactly like something he would have done.

Grei stood there, gathering his thoughts, then reached into his pouch and withdrew the cloth-wrapped Root, careful to touch only the cloth for the moment, not the steel of The Root itself. He hadn't touched it since he'd talked to the Slate Spirit at the edge of the city.

He knelt next to the crushed opening between the two monolithic boulders and touched one of the stones instead. The source of the hissing was in there.

But there was more. Grei could hear the whispers more strongly here. He glanced back in the direction of the distant city, so far now that he could only identify it by the cloud that covered the stars. Was he was far enough away from all that Venishan magic that the natural world was speaking to him again?

"Let's see what's at the end of the road, shall we?" Grei murmured to himself.

He flipped open the cloth, revealing the rust-colored cylinder of The Root and its four hatches.

"Let's find the truth." He touched the artifact.

"Grei?" The Slate Spirit voice immediately slithered into his mind.

"I'm here."

He flipped open a hatch. A hole opened next to him. A minor landslide of rocks slid down into the darkness.

"Bless you, Whisper Prince. Bless you," the Slate Spirit said. *"I will guide you."*

He jumped into the hole, preparing to land like a normal person would, but whispering to the air to break his fall, just to test it. The air swirled, pushing at him. He landed on the bottom of the tunnel created by The Root, not as softly as he'd requested, but not as hard as he would have.

There were whispers here! Confidence filled him. They were muted, yes, but at least here he could use some magic!

But this was…different. The whispers weren't coming from the stone or the air. They seemed to be coming from deeper in the mine, from a specific point down the tunnel before him.

"I am close," the Spirit said.

"What else is down here?" Grei moved into the dark tunnel, listening to the hiss and, behind it, the Faia-like whispers that pulled him forward.

"I am just ahead to your—"

The voice suddenly cut off.

"Slate Spirit?"

There was no response, and that gentle feeling of having another presence in his mind had vanished. The Slate Spirit was gone.

A chill scampered up Grei's back. A host of questions rose in his mind. It felt like someone had cut off the Slate Spirit's voice.

What else was down here? Or was it the Slate Wizards, finally pinpointing where he was because of The Root? Had Pliothe taken control of her artifact?

Except the corridor still went down into the earth. There was only one way to find out the truth of this place. And finding the truth was what the Whisper Prince did.

Grei whispered to the air to light his way, and he moved forward into the dim passage.

Chapter Thirty-Four

REE

Ree jerked and sat up. As a Ringblade, she had been trained to awaken and orient herself immediately. The Ringmaidens had called it the sleep shock drills, two weeks of intensive exercises where the Ringmaidens were required to sleep in a different bed every night within the Sanctum, as well as sometimes outside in the wilderness. They were then, at random, shocked awake in various ways. Sometimes it had been with a loud noise. Sometimes with a sudden attack. Sometimes a Ringblade would sneak in and move around the room to see how long until the Ringmaiden sensed they were there.

Many of the girls had washed out during the sleep shock drills.

Ree had awakened now because her training told her something wasn't right in the room. But she came to consciousness sluggishly. Something wasn't right in her body either. Her senses were dulled, her reflexes slowed. She had never been this exhausted before. The little girl's mechanical rats had hurt her more than Ree had let on. Some had cut deep, and she hadn't had time to properly clean the wounds. The room felt chill, her skin hot.

An infection. Dammit.

"If you do not tend to the necessary now, there will be no later." She heard her Ringblade instructors in the back of her head. Danger had come, and she wasn't ready.

Blinking gummy eyes, she peered into the gloom. Grei was nowhere to be seen. Adora as well. They had either left or been taken, and she hadn't awoken for it.

But Ree was not alone. The beautiful female Slate Wizard stood in the center of the room underneath the open roof. The frantic illumination from lightning lamps danced across her burgundy cloak, her flowing dress, and her perfectly fitted embroidered vest.

Painstakingly, Ree got to her feet. She swayed, gritted her teeth, and kept herself from stumbling. The cuts burned all over her body.

They took him while I slept, she thought. *Now I barely have the strength to rise, let alone fight. I've failed him.*

The beautiful woman appeared to have come alone, which meant she probably hadn't. Tiny noises reached Ree's ears and confirmed her suspicions a second later: the barest scrape of a boot on cobblestones outside, the creak of a grip on a sword hilt, the muted huff of a breath....

Ree guessed there would be anywhere from a pair to a dozen fighters outside. This told her a number of things.

The thunderous swordsman—the man who had nearly killed Emperor Baezin in single combat—wasn't here. Ree knew fighters, and that man would never hide outside while someone else did the talking. The woman was here without him at least.

It also told Ree that this female Slate Wizard felt she needed a mundane guard. That was the most interesting bit of information by far. For some reason she didn't feel she could handle Ree alone.

"You look ghastly, dear," the pretty woman said.

"I missed my bath." Ree thought about her options. She was in no condition to fight more than a single opponent right now. By the Faia, she wasn't in much condition to fight a kitten. But maybe she could get this woman to underestimate her, perhaps drop her guard. If that opportunity presented itself, Ree was going to take it. She walked shakily along the wall, letting some of her feebleness show, wishing she was faking it more than she really was. By the Faia, her whole body hurt.

"I can help you with that. There are baths in the Slate Temple that would make you shudder in ecstasy." The woman had the poise of Empress Via, and her beauty radiated from her like heat. It was compelling, distracting, and Ree found her gaze lingering on the curve of the woman's neck, on that perfect jawline, on those large, dazzling eyes—

Ree jerked her head, blinking.

Ah… she thought. *So her magic is one that snares the imagination, the desires…. She's a seductress. No wonder she has a guard.*

Ree had never faced anyone with this kind of magic before, but she had plenty of practice seducing normal people. Perhaps she could put that to work.

"You're the Ringblade," the woman said.

"What's a Ringblade?" Ree asked.

The woman laughed. It sounded like chiming bells caught in a breeze, and Ree almost looked at her face again. She wanted to. The urge was so compelling it spooked her. Her heart pounded faster.

"The Thiaran Ringblades are legendary," the woman continued. "The most efficient assassins in the world. It is said you can sneak through the darkness like a shadow. I've heard tell you are accomplished lovers and diplomats all wrapped into one." The woman gave a coy smile. "But no one mentioned you were funny."

"Always leave them with a smile on their faces," Ree said.

"The dead ones?"

"I don't kill them all."

The woman's easy smile remained in place a beat too long. A normal person would have missed the disappointment, but Ree caught it.

"I haven't properly introduced myself. I am Fylomene." The woman gave a fluid, graceful curtsey.

Ree said nothing.

"And unless I miss my guess, you are Ringblade Ree. You are lucky I found you, Ree. Vaeron would not tolerate this obstinance."

"The swordsman was Vaeron?"

"The king of Venisha."

"I know who Vaeron is," Ree said. "And you're the queen?"

That scored a hit. Fylomene's eyes tightened just a little. So, she was *not* the queen. And she was not happy about it.

"I'm a Slate Wizard," she said, for the first time without that fake kindness in her voice, for the first time seeming to try to impress, rather than just exuding impressiveness. Ree caught a glimpse of the little girl inside the dazzling woman.

Ree wished she had more of her faculties about her. She was trying her hardest to catch all the nuances she'd normally have picked up as a matter of course. She also regretted her current situation, and blamed herself. She shouldn't have fallen asleep. She had no idea if Grei and Adora had been captured or not. If they were dead or not.

In her almost delirious state, she was tempted to mention Grei, to test whether Fylomene had any idea where he was, but decided against it. Ree longed to know what had happened to him, but asking about Grei would tip her hand, reveal she *didn't* know where he was.

Which, if Fylomene was looking for him—which she almost certainly was—would give her critical information. Let her dig for it on her own. No reason to help her.

Fylomene cocked her hips and put her hands there. "The Ringblades are legendary, but I confess you look bedraggled, dear. I expected more. A steel-eyed, steel-armed woman with burning coals for eyes and razors for teeth, perhaps."

"The razors kept cutting my tongue. I left them in Thiara." Ree finally found a way to look at the woman through her peripheral vision without facing her directly. That seemed to cut down on the dazzle.

Fylomene sighed. "So it's going to be cat and mouse? I had hoped we could have a civilized conversation. If you give me what I came for, I have no reason to hurt you. Is it, instead, time for me to test the legend?"

"Isn't that why you came?" The world swayed to the left, and Ree clenched her teeth, forcing herself to stay upright.

"Vaeron wants the Whisper Prince."

Relief flooded through Ree. Her patience had paid off. They didn't have him. "Then you're too late. He left with Blevins."

"He left you behind?"

"I was slowing him down."

Fylomene cocked her head. "See? Why don't I believe you?"

Ree shrugged, trying to sell it. "It's the truth. I disappointed him."

Fylomene clearly didn't buy the lie. "How do you like this truth, dear? You're burning up with fever. You're desperate to hide it, but it is laughable to try to hide anything from me. I will get what I came for. It's only a matter of time."

"I had too much to drink last night," Ree said. "That's why he left. He doesn't tolerate mistakes."

The woman gave a mirthless smile. "Pliothe's creations carry all manner of infection, most of which you probably don't even have in Thiara. I've seen this before, Ringblade Ree."

This conversation had only lasted a few minutes, but already Ree felt like what was left of her strength was leaving her body. If she didn't make her escape soon, she'd have nothing left, so she began the calculations in her head. There were probably a dozen soldiers outside. Fylomene would have assumed she'd need at least that many to take down the Whisper Prince, especially since she didn't have the murderous Vaeron with her.

So if Ree went crashing through a window, if she was fast and accurate, she could put down two and slip into the night.

Unfortunately, she was sluggish, fighting even to keep her vision in focus. Two opponents was a tall order. And she gave herself practically no chance of beating anyone in a footrace.

"I want to help you," Fylomene said. "Just tell me where the Whisper Prince is, and I will let you live."

"Isn't that the deal the king would have given me?"

"Except I'm telling the truth." She pitched her voice quietly, as though she didn't want the guards outside to hear. "Vaeron likes to kill people."

"What you're saying is I can trust you, is that it?"

"Yes, dear."

The woman was good. She sounded completely honest. Ree wanted to believe her. She fought the feeling. "So, I tell you where the Whisper Prince is, and you let me go?"

"That's what I'm saying."

"How do I get past your soldiers?"

Fylomene smiled. "They are men. I can make men look where I want them to look."

That almost made Ree smile, and she realized she had forgotten to keep Fylomene in her peripheral vision. Ree felt a sudden lassitude and an attraction to Fylomene that bordered on that giddy, flowering feeling of falling in love. She shut it down with a twitch of her head.

"Where is he, dear?" Fylomene asked conspiratorially, like they were friends, like they'd broken a barrier and could share secrets now.

"I..." Ree felt such a strong affection for the woman that, if she'd known where Grei was, she might have actually said so. The most likely guesses popped to her mind. Grei had left her behind to protect her somehow, perhaps thinking he would draw the pursuit away from her. Or he was looking for the heart of the Slate Wizards' power, so he could attack it. Or he had sensed a key to learning the magic of the Slate Wizards and had gone to chase it.

Ree almost blurted her theories, but instead she bit down on her tongue until she drew blood.

The pain washed through her, momentarily throwing off whatever spell Fylomene was casting.

"I don't know," Ree croaked.

Fylomene sighed. "You poor thing. You don't realize I am giving you the best deal you're going to get."

"I would die for Grei," Ree grunted, and she realized she was stooped over now. Sparkles danced in her vision. She hung tight to her evaporating sense of self. She swayed back and forth, struggling to stay upright. "Even if I knew where he was...you could torture me...chop my head off...I won't give him up...."

The room just wouldn't hold still, and Ree finally stumbled. She couldn't gauge where the ground was anymore, and she fell onto her side. Everything was so cold....

Through blurry vision, she watched Fylomene gracefully glide across the floor to stand over her.

"Well, one thing lives up to legend," Fylomene said, descending to her knees next to Ree. "Your loyalty is impressive. As is your willpower."

Ree felt she should pull a dagger, should roll to her knees...but all she could manage was an uncontrollable shiver. All she could do was glare pitifully at the woman.

At first Ree thought she was glaring back, but the woman had a compassionate look on her face like she was going to protect Ree, like she cared. That expression flowed over Ree like warm water, and she felt safe.

It's over, she thought. *Her spell has me. I've lost.*

"Sleep," the woman murmured. She reached out and touched Ree's forehead.

That was the last thing Ree remembered.

Chapter Thirty-Five

GREI

The Root had taken Grei down into the earth. Ever before, it seemed The Root's tunnels had been level, traveling straight to whatever destination Grei had envisioned, fifteen feet below the surface of the earth. But then, Grei had never wanted to go anywhere that wasn't above ground.

This tunnel, however, went down at an angle so steep he almost couldn't walk it. He kept his arms out at his sides for balance, his boots scraping on the slate as he caught his balance again and again.

The Slate Spirit was still quiet. Grei tried to contact him periodically, but it was as though something had cut him off. Urgency rose inside Grei. The only person who could do that was Pliothe, and that meant she might be tracking him. He had to hurry.

He navigated his way deeper and deeper, and finally the corridor evened out into a flat passage. The Root's passage ended a hundred paces later when it opened into a huge cavern.

Grei entered, looking up and up. The top of the cavern was so high it was lost to the darkness. The light he had asked from the air wasn't strong enough to illuminate it. To his right was a huge passageway, much larger than the corridor of The Root, and he moved toward it. The scrape marks of chisels and axes marred its sides and the ceiling, unlike the smooth tunnels of The Root.

He peered inside. The field of light that followed him showed rubble not far ahead. He surmised this was how people had once come and gone, but the entire passage had been collapsed at some point in the past.

He left the collapsed tunnel and explored more of the cavernous room. There was a mound of something in the center. As he neared, he spotted a broken wagon wheel. The wood spokes were dry and splintered, jutting up like cracked teeth. The steel band that had surrounded it had fallen to the side. Beyond them, he spotted the rusted metal that had been the cab of a carriage, half buried by the rocks and dust of a century.

Recognition washed over him and Pliothe's vision returned to him. He spun around, looking at the huge passageway, then back at the rusted carriage, putting the fragments of the vision into place.

This was the place. This was where Pliothe—where all the Slate Wizards—had met the god Venisha.

He went to the carriage. The whispers were stronger down here, which seemed odd to him. This was the lair where Venisha had once been strong. If anything, it should be filled with the hissing of Venishan magic, not the whispers of Devorra's magic.

Ever since the Slate Spirit's voice had vanished, a foreboding had been growing inside Grei. At first, he thought it was because Pliothe was certainly in pursuit, and with her Vaeron and Fylomene.

But a new thought floated up inside him, and he had to know the truth.

The door of the carriage had been bent and jammed into the casting. He whispered to the steel, softening it until the door would move, then he bid it open and looked inside....

A chill went up his back. There were skeletons in there.

Two skeletons.

A cold fear settled in Grei's belly, and his body ached with the realization that he'd made another mistake. He gripped The Root.

"You're not Mezzryn," he said, breathless. "You never were. Who are you?"

From the darkness something huge approached. The ground shuddered so violently that Grei stumbled. Bits of rock dust drifted down from the ceiling. He could not see far, but he felt the immensity of the creature. He braced himself against the broken wagon wheel, shining his sphere of light toward the back of the cavern....

The thing descended into the blue glow. Enormous spines of slate jutted out from its craggy head, which was as big as a house. Its jaws were the thick mandibles of a giant stone bug, split in the middle. Its snout was flat-nosed, like a rock face that had been cleaved in half with two oblong holes for nostrils. Its eyes burned turquoise in the darkness above. Glowing ephemera wafted up from them, circling around the great stone horns that jutted straight out from its temples.

Grei had seen Slinks tear people limb from limb. He'd seen powerful magic overthrow an entire city. He'd seen the burning fury of a demigod nearly destroy an entire continent, but he had never seen—had never felt—anything like this.

It was one thing to be in the presence of a demigod.

It was entirely different to be in the presence of a god.

He couldn't catch his breath. He wanted to scream the god's name, to say it aloud, but he couldn't make his lungs work.

The thick slabs of the dragon's mandibles moved down and opened in an entirely alien fashion. Before Grei could wrap his mind around the reality of what he was seeing, the dragon spoke.

"I am Venisha."

Chapter Thirty-Six

GREI

"You want the truth," Venisha rumbled, his impossible mouth opening a triangle in his maw. "Well now you have it, Whisper Prince. I am Venisha, creator of the world."

Grei slowly backed up, eyes wide. The dire warnings of the White Tree thrummed through him. This was the god who had tried to destroy the goddess Devorra. This was the god who wanted to take over the entire continent. His continent. The Slate Spirit wasn't some Slate Wizard who'd been betrayed. The Slate Spirit *was* Venisha.

The flurry of thoughts in Grei's mind solidified into certainties. The warnings of the White Tree. The vicious, violent nature of King Vaeron. The powers each of the Slate Wizards possessed, powers meant to manipulate, to subjugate, to destroy.

All creations of this creature.

When Grei had bound himself to The Root, he had sold his soul to a horror.

"Your nature is to dig, Whisper Prince. Dig dig dig..." Venisha said. "It was how I knew I could get you here."

Everything the Slate Spirit had done was designed to bring Grei to this place. Venisha had told Grei half-truths. Yes, he was trapped. He was a prisoner, but the Slate Wizards weren't his jailors.

"Something else is holding you here, something the goddess Devorra did," Grei said.

"Cease your retreat," Venisha said. "Take a moment and think."

He spoke in the same voice Grei had heard in his mind time and again, but it no longer had the tone of a gentle mentor. This was the tone of command, of a vast being used to getting his way.

"You are of great value to me," Venisha continued. "The one destined to free me. Be smart, Grei, and we will rule your land together. You will be the first among my Slate Wizards. The Overlord of the continent you call Devorra."

Venisha stopped at the threshold of the broken wagon, and his jaw worked, grinding stone. Little flecks of rock dust sifted down from the split in the mandibles of his chin.

Grei backed further away.

"You can do something my Slate Wizards cannot. If I could have given them your power, your deliciously versatile power, I would have. But you…you can bend nature. That is what the Whisper Prince was made to do. You can free me."

"You lied to me." Grei's teeth chattered saying just that much. The sheer presence of the god was crushing. Magic emanated from him, filling Grei's mind with waves of hissing. He continued backing up, almost to the opening of The Root's tunnel.

"For your sake, do not sour our meeting," Venisha said.

"I'll never free you."

"Don't make me force you."

"Force me…." A chill ran up Grei spine. He still owed the "Slate Spirit" one final request.

What kind of hooks were in Grei's mind that caused him to feel so good when he fulfilled a promise to…the entity he'd *thought* was the Slate Spirit? And what would the punishment of refusing be?

Alternatively, what if the spell that bound him to The Root could *make* Grei free Venisha?

The Slate Wizards

Grei's retreat had taken him to the edge of the tunnel made by The Root.

"Free me, Whisper Prince." The turquoise light in the dragon's eyes burned. "Free me."

Grei turned and sprinted into the tunnel. The idea of capitulating to the god was unthinkable. Nothing Grei knew or had heard about the god Venisha was good. He'd masqueraded as a helpless spirit and brought Grei here on false pretenses. He'd created the Slate Wizards, a bloodthirsty clutch of tyrants bent on conquering the Thiaran Empire. And, if the White Tree was to be believed, Venisha had destroyed the goddess who'd given birth to the world.

Grei had to find a way out of this. He had to figure out how to resist. He was in over his head again, and he didn't know what to do.

As he sprinted down the smooth hall, clutching The Root, he recalled visions of when he'd told Selicia that he would find "some way" to defeat the emperor even though Grei didn't know how to do it. He remembered Adora floating face down in the waters of the Temple of the Faia, dead because he hadn't known what he was doing. He thought of how he'd created Velak's red mist when he'd insisted on using his magic even though he knew it was out of control—

"Do not force my hand, Whisper Prince." Venisha's voice was so loud in Grei's mind it was like someone had smacked him in the forehead. He stumbled, canted sideways and hit the side of the corridor. Where his shoulder struck, the passage opened, rock dissolved away as though it had been eaten by acid, sending him staggering into a new tunnel even as the tunnel that led back to the surface squeezed together...

And vanished.

"No!" Grei ran and slammed a hand flat on the rock—now just a wall in the new corridor. He squeezed The Root in his hand, concentrating.

Open... he thought. *I wish to return to the surface. Open to me....*

The wall shuddered, then slowly opened up again.

"You are indebted to me," Venisha spoke in his mind. *"Don't make me force you...."*

Grei ran up the tunnel, clenching The Root, keeping his mind focused on that moonlit plain, on that tumble of rocks on the surface. The tunnel narrowed, and he felt Venisha's will against his, using The Root.

The tunnel shuddered around him, squeezing to a tube that made Grei crouch, then expanding again as Grei gasped. Every time the corridor shrank, it felt like a hand was squeezing his head. When he pushed back at it, using all his will, the corridor expanded again, just wide enough to let him through.

The ordeal became a battle within his own mind. Grei's bluish glow of light followed him, but it was waning. Every time he exerted his will, it seemed the light faded a little bit more.

Grei could feel the strength of the god in this underground warren, strength he'd not felt when he had stood above. If Grei could just reach the surface, he thought he could fend off the god forever. Or abandon The Root completely.

The corridor bent to the left, and Grei stumbled half-blind with concentration down it....

Except that wasn't right. When he'd come down to the Slate Mines, there had been no left. As always with The Root, the tunnel had been perfectly straight.

Grei grunted, imagined the tunnel straight to the top again.

Straight, he thought. *Straight....*

The will it took to straighten the corridor caused sweat to bead on his forehead, but then he realized that he hadn't been making the tunnel go upward at all. He'd come down at an extreme angle....

He stopped, breathing hard, and looked back the way he had come—

The tunnel ended about twenty feet behind him.

Fear trickled over Grei like cold water. He was deep underground. He was making tunnels into pure rock, and he didn't know where he was.

"You see it is futile it is to fight me," Venisha said in his mind. *"I urge you to come back to me while I still think fondly of you. We can work together. When I rise again, you will have as much power as you wish. Emperor of Thiara, as Vaeron is king here."*

"No!"

Grei redoubled his efforts. The surface! He just needed to go up. It didn't matter if he came up in the same spot. Once he reached the surface—anywhere on the surface—he could be free of The Root.

With a shout of effort, he imagined what he wanted. The tunnel rumbled, then angled upward. He ran, but soon the tunnel began to feel flat again. With a gasp, he focused again, and the tunnel angled upward once more.

But the moment he lost his focus, the tunnel flattened out again. Panting, Grei stumbled, fell to his knees.

"This is all so unnecessary. You are here now, and I will never let you leave."

"Rrrrrgggh!" Grei lashed out with his mind. He pulled the hissing sound all around him into himself and envisioned the triangle lights.

The triangle lights exploded around him like sparks, just like they had when he'd fought Pliothe. He lashed out blindly, imagining them whipping the corridor in front of him.

Up, he thought. *Up!*

Rock exploded away, making a jagged opening like he'd blasted it with lightning. He stumbled up the incline toward—

It opened into a cavern. Despair knotted in Grei's stomach as he thought that, somehow, Venisha had tricked him into making a full circle, had brought him back to the huge space where the steel carriage was.

But this was different. A green light glowed in the center of this place.

"*Grei!*" Venisha's voice boomed.

The voice drove him to his knees, and he hit the sharp stones. He forced himself upright again, peering through the blinding pain, and staggered up the incline toward the green light.

"*Stop!* *Do not force my hand! Stop!*" Venisha thundered.

If Venisha hated this course, this was where Grei wanted to go. He charged upward. He felt the squeezing hand on his head, so fierce this time he feared it would crush his skull—

Then it was gone.

Stumbling blindly forward, hand extended, he waited for the next assault, for Venisha's booming voice to return, to punish him.

But it didn't.

Grei stopped, sweat dripping down his face, and blinked blearily at what lay before him.

Green grass, as thick and lush as he'd ever seen it, covered the cavern floor. A muscled grassy knoll rose up in the center of the space. A trickling waterfall lined by a riot of colorful flowers—red, blue, purple, orange—cascaded merrily down from its top, winding along rounded crevices, across the verdant swarth, then finally disappearing into a mossy crack in the wall.

Mist hung thick in the air, and the grass climbed halfway up the cavern walls. Softly glowing green creatures flicked through the air like fireflies—

Those were fyds! The winged, faceless little creatures that had filled the cove air beneath Fairmist Falls now fluttered about the green knoll.

Grei hadn't seen fyds since Velak destroyed the Blue Faia's haven and stripped away its magic.

He walked forward, and whispers clustered all about him. He hadn't heard them this loudly since he'd first arrived in Venisha, and he was suddenly certain the strength of the whispers in the Slate Mines originated here. Not only had Venisha's voice vanished from his mind, but the hissing was gone as well. With a wash of relief as profound as any he'd ever felt, Grei soaked in the whispers, feeling the repeating desires of the air, the stone, the grass, even the fyds themselves.

There was no way it could exist so far underground, away from the sun and sky, the fresh air and all the other pieces that living things required. It was like a part of Thiara had been taken across the Sunset Sea and plunked right here in this cavern.

"What is this?" he murmured, letting his voice ripple out to ask the question of the knoll, the air, the fyds.

Dozens of fyds turned, their bulbous eyes fixing on him. They fluttered toward him, surrounded him. When Grei had been a boy, such a thing would have terrified him, but he knew now that the fyds were simply attracted to magic, that they...fed off of it, catching little unused swirls like food.

*Magic...magic...magic...*they whispered, as singular in their thoughts as the grass and stone.

Grei approached the knoll, and the fyds followed like a glowing, shifting cape. He knelt at the edge of the stream and put two fingers into it. The water was warm like it had come from a hot spring deep beneath the stone. In the chill of the cavern, the warm water reassured him like the arms of a mother.

He stood and worked his way around the enormous knoll, taking it in from all angles. If he didn't know better, he'd say this was the haven of some Faia, but there were no Faia in Venisha....

Grei stopped, eyes widening, as he came to an enormous, elongated ridge of the knoll. He walked around to one side of the end and then to the other side, then backed away quickly to see it at a distance. That wasn't a ridge at all…

That was a dragon's head!

The profusion of green grass had all but obscured its features, but the elongated ridge was a neck, and at the end was a large, curved head with pointed ears, a rounded head, and a long snout with wide nostrils.

A trickle of pink smoke drifted up from both nostrils, mixing perfectly with the misty air of the room—

Except that wasn't smoke. It was the mist itself, life-giving moisture that permeated the cavern.

"By the Faia," Grei murmured, moving closer. He could see it now, the entirety of the dragon. He could see the tail snaking away from its body, buried beneath an inch of soil and grass. The body of the dragon formed the entirety of the huge knoll.

He crouched next to the immense eye. It was closed, and for all the world the dragon looked like it had curled on the verdant floor, went to sleep, and let the centuries cover it over. There was no dividing line between the dragon's body and the grass, just one continuous green sward.

Grei reached out through the whispers, beseeched the grass to grow next to his foot, to reach taller.

It obeyed immediately, growing quickly to reach his knees like it wanted to sniff him. Grei reached out and put a hand on the dragon's head just above the eye. The grass there seemed to sense him, quivered, and reached up at him.

He brushed his fingers over the dragon's eye, ruffling the grass. His body filled with power, bursting with the vitality of this place, this Faia-like haven. He asked the grass to move, to reveal what was beneath. As his hand moved over the spot, the grass retreated, pulling backward to reveal smooth, shiny scales as bright and translucent as emeralds. They were like green beads of glass. He stared at them, feeling that if he looked deep enough, he would see something deep within the scales.

The impossibility of it caught him, held his gaze as though he was falling into that translucent depth, falling into the facet of a gemstone.

He continued whispering to the grass, continued brushing his hand across the dragon, uncovering more scales, continuing along the long neck. The grass obediently retreated as he bid it show him the entirety of the prize it had hidden for centuries.

The grass drew away like a blanket sliding off the magnificent creature. Its translucent emerald scales glowed in the darkness, and he could see every detail in its enormous back legs, the dark wings folded along its back, the coiling, seemingly never-ending tail, and finally the entirety of its majestic head and the thick stone collar around its neck.

When Venisha had risen up in front of him, Grei had felt terror. This dragon was equally as large, equally impressive, but instead of feeling fear, he felt…safety.

"You…" he murmured to the sleeping dragon. "You're Devorra."

Chapter Thirty-Seven

GREI

He stood in wonder before the sleeping goddess, and suddenly the entire cavern shook. Rock dust sifted down from the ceiling. The ground shuddered.

A voice thundered from the corridor where he'd entered, a powerful blast that had come from a long distance.

"Grei!" Venisha boomed.

Was this here...? Was this what the White Tree had predicted? Was this where she'd fallen after coming to this place to battle Venisha? Somehow, during their battle, he had trapped her here after she'd caged him in that cavern below.

Grei studied the thick stone collar around her neck. A chain meandered away to some point far back in the cavern where he couldn't see.

"GREI!" Venisha's voice boomed up the tunnel. The cavern shook again. *"YOU DON'T KNOW WHAT YOU'RE DOING!"*

I know that you are a liar, and if there's anyone who can defeat you, it's Devorra, he thought.

From the moment Grei had arrived back in Fairmist to try to set things right, the last thing he would have imagined was loosing yet another godlike creature on the world, but he realized this was exactly what was needed to restore the balance. The White Tree had begged him to come to this very juncture, to do this very thing, to restore the balance that had existed before the rise of the Thiaran Empire, before the coming of the Faia and the Slinks.

It had begged him to mend that which had been broken so long ago.

"I'm going to set you free," he murmured to Devorra, letting the essence of the rock collar vibrate in his hands. He heard whispers from Devorra's body, and he heard the hiss of Venisha within the collar.

"GREI! DO NOT RELEASE HER! YOU DON'T KNOW WHAT YOU ARE DOING!"

The god's desperation shook the cavern so fiercely, Grei thought the roof might come down. He ignored it. The thick stone collar was bound with lines of Venisha's hissing magic wrapped tight around the Faia-like whispers of natural rock. So intimately woven together, they created a new kind of element: Devorra's magic and Venisha's magic intertwined like vicious lovers.

"Dissolve," he whispered, beseeching the stone to become the opposite of its nature, to turn into misty air.

The rock heeded him immediately. It became muddy, sagging against Devorra's neck. The lines of Venisha's magic became visible as strands of frantic lightning, crackling, spitting, and hissing around the dragon's neck. The lightning lines seemed to hold together, interwoven in the trembling, watery stone for one desperate instant...

...and then the stone evaporated, becoming a gray mist. With nothing to bind, the lightning lines flew apart like angry whips. Grei threw himself to the side as one arced past his face. He rolled away as the lightning whips thrashed about, slapping the ground and scorching it.

For a terrible instant they thrashed and slashed...

then they trembled...

then they vanished.

"GREI!" Venisha's voice thundered through the cavern, then fell silent.

The green dragon took a breath, long and deep. It seemed to go on forever, like she was inhaling the entirety of the cavern's air, and then she opened her eyes.

They sparkled gold and orange like a blazing sunset. Grei felt like he was falling toward those eyes, like he could see all the way to the center of the world if he looked too long. She blinked, breaking the mesmerizing spell.

Grei wobbled on his feet, shaking his head as the dragon stared at the scorch marks on the ground all around her. Her enormous jaws slowly opened, revealing pearly teeth as smooth and round as polished river stones.

"Human," she said, as though just recognizing what he was. Her breath flowed over him, smelling of wildflowers.

"I'm Grei. I'm...the Whisper Prince."

"What..." Her foggy eyes blinked again, slowly focused, and then she said, "What have you done?"

"Venisha had chained you here. He was holding you captive. I freed you."

"No..." she murmured. "He...was not holding me..."

"What?"

"I was holding him." She blinked again, and her bewildered expression changed, sharpening. Her eyebrows slanted down over her eyes. "No, little one.... No no. You should not have come here."

The cavern shook again, this time so violently it knocked Grei to his knees. Chunks of rock slammed into the ground to his left and right. He shot a look upward—

The ceiling was coming down. Rocks as large as houses dropped toward him.

"Oh, little human..." the dragon said, and she leapt.

Chapter Thirty-Eight

GREI

Grei shouted as the dragon leapt upon him.

Her bulk covered over him, and he thought he must be crushed. Instead, she protected him from the stone, shuddering as tons of rock pounded down on her and on either side of her body. She took the relentless punishment.

The glowing light of the cavern winked out. Only the space beneath the dragon's emerald belly remained, big enough for Grei to huddle as rock shook her body, dirt and smaller rocks sliding in slopes in around the dragon's legs.

As quick as it had begun, the cave-in ended. Grei coughed, blinking at the tiny space beneath the dragon's belly. The light he had created was gone, but a green glow still emanated from the dragon's belly scales, illuminating the thick dust. The space was as wide as Grei was tall, and three times as long like a hallway. On the far side, the dragon's head, tucked under its own belly, rose to regard him. She opened her glorious orange-gold eyes, and they lit the gloom like a sunset.

He could barely breathe for all the choking dust hanging in the air, but then the dragon exhaled, and the dust settled. The little space filled with pure, life-giving air. Grei took a deep breath. It smelled of wildflowers.

He could only imagine the immense pressure of the stone overhead, but the dragon acted like it did not hurt her at all, like the weight was nothing.

"You came to save me," she said.

"The lands need you. The Thiaran Empire needs you."

She sighed. "It was the one thing I feared…."

"What one thing?"

"That someone good-hearted would try to find me."

"You are…Devorra. The goddess of…well, of Devorra."

The great line of her scaly lips pulled back, extending further toward her pointed ears, and he realized it was a smile. "I do not have a name, not as a humans do. But I understand naming is important for your kind. Devorra will suffice."

"You need to come back to the Thiaran Empire."

"Thiaran Empire?"

"It's…where you came from. Or, well, an empire on the lands you created. There's also Benasca…and…" He trailed off, realizing that if she had been here for centuries, she wouldn't know anything about his world, about the events that shaped everything he knew. And it seemed ridiculous to give her a Thiaran history lesson right now.

She let out another sigh, and a breeze of wildflowers blew past him. "I have dreamed. Oh, I have dreamed for so long. How many turnings of the seasons?"

"I…I don't know. Centuries. Many centuries."

"That is a measurement of time," she said, as though recalling a distant memory. "Many turnings of the seasons. A hundred turnings of the seasons?"

The question threw him off balance. It was as though the notion of a year, a century, was a new and barely remembered concept to her. How long had she really been here?

"I fell into a dream," she continued. "It was the only way I could hold him."

"Hold him? He had *you* trapped here. He had you chained."

"No, beautiful human. The chain was of my making. I had not the strength nor the desire to destroy him. We built this world together, he and I. But I knew if I bound myself to him, I could anchor us both to this place. It was the only way to keep him from ravaging that which I loved. Tell me, Whisper Prince, how did you come to find me?"

"The White Tree told me of you."

"Ahhh…" That seemed to make her happy. "She lives in the grove still. That is good. And…my other? My little sundrop? My curious one? She lives as well?"

"Who?"

"I left her with my blue roses to protect her."

"Do you mean Cavyn?"

"Is that how she named herself for the humans? Yes. Cavyn. Does she still live in her grove?"

"Cavyn is…no. She…her son killed her."

"Her son?" Devorra didn't seem the least bit perturbed that her daughter was dead, only curious about her grandson.

"She…well, she married a human."

"Married? She made a life bond?"

"A life bond, yes."

The dragon smiled. "Of course she did. She was always fascinated by humans. And she no longer lives like them? She has changed form?"

"Changed…well, Velak killed her. She had trapped him, and he escaped. He was angry at…at everything."

Sparkles rose from Devorra's round, pearly teeth. "And you unwound him?"

"Unwound him?"

"What you call killing. You removed him from this land."

"Me and…Cavyn's husband. A man named Blevins. Or, well, Baezin." He shook his head. She wouldn't know either name.

"Her husband. Ahhh." She seemed to marvel at the word. "My little sundrop bound herself to a human. She fulfilled my every hope."

"She did?"

"She and what you call the White Tree were my attempts to give abilities forward, to interweave them into the world. That integration was…problematic. The lives that sprouted evolved, but many could not wield the life-giving power."

"You were *trying* to make the Faia?"

"The Faia?"

"Your…uh, your granddaughters."

"Ah. Cavyn's creations. Her attempts to interweave with the lands."

"She…she had babies with a human. Baezin."

"Marvelous. Oh, marvelous. And you are then the…son of the Faia?"

"Well…. No. Or, maybe yes after a fashion. Your grandson Saebin—"

"He was a Faia?"

"More or less. He was the same type of creature."

"Born of Cavyn and Baezin."

"Yes. He did something to me, to enable me to hear the whispers."

"The whispers?"

"Devorran magic. The voices of the lands, the elements."

"Ah. Yes." She smiled wider. "Then the sacrifice was worth it. You have the ability now to protect yourselves. That was what I had hoped for. I knew if I just gave you time…"

"You trapped Venisha here to…to give time for the Faia to be born?"

"And you, yes. Those like you. If there are enough of you, then you can chart your own destiny. Do you see?"

He blinked, seeing what she was saying. For a brief moment, he looked at the world the way someone like

Devorra might look at it. Not at individual lives, but at the trend of those general lives, building toward…

"You gave magic to the lands," he said. "You gave it to your creations so they wouldn't have to rely on you. So they could build themselves, make mistakes themselves, save or destroy themselves."

"Yes," she breathed.

"And you came here to protect them. To give us time to grow. To learn how to protect ourselves from Venisha."

"Venisha…" she breathed, and the tiny coffin-like space smelled like a fresh meadow. "He does not agree with me. He will ravage the world if he gets the chance. He thinks he is making it better, of course, but he will undo all of our work in his drive to assuage his pain. He refuses to see what is right in front of him."

"What's that?"

"That all is exactly as it should be. The struggle, the seeming chaos. Death and rebirth. Happiness and despair. Sunlight and darkness. It is all in a beautiful balance. A cycle that turns and turns. Venisha does not see this. He longs to 'correct' what we have created. He longs to make it 'perfect.' But in doing so, he will eradicate it. The balance is hardy. It will absorb and overcome just about anything. But not my lover. Venisha alone has the power to break the cycle and bring our creation to ruin. And so I had to stop him. I took myself out of the cycle in order to take him out of the cycle. I crafted a chain that was made of myself, and I intertwined it with him. I tethered myself to him, if you will, held him down like a rope around a cloud." She sighed. "But no longer. You have changed that, Whisper Prince. It was my one great fear, that someday curiosity would lead one of my…children…to this place. And that you would take a mistaken pity upon me. This is my regret…."

Her voice lowered, so low that in fact she wasn't speaking at all. But Grei heard her through the whispers, like he could hear the stone and the air.

"But it is not wholly unexpected. Perhaps it was meant to happen. Perhaps the cycle is turning exactly as it should. Do you hear me?"

"Yes, I do."

"Ah, Whisper Prince indeed." She switched back to talking aloud. "You *do* hear the whispers of creation."

"Yes, and I can help you. Together, we can preserve the cycle. Venisha is back, yes," Grei said. "But so are you. You can fight him!"

She closed her eyes, seeming sad.

"You can stop him for good."

"Of course I can," she said with resignation. She did not seem to believe the words. "The cycle turns, and so must I."

"What?"

Her strange dragon smile spread across her long face again. "Venisha awaits us, Whisper Prince. He has waited a long time. I think we should not make him wait any longer."

"Wait, what—"

She stood up like there was no mountain above her. Rocks tumbled down around her legs, bouncing toward Grei as she lifted a thousand tons of stone. He whispered to them as they almost hit him, changing them to water, and the rocks responded immediately. He'd never had such swift response before. The whispers surrounding Devorra were so loud. He felt like he was in command of the blue roses again. In command of a dozen fields of blue roses!

"Yes…" she whispered. She lifted her head out from under her body into the crush and tumble of the stones, but even as she did, the stones turned to water. The crash of blue ocean swirled in, lifting Grei up before he could think of what to do.

"Yeeessss…" she repeated. The swirl of the water lifted him up, bringing him next to her head as they cut through the sudden water that had once been stone. Unlike when Grei turned stone to water, this turned the blue color of the ocean, like it had been truly transformed. A bubble of air opened around Grei's head so he could breathe. It was like they were suddenly in the middle of the Sunset Sea.

The elements changed for her, reacting to her desires automatically. She didn't even have to whisper to them. It was like the elements were part of her own body.

He barely had time to marvel at the miracle swirling around them before they burst through the surface like a breaching whale, water spraying around. Grei spiraled, thinking he would crash into the ground, but before he could whisper to the sparkling air for assistance, it cradled him like a dozen soft hands and set him gently down on the earth at the edge of the new sea Devorra had created.

Devorra spiraled into the air and opened her wings above him. Water droplets shimmered in the air like diamonds in the moonlight, and she stretched luxuriantly like she hadn't moved in a thousand years. Her wings never flapped, but Grei knew they didn't have to. The air was hers to command. It was possible that the air actually *was* her.

She hovered above him, hanging weightless. Then the moment passed.

She spiraled to the ground and landed gracefully next to him, folded her majestic wings against her sides. The water settled around them, coming down like a sheet...

...to reveal the immense form of Venisha a hundred paces in front of them.

He stood like a mountain. Grei had had the chance to see his threatening, horned face come out of the darkness, but he hadn't seen the entirety of the god. Now he did.

He was twice the size of Devorra, made of striated stone from his horned head all the way to his spiked tail, which extended a hundred feet behind him.

"Welcome back from your dream, Devorra." Venisha rumbled, his voice like the scraping of rocks. "Did you sleep well?"

"A dream of necessity, my love."

He shook his great head. "As ever, you are delusional. I am not your love. Not any longer."

"You will always be," she said.

"You trapped me for an eternity, *lover*." The word dripped with hate.

"To save you from yourself. To save what you love from your own anger."

Suddenly Grei understood Venisha's master plan. Drawing Grei here. The confrontation in his cavern. Grei fleeing. Venisha hadn't wanted Grei to stay away from Devorra. He'd driven Grei into The Root. The struggle to maintain the tunnel, to make it go upward, it had all been an act. He'd wanted Grei to run straight into Devorra's arms, to destroy the collar. It had all been to the plan, and Grei had fallen for it.

"You sent me to her." He looked up into the sky at Venisha. "You wanted me to free her."

Venisha ignored Grei, glaring with his burning turquoise eyes at Devorra. "You thought you could trap me forever, but all I needed was one crack. All I needed was one flaw, and you gave it to me as I knew you would. You with your sentiment for these worms who crawl upon the face of the lands. You with your pity and your cloying compassion for them. Your progeny…"

"She was part of the cycle, just as you are," Devorra said.

"I am not part of any cycle of yours! I *am* the cycle. I made the cycle!"

"I know you believe that, but it is not true."

"I created this world. You only added to what I made."

"It has grown beyond us, my love, if you would but see it."

"This. This is how I knew you would hand me my chance. Because you invested your power in your 'daughter.' You gave her the blue roses, weakened yourself. I knew I had only to wait long enough. Soon, she would make a mistake, hand her power off to someone strong enough to come looking, to set you free."

"Yes, my love."

"That bitch held the line for centuries, much longer than I thought. But it was only a matter of time until she fell to her inevitable flaws. I thought it would be the Faia, but it was the one called Saebin. He made the final mistake I had been waiting for." Venisha's burning gaze turned toward Grei. "He made you."

Grei clenched his fists. The god snorted, then turned back to Devorra.

"Once your daughter fell to Velak, once he slaughtered the Faia, I knew my moment had come. The time for me to finally take everything that belongs to me."

"It doesn't belong to you, lover," Devorra said. "It never did. And the more you squeeze it, the less it will give you. Can't you see what you've done here?" She lifted a wing and indicated the city in the distance with its low-hanging haze, its dirty buildings. "Don't you see what you've done?"

"You trap me for a millennia, then you point to my city in shambles and blame me?" His mandibles opened up, creating that triangle maw with sharp teeth within.

"It does not need repairing," she said. "It needs nurturing."

"You're a fool," Venisha said.

She sighed.

"But I don't need to argue with you anymore. I'm free, and you will never get that chain around my neck. Not ever again."

"I know."

"Do you know what happened to me while I've been held down by your insidious spell?"

"You've grown stronger," she said.

His mandibles worked. "Yes," he ground out, clearly annoyed that she had guessed. "Do you know why?"

"It was tangential to the spell I made. It turned your magic back on you."

"It lanced me. It skewered me. It flared and fought inside me until I thought I would explode. And you rebuffed every attempt for me to push it out into the world. It was like trying to push an ocean through a dozen pinholes. Do you know how frustrating that is?"

"I am sorry, my love."

"No you're not!" he raged. "You never were! If you actually had the compassion you claim, you would never have done such a thing to me in the first place. You would have turned over what was mine from the beginning. You would have honored me."

"You were going to destroy the world."

"I am going to mend what was broken!"

"No. You don't see it. But you will before the end."

"I suppose this is where you will make your predictions," he said derisively. "Tell me, *lover*. Tell me how this will end."

"I—"

Venisha lunged forward, moving so fast he blurred in the moonlight. Grei was ready for an attack, but he wasn't ready for the speed of the god. It was staggering. He moved so fast that he pushed a solid wall of air before him.

Grei flew backward, a hurricane wind slamming him off his feet.

He crashed to the rocky ground and rolled. The impact knocked the wind from his lungs, and he gaped like a fish for a critical second. Dirty clouds scudded over the moon, silver and mud. He heard rock slamming, the sounds of flesh rending, bones snapping. But there was no roar. There was no scream, no outcry of pain.

Finally, Grei's spasming lungs went to work. He sucked in a blessed breath.

Help her, he thought. *I have to help her.*

He rolled to his belly and craned his neck up. Venisha's great spiked head rose and fell, rose and fell over the green-scaled body of Devorra. Venisha snarled and growled as he came up, blood flying from his open mandibles. Blood and gore flecked his face, dripped from his pointy teeth.

"No!" Grei fought his aching body, pushed himself to his feet.

A knife stabbed through his calf and he went down with a cry. Rolling over, he looked at his left leg. Bone stuck out of the front of his shin, and his leg bent at a ghastly angle.

"By the Faia..." He gagged on the pain.

No, I have to help. I have to help!

Gritting his teeth at the pain, he rose again, standing on one leg. Lightning and fire lanced up, jolting his entire body as he hopped toward the vicious, striking god.

But it was too late.

Devorra lay dead on the ground. Venisha had bit through her entire neck. Gore covered the stone beneath her, and her neck was only connected by the bones of her spine.

"Devorra!" Grei reached into the whispers, which were still strong, and he commanded the air to become a spear that drove into Venisha's neck behind the spikes fringing his head.

Venisha jerked as the air pierced him, but he didn't stop. He closed his jaws on the bone, crunching through the last thing that connected Devorra's head to her body....

Devorra's body lay limp, much like Grei had found her, but the green glow of her scales slowly faded.

Grei screamed. Forming another wind spear, two of them. He shot them at—

A gale force hissing exploded in his head, and he lost all concentration. His wind spears swirled away and he fell to the ground, hitting his good knee and then falling over onto his side.

An enormous stone claw slammed down around him, picked him up, and threw him onto the bloody body of Devorra.

He tumbled, groaning at the pain of his ruined leg as he rolled, flopping down the slope of Devorra's side. He crumpled into a heap against the ground and Devorra's scaly belly and screamed. The pain was overwhelming.

You're going to die, he thought. *If you don't get up, he's going to kill you. Fight him!*

Grei grit his teeth. He pushed past the hissing that tried to dominate his mind, seeking the whispers. They thrummed from Devorra's body as though she was still alive. He could still access them.

And that meant he could still do something.

The stone beneath Venisha turned to water, and the god sank down to his crouched knees. But he was too large. Grei didn't have enough strength to make the lake deep enough.

"Whelp," Venisha growled. Two huge claws pinched Grei's shoulder, piercing all the way through and clicking together inside his body. He screamed.

Venisha hauled him upright, like a rag doll on a string.

"You were chosen by Saebin because you have heart," Venisha growled. "That's why you hear her whispers. That's why you wield the power you do. But…"

Venisha's tail whipped out of the shadows, the tip of it as long and pointed as a lance. It plunged into Grei's chest, punching through his ribcage, spearing his beating heart and driving it out his back.

Grei rocked with the brutal strike, looked down wide-eyed to see the spear of stone straight through him. He looked over his shoulder and saw his own bloody heart. The tail pinned it to Devorra's scaly belly. Grei tried to draw a breath, but couldn't. He looked up in astonishment at Venisha.

"Take away your heart," Venisha continued through his clenched mandibles, "and you are nothing."

Darkness came down like a shroud sliding over Grei's face.

And then he was no more.

Part IV

Devorra's Legacy

Chapter Thirty-Nine

ADORA

Adora ran. Her bare feet slapped the dirty cobblestones of the Venishan streets, and she angled toward the ocean. She knew its general direction, and it was as good a place as any. She was free.

But for how long?

When Grei had told her she could go, she had cautiously backed away from him, slipped through the window into the night. She had expected him to come after her almost immediately, to change his mind and deliver yet another speech about how their future could be so wonderful, about how she would come to love her wreck of a life. Some platitude that would feel like a punch to the gut.

Of course, he had genuinely seemed worn down by her absolute refusal to give in to him, to give him the face of the Adora he wanted.

It had been half an hour now, and he still hadn't come after her. A block passed, then another. Her feet were cut and bleeding and she didn't know where in the city she was, but she didn't care.

Grei couldn't keep track of her like he once could. The blue roses had been taken from him. And here in Venisha, his Whisper Prince powers were clearly muted.

It felt like someone had cracked a hot egg over her head, and it oozed slowly down her scalp with the realization that…

…she might actually be free!

That flicker of hope, of excitement, seemed a foreign and fragile thing. What if this was actually her moment? What if she could go somewhere he would never find, end her life, and he would never recover her body, never be able to pull her back from the other side.

She ran for another half an hour through the streets lined with lightning lamps, down to the streets that had no lamps, and finally to the grimy streets slick with the moisture and smell of rotting fish.

She ran past the scant few people lurking in alleys. It had to be hours past Deepdark, but there were always carousers, whether in Thiara or Fairmist, Benasca or Venisha. The dregs of society. The wretched looking for warmth. The lethal looking for victims. She ran past them all, and for some reason, none of them chose to follow her. A scantily clad woman in a sash bra, short skirt, no boots, and a floppy hat on a string with her hair flying behind her. Perhaps it was simply too odd for them, and when odd things happened in a city of magic, perhaps it was best to leave well enough alone.

Her lungs burned. Her legs cramped with pain. Her bare feet were wet with blood, but she kept running.

Then, through the stone and metal buildings, she saw the sea, moonlight flickering on the waves. She ran to a rotting wooden dock, obviously abandoned long ago for the newer, thicker, sturdier docks further up along the shore. This rotting one jutted from a cliff, tall on leaning pillars that lifted the broken end of the dock at least three stories into the air.

With the tide out, only half of the dock's pylons poked into the water, and she ran almost to the broken edge. It was at least two stories in the air. Plenty tall enough to kill her if she jumped headfirst.

She stopped there, chest heaving, her breath ragged. She let the pain course through her. She didn't care. Only one thing mattered now.

Her heart thundered as she swayed drunkenly over the drop. She had to do it fast. Grei was resourceful. If he changed his mind, he might be able to get to her in time.

She ripped off her hat, threw it away. She unhooked her belt with the dagger Grei had given her in case she needed to protect herself.

Here. Something to protect yourself, woman who wants to be dead.

She had gone along with it, though. Playing the carefree persona had been the only way she could keep her sanity. It had been the only way to keep him at arm's length: to pretend that nothing in the world mattered.

And it had worked. She had finally driven the wedge between them. He'd released her.

So do it, she thought. *Do it now.*

She stared at the rocks far below, the ocean withdrawing, splashing forward, withdrawing, splashing.

What are you waiting for?

"I don't know," she murmured.

"You don't know what?" a deep voice asked.

She whirled. At the other end, the beginning of the rotted dock, stood the swordsman king Vaeron, the one who had bested Blevins in Thiara, the one who seemed like a cross between Lyndion, Archon Felesh, and Jorun Magnus. A winning combination, to be sure.

"You've cast aside your weapon, your hat," Vaeron said. "You're staring at the rocks like a lover. What, exactly, are we doing here, Consort of the Whisper Prince?"

Behind him, a half dozen of his soldiers approached. Vaeron was a huge man, just like Jorun Magnus. Well over six feet tall, the king had those same impossibly wide shoulders and muscled arms. Vaeron towered over his minions, each in chainmail armor with slate gray plate mail pieces on the shoulders and chest.

"Oh, what *is* this?" Adora said, genuinely annoyed.

"We found you."

"You're not looking for me."

"But we're looking for your lover."

"He's not my lover."

"You called him your lover."

She sighed in frustration. Was this really happening? After her struggles to escape Grei, now she was caught by this posturing thug. "I was faking it."

"I don't think so. Where is he?"

"As far away from me as he can get," she said.

He cocked his head. "I don't believe you. I think he's going to come looking for you at any moment. You see, I understand lovers quite well."

"I doubt that. You strike me as a person who thinks holding a woman down while she screams is a good time."

That seemed to amuse him. "I like you."

She rolled her eyes. "I don't care. Not about you. Or Grei. Or any of this." She turned to leap off the dock. Not even that beast of muscle and speed could reach her in time to stop her—

She caught a movement in her peripheral vision just as a black fist smashed into her cheek. Stars exploded in her vision. The world turned sideways and she sprawled across the wooden planks of the dock.

The hit was so hard that for a moment she couldn't feel her arms or legs, like she wasn't even connected to them. By the Faia! *Ow...*

The side of her face felt like a fuzzy bit of fire.

She groaned, blinked up at the enormous man standing over her. He was every bit as tall as Vaeron himself and covered head to toe in black-enameled plate mail armor. His visor was a thin slit in an imposing wedge of black steel. This hulk had somehow come up behind her. How had he managed that? Had he climbed up one of the pylons?

She wanted to scramble to her feet, dodge past the man and leap from the dock, but her face was planted against the wet plank, and her body was limp. She was still negotiating with her brain to determine exactly which way was up.

The big mute warrior stood over her, jerking strangely in place. His arms twitched, like he wanted to grab his weapon. His legs twitched, like he wanted to jump on top of her. But he did neither.

Vaeron and his half-dozen henchmen clustered around her. He leaned in, smiling tightly.

"I don't hold my women down," he said quietly. "I tell them to lie still. If they don't, then I make them lie still. See?"

"You're…an innovator," she grunted, tonguing a loose tooth in her mouth.

"Where is the Whisper Prince?"

"By the Faia, he's going to kill you," she murmured.

He chuckled. "Is he?"

"Like a bug. Under a boot. That would almost be worth living to see."

The mirth faded from his face. "I study my opponents, wench. I know all about the Whisper Prince. I've stripped his power, brought him to *my* city. He's all but helpless. You think I don't know what I'm dealing with?"

"You are…ridiculous." With an extreme effort of will, she managed to prop herself up on one elbow. "Bragging? You're running around *your* city looking for him. You're beating on his companions to find him. You reek of desperation. Like a little boy who can't find his ball. Do I think you don't know what you're dealing with?" She laughed, even though it hurt her face to do it.

"He has no powers."

"No powers. See, that's the problem with little boys like you. You think with your big swords, not your brains. Grei didn't become the Whisper Prince because he was handed the biggest sword. He waded through a lake of pain. He died and brought himself back to life. He turned the whole world upside down to match his will. Do I think you don't know what you're doing? I don't think it. I know it. You don't have a clue."

"I will crush him."

"Crush him—?" She cut herself off with a chuckle. "Yes. I see. Very well. Let me tell you what's going to happen. Grei is going to find the heart of your power. He's going to find it because that's what he does. And then he's going to pull it all into himself. Because that's what he does. And then he's going to bring justice to you and everyone around you. Why? Because *that's what he does.*"

"Listen to me, bitch or—"

"Or you'll kill me? Torture me? Be sure to stick the knife in well, Vaeron, or you're only going to be fifth in line of the men who have hurt me."

His eyes flashed. He reached down and put his huge hand over her throat and began to squeeze. She laughed mockingly until she choked, holding his angry gaze, letting her bulging eyes say everything.

Do it. Kill me, you moron.

He seemed to actually understand her unspoken message, because his lips pulled back to show clenched teeth. Then his eyes narrowed and a wicked smiled bent his mouth. He released her.

She drew a shuddering breath and coughed spasmodically.

"Faia curse you," she choked. "Not one of you can do the job…correctly."

"You've issued me a challenge, consort of the Whisper Prince, and I never turn away from a challenge. Fifth in line? I've never been fifth in line for anything."

"I find that—" she coughed. "Impossible to believe."

"We'll just see about that." He rose to his feet.

Adora sighed through her raw throat, wondering what she had ever done to any gods or demigods—Faia or Slinks or all the unseen supernatural creatures who pushed this world forward—that they would so cruelly deny her something so simple as death.

"Bring her." Vaeron clomped back down the dock.

His soldiers bound her hands and her legs and the big henchman, the one in black-enameled plate mail, slung her over his shoulder like a sack of meal. He never spoke and she could barely hear him breathing as he carried her away.

She found herself retreating into her mind again. For a brief moment on that dock, as she was about to jump, she'd felt herself. Now she was caged again, under the power of yet another man. Rage kindled in her.

Fiercely, she stamped it down.

She couldn't get angry. When Velak had pushed himself into her body, she had felt more rage than a person should ever have to endure. She had made innocent people the target of that rage, and Velak had gleefully approved as she had incinerated them. She couldn't do that again, couldn't go to that evil place ever again.

So she fell back into the persona she'd created for Grei. She insulted King Vaeron, called him a moron, went on again about how Grei was going to find him, ride him like a pony about the city, and then bury him in a coffin of solid stone a hundred feet straight down in the earth.

She thought Vaeron would get angry, spit vituperations at her, or brag again about how he was going to crush Grei. Instead, without a word, he walked back to her, looked her in the eye, and punched her precisely in the jaw.

The lights went out and Adora knew no more.

Chapter Forty

ADORA

Adora awoke strapped to an inverted pyramid made of bronze. It had some kind of vast scene on it in bas-relief. Her wrists had been firmly secured in leather straps with buckles attached to chains that had been pulled tight through holes at the points. Her ankles were strapped firmly together and secured through the third hole at the bottom.

A too-familiar rage rose within her. Memories of Lyndion flashed through her head. His mocking, hateful smile. His knife cutting into her....

She glared at the two henchmen, checking the restraints as though she had just been put up here. The room was some kind of dungeon, low-ceilinged, built of what looked like slate. The Slate Temple. They were in the stronghold of the Slate Wizards.

The walls were made of granite and there was only one door. Of course. Every prison cell or torture room she'd ever seen—which was really far too many, in her opinion—had only ever had one entrance.

A short, squat table sat to her left covered with a black cloth that had been folded over itself, hiding insidious-looking lumps. One of the items poked out of the black cloth on the right-hand side, revealing the gleam of steel and a serrated edge. Torturers' tools.

Vaeron stood near the door talking to one of those Slate Priests dressed in red robes. The only other person in the room was the mute thug in the black-enameled plate mail. He didn't speak, but he continued to jerk irregularly. His arms twitched like he couldn't get comfortable. Or like he desperately wanted to kill someone and could barely contain it. Of all the people in this room, that man struck Adora as the most dangerous. Violence exuded from him.

Vaeron stopped talking to the priest and glanced at her.

"Oh good, you're awake." He turned back to the priest. "Fylomene is doing me no good on the hunt, clearly. Go find her, bring her here. Don't come back until you have her with you."

"Yes, your majesty." The priest bowed and rushed from the room.

With theatrical flair, Vaeron flicked the door closed. It boomed in its casing. The door was heavy, thick wood, banded with iron, and Vaeron seemed to want to impress her with his strength.

"You're an idiot," she said.

His lips tightened. "Tell me what you were doing on the dock."

"Going for a swim."

"You looked like you were going to commit suicide." He smiled like he liked the idea.

"You figured that out, did you? What gave me away? That I was standing on a tall dock, looking at the rocks? Or that I actually tried to jump? You're quick. It would take most people three seconds to figure that out."

His joy froze on his face, and his smile seemed like a dead man's rictus. Her needling had such swift effect that it surprised her. He truly was like a spoiled child with no control over his emotions. She suspected it had been a century since anyone had refused this man anything. How did people like this ever become king? What was wrong with the world that someone like this could become king?

Vaeron moved forward and stopped next to the stout wooden table. He flicked aside the black cloth, revealing six steel implements. They looked a lot like the twisted weapons in her father's laboratory right before the Phantom War. One was just a thin polished stake sharpened on one end. The next was a miniature scythe, curved like a question mark with a deadly point. Another looked like a giant key with a dozen tiny spikes sprouting at the part that would ostensibly go into a lock.

"You say you want to die," Vaeron said.

"I actually didn't say that. You said that."

Vaeron slipped the thin stake from the table and sauntered toward her. "But death and pain are two very different things. What's your name?"

"I am Niladantilusia, Faia Queen of the Forest of—"

He stabbed her in the side. She cried out, then clamped her mouth shut. She looked down to see the thin spike sticking out of her flesh just above her hip, an inch inward from her left side.

"What is your name, girl?"

She huffed, trying to master the pain. "I...don't have a name."

He grabbed the rod and shoved it deeper. She gagged and bit her lip as it burst through the flesh of her back.

"It's a small thing. A name. I just want to know what you are to the Whisper Prince. If you're not his lover, what are you?"

"I'm...no one."

Cold sweat coated her scalp, her face. She tasted salt in her mouth. It felt like someone had heated sharp tongs in a smithy's forge, then clamped them on her side. She resisted the urge to shift her body to try to make the agony bearable.

That was useless. She knew that would only make it hurt more, so she held herself still.

At the back of the room, the mute knight continued to twitch, shifting to one foot and going completely still, then thrashing his arm, going still, then shifting to his other foot.

"Oh, you don't actually think that." Vaeron ignored the man's odd behavior. He now sounded reasonable, like a solicitous friend trying to boost her confidence.

"I actually do, you vicious mongrel—"

He rotated the rod.

She screamed.

"What. Is. Your name?"

"Velak. The First Blessed. Adora. Mialene. Lyndion's sacrifice. Grei's prisoner. Take…your pick."

"Mialene." Vaeron glanced over his shoulder at the mute warrior, then back to her. "Mialene Doragon."

The black armored warrior twitched so violently that his hand almost reached his sword before he stopped and shoved his arm back down. He skittered to the side, stopped, stamped his foot, and stood still.

Adora breathed hard like she'd run a mile. Her body was soaked with sweat. Her hair hung limply against her forehead.

"You're the Princess of Thiara," Vaeron said incredulously. "Well that's…that's…you're the Lost Princess?"

She said nothing.

"That makes you…you're Baezin's great-granddaughter."

The black warrior twitched so violently he backed into the wall, but then he stood stock still.

"How did you survive?" Vaeron asked.

The pain of the torture had swept all of Adora's sarcasm away. She didn't want to play this game anymore. She didn't want to play any games. Not for Grei or Lyndion or this trumped up, jumped up, muscled up idiot king. She just breathed, glaring at him, and she let the rage build up within her. This was a man she truly wouldn't mind killing.

The thought brought images of the Seekers of Baezin's Order, burning. Running around in their white robes, flags of fire flying behind them. The screams. The smoke. The cries of the dying.

She shut her eyes and told herself to calm down.

She opened them again to find Vaeron right next to her. She could smell his smoky, meaty breath, like he'd just eaten a grilled steak. She wanted to vomit.

"My apologies, your highness," Vaeron said. "If I'd known you were royalty, I'd have taken better care of you."

"Would you."

"Of course." He yanked out the thin stake. She screamed, tried to cut it short, and bit into her own tongue. Blood leaked into her mouth. She breathed fiercely through her nose and felt the wet trickle on her hip. She looked down at the small, puckered hole in her side. A rivulet of crimson snaked down her skirt, soaking the red cloth a darker red. She felt a burning inside, in her heart, completely different from the pain in her side.

It felt warm, and good, and it fed on her anger.

"What an amazing fortune this is," Vaeron said, just like Velak had said before him, just like Lyndion had said before that. Adora the coveted jewel. Adora the perfect piece on their game board.

The heat in her chest grew hotter.

"You will suffer no longer at my hand. I can see the future." He put a hand on her naked thigh and leaned so close she thought he was going to kiss her with his meat mouth. "At long last, the King of Venisha will marry. He will join with the house of Doragon."

She glared at him. She could see him burning, could see him running around with a flaming cape like the acolytes of Baezin's Order.

"We all do what we must for our kingdom...." He whispered, his lips close to her ear. "But I confess that, once we get you cleaned up, I am going to enjoy this duty."

She blinked slowly, staring straight ahead with a stony expression. The twitchy black knight smacked the wall with his hand, then settled it again at his side.

"Think of it like this," Vaeron continued with a smile in his voice. "It's better than dying, isn't it?" This seemed to be very funny to him, and he chuckled softly in her ear. His hand moved up her thigh—

A knock sounded on the door, and Vaeron's hand went rigid. He backed up, annoyance on his face.

With a snarl, he spun and lunged at the door, flinging it open. It banged against the wall, revealing the red-robed priest outside, the same one he'd been talking to before. His eyes were wide, his hair tousled and his face white like he'd seen his mother's own ghost.

"You have Fylomene already? Because that is the only reason to be disturbing me. And I don't think you've found her that fast." Vaeron growled. He grabbed the priest by the neck, lifted him in the air. The man's legs thrashed and he futilely tried to pry Vaeron's hand from his neck. "I told you not to come back until—"

"VAERON!" A voice thundered down the hallway and the entire room, probably the entire temple, shook. The voice was deep with command, and the effect on Vaeron was immediate. He dropped the priest, who crashed to the stones and kicked his legs, thrusting his body backward until he hit the wall. He rubbed his throat, coughing and choking, but he rasped out three words.

"Venisha has come…."

Vaeron stepped out into the hallway, looking left at something Adora couldn't see.

"He's…here," the priest gasped. "He has returned at last, your majesty."

Vaeron looked back into the room, at Adora, then flicked a glance at the twitchy black armored warrior. "Brother, with me."

Brother?

"You two stay here, tend to that wound. I won't have my bride spoiled." The king vanished into the hallway without another word. The twitchy warrior jumped, stepping sideways, then walked haltingly into the hall and vanished.

Venisha was a city. But Adora had read enough history to know about the Slate Spirits. They supposedly worshipped a god of the same name as their city. A god. That voice had shaken this entire structure. Was this the city's version of the Faia?

Or probably more like Velak.

She should care about that. She could care that this appearance of Venisha had caused the priest to practically faint from fear. It had caused Vaeron break off from his vile assault.

But she didn't care about the priests or their god. Her mind was running around in a circle. All she could think about was Vaeron's hand on her leg, his promise about her future, the darkest reflection of the same kind of promise Grei had made. In short, Vaeron planned to put her in yet another cage. Once again, she was the possession of a man.

Something snapped inside her.

She couldn't hear the sound of the medical supplies the remaining guards brought and set down on top of the torture instruments. She didn't hear their boot falls as they took up positions on either side of her.

Again, she heard the screams of Baezin's Order dying. She heard her own heart thundering. She felt the growing rage, the heat that swelled with it.

Whispers filled her mind, just like they had after her first death, after the Phantom War, back when she'd still had hope, when she'd actually been glad of Grei's intervention.

Her mind, her heart, her ears; they were all full of whispers.

So when the guard touched her, when his fingers came in contact with her flesh, she turned her dead gaze on him. She clenched her fist and pulled against the thick leather strap that restrained her.

"Well *you* got a reprieve, din't ya?" The guard pulled a cork from a dark green bottle and poured it onto a clean cloth.

"Your lucky day," the other guard said in a coarse, rough voice. "All you got to do now is just shut your face and—"

"She's gonna be our queen, Glyndek. Watch your tongue."

The rough guard shrugged.

"I got a reprieve," Adora echoed numbly. "My lucky day."

"He's got a point," the first guard began, then looked up at her hand. "What—"

Adora's fist burst into flame. She felt the heat, but it didn't hurt her, not like the burning of the wound in her side. It felt warm. It felt safe. The leather strap curled, blackened, and turned to ash.

"Holy slate!" The first guard leapt back.

"What did you do?" Glyndek demanded. "What did you—"

Adora lowered her hand and pointed it at the first guard. Flame arced from her finger and engulfed the man. He screamed, but only for a second. The flame was so hot his skin melted off his skull. His eyeballs ran from their sockets like runny yolks.

Her other hand burned free of its restraint and she turned her dead gaze on Glyndek, who had foolishly thrown his hands up in front of his face at the intense heat of his friend's immolation.

"You should have run," Adora said in a dead tone.

The guard screamed. Already his armor was turning orange with the heat. His linen clothes smoldered. Now, far too late, he ran toward the door.

"You don't get a reprieve," she said, pointing. "Not your lucky day."

Fire arced toward the man.

Chapter Forty-One

GREI

"No..."

It was the first word Grei heard. It reminded him of when Devorra had said *"Yes..."* just as she turned a thousand tons of rock into an ocean. It had the same tone. He felt the same sudden sense of...safety.

"I'm sorry, beautiful human. But not yet. Not yet."

Grei looked down.... Except, no. He didn't look. He didn't have eyes.

He floated on a sky of pure green. He had no eyes, but there was green. There was no ground, no sky, just shifting hues of green slithering past him, over him and under him. Except there was no *him*. Not really.

This whole feeling was familiar. He had felt like this before, something similar. A Velakkan in the body of his brother Julin had used a magical wand on him, had turned him to stone. During that seemingly eternal moment, Grei had had no body. He had floated inside the darkness much like he now floated in this sky of green.

Except then, there had only been terror. There was no green, no sense of safety. And no voice had talked to him.

"You deserve to rest, beloved Whisper Prince. But not yet. Not yet."

"Who are you?" he asked. Except he didn't, because he didn't have a mouth.

But she heard him. Because she laughed lightly in his mind like a mother might to a child learning how to walk.

She. It was a she.

"You must find your strength again, Whisper Prince."

The green flowed around him, distracting him with its beauty and safety. "But I'm dead. I don't have to find my strength anymore, do I?"

"Time is short," the voice said. It sounded so familiar. He knew that voice. He knew this sense of lassitude, this sense of safety. *"You are close to crossing the final line."*

The final line.... It sounded wonderful. He'd never felt so relaxed.

He'd also never realized how many pains came with having a body. *Everything* it experienced, in fact, was painful to a degree. The chill of the air on skin. The scalding of a tongue from hot soup. The way air filled lungs, expanding them, pressing the body outward. So many pains had been transformed into comforting sensations simply because the mind would go mad otherwise. Compared to the lassitude of where Grei now was, everything about living was pain.

"I know you want to rest. But there is more for you to do."

"I did everything I could. I never wanted to be the Whisper Prince."

Ripples of smoky charcoal slid past him at the thought. The Whisper Prince. So much loss and pain. It flowed around him in charcoal colors.

The thickest charcoal stream twisted. Instead of going around him, it went directly into him. He felt Adora again, felt her as though she was right here with him: her coy smile behind the bar at the Floating Stone, the way she swung her hips beneath that swishing skirt as she led him outside, the happy look she'd given him at the palace just before she'd made love to him for the first time, that hollow glance she'd given him as the Lowlander lifted her into his arms and carried her to his room.

"Stop." Grei said.

"You're the only protection they have. Venisha is coming. There are none who can stop him. None save you."

"Adora was the one I wanted to protect. But she wants to die." In fact, wherever she was, wherever she had gone, she was surely dead by now. "I go to see her now. I'm going back to her."

He pushed the charcoal flow out, let it pass him and slither away. Further ahead, there was a deeper green, a richer green. He reached for it. If Adora was anywhere, she was in that green. He wanted to go into the green.

"Grei..." The voice was softer now, gentler, like he was leaving it behind. Good. That was good. He didn't want to listen to her anymore.

"Adora lives," the voice said.

Charcoal swirls leapt toward him, swirling in a corkscrew around him, flowing into him again. He stopped.

"No. She killed herself."

"She was going to, but Venisha's Slate Wizards captured her."

The charcoal wind swirled faster, obscuring the green almost completely. "Who captured her?" he asked, and this time he could hear something different in his own voice, something hard.

"Vaeron. He is going to make her his queen."

The green faded away, and now Grei hovered in the darkness of the charcoal wind.

"The world needs you, Grei. Adora needs you."

"She wanted to die."

"She no longer has that choice."

For the first time since he'd come to the green, Grei felt a pain. If he'd had a chest, the pain would have been in the center of it. He knew exactly how a person could be kept alive against their will. He'd done it to Adora, hoping she would see that living was preferable to dying. He'd done it for her…until she'd finally prevailed upon him to believe that she'd rather be dead, until she'd finally convinced him.

The thought that someone else would hold her against her will was unthinkable.

"But I'm dead," he said.

"The lines of life and death are…different for you. The Whisper Prince has other means."

"Venisha ripped out my heart."

"But it has not beat its last."

Grei didn't answer that. The idea of going back to the constant pain of living…

…but Adora was back there. He had stopped her from coming to this beautiful place. He'd held her back. He couldn't just leave her there all alone at the mercy of that mad king.

"I'll do it," he said reluctantly.

"I know," the voice said softly.

"How do I…?"

"Follow my voice."

He dove down, down into the darkening, smoky charcoal wind.

"The pain will be your guide," she said.

Now he could barely see anything at all. The green was completely gone, and all that was left was that drab gray. Even now, he could sense the pain, sense it just in front of him like a lake of needles.

The pain will be my guide.

He wanted to ask her if there was someone else, some other person who could save the world, but somehow he already knew the answer to that.

He went toward the pain. The charcoal wind became agitated. It felt like those needles hovered over him, poking, poking at him. The voice now sounded like it hovered next to him. Then it was behind him.

"Keep going," she said.

The wind funneled into a cone, and the going became more difficult. More pins poked at his chest. It began to feel like he actually had a body again.

"Keep going." Her voice was fainter now.

"Wait. Wait! Who are you?" he shouted back.

"My name is Pyll."

The name, the last of her, swirled before him, one final ribbon of green in the swirl of gray. The pins pushed deep. A horrible hissing rose, obscuring Pyll's voice.

He'd heard the name before, but he couldn't remember. There were so many names in his memories.

Her voice drifted to him, barely audible now. *"You knew me as the Green Faia."*

And then she was gone.

The hissing pierced his ears. The needles rammed home, and the only thing he felt was his body. The only thing he felt was pain.

He screamed.

Chapter Forty-Two

GREI

The pins stabbed him over and over, pushing into his flesh, then coming out, then pushing in, then coming out. He screamed again.

"You must be quiet," a new voice said, a young voice, decidedly not the Green Faia.

Everything hurt. It hurt so much that Grei arched his back. He could feel his arms again. He could feel his legs. He could feel the pain and injuries in each of them, the rocks that had hit them, bruised them, broken them, the cuts they had sustained.

But his limbs were nothing compared to the squeezing, crushing, horribly wrong pain in his chest. It felt like Venisha was still stabbing him, still wrenching his heart out of his chest.

But his heart was beating sluggishly, like it was surrounded in thick mud, barely able to move.

Grei drew a shuddering breath. Fire in his lungs. Fire in his body. Stabbing, slicing, awful agony. He screamed again.

"No," the little voice said again. "No no. You must not. He will hear. He will hear."

Something furry and metallic crawled across his mouth, sat down, muffling his voice. Cold little claws gripped his cheeks on either side of his mouth. He drew another ragged breath and screamed again.

"I am almost done," the little voice said. The poking, searing horror continued, pins sewing into his flesh, into the bones of his ribcage, into his heart.

Stop! Grei tried to shout, but it only came out as a muffled cry. *Stop please! Stop hurting me!*

"Almost done…almost done…" the voice fretted.

He forced his gummy eyes open, looking wildly about. A grimy, half-mechanical rat sat on his open mouth, gripping his face with its little metal claws, muffling his screams.

"Grfff Offff!" *Get off!*

He tried to pluck the creature from his face, but his arms were too heavy. They didn't lift. He shouted and tried again. His arms lifted from the ground, but then it felt like someone had stomped on his chest. He cried out and let his arms fall back to the velvety ground upon which he lay.

"Almost done…almost done…" the little voice repeated.

The pins did their terrible work, and Grei sobbed into the rat stuck on his mouth. He tried focusing on his body, on making it work. He tried more slowly this time, flexing his fingers as tears tracked down his temples. There was a gentler pressure on his chest this time.

He bent his arms at the elbow, lifting his hands off the velvet ground. No spasm in his chest.

"Done!" the little voice cried triumphantly.

Grei lifted his arm. A horrible ache remained in his chest, but the overwhelming, excruciating pain had decreased to manageable.

Questions jumped to mind, the first and foremost being: who was helping him?

He craned his neck upward. A warning pressure squeezed his heart. With a gasp, he fought through it and spotted his benefactor.

Pliothe stood four feet away, wringing her hands in front of her dirty little dress, which fell all the way to the toes of her scarred and scraped brown boots.

With effort, Grei reached up to remove the rat from his mouth. But it fled before he could touch it, scurrying out of his grasp. He looked down.

A network of wires crisscrossed over the center and left side of his chest, all different thicknesses, made of different metals. Gold, lead, brass, steel, copper…they crossed over each other again and again, thin and interwoven, knitted as tightly as flesh. They dug into his actual skin and bone on either side of the hole that had been left by Venisha's spear-like tail.

"By the Faia…. What did you…what have you done to me?"

Pliothe put one booted toe on top of the other, twisting, creating more scrapes on her boots. "I'm sorry. I'm sorry. I don't know your kind of magic. I only have my own."

"You…." He looked in horror at the interweaving of flesh and metal across his chest.

The pressure on his chest eased with each moment that passed, as though the wound was still magically healing, as though what Pliothe had set in motion was still working through him, fusing his body to this chaotic cluster of wires.

"You are…alive," Pliothe said. "You need to be alive."

Grei laid back, closing his eyes. He longed for the sweet green he'd been floating through just moments before. Such peace. Such…contentment. From that vantage, this world seemed horrible.

He swallowed down a raw throat. He'd come back because Adora was still trapped here, because she was at the mercy of Vaeron. Grei had made a mistake, had followed in the footsteps of the demigods he'd reviled.

Because he'd had the power to keep Adora alive, he had done so and ignored her wishes. He'd believed he knew the truth, that she didn't really want to die, that she just needed time to see what he saw, and he'd held her against her will. He'd used his power to bind her, to cage her.

It was the worst kind of crime. Grei had become exactly what he'd sworn to protect the world from.

"Maybe it's never perfect," he whispered to no one. He thought of Devorra, of how he had ruined her plans, had set Venisha free, and yet she hadn't once shown any anger about it. Instead, she had fought to save his life. And when Venisha had spat vituperations and condemnations at her, she had called him "lover." She had genuinely seemed affectionate toward him right up to the moment he'd killed her.

That was a grace Grei had never seen before. Devorra had—

He sat up. He had seen Venisha chomp Devorra's neck in half, but she was a creature of such vast magic…could she have somehow survived? With a grunt, he got unsteadily to his feet. The ground he'd been lying on was the body of the goddess. It had already been covered over with a thin layer of soft, short grass. The bulk of the body rose up before him, and he could identify the bump of her knee, the mound of her foot. Just like in the cave, a profusion of life—grass, ferns—had moved to cover her.

"Is she…?" he murmured. "Is she actually…" He walked around to the side, to where the head had been separated from the body. She lay just as she had fallen, only with everything covered in the soft grass.

Pliothe squirmed as Grei inspected the body.

Devorra was still alive. She had to be.

"I still hear the whispers," he said. As the ache in his chest continued to fade, Grei felt stronger. He could hear the strength and profusion of the whispers all around him, just like he had when he'd stumbled into Devorra's cavern. "She has to still be alive. I hear her whispers. They're stronger than ever."

He didn't have the heart to touch the severed head. He hoped that her neck would somehow…grow together again, that she would rise and tell him all was well, that a force of nature like her couldn't be killed by such a mundane physical death, that they had work to do, that they must chase down Venisha and cage him again.

The short grass continued to grow, spreading across the barren rocky terrain like water poured over a tabletop. Hope grew inside him along with its spread. Surely that was a good sign. Surely she would awaken.

He made a complete circuit of the body—

And stopped where he'd originally started.

In the center of the grass-covered dragon's body was a single patch of missing grass, where Venisha had stabbed. The fist-sized hole in the grass was brown and dead, high on the dragon's side. He came closer, dread growing in his chest. The brown was spreading, slowly creating a larger patch of brown.

"No…" he murmured. He spoke to the grass, using the whispers, beseeching them to fill in that hole, to regrow.

The brown spot spread faster, reaching out across the dragon's vast belly. The whispers became louder in his mind.

"What's happening?" he murmured.

"That is where your heart lay," Pliothe said quietly.

"What?" He turned to face her.

She flinched, lowering her head and looking down at her boots. "That was where I found it. It was behind you, on the dragon, covered in the…the green. I had my friends carry it to you, put it back in your chest."

He put a hand to his intricately wired chest, and he realized that he felt no pain there anymore. In fact, the more the brown spread, the stronger he felt.

"You put my heart back into my body with the moss on it? With the grass?"

"I didn't have time to clean it," she said. "You needed your heart. You can live with grass inside you. You can live with many different things inside you."

He spun back around. The brown continued to spread, faster and faster, as though it were eating the green.

"No," he said. "No!"

He focused on the living grass this time, begging it to stay strong, to hold off the approach of the dying, to grow tall and flourish and—

The brown grass raced over the body until there wasn't a patch of green left on the dragon. The grass had spread across the flat land a hundred yards in every direction, but the withering now raced across the plain as though trying to catch up. The whispers became louder and stronger as it did, and Grei clenched his teeth. He fell to his knees, watching as the last of the green died.

Then it stopped, and inside he swelled with power. He felt stronger than he ever had, stronger even than when he'd taken stewardship of the blue roses.

Devorra's power, whatever had been left in her dying body, had now become his.

He bowed his head, falling to his knees and offering a final plea to the person he'd once been. To the person he would never be again.

"No...."

Chapter Forty-Three

FYLOMENE

Fylomene stopped short five blocks away from the Slate Temple, mouth open in stunned surprise.

Towering above the buildings, almost as tall as the apex of the pyramid, rose the dragon that had haunted her nightmares for three hundred years. The massive creature that had transformed her into an immortal looked down at the comparatively tiny figure of Vaeron. They were having a conversation. A dragon god and a man. Conversing.

Fylomene quickly hid behind the nearest building, her heart pounding. She stayed there for what seemed an eternity, back pressed against the steel-banded metal of the wall, at a complete loss for what to do.

Venisha had returned. Was this somehow a response to her recent betrayal of Vaeron's trust?

No. That was crazy. She had betrayed Vaeron in countless little ways over the centuries. A betrayal so comparatively small wouldn't have summoned their patron god.

Or was her seemingly small betrayal actually much more important than she thought? Clearly events were moving, and Fylomene didn't pretend to know exactly what they were. The god had awoken. The god had *awoken*!

The ground shook.

She peered around the corner in time to see the massive creature leap into the air. His wings unfolded, and she watched in stupefaction. There was no way stone wings could hold any creature aloft, let alone a creature that weighed as much as a mountain. How did rock even cup or beat against the air?

She thought she might go insane watching the dragon god lift himself into the sky, then fly over the city.

Fylomene now regretted what she'd done. It was stupid. There was no reason for it, none that she could even discern herself. She had just…done it. Now she only had two choices. She could run away, or she could run the gauntlet of Vaeron's ignorance.

After too long frozen in indecision, Fylomene came to the conclusion that the safest place for her was still to run the gauntlet. If she didn't return—if she fled now—Vaeron would come after her.

So she turned the corner and approached carefully, readying her story….

But Vaeron didn't see her. He gazed after the impossibly flying god, who was barely a speck on the horizon now, then stalked back into the temple without a backward glance.

Fylomene hurriedly followed. She passed through the tall archway and forced herself to keep her composure. It was something she did quite well by now.

Vaeron was doing his pacing. It was an affectation of impatience. Whenever he had decided upon a course of action, but was waiting on another person, he paced. Usually he was waiting on Pliothe, who was notoriously fickle about punctuality.

He saw her the moment she entered the great room, and as usual, he turned his ire upon her.

"Where the hell have you been? I sent someone to look for you!"

"How long ago, my love?" she asked, putting on a barely-interested expression. "Two minutes? Five?"

"Do not mock me, Fylomene. I have no patience for it. Our patron god has returned, and he has orders for us."

"I saw."

"He has ordered us to make ready and meet him in Thiara."

So the war had begun in earnest. Of course it had. There would be no delaying now.

"Did he say why he has arisen after all these years?"

"Because the time is now," Vaeron said. "Where is Pliothe?"

She shrugged.

He clenched a fist in frustration, picked up a candelabra and hurled it across the room. The three-pronged spire of brass clanged loudly as it hit. Candles skittered across the marble floor, spraying wax, their flames flaring and then winking out.

Fylomene took in the room at a glance. As usual, there were Slate Priests standing guard, two at each of the exits from the room, except for the doorway that went down to the torture rooms. It was unguarded. That caught her attention….

But not nearly as much as the enormous man wearing Pliothe's Night Cage, the magically enchanted armor, so named because of the black enamel of the plates. The man inside twitched every now and then, trying to fight the armor.

The Night Cage was a torture device Vaeron and Pliothe had created an age ago, back when Pliothe was still eager to please Vaeron. When a person was put into the armor, not only did it grow to fit them, but it gave Vaeron complete control over them.

The armor resisted any attempt from the prisoner to move of their own volition. It responded only to Vaeron's commands. Not only that, but it engaged the prisoner's full faculties. Not just body control, but a kind of mind control.

So…Vaeron had found his brother. It could only be Baezin in the armor. There weren't many who cut that same tall, wide-shouldered silhouette.

Vaeron must have been giddy at that victory. Back when the brothers were mortal, Baezin had always been the better fighter. Being able to yoke those natural abilities, and the vengeance of having his brother as a puppet, must have been deeply gratifying for Vaeron. Not to mention an enslaved Baezin would be very useful in the coming war.

Of course Baezin was struggling against his prison, but that was folly. He didn't know it yet, but he would be in that armor until he died. It was designed only to come off when the prisoner was dead. Baezin would do Vaeron's bidding, kill whomever needed killing, until the strain of resisting and failing finally became too much for even his massive, powerful body. Then he would die. Afterward, the armor would fall off like leaves in autumn. Fylomene had seen it a dozen times.

But Fylomene couldn't worry about that. She had to figure out what to do about her betrayal, or today might actually be the day she died.

She had protected Ringblade Ree. She didn't even know why she'd done it, but she'd disobeyed Vaeron, taken the feverish Ringblade to an inn, put her abed and had her guards tend to her.

It was ridiculous. Some kind of momentary insanity. And yet somehow, she still felt a little warmth at the thought of rescuing the Ringblade.

While Vaeron raged to himself as he paced, Fylomene surreptitiously bit her lip. She had defied Vaeron in little ways over the centuries, but never outright. Not once.

Vaeron could never know.

She had used her magic to ensure the captain of her guards was devoted to her. She'd used whatever energy she'd had left to ensure the captain's men also felt quite well-disposed toward her.

But stretching her abilities over that many men was tenuous at best. Without directly applying her wiles to the captain, he would stay loyal to her for about twenty-four hours, maybe more if he had been attracted to her before she'd sunk her magical hooks into him.

Because of how important Ree was to Vaeron, she couldn't count on her influence on the rest of the guards to last more than an hour, and that hour was half over. Really, at any moment one of those guards could suddenly have a revelation. Keeping a prisoner from Vaeron's notice—especially one for whom the king was actively looking—based solely on Fylomene's entreaties was a mortally unhealthy idea.

Once that happened, Fylomene's life expectancy would shorten dramatically. To minutes. Or seconds.

"I told her to find the Whisper Prince," Vaeron growled. "Did I not tell her to find the Whisper Prince?"

"Perhaps she is still—"

"The Whisper Prince is dead!" Vaeron whirled on her. "Venisha killed him personally, since we could not manage it. Our god has awakened, and don't think he hasn't noticed that colossal failure. So I ask you this: if the Whisper Prince is dead, then what the hell is Pliothe doing?"

"Transforming some poor alley cat into her best friend?" Fylomene said, modulating her voice to sound bored, though she could barely hear over the thundering of her own heart. Acting solicitous, agreeing with him, showing interest in his tantrum was far more dangerous. It would have been out of character. She always responded to his anger this way. Doing otherwise would pique his interest, and Vaeron was brilliant at spotting weakness. He'd been good at it before his transformation but after, well, she wouldn't be surprised if his supernatural gifts included an enhanced ability to sniff out an enemy's flaws.

She had to play this perfectly.

Vaeron stalked another candelabra. The orange-robed Slate Priests that stood guard had shrunk back into the shadows, doing their best to seem like statues. The priests knew Vaeron's moods; they, too, were acting to type. "I told her to search for two hours, and if she found nothing, to return to the temple."

"You did," Fylomene agreed.

"So where is she?"

"Finding another grimy dress to put on?"

Vaeron ground his teeth, fists clenched, and he paused before the next candelabra, as though thinking. He peered sideways at Fylomene, and she braced herself. Was this where his erratic, supernatural senses sniffed out her secret? Fylomene should have just killed the Ringblade. Or brought her back in chains.

What had she been thinking?

"Well I'm not waiting on her," Vaeron said. "Venisha is flying over the ocean. I'll not be left behind."

That was the first he'd mentioned the dragon god's intentions. Fylomene was dying to know what they'd talked about, but to ask Vaeron was to invite an explosion.

"You realize," he continued through his teeth, starting toward her. "He has no need to keep us around. We must prove ourselves to him. He has risen, destroyed the Whisper Prince, and he will take Thiara for his own as he promised, as *we* promised we would do *for* him. Do you see how this makes us look?"

"Because we didn't kill the Whisper Prince ourselves?"

He showed teeth.

Strangely, this made Fylomene begin to relax. The main objective was no longer the Whisper Prince, which meant—especially now that Vaeron had his brother in hand—that the others didn't matter so much. He might even forget completely that there had been a Ringblade in the Whisper Prince's group.

"We must earn our place at his side again," Vaeron continued. "And here we are waiting for my idiot sister. Again!" He paced away from her and then back, and something seemed to occur to him then. He glanced at the eastern door of the audience chamber, a door that went down to the subterranean torture cells, and a small smile flickered on his lips. He glanced at her, and the smile vanished.

She raised an eyebrow, and regarded the door, the one she'd noted had no Slate Priests guarding it. When she looked back at him, Vaeron was stalking away once more.

Had that been guilt on his face? Was there something in the cells that he didn't want Fylomene to know about?

"I'm done waiting. With Venisha, we hardly need Pliothe's skills. I wouldn't be surprised if he stripped her of her powers for her negligence. Come. We're leaving Pliothe behind." He pulled Pliothe's teleportation square from his pouch and set it on the ground. "When Venisha hands out rewards, I plan to ask for her powers. I'm tired of always having to coax her along. It's been an annoyance for three centuries. Now it's nothing short of an embarrassment."

"Of course, my love," Fylomene said, stepping closer.

"I'm glad you had the sense to wear something practical. We're likely to be walking into a war. Venisha will take what is rightfully his, and woe to anyone who stands in his way."

"I am ready to serve, my love. As always."

"Good."

"I do have one question, though. Who's in the torture rooms?"

He actually twitched, then tried to look like he didn't know what she was talking about. "The torture rooms?"

"You found someone in your search. You brought them back. They're in the torture rooms. Who are they?"

His expression was caught somewhere between surprise and anger. His face couldn't seem to decide which to fall on, so she took the decision out of his hands.

"It's not the Whisper Prince. Did you find the assassin, or the drunken girl with the wisps of clothing and the hat?" she said, when she knew exactly which it must be.

It was a risk mentioning the Ringblade, of course, but a low-burning anger was building inside her. The Whisper Prince's drunken companion was beautiful. Crass and boorish, but truly striking. It would be just like Vaeron to take a fancy to her.

"Was there a girl with a hat?" he said.

She checked the urge to roll her eyes. By the Spirit, he was an abysmal liar.

"The one with the single red sash across her breasts and the skirt up to here." She placed two fingers high on her thigh. "And the hat. Surely you noticed the hat."

To her surprise, a bit of color came to his cheeks. He jutted his chin out.

So that was it. But why would he be embarrassed? Vaeron had had his share of women over the centuries, just as she'd had her fair share of men. Why would he feel guilty about this one? Had he raped the girl? He hadn't cared about such things in the past. This had to be something else. This had to be—

It hit her then. He'd found himself a queen. It was the only thing it could be, the only thing he would be reluctant to tell her.

Over the course of all these years, despite Fylomene's continuous devotion, Vaeron had never made her his queen. She had pouted over it for about a hundred years before she'd just accepted it. The only thing that had made it tolerable was that he had never married anyone else either. Probably because he'd known—rightly so—that Fylomene would have killed any mortal he'd chosen to take to wife.

That had just changed, and suddenly Fylomene didn't care about the danger of hiding Ree the Ringblade away, the danger of Venisha's return. Her focus narrowed down to a pinpoint, and the only thing she could think of was…"Who is she really?" she asked. "The drunken girl?"

"Drunken girl?" He tried to maintain his poor facade.

"The person in the torture cells isn't your brother. Clearly you found him." She nodded at the twitching hulk in Pliothe's Night Cage. "The Ringblade is just a Ringblade. But we don't know who the drunken girl is. I'm guessing she's royalty. A political piece of power. Somebody the King of Venisha could marry. Someone of consequence—"

"She is." A new voice came from across the room.

Vaeron and Fylomene whirled. A molten figure stood in the doorway that led to the torture rooms. She had the distinct silhouette of a woman, curved hips, breasts, but aside from that there was nothing human about her. Her flaming hair flowed down her head, and her body seemed comprised entirely of lava.

Even at this distance, Fylomene felt a wash of heat.

"I don't have a name," the woman said, "but I have been called many things. The name that caught your lover's interest, the name that made him want to use me for his purposes, is Mialene Doragon."

A quick glance at Vaeron told Fylomene he was just as stunned at the woman's molten appearance as she.

"But I'm done being used for another's purpose. That's not going to happen," the woman said. "Not ever again."

Ripples of flame licked up her body wave after wave as she stepped into the room, leaving melted footprints in the marble. In the marble!

She passed a pillar with the standard of the King of Venisha embroidered on it. It burst into flame, licking up the column.

Fylomene knew that if that woman got close enough, the heat alone would kill her. She backed up.

The molten woman flicked a glance at her. "Good choice." Then she turned her glowing yellow eyes to Vaeron.

"He's going to die. And if you're anywhere close to him, you're going to die as well."

Chapter Forty-Four

ADORA

Adora's soul wept when the fire awoke within her. She'd thought it had been taken away forever. She'd prayed she'd never feel again the way Velak had made her feel when he'd taken control of her: Righteous. Justified in doing murder. And so powerful that none could stand against her.

The fire had been ripped from her during Grei's fight in Benasca. He had demanded Velak let her go, and the Faia of Vengeance had done just that. He'd pulled his fire from her and, in his cruelty, returned her to what she'd been before he'd taken her: a ravaged body ripped open from neck to groin by Lyndion's knife.

The loss of that magical fire had been the most exquisitely painful thing she'd ever felt...until Grei brought her back to life. She'd been forced to look directly into the face of what she'd done.

That was the main reason she'd tried to kill herself. Because of what she'd done. But also because of a fear that, deep inside, some part of Velak remained, some residue that could never be purged.

And if she ever got angry again—truly angry—would she be able stop herself from murdering again?

So in the wake of her inability to take the final trip beyond this life, she'd turned her face away from her rage. She'd drunk herself silly and adopted a personality that never got angry, a personality that just went along wherever Grei led her.

And she'd been right to fear. Velak's fire *was* still there, locked behind a thick door inside her, but Vaeron's domination of her inserted the key into the lock. His torture blew the door wide open.

It was the last thing she wanted, the thing she would have killed herself to stop. So Adora's soul wept as the fire swept through her.

The rest of her wanted to kill.

After burning the two guards and the priests, she'd gone hunting for the focus of her rage, and she'd found him. The woman with him—Fylomene, was it?—backed away, obviously feeling the heat of Adora's rage even at this distance.

"Good choice," Adora said. "He's going to die. And if you're anywhere close to him, you're going to die as well."

Vaeron snarled, drawing his sword and a dagger.

"Oh yes. Please yes."

"I am King Vaeron, Slate Wizard and chosen of the god Venisha. You will heel, bitch, or you will die." He flung a dagger at her. The man knew his craft. It flew in a blur, flipped expertly end over end, straight toward the shoulder of the arm she'd raised—

And melted, molten steel running down her arm and side.

She laughed, pointed a finger at him. Fire burst across the room. It obscured her vision for an instant, and when it fell away, she expected the bastard's eyeballs to be running out of his skull.

But the spitting, hissing bolt of fire hit the pillar behind him instead. A six-foot-tall candelabra flashed into a bronzy vapor. The rock pillar bubbled and melted, a six-foot section of it dripping and falling away entirely, leaving the top of the pillar sticking down like a broken tooth. The vaulted ceiling high overhead shuddered.

Vaeron wasn't there.

Had he vaporized?

She tracked right, caught him running toward the woman, Fylomene. His armor glowed with the heat. His hair smoldered. Somehow he had moved fast enough to avoid the fire.

Adora had been certain he would stand and face her, that he would arrogantly rely on his supernatural abilities. It would have been so satisfying to watch him burn up, an idiot to the last.

She had no idea how he'd moved so fast that he'd evaded her vision, but his escape wouldn't last.

He dove, snatched something off the floor, rolled, and came to his feet still running. He caught up with Fylomene, who'd had the good sense to flee but the ill luck to have Vaeron run in her direction. Well, that was too bad.

Vaeron grabbed her arm, jerking her forward. She stumbled at his inhuman pace. He ducked behind another pillar, keeping it between them and Adora.

"Don't you want to 'bring me to heel,' your majesty?" she demanded, moving into the center of the room. "You seemed so eager to play with me when I was tied down. Come, King of Venisha. Come touch my leg now!"

He literally picked Fylomene up by one arm now. The air rippled with heat waves. The tapestries on the pillars between Adora and Vaeron burst into flame.

She lunged to the left and saw them both. Fylomene looked terrified. She squinted at the heat. Her face was flushed. Her clever little cape was smoldering. Too bad.

Adora pointed. Flame arced toward them.

But again Vaeron was faster. He hauled Fylomene into a dive, wrapping her up in his big arms and awkwardly rolling over her as he half-protected her from the tumble, then came to his feet and kept running like she was some life-sized doll.

A six-foot tall chunk of the pillar melted away. This time, the pillar above the melted section cracked off at the top, unable to support its own weight, and crashed point-first into the ground. The entire building shuddered. Chunks of ceiling began to fall.

"There's nowhere to go," Adora said.

Vaeron ducked behind yet another pillar, but she anticipated that, sidestepping the opposite direction. She caught him as he rounded the pillar.

Their gazes locked. She lowered her finger.

The hulking black knight, twitching and spasming, leapt in front of Vaeron and Fylomene.

Adora hesitated.

She had overheard a snatch of conversation as she'd come up the stairwell from the torture room. Fylomene, clearly angry with Vaeron for the "business" he'd attended in the torture rooms, had let slip that the black knight was Blevins.

The kingdom of Venisha loved its magical artifacts, and it took Adora all of a second to realize that the armor was magical. Probably some kind of torture device itself, meant to turn the person inside into a puppet. All that twitching was Blevins trying to fight his way out.

Now he stood between her and her target. Her heart flared, wanting to just incinerate him. He was in her way. That was what he deserved.

"No..." she growled, her arm trembling. No, she couldn't incinerate Blevins.

Vaeron threw something square on the ground, the thing he'd snatched up in his spectacular dive roll.

He was fifty paces away, but she'd seen that artifact before. Lyndion had used a metal box just like that to teleport her to the Night Mountains. Right before he gutted her.

The artifact spat pale blue lightning. The doorway opened up.

"No!" Adora shrieked. She shot an arc of flame.

Vaeron dove through the portal, yanking Fylomene with him. Blevins charged after. The fire reached them. The portal crackled and closed.

The flame roared into the ground, melting the stones and slamming into the wall behind it, which also melted. Adora blinked, hoping to see Vaeron's melted corpse, but there was nothing there.

They had escaped.

She turned her face to the ceiling and screamed. Fire erupted from her entire body, shooting upward in a column as wide as the pillars she had melted. It struck the ceiling, blowing a hole through the top.

The ceiling shuddered and collapsed on top of her.

Chapter Forty-Five

GREI

Grei stared at the dead grass on the fallen corpse of Devorra. The whispers thrummed through him. The magnitude of the moment hung heavy in the air. Devorra's vitality—the life-force of a goddess—had flowed into him. Pliothe had shoved his heart, covered with Devorra's essence, back into his body and sewed it up. Somehow, whatever had been left of Devorra had entered him. That moss or grass had acted like a reservoir, and the goddess's potency now poured into Grei like water siphoned through a tube.

He felt like he was standing outside himself, like his "soul" hovered ten feet over his head. He looked down on the corpse of the dragon from that height. It appeared more like an ordinary hill with every second that passed. He wondered if there had once been a thousand gods and if, one by one, they had all laid down to die, creating grassy meadows. Mountain ranges. Oceans.

He should have raged at her death. Should have cried. Something.

Instead, he felt a strange, pervading peace, perhaps for the first time in his life.

His overwhelming fear from just a moment ago—that

Grei the mortal man had died forever—suddenly seemed petty. He could still feel that fear fluttering about him, but it was outside himself, like butterflies he could choose to ignore.

He knew exactly what he needed to do.

He was no longer worried about correcting the mistakes of the Faia, of Kuruk. He wasn't concerned about mending the destruction Velak had wrought across the Thiaran Empire, or even the ugly mess the Slate Wizards had made of the kingdom of Venisha.

He felt like he had one hand still in the flowing green he'd been immersed in after his death. Everything was going to be all right.

Only one thing prickled him, a need with a sharpened point. It itched between his shoulder blades, a wrong he had to set right.

Adora.

If he could do right by Adora, he must. If she was Vaeron's captive, he must free her. If she wished to die, he would protect her while she made that decision. He owed her that much. He didn't need to correct everyone else's mistakes. Just his own.

He would find Adora. That was the first step. Beyond that, all other steps would come in their own time.

He whispered to the wind and it lifted him up, as much a part of him as his own arm. He turned toward the smoky, gray-shrouded city in the distance. The moon lingered along the western horizon. He felt the sun below the distant waters of the Sunset Sea, waiting.

He sensed something else then, a small and nervous little life below him, surrounded by even smaller lifeforms, each of them keyed to her misery.

Ah, yes. Pliothe. He had forgotten little Pliothe.

She looked up at him, head cocked sideways. Her large, childlike eyes were filled with an old sadness, a sadness she did not expect would ever change. The girl lived inside a webwork of scars, longing for one thing she had never received. Her metallic animals—her ghoulish attempts to create friends for herself—clustered around her as though trying to make her feel better.

He should hate her. She was a Slate Wizard, and the Slate Wizards had attacked Thiara. She had mutilated and transformed Uriozi. She had tried to transform Grei. But in this sublime moment where the peace of a dying goddess had seeped into Grei's blood, he saw her clearly without the obstruction of fear or hatred. She had committed atrocities, it was true. But so had he.

He thought of how he had played the villain in Adora's life. He thought of how many people had been killed by the red mist Grei had let loose.

"We are two of a kind, aren't we?" he said to her.

He bid the wind lift her up, and she rose into the air alongside him. As an afterthought, he lifted up all of her little creatures as well. They squeaked and swirled in the wind, but the look of gratitude on Pliothe's face was like watching a flower open its petals. She smiled shyly, and he wondered just how much this poor girl had endured.

"Friend..." she murmured.

"Let's go do something good, shall we?"

"What is good?" she asked earnestly.

He opened his mouth to answer, then stopped. "Yeah. I suppose you're right. Then let us do something that feels good to our souls."

"Soul," she said, and she smiled.

They flew toward the city. The wind held them aloft in a gentle, buffeting embrace. They soared toward the last place Grei had seen Adora, that old factory.

When they'd been in Fairmist, Grei had kept one piece of his attention on Adora at all times, just in case she tried to sneak away and kill herself. He thought about doing the same thing, about trying to reestablish that connection, but that method felt tainted. It felt like picking up the end of a leash he'd already let go.

No. He would find her without having to create any unholy attachments.

The city was coming to life, early risers getting up before the sun, preparing for the day. Grei brought his little group to hover over the old factory with the hole in the roof. There were no lifeforms in there. Adora had not returned.

The butterflies of urgency flapped close to him, but that sense of destiny still pervaded him. Everything was moving in its own time.

"Where do you think she went?" he asked Pliothe. Her beatific smile had grown smaller, but it still remained at the corner of her lips, like she was happy about something she'd thought she'd never be happy about again. She pointed.

He followed her gesture toward the massive pyramid that crouched in the center of the city. The Slate Temple.

"Is that where he'd take her?"

She nodded.

"Then I guess that's where—"

In the predawn light, he spotted a flicker of flame at the edge of the pyramid. A window in the side of the sloped wall flickered orange and red. The glass blew out, and a tongue of flame licked up the side of the pyramid, then vanished.

Grei narrowed his eyes.

"Do they light big fires in the pyramid?"

Pliothe's serious expression had returned. She shook her head.

"I think that's where we need to—"

The pointed top of the pyramid glowed, smoked, and then erupted, blowing chunks of molten stone into the air.

"By the Faia!" Grei murmured. For the first time since Devorra's spirit had infused him, the veil of serenity pulled back, and he felt surprise. His first thought was that this was some bizarre ritual created by the Slate Wizards, but what kind of regular ritual would blow the top off the entire ancient pyramid?

"Fire," Pliothe said.

"Come on," Grei replied.

The wind pushed them toward the Slate Temple.

Chapter Forty-Six

ADORA

Adora's rage melted solid stone. Everything flammable in the entire audience chamber burned to ash. The stone overhead cascaded like a molten waterfall. The ceiling yawned open, revealing the predawn sky.

She screamed again and let all of her rage course through her. A column of pure fire shot through the fifty-foot hole above her.

She let her hands fall to her sides and glared around the audience chamber. The priests had fled. There was nothing left except the slate throne at the far end of the chamber. The thick rug that had extended from the double doors on one end of the room to the dais on the other had burned up, leaving only smoldering nubs close to the door and the steps. All the wall hangings had burned away or were in the process of doing so. She moved her baleful gaze around the room, looking for anything to focus her anger on.

Something moved above. She clenched her fist, looking up—

Grei and the girl Pliothe, along with her little entourage of mechanical vermin, descended through the center of the glowing ceiling. The heat didn't seem to bother any of them.

Grei. Floating. Grei, immune to the heat. That could mean only one thing. He'd found his whispers. How did you burn a man who could ask fire to be cool?

He and his group alighted softly on the ground.

"You just make friends wherever you go, don't you?" she asked.

Now that he was closer, she could see he didn't look to be in the best of shape. The front of his tunic had been ripped open, exposing his chest. Except it wasn't his chest. It was a mess of tightly woven wires that plunged into his flesh. Adora glanced at the girl, back at Grei, and narrowed her eyes. "Did she get you, Grei? Like Uriozi. Who am I talking to?"

"It's me," Grei said. "Or most of me, anyway. Or maybe it's not me at all. I'm beginning to think that I never really was *just me*. I might actually be the lever of destiny your prophecy painted me to be."

"Not my prophecy."

"Regardless, I'm not sure I ever really had a choice about anything, least of all who I am."

She raised an eyebrow, which he probably couldn't even see. Adora had looked down at herself after she'd burned out of her restraints in the torture room. Not only had her skirt and top immediately burned off—even her hat, hung in the corner of the room, had turned to ash—but her entire body looked like molten lava. Which probably meant no eyebrows.

"I'm not going to get rid of you," she said, "am I?"

He became solemn. Pliothe seemed like she was trying to curl into herself and vanish. Her head was down, her neck bent almost at a comical angle, and she stared at the floor.

"Actually, I came to rescue you," he said.

"Of course you did."

"From Vaeron. So you could make your own choice about living or dying."

That made her pause.

"I've seen it, what's on the other side. I'm not afraid for you to take that step anymore. It's a better place than here." He paused. "In some ways. I had a taste of it."

"Did you?" She glanced at his chest, then at Pliothe. The girl continued to stare at the floor.

"It's beautiful. It's…the opposite of here, the opposite of struggle. And you've struggled so much." He closed his eyes as though the thought pained him. "I wronged you. I was so bent on serving what I thought was justice. I wanted so much to give you what I thought you deserved, I ignored what you wanted. That was a villainous mistake, and I came to make sure that no one could ever cage you again."

Her brows came down, and she watched him.

"I'm sorry, Adora," he said. "By all that's holy, I'm so sorry. I told myself I didn't want you to die because I was helping you. But the truth is, I didn't want you to go because I didn't want to be alone. It was selfish, and I'm sorry."

Adora tried to get a handle on this situation. Grei had left with his power in shambles, barely able to pry his grip from her. Now he had returned with as much magical ability as ever, telling her he'd just stand back and let her die.

"You've had a change of heart," she said, casting a wry glance at his chest. The heat coming off her arms and shoulders lessened.

He smirked, and she felt its warmth. "I met two gods. One killed the other, then killed me. Pliothe brought me back."

"So you've had a day," she said.

"I did."

"And you regained your Whisper Prince abilities."

"And then some."

"Really?"

"Yes."

"So…what are you going to do?"

"Apologize to you. Make sure no one can stop you from doing what you want to do. That was the extent of my initial agenda."

"And after that?"

"I hadn't thought about it. You were the only thing that was important enough for me to come back."

"From death?"

He nodded.

She sighed. "You make it really hard to hate you."

"It's a romantic line, isn't it?"

Her flames lowered a little more.

"I love you, Adora. If you tell me to go now, I will leave. Clearly, you don't need me to protect you."

"You'd better stop saying such nice things, or pretty soon I'm going to be standing here naked." The hate in her heart quieted further. The flames receded. Now her body was a swirl of lava with a flash of naked flesh across her legs, her belly.

"Ah. Your clothes were the first casualty."

He pulled off his ragged tunic with the giant hole in the middle, handed it to her.

The orange and yellow molten color of her skin solidified, returning her skin to its natural bronze color. She took the tunic, pulled it on. Grei was larger than her, and the tunic made a dress that was a bit longer than the brief skirt that had burned away. She held the gaping hole in the front together with one hand.

"This is disgusting." She daintily touched the blood-soaked edges of the hole in his tunic.

He watched her, and the silence became uncomfortable. She felt she should either kiss him or scream at him to leave. Neither seemed quite right. So she spoke instead.

"A god just landed outside this temple," she said. "Vaeron and Fylomene have gone to Thiara."

He shook his head. "I'm here for you."

"So if I tell you to leave me here—"

"Then I'll leave you here."

"And go where?"

He shrugged. "Find Ree. Find Blevins."

"And you don't care about Thiara."

"I've decided to care about one thing at a time."

"Grei, what are you going to do?" she pressed.

"What are *you* going to do?" he countered.

She hung her head. Her heart warmed, and a flame flickered across her hand, but this time she wasn't angry with anyone but herself. She kept asking what he was going to do, but she hadn't yet made her own choices. She'd wanted to die after what she'd done with Velak's power, but here she was doing it again. And it actually didn't feel horrible this time. Vaeron had deserved to die, and she didn't feel bad about attacking him.

And she had to face the facts. She'd had a chance to kill herself at the dock, and she'd hesitated. She'd paused just long enough so that the decision had been taken from her. When she'd had the chance to end it all, what had she done?

She'd thought of Grei.

She sighed softly, and raised her head. "You win."

"Adora, I didn't come to win—"

"You kept me around long enough that when I had the chance to kill myself, I didn't want to. You made me remember that there were still things I wanted to live for."

"I'm sorry."

They stood there in silence. Pliothe hadn't moved. Finally, with a sigh and a smile, Adora extended her hand.

He looked at it, startled.

"Maybe we can be sorry together," she said. "Talk about all the things we're sorry about."

He swallowed, eyes wide.

"Take my hand, Grei."

He did. His callused fingers were warm and strong in hers.

"Let's do this together," she said.

"Do what?"

"Oh don't be stupid. You're the Whisper Prince. We're going back to Thiara. We're going to destroy Venisha."

"Is that what we're doing?"

"Yes." She started walking toward the double doors, hand in hand with him. Pliothe followed, her head finally raised.

"Let's get Ree first," Grei said. "And Blevins."

"Vaeron has Blevins."

"Let's get him second."

"And some pants," she said.

He laughed. "Yes. Pants first."

Chapter Forty-Seven

REE

Ree's entire body hurt. The room was so cold, the blanket so rough. She shivered uncontrollably beneath the thin blanket made out of, it seemed, nettles.

On a bench at the foot of the bed lay another thick blanket. She felt she should sit up, try and pull it over herself, but she was too weak. She could barely muster the strength to keep her eyelids open. Closing them would have been fine, except she couldn't sleep. She longed to slip into a deep slumber, but her body hurt so much she couldn't. Her muscles ached. Her neck felt two times too thick, and it was getting hard to breathe, like her chest was getting smaller and smaller.

Her teeth chattered. She really should sit up and get the blanket.

I will, she told herself. *I'll get up in a moment.*

But she didn't, and a part of her began to think she would never get up again.

The woman, Fylomene, had said she would send help, would send someone to care for her, but no one had come.

I'm getting weaker. Soon, I'll just...die.

She opened her mouth, trying to get more air. She thought about Grei. She'd tried to protect him, but she had failed. He was somewhere in this city, wandering around, doing his Grei thing. Not thinking about consequences or any kind of strategic approach to his adventures, just bumbling into something, relying on his magic—or luck—to save him. She needed to be there to help him. He needed her. But she couldn't move.

She saw his visage on the ceiling, saw him get blasted out of the Blue Faia's cavern, saw him fall into the lake. He'd have drowned if she hadn't been there. She saw him fighting Velak. She'd been there to pull him to safety. Who was going to pull him to safety if she died?

She saw Grei walking toward the Blue Faia's waterfall. Except this time Grei was blue. Blue hair. Blue eyebrows. Light blue skin. He was trying to convince the Blue Faia of something, but she shook her head.

Ree's gaze drifted to the other side of the room. Grei was there, too. She saw him creeping into the window of the Lateral House. He startled as he saw her, her deadly ringblade in hand. This time he was green. Green eyebrows. Green hair. Light green skin. He held his hands up in surrender. But then he was talking to the Green Faia, not to Ree. His words were gibberish, but the Green Faia seemed to understand him. Whisper Prince speech.

Her gaze drifted down to the far side of the room, the wall. Grei was there, too, beyond the foot of the bed. This time he was red. Red hair. Red eyebrows. Pink skin. And he was talking to Velak, who shook his finger.

I'm hallucinating, Ree thought.

The fact that she hadn't noticed she was hallucinating until the third Grei apparition was concerning.

What was I doing before? I was going to do something. I should focus on that. Something other than illusions of Grei.

Teeth chattering, her gaze fell on the foot of the bed. The thick blanket lay there, easily within reach if she could just sit up.

That's right. I was going to get the blanket. I should get the blanket.

But the very thought of sitting up was exhausting.

I'll get it in a moment. I'm just going to wait...just a moment.
She let her gaze drift to the ceiling again.

Green Grei smiled at her, looking innocent and frightened like he had in the Lateral House. But determined. By the Faia, the boy had been determined even when he was shaking in his boots.

"You shouldn't be in here," she murmured to him. That was nice. That was better than letting her teeth just chatter. Except it was wrong. That wasn't what she had said to him in the Lateral House. He had grinned like a boy after he'd climbed through the window that no one should have been able to climb through, no one except the Ringblades. He'd been grinning at the way the city had been sideways. He'd been grinning, and she had said what? What had she said...?

"Are you amused?" she murmured.

Yes, that was right. That was what she'd said to get his attention. Talking was so hard. She imagined it was almost as hard as getting that blanket. She let her eyes slide shut, but then the pains in her body increased, so she opened them again.

Right. Right. She had to focus. She had to get that blanket.

What had she said next? He had stood there, quaking in his boots, and she had prompted him again.

"How did you get through that window?" she whispered.

A new Grei approached her bed, leaned over her, closer than the others. This one wasn't a specific color. Just normal-person color.

What did Grei say then? He'd said something then.
Kill me then.
That's what he'd said.

"Are you slinked?" she had replied.

No. No, he'd said something before that. He'd told her to kill him after she'd ricocheted her ringblade off the walls and it had rebounded into her hand. He'd said something before that. What was it?

"How did you get through that window?" she whispered again, trying to remember. Yes. Yes. What had he said?

Grei leaned closer, the one that wasn't blue. He actually had brown hair, normal skin, and dark eyes. Like the real Grei.

"I'm looking for answers." He smiled.

That's right! That was what he'd said. Except Grei hadn't smiled. She'd kept him on his heels, dazzling and dismissing him. A kiss and a cut.

"A kiss and a cut..." she murmured.

"A kiss and a cut," he repeated, copying her tone. "I remember. Just hold still."

It felt like someone was pouring warm water inside her, chasing away the chill. As it spread, the delusions of Grei popped like Fairmist droplets. All save the one leaning over her bed. Behind him, Ree now saw Adora. The princess was dressing quietly in the corner of the room, hiking a pair of breeches the last little bit over her hips. She then stripped out of a tunic, one with a bloody hole in the middle, and reached for a fresh one.

On the other side of the bed stood the creepy little girl who had sent an army of metal roaches and rats to bite Ree.

She blinked. Strength returned to her extremities.

"By the Faia," she gasped. She sat up, but she no longer wanted the blanket. It was actually hot in this room.

"That was a nasty infection." Grei raised his hands, and that blessed warmth receded.

"A gift from her." Ree nodded at Pliothe. "Are we friends now?"

Grei glanced at the girl. "Some enemies are more so than others."

"You wouldn't be you if you didn't keep changing the rules," Ree said.

"This is Pliothe."

Adora came forward from the back of the room. She'd switched her bloody tunic for a black one. It was a little big on her, but she'd belted it at the waist, making it a kind of dress over the breeches. She pulled the drawstrings on the shirt tight, knotting it at the top. No floppy hat. No short skirt and sash anymore. No wineskin of ale. And Grei was acting like the Whisper Prince. Clearly, they'd undergone some transformations while Ree had been quietly burning up.

She turned, put her feet on the ground where Pliothe was, and stood up. The girl backed away, looking at the floor. Her army of bugs and rats clustered tightly around her, as though ordered to stay as far away from Ree as they could. A peace offering?

"I'm sorry," Pliothe said in a tiny voice.

Ree extended her hand. "If Grei trusts you, I will."

Pliothe looked up shyly, then extended her little hand. They shook. The girl beamed, and Ree logged the information away. The girl wouldn't be the first to have been pressed into service doing something she didn't like. Ree had been in that position before. She'd betrayed Grei over it. And now she was his loyal comrade. Perhaps Pliothe had taken the same journey. Grei had a way of doing that to people.

"Where's Blevins?" Ree asked.

"King Idiot has him," Adora said.

Ree raised her eyebrows. "Oh, I think I like that name."

Adora grinned.

"And the woman? Fylomene?" Fylomene had been kind to her. She'd put Ree here, and that had probably saved her life. "We may have another ally in King Idiot's court."

"Really?" Grei raised his eyebrows.

"She could have killed me. Could have tortured me. Where are they now?"

"We aren't sure—"

"They're in Thiara," Adora interjected.

Grei gave her a sidelong glance.

Ree looked at Adora, then at Grei, then at Adora. "You two patched things up?"

Adora shook her head, but she was smiling.

"Not a patch," Grei said. "Let's call it the beginning of a whole new garment."

Adora gave the sidelong glance this time.

"Well aren't we domestic?" Ree said, but relief spread through her. Watching Grei and Adora at the Thiaran palace had been like watching the fragile bud of a flower get stepped on and ground into the dirt. It had hurt deep in Ree's bones.

To now see them being playful with each other was like spring had come again, a second chance.

"So what are we doing?" Ree asked.

Grei shrugged. "I suppose we return to Thiara, perhaps somewhere out of the way, somewhere that we don't have to be in the conflagration—"

"We're going after King Idiot," Adora said.

"I don't know that creating a magical war that could result in untold destruction upon—"

"I think you're funny pretending that you aren't aching to thump King Vaeron on the nose," Adora said. "Tell me you're not."

"That's not—"

"Go ahead. Try to convince me you're going to leave Blevins encased in a suit of armor that yanks him about like a marionette. Go ahead."

Grei looked plaintively at Ree, who could not hide her smile. "She's become a little snippy, don't you think?"

"I'm not getting in the midst of your bickering." Ree held up her hands. "So it's Thiara?"

"Apparently it's Thiara," Grei said.

"*Apparently*," Adora murmured under her breath, shaking her head.

"How?"

Grei held up The Root. "This."

"Isn't that what threw us into Venisha in the first place?"

"Yes. It drove me to Devorra. It caused me to free her and thereby free Venisha."

Ree wrinkled her brow. "The city?"

"The god."

"The god?" Her eyebrows went up.

"It's a story. Imagine the great-grandfather of the Faia. Except mean like the Slate Wizards. And really angry."

"That doesn't sound good."

Grei grunted and nodded.

"And that thing brought you to him."

He nodded.

"So why are you holding it?"

"Because I've learned a few things since Venisha lured me here. I've kept it, but I haven't actually touched it." He turned his hand sideways to show that there was a pocket of air between his fingers and The Root. Solid air. That had been one of the first tricks Grei had learned.

"I see."

"I'm going to have to touch it to use it. If I'm quick, I am betting he's not going to have time to react."

"Why not?"

"Well, for one, he thinks I'm dead because he did, in fact, kill me." He nodded at Pliothe. "I'm only alive because of her. Second, I'm pretty sure he's going to be focusing on whatever he's doing in Thiara. It's taken him a long time to get there, and now he thinks he has eliminated all his opponents. Third, I'm convinced he meticulously planned the lure that brought me here, and he hasn't planned for my return. If we move, we'll have the element of surprise."

"Well, all right," Ree said.

Adora winked at her. "Whisper Prince stuff. He's good at that."

Ree chuckled.

"We have to be fast," Grei said.

"Fast?" Ree said, getting into the mood of the room. "You're talking to a Ringblade, sir."

"They're going to kill us," Pliothe said in her small voice.

"You don't have to come, Pliothe," Grei said. "You should stay here—"

Even as he said it, Pliothe moved to his side, worming between him and Adora like she was afraid she would get left behind. Her creatures scurried over to form a cluster behind the three of them. "Friend," she murmured, looking at her boots.

Ree moved around the bed, pulling her weapons belt from the foot of the bed and belting it around her waist. She came to stand next to them. "I think that says it all."

Grei let The Root drop into his hand. "Is everyone ready?"

"You said fast," Adora said. "Stop yapping."

He chuckled, then flipped open the hatch.

Chapter Forty-Eight

FYLOMENE

The killing fire roared overhead, then cut off abruptly as the teleportation cube crackled and the magical doorway blessedly slammed shut. Fylomene hit the cobblestones hard. Pain fired into her elbow, her shoulder, and her hip as she awkwardly rolled. She smacked her head against the stone, and stars burst in her vision. Groaning, she turned over on her side, frantically patting her hair and face. The heat had been so intense at the Slate Temple, practically everything had burst into flame. She was stunned, and gratified, that the hair on her head was still there.

It was still uncomfortably hot, as was her face and every part of her body, but miraculously she didn't seem burned. She drew a blessed breath of the now-cool air, blinked, and looked about for Vaeron.

Her lover was on his feet already, fists clenched, casting about for someone to rage at. His gaze hadn't fallen on her yet, and she looked quickly away. Looking dazed and helpless wouldn't stop Vaeron from abusing her, but it often helped.

His newfound princess had humiliated him. She'd chased him around his own audience chamber, in his own temple, and almost killed him at least three times. And he'd fled her like a frightened child.

Smoke rose off him in patches where her killing heat had struck him. His right forearm was blackened, his tunic had been burned onto his back, and his left cheek smoldered.

Vaeron had never been so thoroughly beaten. Not since his spats with Baezin when they were young men.

Still trapped with the Night Cage, Baezin lay on the cobblestones, arching his back in pain. His backplate glowed orange where he had taken the brunt of the last strike, shielding her and Vaeron. Baezin's armored hands lifted helplessly, unable to reach his back nor remove the armor that was now burning. He made no sound because the Night Cage would not let him.

Vaeron's gaze fell on the writhing Baezin and stalked toward the suffering man. Vaeron drew his sword and tucked it underneath his mute brother's chin. When Vaeron suffered, someone else always had to pay for it. His shoulders hunched as he prepared to bring the sword around in an arc to lop off Baezin's head.

"Don't do it," Fylomene said. She couldn't believe the words coming out of her mouth. What was wrong with her? She had already risked her life for one of the Whisper Prince's companions. Surely that was enough for the day, enough for a lifetime. The most certain way to bring Vaeron's wrath down upon herself was to interrupt his tantrum.

Vaeron spun, forgetting about Baezin and stalking toward her, sword held low and deadly.

"You don't want to do that," she said, trying not to sound panicked and grasping at the only thing that might stop him.

Vaeron grabbed her by the throat and lifted her into the air. She gripped his thick forearm, choking.

"You told me…" she wheezed past his grip "…that you wanted to make him suffer…when you finally caught him."

Vaeron's face was burned along the left side, the skin red from cheek to ear. The hair on that side had also been singed down to the scalp.

"What?" he roared.

"If you...kill him now," Fylomene choked, "he...stops suffering."

Vaeron showed his teeth.

"Let him...suffer...."

That thought punched through Vaeron's rage.

His grip loosened, and she knew the danger was past. "Later?"

"Yes, my love," she choked. "Don't end his suffering so...quickly."

He nodded once, curtly, and dropped her.

She fell awkwardly to her feet, stumbling and gasping, but she managed to stay upright. She rubbed her throat. It wasn't the first time he'd choked her.

What was she doing? What did she care if Baezin lost his head? Why was she risking her life on these whims? Baezin. Ree. There was no reason for her to continue flirting with death. Why was she doing it?

"So...your princess?" She massaged her throat gently. "Did you know she could do that?"

"A woman with such powers burned her way across Amarion, killing the Faia. My spies had told me as much. I didn't know it was her. These Thiarans make me want to raze this empire to the ground. What kind of place is this where magic pops up at random?"

As opposed to being put squarely into your hands, my love? she thought, but did not say.

"How long will it take Venisha to fly here, do you think?"

"He is a god. It will take him as long as he wants it to take him."

"So...soon."

He grunted again. Baezin had stopped writhing. His armor had cooled, and he stood up again. He didn't twitch now. Perhaps the pain of his burns had tamped down his desire to fight.

"How would you like to play this, my love?" she asked. "You have the Black Faia stashed in the palace. Should we make her ready for his consumption? Or…"

She left the sentence hanging, but the meaning was clear. Did Vaeron want to offer the blue roses up to his god? Or try to keep them? She knew he didn't relish the idea of relinquishing power. The question was, would he bend the knee in all things, or try to hold back?

Vaeron stood still, in thought.

"Let's get her," he finally said.

People wisely fled before them as they entered the palace. It was still in disarray after their attack and, previously, the Whisper Prince's coup. With Vaeron seething and the forbidding Baezin following in his black armor, no one challenged them. They vanished so thoroughly, the palace seemed deserted.

The three of them swept down the hall toward the room where Pliothe had secured the Black Faia.

A charred skeleton lay outside the door, face-down and grinning at the floor.

"Someone tried to get in," Vaeron said with satisfaction.

Pliothe had placed an artifact on the center of the door which incinerated any intruder with lightning if they tried the handle and did not speak the password.

Vaeron kicked the skeleton out of the way, watching with a grim smile as the charred bones tumbled and scattered. But his smile soured when he was forced to speak Pliothe's childish password.

"Friend," he growled. It was the word she always chose.

He turned the handle, and no deadly fork of lightning leapt from the box. He pushed the door wide, and it slammed into the wall.

Inside there was a canopied bed, a chest of drawers, a wardrobe, and a basin with a mirror. The giant arched window overlooked the Sunset Sea and the courtyard below,

# The Slate Wizards

and Uriozi huddled in the corner where they'd left her, a web of razor lines trapping her in the corner like a metal spider's web. They originated from another of Pliothe's boxes. It sat on the floor about three feet in front of the transformed Uriozi.

The Faia didn't seem interested in moving, though. Pliothe's creatures were never the same after she had infused them with her metal-and-flesh transformation. Pliothe's control over them seemed exactly like the Night Cage.

Vaeron paused inside the doorway, thinking as he stared at the tiny creature. Uriozi's metallic eyes flicked up to look at him.

Fylomene risked speaking. "Is your intention to betray—"

"Hold your tongue," he said.

"Yes, my love."

"We play a long game here."

"A short game, in point of fact."

He glared at her.

"If you give him control of the blue roses now, you will never get them back. This is the moment. There won't be another. We were created to be his servants. But if you absorb the power of the blue roses, he will have to make a choice. Destroy you to get them, or allow you to wield them in his name."

"But second to him," he mused.

"Surely you did not expect anything else."

The idea of being second in anything was a bitter draught to Vaeron. It was inevitable the moment Venisha awoke, of course, but it was just like Vaeron to not have considered this before now.

And what about her? Had she truly considered what she wanted before this moment?

She thought of the determination in Ringblade Ree's eyes, the fierce love and loyalty she had for the Whisper Prince. It was the kind of devotion she'd always wanted to have for Vaeron. It was what she told herself she *did* have, that she would wade through his tantrums and tortures to serve him. That she would do anything for him. That her sun and moons hung in his orbit.

But Ree's devotion had shown Fylomene something different, that she had constantly been reaching for what she wanted from Vaeron. For three centuries she'd wanted to see herself as indispensable to Vaeron and his purposes, and there were fleeting moments she felt she'd succeeded. It was a constant aspiration. She wanted it, worked toward it....

Ree had it.

Fylomene suddenly realized this was why she hadn't captured or killed the woman. It was why Fylomene had protected her, hidden her. She'd seen something in Ree's eyes. A certainty. A willingness to die for the Whisper Prince without regret. A devotion of unquestioning love, and not hopeful desire.

That had sparked a question in Fylomene's mind that she had been mulling over ever since: What would her life be like if it wasn't centered on Vaeron?

"Let's move her," Vaeron said.

Fylomene snapped out of her reverie. "Where?"

"To a hiding place, woman," he snapped. "Somewhere Venisha will not know. Somewhere that will give me time to understand this Thiaran magic and take the roses from her. If the Whisper Prince can do it, then surely I can. Then, as you suggested, we will negotiate with Venisha for our place in the new order."

"Might I suggest—"

"No you may not," Vaeron snarled. "You will—"

"VAERON!"

Fylomene jumped. The voice was in the room, as though the air itself had shouted. Vaeron spun, his sword flashing out. Baezin did the same, pulling the two-handed sword from over his shoulder. His arms twitched.

But there was no one in the room except Vaeron, Baezin, the trapped Uriozi, and herself.

Her first thought was that it was Venisha's voice, but it didn't sound like him. It sounded like—

"The Whisper Prince," Vaeron completed her thought, moving to the window. She followed and saw four figures standing in the courtyard.

The supposedly dead Whisper Prince, Ringblade Ree, and Princess Mialene—now human again and dressed in oversized men's clothes—stood below.

And Pliothe was with them.

"Little traitor," Vaeron said through his teeth.

"So here we are." The Whisper Prince's voice spoke right next to them like he was in the room. Down below, a hundred yards away on the cobblestones, the Whisper Prince glanced around where their first battle had played out, where he had lost decidedly, barely escaping with his life and the lives of his friends. "Except this time I'm ready. This time we know each other's strengths. Shall we try this fight again?"

Vaeron glared down at them, and he said nothing.

"Or would you like to negotiate the surrender of Thiara back to me," the Whisper Prince's voice floated in the room.

Vaeron snarled. Across the distance, the Whisper Prince smiled.

"My love, wait—"

But there was no stopping Vaeron. He didn't see the odds stacked against him. All he saw was his anger. All he imagined was that he'd beaten the Whisper Prince once and could do it again.

"Vaeron!" Fylomene shouted as he leaped out the window. Baezin followed closely, both of them with swords drawn, as though swords were going to do anything against the Whisper Prince. Fylomene rushed forward, slamming into the windowsill as she watched helplessly.

Vaeron and Baezin hit the ground together, neither seeming to take any injury from the twelve-foot fall.

The Whisper Prince spoke again, his voice now coming from his actual mouth, rather than the air in the room. He said only one word as Vaeron and Baezin charged toward him.

"Good."

Chapter Forty-Nine

GREI

"It's almost like he wants us to win," Adora said as Vaeron and Baezin landed on the courtyard a hundred feet away.

"Perhaps he's implementing some strategy we can't see."

"I'm certain that's it," she said, raising an eyebrow.

Vaeron had attacked masterfully the first time they'd clashed: cut away the blue roses, bludgeoned Blevins nearly to death, and slashed Ree up good. Vaeron had nearly wiped out Grei and his friends in a matter of moments with strategic genius. But every move he'd made since then seemed the opposite. He kept using his strength and fighting prowess, like a musician who could only play one tune.

It dawned on Grei that Vaeron wasn't the strategist. It was Venisha. It had always been Venisha. The god had laid the plans here, had wielded the king like a sword, just as he'd wielded Grei like a knife to cut his bonds.

Grei focused his attention on the hissing that permeated Vaeron's body. He'd been studying Pliothe's creations, the way she wove magic together. The hissing was a demand, not a request like the whispers.

Grei had discovered early on that if he tried to lash the whispers to his will, the effort stole his intellect. If Venishan magic was the opposite of how to effectively use the whispers, it would explain why it was so difficult for Grei to master it.

He changed his perspective, thinking of the hissing like a web of wires lashed to a beast, forcing it to do whatever was demanded: the elements turned from willing partner to bound slave.

This was the nature of Venishan magic. *This* was what Pliothe used, what all the Slate Wizards used!

"Pliothe, can you release Blevins? Can you make that armor nothing more than armor?"

Pliothe nodded.

"Please do it."

"I'll take Vaeron." Adora leaned forward as the warriors sprinted toward them.

"Don't turn into flame," Grei said.

"Oh, *you* get to kill him?" Adora retorted.

"I'm not killing anyone."

"You always say that, and yet…"

"Stop. I never tried to kill anyone."

"Trying and doing are two different things. Look at me, for example—"

"Adora, stop."

"Fine."

Vaeron roared, bringing his sword down at Grei's head, but as fast as the man's sword was, it wasn't faster than a whisper. It cracked into air as hard as stone.

The blade rebounded, glancing off Vaeron's own head and nearly cutting off his ear.

Grei shrugged his shoulders, whispering, and the hard wall of air slammed into Vaeron, shoving him back violently. He skittered across the cobblestones like a turtle on its back.

Blevins's approach slowed to a walk, and he stopped right in front of Pliothe. She made little clenching gestures with her fingers, and her face squinched up. Blevins twitched inside the armor. The tip of his sword clinked to the ground.

Grei delved into the hissing that wrapped around Vaeron, who finally slid to a stop and flipped up to his feet.

"There it is," Grei murmured. With the great influx of power and knowing from Devorra, he could see the powerful and complicated spell that Venisha had woven around Vaeron. It was like little wires tightly wound around—and piercing through—every part of the king's body. They went through his muscles, organs, and bones. Those unseen magical wires sucked vitality from the life around Vaeron and pushed it into his muscles, bones, and blood, creating supernatural strength, speed, and the ability to regenerate.

Vaeron charged.

"King Idiot," Adora growled, clenching her fist.

"Stay beside me. Don't change," Grei said.

"I heard you the first time."

Grei held up his fist as he concentrated. Just whispering to the wires didn't do anything. They only shuddered and did not honor his request. Grei could understand the magic, but he needed to study it more to be able to use it. If he ever wanted to use it. The idea of enslaving the elements made him want to vomit.

Well, there was more than one way around a problem. He might not be able to work Venishan magic, but he could offset Vaeron's powers. He beseeched the wind to hit Vaeron, to drive at him, to constantly knock him off balance.

Vaeron faltered, stumbled, and crashed to his knees. His sword rang as it hit the stones, but he kept hold of it. He rolled and came to his feet. The king growled his displeasure.

Vaeron roared and charged again, bringing his sword overhead. Grei waited. The sword came down—

Blevins blocked it. Steel rang and the blades sparked.

Blevins shrugged powerfully, throwing Vaeron's blade back. He yanked the black helm off his head.

Vaeron glared furiously at Pliothe. "I'll kill you for your betrayal, sister!"

Pliothe hid her head between her own shoulders and looked at her boots guiltily.

Grei threw another invisible wall in front of Vaeron and took the brief respite to whisper to Blevins's horribly burnt body. He healed the skin and muscle that had melted to the inside of the black armor.

Blevins drew a long, slow breath. "Ah, Stormy. One of these days we're going to have to let each other die."

"One of these days," Grei said.

Blevins glanced at where his brother fought with Grei's wall of air, gave a death's head grin, and raised his sword again. "Let him go."

Grei whispered to the air wall. It dissipated. Vaeron, predictably, charged. Grei's standing spell knocked him sideways. He recovered. The wind shoved him forward. His supernatural reflexes compensated, but Grei gauged that the extra effort and unpredictability put Vaeron and Blevins on roughly equal footing.

"Shall we try this again, brother?" Blevins said.

"I will kill you this time!" Vaeron said.

Blevins brought his blade around, swinging low and then cutting upward. Vaeron shifted but was blown off balance by Grei's wind. Vaeron staggered back and, even with his supernatural speed, barely blocked the strike.

"You're just going to stand there and watch?" Adora asked Grei.

"I leveled the battlefield."

"And you feel that is enough?"

He hesitated, then nodded.

Adora glanced sidelong at him. "You really don't care about the outcome?"

He hesitated again, trying to understand the calm he felt. "I do…. Yes, I do care. Just not the same as before. I did what I could to restore the balance between them. That seems to be—"

"Enough?"

"It's a good word. This is the culmination of a pressure building between them for centuries. This is what needs to happen. It is—"

"Inevitable?"

"Another good word. Yes. That's what it is. After Devorra…I feel a drive to move toward the inevitable."

"How do you feel about the inevitable moving toward you?" She put a hand on his shoulder and pointed at the sky over the Sunset Sea.

The newly rising sun lit the enormous dragon as he landed in the surf. Water exploded on either side of him, throwing a thousand diamonds into the air.

Chapter Fifty

GREI

Grei felt a cold hand grip his guts. The stone dragon was at least as tall as the palace, casting a shadow that seemed to extend across the entire Sunset Sea as he stood, the waves churning around him. Grei's calm trickled away, and all he could think of was the god's tail spearing through his chest.

All of his mortal foibles suddenly seemed visible to him. Grei was just a boy from provincial Fairmist, the son of a shoemaker.

Venisha was a god.

"Little Whisper Prince." The dragon's jaw split open in that triangle maw. The pointed teeth inside looked even more malevolent in the light of day. "You survived. How did you do that, I wonder?"

Venisha's turquoise eyes burned, and he looked at the mass of interwoven wires on Grei's chest, then at Pliothe, who had curled into a tiny ball. Her animals climbed over her, trying to cover her.

"I see," Venisha continued. "Little Pliothe tried to reconstruct you as one of her own, but you are not enslaved to her."

Grei wanted to say something, but the words had frozen in his head.

"Resourceful," Venisha said. "Kneel, and you may serve me in the new world order."

Grei shuddered, and he suddenly realized that his reaction was far too contrived to be natural. He'd been caught in the grips of a spell, some spell he'd not yet had the chance to analyze, to understand. He knew it...and yet he could do nothing to stop it.

A warm hand slid onto his shoulder, squeezed gently. Adora turned him to face her, breaking his gaze from Venisha, and pulled him into an embrace.

"This is Venisha?" she whispered into his ear like she was asking if he was a cockroach. "He doesn't look like much. Come, my Whisper Prince. Do what you do best."

Her irreverence voice broke the spell. Grei's icy terror cracked and fell away.

He blinked, looking into her eyes. "I love you."

She let go of his shoulder and her body erupted into flame. Her newly donned clothes burned to ash and drifted away on the breeze. Grei turned and opened his mind to Devorra's whispers.

They flooded into him as though vying for his attention. With the blue roses, Grei had felt more power than he'd ever experienced, but this was different. They were all the same elements as before, but...louder. They were more complex, like each bit of the world around him had a personality and a history. He not only heard the stone beneath his feet repeating its identification of itself, but each stone had its own identity, slightly different from those around him.

Devorra's magic had been powerful at the Slate Mines, but this was the land she had hailed from. This was the land she had built stone by stone, breeze by breeze, creature by creature. Devorra's face reflected back at Grei from everything around him. The whispers of the elements crowded to him, as though recognizing him for the first time, as though recognizing Venisha as their opposite number and clamoring to meet the challenge.

It overwhelmed him, but he managed to hold on. It wasn't his first time absorbing powers that seemed so far beyond his reach. It was always overwhelming in the beginning, but he had soaked up more power than he'd thought his mortal body could hold. Three times now.

With the magic of these lands, Devorra had turned Venisha back again and again. She had followed him to his land, buried him in the ground and held him there, all so that her beloved continent could live free of his tyranny.

"Grei?" Adora's voice came to him from far away, and he realized he had tumbled into the rush of the power, that his mind had gone far away. Her voice caught him, held him, brought him back.

He withdrew his consciousness from all the elements, letting them settle from an overwhelming surge to a manageable presence, like extensions of his own body. The stone in the palace behind him and of the courtyard became his anchor to the ground. The breeze coming off the sea became his senses. The sun overhead and the water curling and splashing on the surf became the beating of his heart.

Grei laughed, unbidden. It felt like his body was the entire world.

Venisha seemed to sense the change in him. He lowered his enormous head, opened his triangle maw and roared at them. The wind was a hurricane, but Grei whispered, blunting the impact. It swirled around them like a breeze.

Adora turned her fiery head against the expected wind, and when it didn't hit, she grinned at him.

"Whisper Prince indeed," she murmured. She raised her molten hands toward Venisha.

Twin arcs of flame slammed into the god's face and chest. Geysers of steam billowed up from the Sunset Sea. Deep within the white cloud, Venisha roared.

Grei didn't hesitate. He asked the mist to become as hot as fire. The steam became like flame. Venisha roared again.

"He is as vulnerable to magic as we are," Grei murmured. "All we have to do is keep hurting him."

"Lucky me. That's exactly what this power was meant to do." She glanced at him, molten eyes glowing, then shifted her gaze to the sky over Venisha where the steam was still rising. "Get me up there."

"What?"

"Above him. He can't see us. Get me up there and I'll attack him from above."

Grei whispered. The air grabbed Adora and shot her up into the sky like an arrow. At the same time, Grei opened a hole straight through the super-hot steam so that Venisha could see him, while keeping Adora hidden above the cloud.

"I have waited a millennia for this moment," Venisha growled, lowering his head. Burn marks blackened the top of his ridged brow along the side of his flat-nosed snout. "Join me or die, whelp."

"I'm not your whelp." Grei raised his hands theatrically. "I'm the Whisper Prince."

Venisha charged out of the ocean onto the beach. Twenty-foot waves surged off him, smashing down as his claws churned the sand. He crushed the stone wall bordering the courtyard like peanut shells and rose up above Grei.

"I was too eager to get on to my conquest to finish you off properly," Venisha said. "This time no amount of magic will bring you back—"

A column of pure fire hit Venisha on the top of his head. He roared, jerking his snout upward. The mist fell to the ground, revealing Adora high in the air above the god, pouring out a column of fire that would have melted the entire Slate Temple.

Grei whispered to the wind to pull Adora away—

Venisha's jaws rose in a blur and snapped closed on her.

"No!" Grei screamed.

Fire exploded from Venisha's jaws, forcing them open. Adora shot out of his mouth like a comet, striking the cobblestones and melting a furrow fifty feet long.

Grei leapt into the air and flew to her. Waves of heat wafted up from her, but he whispered to the air, cooling it. Her flaming hair winked out, and her body changed from molten to smooth bronze skin. He hastily cooled the glowing rock around her and beneath. She was still breathing. Thank the Faia! She was unconscious, but alive.

He whispered to the stone and the air around her, made them as solid as steel. He left a standing order for the air and the stone to change any heat or cold to a normal temperature if it should strike his magical enclosure.

He spun back toward Venisha. Grei clenched his teeth.

The god crawled onto the courtyard. Behind him, Vaeron and Blevins continued their epic duel, too intent on one another to take note of anything else.

Venisha had almost killed Adora, and all Grei wanted to do was hurt this creature as much as he could.

The god had been visibly injured. The spines around his neck and the top of his blocky head seemed to have melted. Burns marked his face.

"You and every other living creature crawling across the mud of this world are mine to do with as I wish." He shook his great head. "You're going to learn your place or I will unmake all of you."

"No. You're going to die." Grei sought that calm he'd felt when he'd been flying on the green, aligning himself with the elements, but he couldn't find it. All he could feel was his desire to kill this monster.

"This is your last chance, Grei. Align yourself with me. Be a king forever. Take Fairmist as your prize. Take the entirety of the Thiaran Empire if you wish. Live as this entire continent's Faia, in service to me."

"Devorra was kinder to you than she should have been. But I see now that the only way for the world to have peace is for you to join your lover. This world doesn't need you anymore."

"This world *is* me."

"Not anymore."

Venisha's glowing turquoise eyes narrowed. "Bend the knee."

Grei listened for the whispers of the rock that comprised Venisha's body. It looked like slate—and there *was* rock in it—but it was much more complicated than any living creature Grei had encountered. The hissing that Pliothe's artifacts gave off laced throughout Venisha's body, forcing the rock to stay together, bending their natural whispers. Like the wires interlaced throughout Vaeron's body, stealing external life-force and diverting it to him, similar hissing wires threaded throughout Venisha. But it wasn't supplementing what was already there. It was wrapping the stone up, lashing it into line, creating a creature where before there was none.

Grei could not fathom what Venisha's natural form really was. If his body was a construct of his magic, was he simply a thought? Was he simply an idea of the world that had taken physical shape through sheer force of will?

When he'd first become the Whisper Prince, he would never have been able to hear the stone behind that hissing. Even after the blue roses, the volume of that hissing obscured the whispers. But he could hear everything now and he…understood it all in a way he never had before.

And he knew exactly what he needed to do.

Venisha surged toward him, triangle maw open wide, rows of teeth sharp and deadly.

The human inside Grei wanted to flee, to get as far away from those deadly jaws as he could, but that wouldn't matter in the slightest. In any contest of the physical world, whether running or fighting, Grei would lose. He couldn't defeat Venisha with his body. He had to do it by listening.

Listening….

He pushed through the hissing wires to the slate beneath, beseeching it to become water. For a breathless moment, time stood still. The hissing wires fought. That stone had been bound for millennia.

But the stone was of the natural world. It still bore the whispers at the core of everything, and now that Grei had Devorra's insight, those hissing wires could not stop him from listening to the whispers beneath, couldn't stop him from talking to that stone.

And it listened to him.

The closest teeth inside Venisha's jaw melted. His jaw, still solid, crashed into the ground at Grei's feet, and this time Grei did leap back.

But he didn't let go of his connection.

"To water..." he whispered, focusing on Venisha's front foot. The talons curled and melted, trickling across the cracked and ruined cobblestones.

Venisha screamed, pulling back.

Grei fell to one knee, exhausted. He had gone so deep into the whispers it seemed to have drained his entire mortal body. He felt he could eat a seven-course meal and still be hungry. He felt he needed to swallow a gallon of water.

Venisha raised his head, still drooling the slate-colored water that had been his four front teeth. His turquoise eyes were wide in shock as he stared down at Grei as though seeing him for the first time.

"I will take you a piece at a time," Grei growled.

His three-part jaw pulled back in derision. "You have no idea what you're dealing with. You don't control those powers."

Grei glanced from Venisha's dripping face to his dripping claw. "I'm going to turn you into the sea, let it wash you away, just like you turned Devorra into the earth." Grei pushed himself to his feet and reached again into the whispers of Venisha's body.

He reached deep, past Venisha's claws, his teeth, to his stone heart. It was made of the same thing as the rest of him.

Living stone, bound by hissing wires. Like a human body, it actually seemed functional, pushing liquid stone through slate veins.

Venisha said something, but Grei didn't hear it, kept his concentration on connecting to the god's stone body.

But the second time Venisha said it, the words hit Grei like a lightning bolt.

"I make my last request of you," the god said, his words slurred as they left his toothless snout.

Grei froze. His eyes widened.

"No!" he shouted.

"I request that you not use your powers against me while I conquer your homeland," Venisha said.

Grei's insides twisted. He tried to finish the magic, but the whispers fled. He couldn't even hear the stones beneath his knees, let alone the stones of Venisha's body, hogtied by whips of magic.

"No..." Grei clenched his teeth. The Root. The Root had been his haven when he'd made the pact. He had to destroy the thing.

Grei fumbled with the pouch, but it was like Venisha had fingers in every part of him, in the muscles of his legs, the bones of his ribcage, the blood vessels of his head. Everywhere.

Those ethereal fingers clenched into a fist.

Grei screamed and fell to his knees, gurgling at the pain. His hands were like spiders passed too close to a torch, curled and useless. He couldn't open the laces, couldn't get to The Root.

Venisha loomed over him. "I could have used you, Grei. You would have been far preferable to Vaeron. But that no longer matters. Goodbye." He raised his giant claw over Grei's twitching body.

And brought it down.

Chapter Fifty-One

GREI

Venisha brought his massive claw down, but suddenly Blevins was there, standing over him. The claw fell. Blevins roared, stabbing Vaeron's enormous sword up through stone.

Magical turquoise light flashed and Venisha recoiled, shouting. His sudden withdrawal ripped the blade from Blevins's hand.

Blevins lifted Grei's body in one arm and ran for the palace.

"No," Grei said. "A-Adora…"

"She can't defeat this thing," he said.

"No, *she's* hurt…."

"I know where she is. I saw what happened."

"Then we have to get her."

"No."

"Blevins—"

"She's going to die if you don't defeat this monster. You're the only one who can. So focus."

"He's taken my powers." The pain twisting up his body had vanished the moment he stopped trying to listen to the whispers in Venisha's body. In fact, he could hear the whispers of the stones making up the palace now that they'd put some distance between themselves and the god. "If I try to use them against him, it's like someone sticking hot knifes in every part of my body."

"So take them back." Blevins leapt up the steps. Behind them, Venisha roared and charged.

"I can't *take* them back."

"You're the Whisper Prince."

"He's taken it away from me, Blevins—!"

"Figure it out, Grei!"

"There's no other way to…" Grei trailed off. Blevins was right.

The hissing.

That was it. The hissing was to Venishan magic as whispers were to Devorra's magic. Grei had been cut off from one because of his pact with the Slate Spirit, but he would bet he wasn't cut off from the other.

He just had to learn how to use it. He had seen the makeup of Venisha's physical body. He'd tried to bleed the rocks out from underneath the hissing wires, but if he could only learn how to use Venishan magic, he could snap the wires as well.

Devorran magic was out of reach. He couldn't use it to fight Venisha, but he hadn't bound himself regarding Venishan-style magic. He'd have to face Venisha on his terms.

"Where is Pliothe?" Grei asked.

"She ran. I saw her running toward Fylomene."

"Where is Fylomene?"

"Why does it matter?"

"You told me to figure it out. I'm figuring it out!"

Blevins grunted, set Grei on his feet, then led the way down the hall.

They passed two windows looking out on the courtyard. The enormous dragon was gathering himself. His teeth had grown back, as had his claw. Grei wasn't sure if he was going to charge into the palace and knock it down, trying to kill

Grei, or if now that Grei had been rendered impotent, Venisha would simply resume his conquest.

"What did you do with Vaeron?" Grei asked.

"I kicked him into a broken wall. It collapsed on him. I took his sword."

"I thought you would skewer him for sure."

"Well, I would have, but I had to break away to save your ass one more time."

As they passed the last window in the hall before it went into a part of the palace that had rooms on either side, Grei caught sight of Vaeron. He'd made it back to the courtyard and was approaching Venisha, who seemed to still be assessing his wounds.

Blevins was a few steps ahead now, and had reached the room where Vaeron had leapt from the window.

"This is the room." Blevins reached for the handle. "Where Fylomene—"

"Don't touch it!" Grei lunged forward and batted his hand away. Blevins shot an annoyed glance at him. Grei pointed at the tiny metal square set in the center of the door, then at the burnt skeleton in the shadows of the hall.

Blevins raised his eyebrows.

Grei could hear the cacophony of hisses coming off the door. There was something deadly attached to this. His first impulse was to listen to the whispers of the door, of the stone, of the air around it, but he fought it. He couldn't use that kind of magic against Venisha. He had to speak to the hissing.

He focused on it, holding up a hand to keep Blevins still. He tried to tease out a cooperation from the spell like he did from the elements. Nothing.

Dammit! How had he done it when Pliothe had tried to transform him? It had been an instinctive reaction. Why couldn't he replicate it?

"I'm never going to get this fast enough," he murmured.

"I'm surprised that dragon hasn't come through this wall yet," Blevins looked back down the hall. "He knows you're in here. And he could crush this entire building by jumping on it."

"He seems interested in recruiting me," Grei said. "I think he wants to know how I came back to life."

"You died again, huh?"

"I didn't figure that would surprise you."

Blevins grunted.

Grei crouched before the door. The hisses were definitely concentrated around the handle. He reached out a tentative hand. Maybe if he put his hand close to the hisses, he could hear something different, something that would—

The door opened. Pliothe stood on the other side. Behind her stood Fylomene, and in the corner, behind some kind of wire prison, huddled the half-steel, half-flesh Uriozi.

Pliothe looked up at Blevins with large eyes. He glared down at her, then looked away as if her gaze burned him. That just about made Grei's jaw drop. The only time he'd ever seen Blevins shy away from a confrontation was when Adora had railed at him for leaving her to the Slinks when she was a little girl.

Then Grei put it together. Pliothe was Vaeron's little sister, and that meant she was Baezin's little sister!

"He is going to come for the roses," Pliothe said, using more words at once than he'd ever heard from her. "That is what he wants."

"She's right," Fylomene agreed.

Blevins drew his dagger and closed on Fylomene. "We don't need to hear anything from you."

"Blevins!" Grei barked.

"That's her magic, Grei. She speaks and soon you begin to agree with her."

Fylomene raised her hands, but she didn't stop Blevins as he backed her up against the wall and tucked the tip of his dagger beneath her chin.

"Don't," Ree said from behind them. They all turned to find her standing in the doorway.

"Ree!" Grei said in relief. When the battle had begun, he'd forgotten completely about her and Pliothe. "Where did you go?"

She held out her hands helplessly. "Away from the tornado of mist and fire. Once Adora burst into flame, I couldn't stay next to her. I circled to find somewhere I might do some good. A dagger's pretty useless against a dragon. By the time I'd flanked him, though, you all ran away. Took me this long to get back to you. Blevins, don't kill her."

"Better explain that." Blevins didn't give an inch. Fylomene kept her hands raised and her back against the wall, probably correctly assessing that if she started talking Blevins would stab first and worry about consequences after.

"She saved me," Ree said. "She could have killed me or brought me back to that mad king. She didn't."

"Let her go," Grei said.

Blevins shook his head, and for a moment Grei thought he might stab her anyway.

"Fine, Stormy," he growled. Then to Fylomene, "If I catch you trying to mess with someone's head, catch you saying anything that smacks of manipulation, I'm not going to ask permission from the Whisper Prince. Do you understand?"

"I understand."

"So we're protecting the roses?" Ree nodded at Uriozi.

"No," Grei said.

"We're not protecting the roses?" Ree asked.

"He is coming for the roses," Pliothe reasserted.

"Whether he gets them or not isn't going to change the fact that he's going to win," Grei said.

"Take them back," Pliothe said. "You use them to stop him."

Grei shook his head. "I have to use your kind of magic. You have to show me how."

She blinked at him. "I...I don't know how. I tell things to be the way I want them to be, and they do it."

"There has to be more to it than that."

"I don't know." Her head craned downward, turtling into herself again. She stepped on the top of her boot.

"Take the roses, Whisper Prince," Fylomene interrupted.

"You shut up." Blevins's dagger returned to her throat in a blur.

Fylomene raised her chin, swallowed, and continued bravely. "Venisha has wanted those roses for three hundred years. If he gets them, this fight is over."

"You don't know that," Blevins growled.

"I know Venisha. Vaeron is a pure reflection of him, and I know Vaeron. The only reason Vaeron would ever want something is so that it will give him dominion over others. Venisha is the same. He wants the roses because, somehow, he is certain if he gets them he will rule the world."

Blevins narrowed his eyes and glanced at Grei as though trying to determine if Fylomene was offering information or casting a spell.

"If she was trying to manipulate me with magic, I'd know it. She's telling the truth as she knows it. And she might not be wrong. I don't understand even half of what I ought to in this situation, and now I'm hobbled because of my pact with the Slate Spirit." Grei hesitated only a moment, then he nodded. "Very well, we protect the roses—"

The room exploded.

Chapter Fifty-Two

GREI

Stone, furniture, splintered wood, all of it flew into the air. One moment Grei was in the room, and the next he was falling toward the courtyard below, the new day's light blinding him.

He instinctively whispered, asking the wind to turn rigid around his friends, to shield them from the flying debris. He couldn't see them, but he could track them by their own unique whispers. He bid the wind to set them all down gently.

His guts instantly twisted, and he gasped as he fell onto the ground harder than he meant to.

As the stones crashed down around him, he saw that Venisha had finally clawed at the side of the palace, right at the room's window. The claw had hit so hard that it had felt like an explosion.

Littered on the ground were rocks as huge as vegetable carts, shattered clay shingles from the roof, broken furniture from at least two rooms, and his friends. Despite the horrible twist that had gripped Grei's guts, it looked like his spell was at least partially effective. His friends were moving; they were alive.

Blevins was the first to get to his feet. A cut on his forehead bled freely, covering his cheek. He'd lost Vaeron's massive sword, but his dagger was out. Fylomene lay underneath an unconscious Ree, who looked like she'd protected the woman from a chunk of stone that had fallen on both of them. Neither of them was moving, but he could hear their whispers. Both lived.

The half-mechanical Uriozi also lay among the debris, partially covered near the base of the palace. Above her, where the room had been, a giant hole opened in the side of the palace, as well as a ten-foot chunk of the roof.

Pliothe crawled forward, dazed. She didn't seem to see Venisha rise up before her, eyes glowing.

"Pliothe!" Grei shouted.

She looked up at Venisha and froze, eyes wide. Her mechanical friends had scattered across the courtyard, but a few of them crawled toward her.

The dragon loomed over the girl. Vaeron stood on a chunk of the fallen palace, also glaring down at her.

"I gave you the power of a god, little one, and you betrayed me," Venisha said. "I killed the Whisper Prince, but you brought him back."

Pliothe wrung her hands and cowered, her body shaking.

The mandibles of Venisha's lower jaw began to open, and he leaned toward her.

"Leave her alone!" Grei limped toward the girl, but he was too far away. He wanted to let the wind carry him, but he could barely keep from vomiting after the last use of his power against Venisha.

"What was given can be taken." Venisha's turquoise eyes flashed, and Pliothe screamed. Turquoise smoke rose from her mouth, her eyes, her ears. It also wafted up from each of her creations. They twitched and danced like they'd been thrown on a hot skillet.

The last of the smoke left Pliothe, floating free. Her creations fell as one, like marionettes with their strings cut. The turquoise smoke twirled together like a rope, then drifted over to flow into Venisha's glowing, smoldering eyes.

Grei finally reached Pliothe and picked up her limp body. "You bastard," he breathed, but Venisha ignored him, turning instead to Vaeron.

"Let us get what we came for," Venisha said. His giant talon picked through the debris like he was scattering crumbs, and he lifted Uriozi's unconscious form.

Grei laid Pliothe on the ground and forced himself to his feet. He had to stop this. He had to do something!

He opened his mind to the whispers of the air, of the stones scattered across the ground, and—

He gasped, falling to his knees. Just thinking about thwarting Venisha while calling on the whispers caused his body to twist up like some bony hand was clenching his organs, his bones, his veins. The harder he tried, the more it hurt.

Venisha picked gently at Uriozi's half-mechanical body with his pointed talons. "Ah…there it is…."

I can't use my magic, can't use Devorra's magic…. Grei ignored his pain and turned his attention to the infernal hissing that bound Venisha's body together. This magic didn't respond to requests. It didn't work with the elements; it subjugated them.

That had to be the key somehow. Grei had been trying to blend with the hissing. He kept trying to find its center, to understand it, to move it with a request as he had the whispers.

Maybe with the hissing, he had to do the opposite. He had to unlearn what he had learned about the whispers.

He stopped trying to listen to the hissing, or to speak to it—to them.

Instead, he imagined them as an image. He envisioned invisible hands grabbing the wires.

"Tear," he demanded, and he ripped at them, severing them and yanking them from their moorings.

Venisha, still turning Uriozi's limp body this way and that with his claw, suddenly twitched. Part of his arm sloughed off like a small avalanche of rocks cascading down a mountain. He jerked his head to the side.

Grei left off listening to the hissing altogether, ignoring what he heard, and he tried to *see* the wires. They weren't sounds at all, not at their essence. That was why he could never hear any words or speak to them. They were...images in his head, another kind of vision laid over the god's body. The stronger Grei envisioned those wires, the clearer they became.

It was the same with the imaginary hands Grei envisioned to tear at the wires. He went further, pictured more hands. More tearing. Everywhere he ripped at the hissing wires, chunks of Venisha fell to the ground.

The god roared, spinning and lunging at Grei.

Grei ripped hard at the wires beneath the god's neck. Rock crashed down. Venisha's head smashed into the ground right before Grei, the muscle apparently having come with the rock he'd torn out. Dark, dense blood oozed across the ravaged courtyard.

"Stop!" Venisha gurgled, barely able to speak through his torn throat.

Grei grabbed Pliothe and lurched away, but he did not break his focus. He envisioned his ethereal hands ripping out wire after wire.

Working with the whispers had taught him how to focus on more than one thing, and now he put that skill to work with a vengeance. Venisha thrashed mightily, but Grei yanked wires on his legs, on his back, on his tail—

Darkness enveloped Grei. He couldn't see anything. There was no sky, no ground, no palace, courtyard or Sunset Sea. He couldn't feel Pliothe in his arms. Like when the Highwand had turned him to stone, or when Venisha had ripped out his heart, he floated in a dark place with no body whatsoever.

But this time, Venisha materialized out of the darkness. There were no burn marks on his head, on his snout. His right talon was unmelted, and all of the chunks Grei had torn from his body had been replaced or healed.

One talon slammed down in front of Grei, followed by the next.

"You annoying little insect. You think you can just kill me? Is that what you think?"

"No one wants you here," Grei growled. "No one wants to serve you or your vision!"

"You don't get a choice!" The dragon lifted his talon and brought it down on Grei.

He had no whispers to defend himself; he couldn't hear the elements, couldn't see the wires of Venisha's body. There was only the ever-present hissing of Venishan magic, and it seemed to come from all around. As the talon descended, Grei instinctively threw his arms up to block it.

The enormous claw slammed into his forearms, grinding bone on bone, jarring him to his core. Pain lanced through his whole body—

But he stopped the enormous claw. The strike should have squashed him, but it hadn't.

Because this isn't the physical world, Grei thought, finally putting together what was familiar about this place.

This felt like when the White Tree had taken him to some place within his mind to show him stories about the Lord of Rifts. It felt like when the Green Faia had taken him on a similar journey, showing the Blue Faia's refusal of Lyndion, it felt like when he'd been trapped inside his own arm when the rest of his body had turned to stone.

The hissing...the hissing everywhere. Were they *inside* Venisha's body? Or was this some bridge between Venisha's mind and Grei's? A no-man's land where only Grei's mind and Venisha's could go?

In the physical world, Venisha had been falling to Grei's attack. This felt like a desperate attempt to re-set the battlefield. As always, Venisha wanted Grei to think he was at a disadvantage.

But was it true?

"I don't know how you figured out how to undo my spells," Venisha said, raising another claw. "But it will be the last thing you do." This time, he reared up and two talons came down.

Grei threw up his hands again, but this time he didn't imagine it was his forearms against Venisha's claws. He imagined it was the strength of his conviction against Venisha's. If this really was a place of the mind, Venisha's physical strength counted for nothing. It was Grei's imagination against Venisha's.

Venisha wanted Grei to see the god as monstrous, dominant, unbeatable.

Grei squinted and envisioned himself as larger than Venisha. Much larger. He pictured himself as a towering giant and Venisha as a tiny rock dragon the size of a dog.

Then it was real.

Venisha stood before him in miniature, exactly the size Grei had imagined him to be. The dragon's head came maybe to Grei's shoulder, and the talons hit no more forcefully than the paws of a dog that had jumped up at him. They rocked his body again, and it hurt. But it wasn't the overwhelming deathblow Venisha wanted Grei to see, to believe.

Shimmering and hovering over this new version of Venisha was a silhouette of the enormous dragon he had been a moment ago.

Venisha stared at Grei, eyes wide, then glanced up at the ephemeral silhouette high above.

"Impossible..." he murmured.

Grei slugged Venisha in the jaw.

The tiny dragon reared back, but Grei pursued. He wasn't a combat master like Blevins, but he'd imagined being as deadly a fighter as Blevins plenty of times. He imagined that again.

He kicked straight forward, foot slamming into Venisha's breastbone. There was a ferocious crack, and the dragon flew backward into the darkness.

Grei followed, unwilling to let Venisha out of his sight.

"You brought me here to trick me again, but you aren't a three-story dragon here," Grei said. "This is a battle of wills."

Venisha leapt to all fours and roared at Grei, but with his diminutive size, it came out as a pitiful hiss.

Grei swung at Venisha, who ducked, but Grei's hands slid across the dragon's wings and he grabbed hold, twisted.

Venisha lashed out with his tail, trying to take out Grei's knees. Grei let go of the wing and hopped the tail, then slugged Venisha in the face again. Again, the god flew backward, crashing and tumbling against the black like there was an unseen floor.

As Grei leapt forward, he listened to the hiss that surrounded them.

"When you were trapped. All that time you were trapped," Grei said, "you told Devorra that you were growing stronger. But what you meant was that you were building up your hatred. You weren't actually growing. You weren't actually improving. You stayed as static as the stone you're made of. Craving only power, but not learning. Not actually using your imagination."

"Die!" Venisha shouted, lashing out again with his tail. Grei caught it this time, and yanked the dog-sized dragon onto its side.

"Except imagination is the seed of resilience. Imagination leads to discovery, to change, to improvement. You don't have the upper hand here. Imagination is what I do."

Grei leapt into the air like Blevins might have, like the Jorun Magnus of the legends, and he came down on the wide-eyed Venisha like a falling stone.

He put his fist through Venisha's horrified face, focusing all of his willpower, his determination, his conviction. The dragon's face cracked down the middle, and light burst out.

It flashed and erased the blackness all around.

Grei drew a sudden breath, squinting at the blue sky, the destroyed courtyard. He still clutched the unconscious Pliothe in his arms. To his left, Adora still lay unconscious in her protective barrier. To his right, Fylomene and Ree still lay half-buried under rubble. Beyond them, Baezin and Vaeron had renewed their fight.

Before Grei, Venisha reeled. He backed away, hobbling on his half-crumbling legs, squinting through his Adora-burned face, choking on the half-destroyed neck. All of his injuries had returned.

Grei knelt and laid Pliothe gently on the ground, never taking his gaze from the god.

"I will let you live this time," Venisha growled, shuffling backward down the beach. His back legs plunged into the surf, and he extended his wings.

Grei dove into the construct of Venisha's body, ripping wires free from the joints in both wings. The wings crumbled at the joints, and the huge stone spans flopped back to Venisha's sides with a crash.

Venisha cried out. "Grei, stop!"

"No," Grei said. "No more chances."

"I will give you…" Venisha trailed off, seemingly unable to come up with something he hadn't already offered. "Grei, stop!"

"It's not so bad where you're going," Grei said. "I've been there. It's not so bad."

He ripped the wires out of Venisha's head. Through a rasping throat, the god screamed denial to the sky. One last, frustrated, furious, desperate cry. One name.

"Devorrrrraaaa!"

His slate body crumbled like a rockslide, splashing into the sea piece after piece until only his legs remained, pillars standing in the surf as it splashed over them and retreated, splashed and retreated.

Grei watched, not sure what he was waiting for. Some kind of revivification? Some method by which the god could rise again? But there were no allies coming to Venisha's aid. There was no Slate Wizard or Green Faia to bring him back.

Venisha did not rise again.

Chapter Fifty-Three

GREI

Grei turned, feeling the weight of his fatigue like the thundering of a thousand horses in the distance. Whatever magic he'd used in that battle of wills, it had almost rendered him unconscious. Fatigue was coming in that thunder, and he knew when it reached him, he would collapse. And the fight wasn't done. Not yet.

On an elevated patio on the northern end of the courtyard, Blevins and Vaeron clashed swords. Blevins had found Vaeron's enormous sword, but Vaeron had picked up another blade. And Vaeron had managed to adapt to the handicap Grei had given him. His own magic had finally compensated. He danced with the breeze, anticipating, and staying a step ahead.

Blevins bled from half a dozen wounds in his chest, arms, and legs. It was a miracle he still stood upright. He retreated, and Vaeron drove him toward a section of the sea wall that Venisha had not destroyed. Beyond the wall was a twenty-foot drop to the sea.

Grei figured Blevins could have managed to hop onto that wall and make the jump successfully at full health. But the swordsman's right arm hung limp, and he was fighting with his left, barely managing to fend off Vaeron, in full retreat.

With Grei's new understanding of Venishan magic, he now knew what to do. He knew Venishan magic as well as anyone alive. He reached out, saw the wires that tied Vaeron's magic to his body…

…and ripped them out.

Vaeron jerked off his feet like some giant dog had picked him up and shook him. He crashed across the cobblestones.

Blevins sluggishly reacted, turning his retreat into a dead stop. He blinked, then started after his brother.

Vaeron scrambled laboriously to his feet, moving like his arms and legs were suddenly heavier than they normally were. Horror filled his face. He glanced down at himself, then to where Venisha had crumbled into the sea, then to Grei.

Blevins gave a wet chuckle, blood flecking his lips, and he continued toward Vaeron. The king snapped his attention back to his brother, brought his sword between them, but he seemed abysmally slow. His posture crumpled. He retreated. Blevins slashed. Vaeron frantically parried.

Grei came closer. He whispered to his standing spell, telling the wind to leave off hitting Vaeron. The contest was now even. Two mortal men. Two brothers on an even battlefield.

He also whispered to the air and stone around Adora, releasing his commands. The last thing he wanted was to collapse from fatigue and have trapped her in a coffin of his making.

He also beseeched the rubble covering Fylomene and Ree to melt like water and flow away.

"Brother, let us call a truce," Vaeron said, just as Venisha had done. Fylomene had been right: a true reflection of his creator. He backed up under the onslaught of Blevins's renewed attack.

"Let us ink our final truce," Blevins said. "In blood."

He pressed the attack. Vaeron missed a defense, and Blevins cut him on the arm. Vaeron hissed, missed another defense. Blevins cut him across the ribs. Vaeron stumbled and leapt back, but his feet bumped up against the wall of the palace. His eyes flew wide.

"No, wait—"

Blevins skewered Vaeron through the chest. The thrust was so hard, the blade went into the stone behind the King of Venisha.

Vaeron's mouth opened. His sword clanged to the ground.

Red-faced, sweating, Blevins backed up, leaving his sword stuck through Vaeron. His brother stared at him, eyes bugging out of his head.

"I...I'm the King of..." Vaeron tried to take a breath, but he only gaped like a fish on land. His legs went limp and his body slumped, pinned to the wall by his own sword.

Blevins turned and locked gazes with Grei.

"Live by the sword, die by the..."

He collapsed.

Grei limped toward his friend. The thunderous fatigue had arrived, and it slammed into Grei. He staggered up the three shallow steps from the courtyard to the raised patio like he was climbing ten flights, then fell to his knees next to his bleeding friend.

Blevins had three wounds to his chest and stomach. It was a miracle he had stayed standing.

"Hold tight..." Grei let the whispers flow into him, and he knew it was the last spell he was going to cast. He could barely retain consciousness as it was. One more effort and he would collapse. But it was worth it. "Get you...fixed up—"

Blevins gripped Grei's wrist.

"No."

"Blevins..."

"Don't you do it, Stormy. Don't."

"I have to...." Sparkles appeared in his vision. He didn't have much time. He wasn't even sure he could wield his magic now, but he had to try. "The wounds are mortal.... I have to...."

"Don't...do it," Blevins murmured, closing his eyes. His hand slipped from Grei's wrist. "Don't...."

Grei hesitated. He could heal his friend. He could spend his last little bit....

He didn't.

Instead, he took Blevins's hand, felt the strength in the man's grip, this legendary man who had saved Grei's life more times than he could remember.

"It's not so bad," Grei said. "On the other side."

The strength in Blevins' hand faded. His grip went limp. His chest stopped moving.

Grei bowed his head, clenching the great man's bloody hand. The war was over. All the wars were over.

"Safe travels, my friend. Farewell," the Whisper Prince whispered.

Epilogue

Grei stood in the chicken-scratched yard, low hills in the distance. A few chickens pecked the ground, looking for seeds, at least a dozen paces away from him. To his left was a fenced pigpen with a giant roofed shelter. Three huge pigs wallowed in the mud, reveling in the sunshine. The entire area smelled…well, like a pigpen. He had to be careful not to step in the chicken droppings everywhere.

The smell of the simple life.

Grei could have asked the air to smell like something different. He could have turned all the pig and chicken feces into liquid and sunk it deep into the soil to become nutritious fodder. He could have.

He didn't.

He wasn't a savior anymore. Not a protector nor an emperor nor a wizard. He was just Grei. The balance had been returned. The mistakes would continue, as would the victories, and it wasn't his job to control either.

He looked over at the little girl who stood a dozen paces away, watching him. She didn't have blue eyes or tumbling brown hair like Adora had envisioned a lifetime ago. This little girl's hair and eyes were black. She wore a curious expression and a blue Trimbledown dress with frills.

"You're sad?" Pliothe asked, as though she honestly wasn't sure.

"Not sad," he said. "Thinking."

"It has to do with pigs," she said. "Or does it have to do with the chickens?"

He chuckled. "Both."

"You don't like them?"

"Not particularly, no. Pigs are alright, I suppose. Chickens are terrifying."

She giggled. "The Whisper Prince is afraid of chickens?"

He winked at her, not for the first time thinking how odd it was that Pliothe looked and acted like a young girl even though she was three centuries old. But the children of magic all had their scars, didn't they?

It was possible Pliothe would always see herself as—and think like—a little girl. She had never had a childhood. She'd been frozen in time as the enforcer of a malicious god. She had never had a chance to grow up, and maybe she never would. She'd earned the right.

They had all earned their rights. Blevins had earned the death he'd sought for so many years. They had buried him in the Jhor Forest, deep where no one could ever disturb him. Grei had created the entire tomb with his magic.

He had repaired the palace. He had even put the throne back and released Biren.

He had considered staying long enough to ensure that someone fair and good-hearted ascended the throne, but in the end, he hadn't.

Devorra had shown him that balance wasn't a pretty, polished thing. It was chaos and upheaval, serenity and wisdom, and everything in between. It wasn't his job, nor was it his right, to determine the fate of the Thiaran Empire.

It wasn't his right to change anything, come to that, but that hadn't stopped him. Before he'd left, with Pliothe's guidance, he had healed and returned Uriozi to her former self. Pliothe had lost all of her powers, but her knowledge remained intact.

In the end, Grei had mended the broken things, but only to a point. Blevins had been right about some things after all. If Grei didn't want to wrest away the mantle of emperor for himself, then he had to let go of any political responsibility. And so he had.

He'd left Empress Via and Princess Vecenne to sort out the wreck of the empire with their new advisors, Fylomene and Ree. The last he'd seen them, they had been looking at a map of Thiara, talking about recruiting Highblades and a new army to ensure that someone like Biren couldn't just walk in and take over again.

Only Ree had looked up to see him standing in the shadows of the room, and somehow she'd known he was leaving. Her eyes had twinkled. Whether it was from happiness for him or sadness at his departure, he didn't know and he didn't look inside her to find out.

She had winked and mouthed the words, *Are you amused?*

Those were the first words she'd ever said to him, back when he'd climbed through the window of the Lateral House, looking for answers.

He was no longer looking for answers. He'd finally found the ones he wanted.

He'd raised his hand, then bid the whispers to speak close to her ear.

"Goodbye."

The memory vanished as Pliothe broke him from his reverie.

"Did you come to face your fears about chickens?" she asked. She still didn't know why he was standing here in this yard, contemplating pigs and chickens, and she wasn't the type to let a question lie.

"Adora had a dream once," he said. "This was it."

"A dream of pigs and chickens?"

"Yes. And of you."

"I was in the dream?" She straightened up at that, excited. Pliothe liked being included in anything that felt like family. "As a girl, or as a wizard?"

"A girl. Adora saw a little girl riding my shoulders, laughing. It was a dream about what we would do with our lives after...."

"But it's not her dream anymore," Pliothe said.

"No. It's not."

"And that makes you sad?"

"A little. But actually, I'm glad I don't have to tend chickens."

She came forward and took Grei's hand tentatively. "But the girl on your shoulders? We could do that part, couldn't we?"

He laughed and lifted her up. She scrambled until she sat on his shoulders. She drew a deep breath and giggled. He held her steady by grasping her shins with his hands and bounced up and down.

"Yes!" she squealed. "More more—!"

"Hey!"

Grei glanced down the slope toward the sea and saw Adora. She held up her hands. "We're going to miss the tide."

Pliothe gripped his forehead to keep from losing her balance, squealed and covered one of his eyes with a desperate grab.

Adora cocked her hips and put her hands there. Behind her, their ship cut the blue horizon, anchored just off the coast. A tiny pier with three dinghies sat in the water a hundred feet behind Adora. She wore sailor's boots, billowing pants, and a leather vest over a loose white shirt. Her sleeves rippled in the light breeze. A wide-brimmed hat trapped her black-and-gold hair, keeping it from falling in her face, though errant locks still whipped up every now and then.

"What *are* you doing?" she called.

"Reminiscing." He bounced Pliothe again. She giggled and grabbed his ears this time. He winced. It felt like she was going to rip them off!

"You've never even been to Trimbledown," Adora said. "How could you be reminiscing?"

He jerked a finger over his shoulder. "The yard," he said.

She stared at the weathered old farmhouse, at the pig pen, at the horse stables, mystified.

"Your dream," he said. "What you said you wanted."

Recognition dawned in her eyes, and a smile spread across her beautiful face.

"The chicken-scratched yard...." She glanced at Pliothe, who rocked like she was on a bucking horse, then Adora started up the hill toward them. He watched the way she moved. Her hair swinging. Her hips swaying. He'd always loved to watch her move.

She stopped next to him and surveyed the yard. "Ah. I see it now. You want this?"

"It's *your* dream."

She wrinkled her nose. "It seemed better in my head."

He laughed.

"The ship is ready," she said. "Supplies are on board. Water is restocked. Got that sail repaired. So if you're done with old dreams, would you like to go?"

"Well, I guess it's time for Pliothe to get down off my shoulders," he said, glancing upward.

Pliothe's giggling subsided. She shifted, preparing to climb down, but he held tight to her shins.

"Or..." he said, "...not!"

She squealed as he launched toward the surf, running full-tilt down the sloped, bumpy ground. She bounced and laughed and grappled with his head, trying to stay upright.

He glanced back at Adora—

To find her right behind him, pounding hard and keeping up. He laughed and she put on a burst of speed, trying to get ahead of him. Her face, rosy from the sudden exertion, was absolutely gorgeous. She was happy. He'd dreamed of that look on her face, but he'd never seen it before. He'd seen her passionate, concerned, earnest, terrified, but never just…happy.

They raced to the surf, but Grei didn't feel like stopping. He whispered to the waves and asked them to go solid where their feet struck. Together, he and Adora ran across the sea to the ship, with Pliothe laughing on his shoulders the whole way.

As they neared, Grei bid the wind to lift them up and over the rail. They landed on the deck and lay there gasping until they recovered their breath. Adora was the first to sit up.

"What about the dinghy?" she panted.

"We'll get one at the next port," he said.

"Oh no." She shook her head. "I paid a good price for that dinghy. That's my dinghy."

"As you wish, my lady." He went to the rail and asked the air to bring the dinghy to the ship. The loop of rope lifted free of the pier, and the dinghy whisked toward them, bouncing across the waves.

"Cheater," she said, but she smiled. In moments, he had the dinghy lashed securely to the side of the ship.

"Where to, my lady?" he asked.

"This lady?" She pointed at herself, then pointed at their ship. "Or this *Lady*?"

They had bought the ship in Thiara, a sleek sailing vessel named *The Lost Fair Lady*. Adora had laughed when she'd seen it and had fallen in love instantly. They'd bought it moments later. No other ship would do.

"South," Adora said. "Nobody seems to know what's south of Trimbledown. There's got to be something."

"South it is," Grei said. He had rather enjoyed not knowing exactly where they were going.

Adora set the sail to catch the breeze, and *The Lady* leapt forward. Adora stood at the helm. Her floppy hat whipped off her head, but fell against her back thanks to the cords that caught across her neck. Her hair fluttered back from her face like a gold and black banner.

Pliothe ran to the prow and slid to a stop at the rail, pushing her face into the wind.

Adora glanced over her shoulder at Grei. "This, I think…is a better dream."

"A much better dream."

Author's Letter

Oh my goodness, what to say about *The Slate Wizards*? Shall I start with the fact that I gained ten pounds writing this book? Or how about the fact that I hit writer's block for the first time in my life?

Ending this story damned near broke me at the end of 2021. I actually had to abandon ship and turn to writing Lorelle of the Dark at the beginning of 2022 just to shake the deadlock. I said to myself, "Okay, you started Khyven the Unkillable by saying, 'Just write a crappy book.' So do it again!"

And I did. I wrote Lorelle. And it was wonderful.

Then came Rhenn the Traveler. It just poured out.

As I came down from the high of completing an Eldros Legacy trilogy in a little more than a year, I looked around my disaster of an office. Whenever I get on a writing jag, things pile up. Then when I get done, I can't possibly contemplate writing a new book until I tame the chaos.

So I cleaned.

And when I was done, I sorted my mail.

I paid my bills.

I organized my closet.

I dove into my filing, getting all past documents organized and put away in the correct folders.

I vacuumed.

When I started rearranging my books (I keep stock on hand for comic con selling), my wife came into my office and asked:

"What are you doing?"

"Cleaning," said I.

"Um, okay. You're cleaning by putting the Khyven the Unkillables on the Tower of the Four shelf?"

"Um, well, they are thicker books, and there's more space over here and…" I realized then what she was getting at. I'd hadn't been cleaning for two weeks. I had been avoiding.

"Ah…" I said.

She came up and kissed me and left the room.

I sat down on my newly vacuumed carpet and considered the truth. The Slate Wizards was the next book on my roster. Oh, I had other projects I could dive into, but it was far past time to finish the trilogy, and there was no good reason not to. No new project that had to be done right now. No family emergency I had to run off to. Nothing.

The truth was: I was terrified. I was scared that if I started writing on The Slate Wizards, I'd vapor lock again. So I had been doing anything and everything to keep that from happening. I'd had such a great beginning to the year, I couldn't stand to jump back into that thorn bush.

So I eased in. I started going back over Fairmist, reading passages, and I fell in love with the world again.

I dove in, but it wasn't easy. This book fought me every step of the way until the midpoint… and then it finally broke loose. On a pile of Zinger wrappers and Coke bottles (I crave sugar when I'm slamming out a book), I finally typed the last word, sat back, and let out a long breath.

Getting to the end of a novel is always an emotional experience for me. I go into what I refer to as an authorial postpartum depression.

But this time I didn't.

Ending a series is different than just finishing a book. There is no more building toward the future, no dropping foreshadowing or little plot threads. Everything that you can wrap up gets wrapped up.

So instead of falling into my typical postpartum depression, I began reminiscing.

The journey of The Whisper Prince had started seventeen years ago.

Seventeen years!

That's almost enough time for me to have had two kids and have them both graduate high school.

But some books have a certain nature, I suppose, and the nature of The Whisper Prince has been to, like the droplets of Fairmist themselves, drift slowly toward their destination in their own time.

The Whisper Prince was not only slow to come to completion, but it was slow to the starting gate as well. I began dreaming up the characters in 2005, and it took ten years more before I published it in 2015. I had planned to get The Undying Man out the following year, but my middle grade novel The Wishing World got picked up by Tor Books and all my attention went to that and its sequels.

The Undying Man finally rolled out at the beginning of 2018. I had planned, of course, for The Slate Wizards to follow it up in 2019, but again that plan got hijacked. Threadweavers, which had waited even longer to step into the light than The Whisper Prince, demanded to be released. Then Charlie Fiction hit me out of the blue and I ran with it. Then Tower of the Four. Summer of the Fetch. And finally the three previously mentioned books in The Eldros Legacy.

Seventeen years is a long road for a trilogy, and it's a road that marks many milestones in my growth as an author. So much has happened since I came up the characters of Grei and Adora, and I'm so grateful to have eventually brought them to their final shore.

I hope you enjoyed this story. It remains one of my personal favorites. Whenever I need that cool and cloaked darkness, to see those floating droplets drifting through the streets, I return to Fairmist. I return to Grei, Adora, Blevins, Ree, and to all the characters between these pages who mean so much to me. Thank you for taking this journey with me.

I'll see you in the next world. ;)

Also by Todd Fahnestock

Eldros Legacy (Legacy of Shadows)

Khyven the Unkillable

Lorelle of the Dark

Rhenn the Traveler (Forthcoming)

Tower of the Four

Episode 1 – The Quad

Episode 2 – The Tower

Episode 3 – The Test

The Champions Academy (Episodes 1-3 compilation)

Episode 4 – The Nightmare

Episode 5 – The Resurrection

Episode 6 – The Reunion

The Dragon's War (Episodes 4-6 compilation)

Threadweavers

Wildmane

The GodSpill

Threads of Amarion

God of Dragons

The Whisper Prince Series

Fairmist

The Undying Man

The Slate Wizards

Standalone Novels

Charlie Fiction

Summer of the Fetch

Non-fiction

Ordinary Magic

Tower of the Four Short Stories

"Urchin"

"Royal"

"Princess"

Other Short Stories

Parallel Worlds Anthology — "Threshold"

Dragonlance: The Cataclysm — "Seekers"

Dragonlance: Heroes & Fools — "Songsayer"

Dragonlance: The History of Krynn — "The Letters of Trayn Minaas"

About the Author

TODD FAHNESTOCK is a writer of fantasy for all ages and winner of the New York Public Library's Books for the Teen Age Award. *Threadweavers* and *The Whisper Prince Trilogy* are two of his bestselling epic fantasy series. He is a finalist in the Colorado Authors League Writing Awards for the past two years, for *Charlie Fiction* and *The Undying Man*. His passions are fantasy and his quirky, fun-loving family. When he's not writing, he teaches Taekwondo, swaps middle grade humor with his son, plays Ticket to Ride with his wife, scribes modern slang from his daughter and goes on morning runs with Galahad the Weimaraner. Visit Todd at:

www.toddfahnestock.com